The End of All Worlds

T E SHEPHERD

The End of All Worlds

shepline

First Published in Great Britain in 2012 by Shepline Words, Bicester, Oxfordshire

www.words.shepline.com

British Library Cataloguing-in-Publication Data
A catalogue record for this book is available from the British Library.

PB ISBN: 978 0 9571756 3 1
E-BOOK ISBN: 978 0 9571756 1 7

Typeset in Goudy Old Style by Shepline Creative, Oxfordshire
www.creative.shepline.com

FOR
Emma

ACKNOWLEDGMENTS

To all those who have helped and encouraged me, nurtured me humoured my story writing, and allowed my imagination to take me this far, thank you. I need not name names but Mum and Dad, you know what you have done, and Emma, thank you most of all for 'winking' at me. John Singleton, Mary Luckhurst and Geoff Sutton, I learnt so much from you. Philippa, this isn't University admin and Emma G, I kept smiling and making jam. Helen, your critiques have been invaluable; I thank you for sticking with my story. Sarah, Tina, Sian, and Julian, and all of the lunch time crew – in your own way you have given me the confidence to complete this and Helen B, thank you for putting the finger on it and identifying where I was going wrong – you don't know how much you have helped. Bill Goodyear, your help was obvious. Clare, Louise and Elizabeth, you kept me sane during those long days coping with the VT Tool. And Kirstie, Kirsty, Jane, Richard, Rachel, Rachel and Rachael ... if this list is like a roll call of classes, it is. You were all important. Lest you forget, this dedication is not the first thank you for early encouragement, OJB.

THE WORLDS
The story is set in Iceland in the present day and in the world of the huldulfolk

CHARACTERS

Eleanor Ármannsson	literature graduate and storyteller
Ben Ármannsson	science and geography student, Eleanor's brother
Hanna Katla Baldursdóttir	student, singer-songwriter, Eleanor & Ben's cousin
Kirsten Ball	conservation volunteer, veterinary nurse
Alice Cartwright	conservation volunteer, Kirsten's best friend
Andy Taylor	fell runner, Eleanor's long-term university friend
Bjäkk	research scientist at Hólar laboratory
Finnur	mountain guide
Aðli	mountain guide
Gunnlaugr	stranger who lives in the mountains
Charles Ancell	Alcon developer
Kári	chief engineer at Alcon
Professor William Tyndall	climate scientist
Kathryn	William's British research student
Níls	Professor Tyndall's technician

HANNA KATLA'S BAND

Halldór	keyboard/guitar/vocals
Bryn	Drummer
Jon	keyboard player

THE ALFAR

Solveig	Guðni's ancestor, grandmother to Finnbjörn & Jóhanna
Finnbjörn	Jóhanna's brother and Eirný's lover
Jóhanna	Greipur's lover
Eirný	alfar lady
Greipur	alfar man
Valdís	svart-alfar lady, Gunnlaugr's assistant

THE ÞURS

Baldur	þurs leader
Erik	Archivist
Petur	Boy

THE FAMILY

Guðni Ármannsson	Eleanor and Ben's father
Diana Cooper	Guðni's English wife
Baldur Aðalsteinsson	Hanna Katla's father, and Lára's husband
Lára Ármannssdóttir	Guðni's sister

PART ONE

Lost

1

Eleanor slid the rucksack off her shoulders and swung it down amongst the basalt rocks. Wearily, she pulled a bottle from a side pocket and quenched her thirst with cold, fresh, mountain water. She looked back down across the valley to where the Jökulsárglfur canyon stretched out towards the horizon like a dark stain on the landscape.

She frowned. She was used to hill walking and climbing, but not everyone was like her. There was Alice, sitting on the rock, bent over herself, catching her breath. Alice was the sort of person who was up for the challenge but unused to a full day of walking with no hot shower and no ready-made camp at the end. As she watched, Alice looked up. Eleanor smiled as she continued to assess the physical fitness of her companions. She enjoyed the camaraderie of the hike but found herself secretly wishing that it was just Andy and herself with Finnur as guide.

Andy? Eleanor looked across at her spindly-limbed friend from university. From where she stood, Eleanor could see his soulful eyes and the stubbly beginnings of an unshaven beard that only added to his attractiveness. She cursed herself for thinking this way, for she promised herself last Easter that she wouldn't – not any more.

Next, Eleanor looked towards Finnur. Their native guide grinned broadly in that mischievous way he had, as he approached her and offered her a *mjölkurkex*. Gladly, she reached out for a slab of biscuit and bit through the outer layer to its firm but milky taste. She took a step back and perched on a rock, allowing herself time to relax. Her eyes followed the line of the ridge to the peak that faded into thick, grey cloud – the summit that she now knew she would not reach.

'How many years have you come and tried to climb this?' Finnur asked her.

She smiled wryly. 'Three. First year I was too young; last year, not enough time and now, the weather!'

Eleanor's attention drifted back up the mountain, her gaze full of longing. She was unable to hide her disappointment. One day, she dreamt. One day, the summit, she promised herself.

Ben crossed the oak floorboards of his bedroom, packing another couple of sweatshirts into his rucksack. He kept glancing over at his desk and his computer, surrounded by paperwork. Packing more clothes, he looked again to the computer. Slipping into the seat at his desk, he reached for the mouse. He clicked through several screens until he found what he was looking for. Cursing his stupidity, he reached for a weighty text book. He thumbed through to the correct page before running his fingers down columns of figures. Ben scrawled down notes on scraps of paper.

He remembered the conversations he'd had with his tutor earlier in the summer about the proposal for his dissertation. Back then, with the increasing news stories and prophecies of dread and doom circulating the tabloid newspapers, a proper scientific study into the effects of climatic change on the Icelandic tourist industry seemed such a good idea. That was before he had begun to gather the data together and build his own scientific models to predict trends across the whole of the North Atlantic region. He found there was too much information out there; he had to keep stopping himself to refocus the scope of his study. That is, until he discovered another piece of evidence and read one more scientist's theory on the blogosphere.

He sat staring at his books, pen poised in his hand. Then, tapping further numbers into his calculator, he pieced together the sums. He reached again for his computer and input his findings. Finally, Ben sat back in his chair and watched, content, as his mathematical model integrated the data, and mapped out the new picture. He had repeated this process with differing variations more times than he could remember and yet – he stared as the colours were plotted onto the outline of Iceland – it was as mesmerising as ever.

There. Ben watched the modelling software redraw the temperature and precipitation fields before it plotted them against seasonal variations in population. There, amongst shades of green and blue that he could recognise as the Central Highlands he saw patches of orange and red.

Finnur strode on ahead, leading the party up the trail that climbed gradually along the side of the ridge. On either side, rocks changed in colour; grey giving way to earthy browns and hues of red and green. The weather turned grey and foreboding as it closed in around Eleanor and the party. Downhearted, now that the summit was behind her, she walked on dreaming of their rendezvous with the bus, of a warm shower, and a soak in a hot pool.

The fine mist hastened seamlessly into heavy drizzle. Eleanor pulled her waterproofs over her trousers and her hood around her ears. Andy squinted down at her from behind his hood. She managed to give him one last enthusiastic grin, as water dripped from her fringe.

Pausing for a moment at the apex of the ridge, Eleanor waited with Andy, whilst Finnur discussed the route with Aðli, his fellow guide. They came to a decision and again the party set off, taking a narrow path down the far side of the ridge through thickening rain and lowering clouds. Visibility diminished with every step. With a wall of rock to one side and a chasm of nothingness to the other, Eleanor took careful steps.

Ben cursed his computer, scratched out a hurried calculation and noted down new numbers. Cross-referencing the accuracy of these, he paged through his book.

A phone rang, and he grabbed his mobile.

'Hanna, hi,' he said. As he listened, his gaze slowly crossed the room to the pile of clothes and gear half-packed in his rucksack, 'No it's cool. I'm all packed. Tomorrow morning, já...'

Still listening, he offered the occasional word to let her know he was still there, and crossed the room to distractedly drop items into his rucksack.

'How's work?' he said, repeating Hanna's question. He glanced across at his computer. 'It's going good. I think I might have found a get-around for a nasty fudge that accounts for flux corrections, if so, I may have to change my thesis.'

He sunk back into his chair and reached for his mouse; his mind, as ever, exploring further possibilities. He tapped in the last few figures and clicked to activate the drawing of a new model, 'Sorry – you getting this?'

He sat back in his chair, watching again the beauty of the computer processing his model. 'How's your book?' His question was pure politeness for his mind was set on the vexed question of anthropogenic aerosols. He half-listened to the excited ramblings of his cousin, who had crossed the 40,000 word plateau, and offered skilfully feigned responses as he scribbled down more numbers.

Finnur passed between the group members as they descended through worsening conditions. An icy wind blew horizontal rain into them, which stung their faces and froze against their skin. All along the line he reiterated his instructions to keep one behind the other and not to rush. He looked back down the line, to where, just metres away, Aðli – leading the trek – was already a hazy image in the gloom. The others followed in single file or in pairs, with subdued conversation. Finnur allowed Andy to pass before falling into line with Eleanor.

'That's the thing about this country.' Finnur laughed. 'It can be sunshine one minute and the next – the fiercest storm you've ever seen.'

Eleanor glanced round to look up the mountain, but it was lost in fog. Returning to the path, she fell in behind Finnur, following in his footsteps and being careful always to keep him in view. Ducking her head and shielding her face with her hand she began to see flakes of white. The wind turned, funnelling around them and blowing in snow.

'We turned too late, I'm afraid.' Finnur paused to let Eleanor pass.

'You weren't to know,' Eleanor's voice felt choked, as she spoke against the wind, 'It wasn't in the forecast.'

Eleanor stepped carefully, following the path as the snow fall thickened. The air around her was thick with heavy snowflakes driving onto the ridge and wiping out her whole vision. She reached out an arm as she walked, entranced to watch as her fingers faded into the mist. Her breathing quickened and she hastened to catch up before stopping and realising that she could no longer see the others.

'Finnur!' she called out and continued on down the path.

The wind howled through fog, low and mournful, a collage of voices in the gloom. For a moment Eleanor thought she heard her name. She pulled back her hood to try and make out the words. There it was again, clearly a name. She lingered for a moment on the path, peering out into the gloom, certain that she could see a figure.

'Hello!' she called. 'Who's there?'

The driving snow stung her face and began to creep round the back of her neck and the wind called her again. She pulled her hood up and angrily pushed up the toggles. After striding on for a few minutes she stopped again. Up ahead she saw what looked like the dark outline of a human figure, faint against the whiteout.

'Finnur?' The figure was gone, or disguised by more snow. She moved forward, quickly now, trying to catch up, 'Finnur!' she called again. Eleanor's heart raced as she cursed her stupidity. She knew the rules but she had stopped for only a second and now they had gone. She knelt and felt the ground, searching pointlessly for footprints.

She called out again, desperate. They couldn't be that far. They must be close. She sunk to the ground and sat and waited. *Best*, she reckoned, *to wait for their return than to stumble off into the snow, possibly in the wrong direction.*

*

Ben sorted through his tickets, an envelope of money and his passport. He gathered them together, pushing them into the pocket of a smaller rucksack. Moonlight filtered in through the window. He stood again in front of his computer, staring at the incomplete calculation represented by a map of colours and shades plotted to the graph. The flickering light from the monitor hypnotised him. He frowned, idly dragging the cursor across the screen, killing the programs and saving tonight's work.

He yawned, pulled off his clothes and climbed into bed. Staring vacantly for a moment at the clock, he remembered to set the alarm.

Alone on the hillside, Eleanor shivered as snow settled around her and the blizzard cut out the light to the gully. She pulled her jacket closer round her, swigged down a mouthful of water, and chewed on a couple of dried dates. She stared out into the whiteness and stinging snow. Again, she called out. Her voice wavered with her desperation.

Ben saw his sister sitting alone on the hillside huddled for warmth in the cold Icelandic night. He turned uneasily in his sleep; he curled his legs up and squeezed his eyes shut. He saw himself sitting in a cold, grey corridor, a cup of luke-warm coffee in a plastic cup in his hands. He looked down the length of the corridor in each direction as nursing staff moved like blurs through the hospital. A cacophony of noise echoed down the corridor.

A voice.

His head turned. His father was there, with red, sore eyes and cheeks still damp with tears.

Ben fought the visions, tossing and turning in his bed. He saw his sister – Eleanor – lying motionless against a rock. Sitting up sharply in bed, Ben woke breathless—

'Eleanor—' Echoes of his dream flashed through his mind. He gulped down breath and collapsed exhausted, back onto his pillow, staring up at the ceiling.

Hanna Katla Baldursdóttir sat waiting in the arrivals hall at Keflavik airport, flicking through the pages of a magazine with a vague pretence of reading it. Across the tannoy a flight number was called out and instinctively she looked up at the plasma screen. The flight details she had been hoping and fearing to see flashed up. She pushed back her blonde hair behind her ear and fiddled anxiously with her pony tail. Hanna kept her gaze fixed on a pair of double doors across the room that constantly hissed open and closed as if with indecision. In an hour, maybe less, she would be greeting her cousin through those doors and she would have to tell him. She looked away, remembering the telephone conversation yesterday. How could she tell him that, in the course of one short night his world – their world – had changed forever?

Hanna's attention became diverted by the TV monitors across the room – the rolling CNN coverage of the day's tragic events – still holding back on names, talking around the scenario, news anchors corresponding with experts in the field and spokespersons from the emergency services. Hanna Katla lowered her head into her hands as she struggled to find the exact words that she would use.

Flight FI460 descended over the lava-formed coast of Iceland. Within the cabin the warning lights flashed out the instruction to refasten seatbelts. Ben closed his book and slipped it into the top of his rucksack stowed beneath his feet. He smiled wistfully, removing the headphones from his ears. Slouching back in his seat he gazed out of the window. Streaks of mauve blurred past his field of vision – lupines amongst the lava.

Hanna Katla paced the clean beech floors, stopping occasionally to glance up at the arrival boards as they flashed updates. She fiddled with her hair. Frowning, she approached the glass, and peered through into baggage reclaim. She smiled. Ben stepped off the escalator. When he spotted Hanna he smiled and waved to her.

Hanna lifted her hand but could not bring herself to wave back. How could she tell her cousin that in the time it had taken him to fly from England to Iceland, that his sister...? She turned away from the window. She walked amongst the throng of people; the cacophony of conversation growing louder and louder until it drove out her own thoughts.

Somehow she found her way to the arrivals gate and stood dazed in front of the doors. Her cousin approached through a confused blur of vision. He quickened his pace towards her and greeted her happily. Hanna stood rigid and rooted to the floor. She heard Ben say her name but was unable to answer.

'Where's Eleanor?' Ben frowned, looking beyond Hanna, down the hall. 'I thought she'd be here!'

Hanna could hold back no longer and fell, tearful, into Ben's arms, and blurted the words out. 'I'm sorry. I don't know how to tell you – there's no easy way–'

Ben took a step back, still holding his cousin. He stared at Hanna, confused by her actions.

'There was a storm last night.' Hanna flinched. 'A bad one in the Highlands – they've got rescue teams out but – I'm so sorry Ben, but Ellie – she–'

Ben felt his mouth convulse and legs quiver uncontrollably. Suddenly it was so cold in the airport. 'You're not saying. She's not – she can't be.'

Hanna shook her head defiantly. 'We don't know. We really don't know.'

Ben looked away. He noticed a television monitor high up on the wall opposite displaying a news report with aerial footage of the highlands and a reporter doing a piece to camera.

With the awful, tragic truth now told they sat opposite one another in the small café at Keflavik airport, mugs of steaming chocolate in front of them. Hanna Katla reached across the table and took her cousin's hand.

'I – I don't believe it.'

'We don't know for sure.' She smiled kindly. 'Ellie – she could still be okay.'

Ben looked up; his eyes filled with tears, and swallowed back pain. 'Got to phone Dad—' He pulled away, and fingered the keypad of his mobile.

Hanna Katla breathed in the sweet smell of chocolate and sipped her drink. She sighed as she watched her cousin pace the far side of the room, talking into his phone.

A helicopter swooped low across a ravine. On the ground, mountain rescuers searched the hillside. Finnur stood at the base of the hill watching the next shift scour the hillside. Alongside him Aðli climbed down from the guide's van with a thermos flask and enamel mugs. He passed one to Finnur.

'Nothing?'

Finnur shook his head, 'I've been back up to Hrútfell, searched the track - searched off the track. Nothing.'

'It's a good sign, maybe?'

'Maybe.' Finnur shrugged. 'She obviously found shelter and she's fit, but—'

All the way back across town from the airport to the suburbs of Reykjavik Ben sat beside Hanna Katla as she drove the jeep but he saw nothing. He heard nothing. Hanna needed to talk but Ben's monosyllabic responses killed the conversation at every starter. He looked even worse than she felt. This was not how she had planned to spend the day.

She slammed on the brakes and pulled the vehicle to the edge of the road. Ben started; jolted back into the present. He turned to see Hanna clutching the wheel, her head bowed, fighting tears.

'Hanna?' Ben pronounced her name tentatively.

Hanna sat up straight and pushed back her hair. She sniffed away the tears. 'I'm okay. I just – I was thinking – what I had planned tonight and for when we were to meet up with Eleanor the day after tomorrow.'

'We still might,' Ben spoke before realising the hopelessness of the statement. Hanna Katla shook her head.

'No,' she said firmly. 'Come on. My dad will be back by now.'

Spinning gravel out from under the tyres, they drove off.

Ben climbed into his bed in the small guestroom on the basement floor of his aunt and uncle's Reykjavik house. He lay against the pillows staring across the room at the atmospheric black and white photograph of the volcano at Leirhnjú with steam rising across black craggy ridges. The picture had hung in this room for as long as he can remember; as a child he would arrive here for the annual summer holiday and gaze upon the scene.

Alongside was the second single bed – the bed his sister usually slept in. A vision of her face flashed through his mind. She was looking back at him across a valley with a waterfall, before she turned and bounded up the path at the pace of a gazelle. She couldn't be dead. She mustn't be dead. His rational and scientific brain argued against his optimism and hope.

Ben pulled a copy of *Iceland Review* from the bedside cabinet. Opening it at a random article, he attempted to focus. A story about Icelandic bar talk – and he was there in Blikki's with Eleanor and Hanna Katla sharing tales from their university lives and catching up on news over glasses of Egils beer.

But he was not at Blikki's and Eleanor was not with him. He was lying in his bed in his uncle's house thinking of his sister out there, alone in the highlands, either fighting for her survival or ... already dead.

He replaced the magazine and switched off the lamp. The room sank into Icelandic summer darkness – a washed-out colourless light. He squeezed his eyes shut and tried to sleep.

An hour later, sleep still eluded him. He tried to empty his mind of his thoughts, but every time he was close to succeeding, the awfulness of the day's events loomed larger and bleaker in his thoughts.

The sounds of silence at the dead of night echoed loudly in his head. A clock ticked. In the stillness of the hour, each second reverberated through his mind like footsteps on a wooden floor. Hot water pipes gurgled and clattered. The sound of traffic and laughing and joking voices were as clear as if he was on the street. He slammed his head into the pillow praying for sleep to take away his thoughts.

2

Ben stared at the digital display from where he lay in bed, as the numbers blinked onto 05:31. He couldn't remember how he got to this moment; past the hours of aching for sleep, but awake now, he hauled himself from his bed. He slipped on his clothes, feeling the warmth and comfort of his thick Icelandic woollen sweater and dragged a comb through his matted hair. Ten minutes later he found himself on the doorstep, gently pulling the door closed behind him.

To his right, he could see the tower of the Orthodox cathedral looming over the city with the sides of the tower fanning out like the wings of a majestic bird. He began to head towards it without really thinking and soon found himself crossing the square at the foot of the tower, staring up the lengths of concrete emulating basalt columns. He pushed through the door and into the church.

A few minutes later, he stepped out of the lift and climbed the last flight of stairs that curled around the bells until he was looking out across the waking city at the suburbs and the patchwork of brightly painted roofs.

Beyond the water towers at Perlan, he had a clear view of the mountains. His sister was out there somewhere. He crossed the floor of the tower, to get a view of the mountains across the harbour.

Ben, I'm really sorry, but Eleanor – she's – they've got rescue teams out...

He heard his cousin's words again. Somewhere, out there in the highlands, his sister was alone, cold and starving – injured maybe – or worse.

Behind him, the bells struck the hour; crashing metal against metal that echoed on and on through his mind. He ducked subconsciously and unnecessarily. Out of the corner of his eye he saw sunlight reflect off one of the sculptures by the harbour.

Ben stood in the shadow of the Viking boat sculpted from steel and stone on the periphery of Reykjavik harbour. His hand stroked the clean, polished lines. He remembered years ago when he and his sister first saw this, how they had quarrelled over what it had meant. She'd been lyrical about its artistic beauty and he couldn't stop marvelling over its construction.

He laid his cheek against the curve of the stern. Immediately his skin burned with the sharp, stinging cold of the steel. He pulled back, rubbing his cheek warm. He recoiled as unwelcome visions of his sister entered his mind; of Eleanor out there somewhere in the mountains, feeling the same cold pain. He stepped away from the Viking ship which was no longer a symbol of happier times, but which now rose up against the horizon as a stark reminder of his loss. He turned and ran, down the length of the harbour, across the busy perimeter road and into the quieter old town and the straight line of the High Street.

The people of 101 Reykjavik began to stir; businesses to unlock their doors; bar workers to clean up after the night before. He stopped next to a rack of newspapers outside a bookshop and scanned the front pages. There were a couple of Icelandic newspapers alongside a host of internationals. The *New York Times*, *Le Monde* and a Norwegian or Danish daily with a headline he did not even attempt to translate. And *The Times*, which he pulled out of the rack and scanned the front page. Leafing though it, he stopped on page five where a single column picture of his sister was accompanied by an unnecessarily bleak headline. He allowed his gaze to trail across the lines of text and tears began to form in the corner of each eye. He pushed them away angrily with his fist.

Hanna Katla sat at the dining table, knees hunched up under her to balance her bowl of cereal, drenched in mjölk and topped with fruit and skyr - thick, soured yoghurt. She was reading through the newspaper article, reacting with an occasional shake of the head or grunt of disagreement - an accompaniment to the Icelandic Pop that infused the room. Across the table from her, Ben sat and stared blankly at the sleek graphics and videos of Popp TV.

'Here.' Hanna Katla raised her head. 'It says here that the rescue services still have high hopes for the safety of Eleanor Ármannsdóttir—'

'Eleanor Ármannsdóttir? Can't they even get her name right?' Ben protested.

'Over-enthusiastic news editor I guess,' suggest Hanna, 'They couldn't cope with you and your sister taking your father's name in the English style. Even so, they've still not got the spelling quite right!' Hanna grinned. 'Still, this is good news. We mustn't give up hope.'

Ben looked up from the television screen. 'It's been thirty-two hours.'

Hanna Katla sighed and pushed her empty bowl across the table. She lay down the newspaper and regarded her cousin, her chin resting on her hand.

'I don't know why I bought it.' He flicked the paper with one finger. 'It's not as if I need reminding what's happened and it tells me nothing of what's going to happen.'

'She'll be okay, Ben. You know your sister.' Hanna reached for her mug of coffee and crossed the room. She curled one leg under her at the opposite end of the sofa from her cousin and smiled warmly. 'You've seen Eleanor when she's been out doing her fell running, the climbing. You were with her when she went on the Duke of Edinburgh Gold Award Expedition.'

'That was the Lake District. She knows the Lakes like the back of her hand! These! These are the Icelandic Highlands!' He slammed his finger into the newspaper article. 'Four out of ten hikers who get lost are never found!'

'That's the press for you.' Hanna Katla gave a quick shake of the head. 'It's more like one in four – on average.'

'But Eleanor.' Ben looked up. At this moment he really believed what he said, 'She could be that one.'

Hanna Katla took Ben's hand in hers and gave it a light squeeze. What could she say? The hurt he was feeling, she was feeling also. Twenty-four hours of daylight there may be, but the Icelandic nights could be cold – and now especially—

They both stared vacantly at Popp TV. Eventually, after several songs, Ben broke the silence.

'Before I left, Hanna,' he began, 'I was running some climate models – for college, you know.'

Hanna Katla nodded. Ben's mind was engulfed in science.

'I was looking into the regional cooling effect, as regards Iceland. It's due to a shutdown of the ocean thermo haline circulation—' Ben stopped. Hanna saw him register her blank expression.

'Sorry,' Ben said, 'One of the effects of this is that we start seeing these increasingly inhospitable winters ... and,' he paused. Hanna watched him stumble over the words, 'These colder, stormy summers.'

Hanna Katla nodded, understanding.

'I'm worried, Hanna,' Ben said, 'I'm worried for her.'

Hanna Katla embraced her cousin. She wished she could do more, but confirmed what he already knew – that she was worried too, that she understood how he felt.

'Eleanor can look after herself.' Ben's voice was hyper and beginning to show signs of panic. 'But if she's out there alone, who knows how much food she's got? And if it's been raining, she'll be wet, cold—'

The music died away as a journalist cut in with today's top story fronted by video footage of the rescue effort in the mountains. Hanna found herself drawn with Ben to the images flickering past at twenty-five frames per second. Some news editor with pretensions towards award nominations had spliced in artistic footage of running water and hot springs bubbling, but the news was still grim.

'She's dead.' Ben's voice was flat.

'Don't think that,' said Hanna, 'They haven't found anything. That's a good sign.'

'Hanna, you've just heard it,' he said, 'They found a makeshift bivouac, reflective straps caught beneath rocks—'

'Exactly,' Hanna confronted her cousin, 'Not the work of a dead person is it?' she told him. After a few minutes of silence their attention strayed back to the television news reports.

Ben shook his head. 'Then where is she? She knows the rules. Cous, where is my sister?'

Hanna Katla remained silent. What more could she say?

Hanna led Ben off the main Reykjavik High Street and up a small side street towards the cathedral. A few doors along, they stopped. In front of them was a plain, white-washed building with a green door. A small painted sign with the name of the children's activity charity fixed to the wall.

'This is me,' she said, pointing to the door, 'I'll meet you for lunch, yeah? Blikki's?'

Ben nodded. Blikki's. He was there again in an instant; sitting across the table from his sister, laughing with her. Eleanor. She pushed her shoulder-length, mousey-blond hair behind her ears, smiling at a joke he has just made.

'About one, yes?' Hanna repeated the arrangement. She nudged her cousin.

Ben didn't answer. Still drifting in his own thoughts he slowly became aware of Hanna's persistence in arranging their lunchtime rendezvous. He agreed: Blikki's Bar, one o'clock. She asked him what he was going to do until then.

He shrugged. 'Maybe your Dad's museum, the art gallery, a swim maybe... To be honest I'll probably just head down the harbour and think.'

Hanna nodded, hugged him and told him to be careful. She turned and let herself in through the door.

Suddenly Ben was standing alone in a side street off Reykjavik High Street with absolutely no idea of what to do. He should be tired. He should sleep. Two nights ago he had gone to bed in the small hours fired with ideas and possibilities for his project, only to rise again to catch the seven o'clock bus out of Oxford to make his flight to Iceland and...

It had been fewer than twenty-four hours and he was at a complete loss. His mind was in a half vacant, dark, dizzy place and his body felt like a dead weight of heaviness to it. Only his head was uncomfortably light-headed. He tried to focus on his project, but found it hard to recall what he had been working on. He stopped, realising suddenly that he was now standing in the middle of Reykjavik High Street without any idea of how he had got from the door where he had left his cousin to where he stood now. Ben looked up at the fashion boutique window. He couldn't even remember how he got twenty metres down the street? The whole event had destroyed him. Ben felt the tears on his cheeks, unable to stop them. He sunk down beside the wall, lowering his head into his hands and with his breath fluctuating he tried to keep down stifled tears.

Ben sat in the breakfast room of his cousin's house. Too fragile for the busy streets of Reykjavik, he had retreated to the end of the sofa and a diet of TV. He held a pen poised over a notebook on which he had written three lines of feelings and one mathematical equation. He scanned the room, lingering briefly on the flickering light of the television, before focusing again on the page of his notebook.

For a moment his brain connected with the equation. He puzzled over why he had written it. It was rubbish; meaningless symbols that were no help to anything. He drew a defiant line through the numbers again and again, pressing harder with each stroke until his errors were obliterated and the page began to tear. His gaze drifted upward and across the room. Above an old, battered piano, piled with newspapers, magazines and books, was a photograph – a waterfall on a brilliant summer day – a rainbow arcing out of the canyon. Ben stared at it, admiring its beauty. He got up from the sofa and approached the picture, gradually losing himself in the scene it depicted.

At her desk in her second floor office, Hanna was mid-way through sorting a pile of applications. She glanced up at the clock on the wall opposite. It was fast approaching a quarter to one. Time to go and meet up with her cousin, which was something she was both looking forward to and fearing with utmost dread. Her heart raced with the fear of not knowing what to say to him. She so desperately wanted to make him feel better but how could she – did anyone ever – know what to say in these situations. She felt the grief herself; but nothing like what Ben felt, and what did she have to say to consol him?

Hanna left her office, and walked the short way down the street in the sun, to Blikki's, a café bar on a corner halfway down the High Street between Snorrabraut and the old town. She pushed through the door, setting off a cascade of jangling bells above. She moved into the dark interior of the bar, scanning the tables and leather sofas, scrutinising the faces of those meeting for lunch, searching for her cousin. Ben hadn't arrived yet; he must still be on his way. She slipped into a seat by the window to wait.

After ordering a large beer Hanna took out her notebook and a pen and began reading through song lyrics, scratching out words and writing in alternative lines. She looked up every so often, scanning the dim interior, wondering if she had missed him. He wasn't at any of the tables. She checked her watch again. It was gone one o'clock already. She downed some more of her beer and sat back to wait.

Out of the corner of his eye, Ben spied the keys to his cousin's jeep on the dining table. He stared at them. He turned and reflected on the photograph of Gulfoss. Again, he looked at the keys and in that instant the decision was made. He grabbed the keys and left.

Half an hour later, Ben swung his cousin's truck into the car park, gravel crunching under the tyres. Fine, penetrating rain blended with the spray from the canyon beneath. He stepped down from the vehicle and made his way quickly across the car park and down the footpath, weaving in and out of tourists with their day-sacks and camera bags to where the river plunged over the falls in a churning, rolling mass of foam and water. His feet slid and squelched through the dark volcanic mud to the observation point by the side of the waterfall. His movements instinctively became more wary. The canyon beneath provided some thirty metres of chasm into which he could easily disappear should he take the wet, slippery rocks at just the wrong speed.

Ben approached a point of rock projecting out over the edge of the waterfall. He leaned his head over, looking down past the froth and foam of water at the canyon beneath. The mist penetrated his clothing, seeping into every pore of his skin. His mind was filled with the deafening thunder and the power of the water plunging down, clashing against rock and smashing back up before falling again. The wind and spray hurt as they grated against his face and the roar of water penetrated his ears. The river beneath loomed closer. He fell. All was black. All was silent.

The train slid into the station and lurched to a halt. Ben reached through the window and slid down the handle, swung the door open and jumped down onto the concourse. Moving quickly away from the door, he stopped. He paused to look up and down Crewe station and, scanning the thronging crowd of people, there he saw her – over the far side of the platform, between the telephone kiosks and stairs. He lifted his hand to wave. She had seen him too.

Brother and sister were soon hugging each other. It had been a long time since that weekend just after Easter when Eleanor managed to grab some time off from revising for her finals. Now, she had graduated – although how well, she would have to wait a few months to find out – and he had his last lecture and seminar group of the year still to come. They each stepped a couple of paces back and looked at each other.

'You look,' Ben began hesitantly, 'different somehow.'

Eleanor shrugged. 'Your train's early – would you believe it,' she exclaimed, 'you want to catch a coffee before the Oxford train?'

'Yeah, that'd be great!' Ben's response was enthusiastic. They had news to catch up on and their holiday to plan – email and text messaging could only take you so far. He reached down to pick up his bags again and when he straightened up and looked about for his sister, she was gone.

He frowned, trying to spot her beyond a group of people and saw Eleanor in her blue jacket heading across the platform. She'd dumped her stuff somewhere and could move faster. Again, she was gone. Alone, the snack bar ahead of him, he made his way across the platform.

'Eleanor?' his voice was shallow and empty. He blinked his eyes open. A mixture of rain and spray stung his eyes. He blinked the discomfort away and winced; his left leg was throbbing.

A man's face was close, leaning over his, looking into his eyes, speaking Icelandic. Ben picked up the essence of what was said and responded in English.

'Thought you were going over, for a minute,' the man told Ben, 'You were lucky. Still, if I hadn't caught you – I don't want to imagine...'

Ben nodded. He looked down, beyond the length of his body at the raging torrent of Gulfoss.

'I was lucky.'

Eleanor scrambled almost on all fours over the last few rocks, washed clean after the snowmelt, to the top of the ridge. Catching her breath against a cold, strong wind she looked out at the path she must take. The next valley stretched on to a ridge beyond; the northern slopes still a patchwork of un-melted snow and birch scrubland. She had to go somewhere beyond that farthest ridge. She breathed out heavily, cursing her predicament and reached for her water bottle. It was two-thirds empty. She sipped the smallest amount that would still quench her thirst, licking the moisture off her lips to supplement her meagre rations.

Ben lay awake for the second of his Icelandic nights. Hanna's cross words and justified reprimands at his carelessness up at Gulfoss echoed through his mind. He hadn't planned on telling her. Why worry her? However, he had arrived home soaked through from the rain and shivering – and she had lambasted him for missing their lunch date – so he had had to tell her.

Now, again, he lay awake and begged his mind to let him sleep. He listened to every sound of the night. He listened to people walking the pavements, the cars on wet roads, the gurgling of water in pipes and, on the floor above, the footsteps of his uncle as he made his way back from the bathroom. Every noise was amplified into a cacophony of sound in his head that kept him from sleep. The memories of Eleanor, the conversations they'd had, circled his mind and mobbed his ebbing consciousness.

3

The clattering of metal bins being emptied drifted in from the street outside. Ben started, sitting up in his bed. He was awake. He grinned and almost laughed. Last night he had slept. He had actually, finally, slept. He swung his legs out of bed, stumbled forwards to the window in his boxer shorts and drew back the curtains just slightly. He peered out of the high window at the fine day beyond. He could see patches of blue sky breaking through the cloud.

Hanna Katla stood with her father, Baldur Aðalsteinsson and mother, Lára Ármannsdóttir, outside the front door of their home as the taxi cab drew up at the kerb. Standing to one side, Hanna watched her mother as she compulsively touched and straightened her long fair hair and breathed nervously, as she anxiously clutched and twisted her hands. Hanna's uncle, Guðni Ármannsson, got out from the backseat of the cab, ashen faced and shoulders slumped, his hair uncombed and with dark circles under his eyes. He stooped to help his wife Diana out of the car. She stepped from the car in one fluid, graceful movement. She was tall, with mid-length dark hair.

The taxi driver heaved luggage from the boot and Hanna moved quickly to collect it. From the front gate, she watched her uncle approach her mother and father. Nearer to Lára, Guðni stopped. She stepped down towards him to face her brother. Guðni took another step towards his sister. Awkwardly they greeted each other and her voice broke into sobs as she commiserated with him.

Diana stood a few steps behind, watching her husband and his sister. She smiled nervously, eyes darting from person to person, smoothed down the sides of her dress with the palms of her hands. She waited. Hanna picked up the bags and moved past her mother and uncle. Aware that her aunt was taking the opportunity to follow, she heard Diana speak her name and began to talk about what happened like she didn't already know. Hanna set down the bags and turned around slowly.

'Don't.' Hanna spoke firmly. 'I'm sorry, I don't mean to be rude, but Ellie, she's not been found yet – we don't know – we can't grieve for her yet.' She blurted out the words, feeling the relief of speaking them.

Hanna stopped. Diana looked at her gravely and shook her head. A frosty silence lingered for a moment between the two of them.

'Where's my son?'

Hanna nodded. Ben. Of course.

'Downstairs.' Hanna led her aunt down the flight of stairs to the half basement and through into the day room, where she could see Ben sitting at the table with his laptop and his research, puzzling over figures and graphs.

Hanna Katla stepped tentatively into the room and moved closer to her cousin.

'Ben? Your Mamma and Pabbi have arrived,' she said.

Ben spun round to see Hanna standing with Diana in the doorway. He nodded, and Hanna watched as he turned back to working on the convective-precipitation chart he had shown her earlier.

'Ben?' Diana stepped nearer and laid her hand on her son's shoulder. He pulled sharply away but remained focused on his research. Hanna looked from Ben to her aunt. She shrugged to Diana and shook her head sadly before they left the room, leaving Ben to his figures and his maths.

Ben continued to stare at the notes and calculations and tried to refocus his attention on something other than his sister's disappearance. He glanced over his shoulder briefly. His mother turned off the corridor back onto the stairs. Her presence bothered him. He turned again to his notes. The more he concentrated on them, the more the words and figures slid across the page into one another. They meant nothing. They could be the times of the local bus service, except even that would have had some meaning.

As the morning passed, Ben remained in his seat, his fingers tabbing between screens on his computer; from his modelling software, to the BBC News site, to the Icelandic Met Office. With each task he sat differently; hunched over his computer to plot his research; sprawling back in his chair when reviewing his notes and checking data in books; sitting forward, leaning on his fist as he stared at the screen, hitting refresh on the news site – again and again and again.

Finally, Ben kicked back the chair and quickly moved through to the hall and up the stairs to the ground floor, where his step became cautious as he neared the kitchen to find the rest of the family. Guðni and Diana were sitting at the breakfast bar, whilst Lára grinded coffee beans and prepared drinks. They all looked up as Ben entered and he felt awkward and uncomfortable under their watchful gaze.

'Dad,' Ben said, his voice choked with emotion. Guðni got to his feet and rushed forward to embrace him. Over his Dad's shoulder Ben saw his mother stand, but hold back from approaching. He also saw Hanna watching from across the kitchen as she helped her mother prepare food. Ben felt tears well up in his eyes. He pulled back and looked at his Dad, also tearful.

'Benjamin. I'm sorry that you've had to carry this burden,' said Diana. His mother now approached him and reached to lay a hand on his shoulder. He turned his head away from her and tightened the embrace with his father.

Later, the two families sat around the dinner table in an uneasy silence. In an atmosphere that was a strange mix of family reunion and wake they ate their meal of fried haddock in a wine and feta cheese sauce. Hanna forked up another mouthful of fish and potato. Guðni leaned across the table and asked how the band was going. She frowned, wondering how best to answer this.

'Good, já. We've played at the university a few times – and last month we had a recording session laying down the tracks for a new album. We have a gig at Grand Rokk would you believe – in just a few days' time—' She stopped, stumbling over her words as she realised how inconsequential it all sounded.

Diana lay down her knife and fork noisily. Hanna saw her aunt turning away from the table and hiding her eyes in her hands.

'Your cousin,' Diana began, before turning to her husband. 'Your daughter has disappeared and hopes of her safe return are fading fast and you're talking about rock concerts?! It's bad enough us sitting here eating this meal.'

Diana pushed back her chair forcibly and left the table. Her brother, Baldur, followed her, putting his arms around her, reassuringly. Guðni frowned towards Hanna.

'I'm sorry, Di,' answered Guðni, 'There are no rules here. I'm sorry, but I can't behave like there's no hope. Everything will be alright. Everything *has* to be alright. I can't believe that Eleanor will not be returned to us.'

'How can you be so sure?' Baldur countered. 'You don't know what it's been like this year. More hikers than ever have been lost. Not just tourists either, but Icelanders too - experienced guides.'

Guðni got up and stepped towards his wife. He directed his reply at his brother-in-law. 'We've all seen the news reports - a climate in chaos. The changing planet - I've had the breakfast time conversations with Ben.' He reached out to Diana imploringly. 'It's just coincidence, Di. We're only noticing these things now because it's happened to our own daughter.'

Diana faced him and shook her head vigorously before rushing from the room. Baldur fired him a cautionary glance before following Diana. Guðni was left watching the door through which Diana had left.

'Best leave her, Guðni,' Lará said. 'Baldur will look after her.'

Guðni shook his head as he wandered across to the window. He removed his glasses and wiped away his tears.

'My dear Ellie. She *has* to be okay,' said Guðni, 'She knows the rules - the procedures - she wouldn't do anything stupid.'

Lará, too, now got up from the table and crossed the room to her brother.

'Something is happening, Guðni. The world is changing. I can feel it.' Lará lifted her head and looked at Guðni directly. 'We're not safe anymore.'

Lará reached out to support him. 'What's happened to your daughter? That's proof of it.'

'I know my daughter. She's okay.' He laid his hand on his heart. 'Here. This has never been wrong.'

The honesty and self-belief in his face warmed Lará's heart. She hugged her brother reassuringly.

Hanna's gaze shifted from watching the two adults, to Ben, who watched his father intently. Ben needed to talk to his father alone and express his feelings and his fears. He shook his head and she knew what this meant to her cousin; the incredulousness he felt for the calm and composure Guðni displayed.

Aðli leaned against the side of the van, drawing on a cigarette and staring out over the landscape. At the back of the van, Finnur was stowing ropes and poles and ice picks.

'If she ever was here, she isn't now,' said Aðli.

Finnur considered this. He remembered Eleanor's character and tried to assess her chances. Another night out here and – he studied the weather – in his time working in the highlands as a guide he had known stronger people succumb to lesser conditions. He stepped back from the van and slammed the door shut before joining Aðli in the shelter from the wind.

'Tomorrow we should start out from Tönga,' Finnur said, 'We can try the eastern slopes. And there are caves up that way.'

Finnur glanced at his friend. He saw Aðli consider the proposal.

'If you found a cave to get inside, deep down in – and if you had food and enough water, you could add another day or two to your chances of survival.'

Streaks of orange and mauve from a lowering sun bled through layers of *altostratus undulatus* clouds – layers of colour high above the streets of grey tarmac and pebble dashed walls. Ben quickened his pace, sidestepping past his parents and his aunt and uncle, along the kerb-stones, to draw level with his cousin. With the cord wrapped several times round his fist, he gripped the duffle-tied sports bag by the nylon fabric.

The fading light signalled the shift from Icelandic day into long evening. Beyond the painted roofs and the multitude of little church spires the mountains, shaded by greys, greens and browns, were caught at their tops by another band of rain-heavy clouds.

'You can tell that summer is almost over,' said Ben, 'It's subtle, but you feel it in the air and can see it in the colours.'

'It's going to be another cold night, they say,' said Hanna.

Ben looked out to the harbour. 'That's what scares me.'

They walked on in silence, down the street, tree-lined down one side with the houses set back and a fence down the other side, with the playing field beyond. Hanna trailed her fingers over the bars, until finally they turned into the forecourt at the front of a building and stopped at the door.

'Come on,' Hanna smiled. 'Let's swim.'

Ben lathered soap along his limbs and breathed in the sweet smelling, sulphurous water from the shower that cascaded over him. Guðni stood next to him in the communal showers, bursting forth with occasional snippets of song. Ben put his head back and pushed his face into the force of the water, rinsing the soap from his body. As the last of the water drained away he returned to the bench where his clothes hung on the hook, grabbed his swimming shorts and pulled them on.

Dripping water, he pushed his way out of the changing room, padding barefoot over the cold slabs of concrete that surrounded the pool. He dived quickly out of the cold, grey air and into the deliciously warm pool. His head bobbed up, seal-like, on the far side of the circular pool. Next to him, treading water, hair sleeked back, was Hanna. They grinned at each other and Ben dived again, swimming strongly across the pool.

At the far side of the pool, he surfaced again and levered himself out of the water. Across the low, rendered, unpainted wall opposite the painted roofs of the town and the elegant lines of the cathedral spire stretched skywards.

'I don't know why,' Ben said, 'but this – it's so beautiful.'

He sploshed back into the water and turned to Hanna, once again at his side.

'It's grey. It's concrete. It's cold. But there's something about this that, I don't know–' He stopped, looking to Hanna for help in articulating his thoughts.

Hanna Katla bit her lip. She too looked across at the view. A shaft of sunlight broke through the clouds. She nodded; almost a laugh.

'You see?' Ben tossed his head. 'You get days when there's no natural colour and then suddenly the sun – it does this.'

The cloud had broken in a swathe across the horizon and a sunset was rich in gold, red, mauve and orange. Ben relaxed into the hot tub and sunk below the surface of the water until only his eyes, nose, and ears were exposed to the chill evening air. He listened in vaguely to the conversation in the pool; his father asking Hanna about university; and Hanna's explanation.

For the first time in two days, Ben's thoughts relaxed enough to turn once more to his paper. Staring up from the water, tinged with blue from the refracted light, to the sky above, he saw in the lines of clouds a temperature chart plotted against seasonal tourist numbers – and suddenly his mind was crunching the numbers and exploding with thoughts and scientific processes.

Small waves splashed over his face, as Hanna pushed herself up and with drips of water sliding from her skin as she climbed out of the hot tub. Ben watched with his father as she crossed the floor and dived into the pool. A silence surrounded them as father and son returned to their own thoughts.

'I brought some mail out for you,' Guðni said after a while, 'Research materials I think – Bangor postmarks.'

'Thanks.' Ben nodded. Then hesitantly added, 'I was thinking,'

His father raised his eyebrows, looking interested, presumably expecting a theoretical and deeply scientific discussion akin to those they had shared many a breakfast time.

'I was thinking I'd go up there.' Ben watched his father's expression carefully. 'To the Highlands.' He saw the incomprehension grow on his father's face.

'Why?'

'To do something, Dad! I can't sit here and do nothing. Ellie is out there – somewhere.' His gaze was intense, 'I *have* to help.'

Guðni remained silent.

'I can't explain it.'

'Benjamin,' Guðni frowned. 'The authorities are doing everything they can to find Ellie. There's nothing that you, me, or your mother can do.'

Ben shook his head, unable to comprehend how his father felt.

'I know you feel helpless,' Guðni offered. 'Lord knows I do, too.'

'Then why won't you help me?'

Ben waited for a reply from his father. Eventually Guðni returned his gaze to Ben. 'It's too dangerous. And there are professionals – plenty of professionals. We would just be in the way.'

'It's three days, Dad. If they don't find her soon—'

'Then we've lost her. Yes. I know.'

Ben pulled his clothes off and again found himself standing naked staring at Leirhnijú. Transfixed by the atmospheric shades of black and white in the photograph, he pulled on his pyjama trousers. Returning to him now were his father's words across the hot tub.

In all honesty, Benjamin. Your mother and I – we couldn't lose you as well. We couldn't bear it.

Alone in his basement room, Ben heard his father's words again. He threw his head back in resigned contemplation before crawling into his bed. Ben tucked up his knees into a foetal position and squeezed his eyes shut before he willed himself to sleep.

Hanna stood on the back porch watching the thundering rain flood rivers of water into the street in the dim light of morning. She clasped a mug of freshly brewed coffee and breathed in the strong aroma. Suddenly aware of someone else stepping into the room, she turned – it was Uncle Guðni.

'Have you seen anything of Ben this morning?'

Hanna shook her head, remembering creeping downstairs to use the basement shower room earlier and pausing at her cousin's door to listen to the snoring of deep sleep within.

'I do hope he is feeling better,' Guðni glanced back towards Hanna as the kettle steamed and gurgled in front of her. 'Last night – I could see he had taken this all on his shoulders.'

'He and Ellie were close.'

'They *are* close.' Guðni stressed. 'But it's not his fault. None of this is anyone's fault.'

Hanna found herself nodding, unable to voice a more articulate reply. She sipped her coffee and slowly the conversation shifted into enquiries about current Reykjavik art exhibitions; the progress of a new bypass back in Oxfordshire; how work was; the health of friends and the extended family.

Ben was lost in thought as he traced the rim of his mug with his finger. He held his pencil ready, his research set out in front of him, before jotting down a couple of notes and joining the dots of his argument together. Having taken up the mug he breathed in the rich coffee aroma.

Almost by its own will, the pencil between his fingers began to sketch out a graph and he moved hastily to fill in numbers. A series of crosses, a line drawn between them and the diagram was plotted. He set his mug down and pulled the newspaper towards him, turning immediately to the weather reports. This time he used real source data to plot the diagram and he sat back to study it.

Ben shook his head at the simplicity of the calculation. He turned back a few pages and read through his notes. Forward again to a blank sheet of paper and he re-formulated his hypothesis with the benefit of better data. He directed his pencil fast across the page, as he put down the evidence of his discovery.

With a single click of the mouse, Hanna minimised the booking database; the web browser sat beneath on the screen with the update page of her blog already loaded. Her fingers moved across the keyboard. She paused, sucking in air through her teeth, as she thought. A line of words grew across the page, wrapping onto the next. She was typing fast now, setting down her thoughts and her feelings as they came.

Her fingers paused over the keys. She stared at the words on the screen, but it was a song that haunted her mind. She heard the beat and the chords. She began to mouth the words. A flick of the wrist and she guided the mouse to bring up a new window in the word processor. She was typing again, but this time lyrics, quickly and as she heard them sung in her mind.

Ben pushed back his chair. He sighed with relief, and threw down his pencil, to watch it tumble across the paper and roll across the table, stopping just before the edge. He reached for his mobile and keyed through his address book until he found Eleanor's number. At the moment of pressing call he remembered and froze. The phone slipped through his fingers and hit the notebook with a dull thud, still ringing.

'Eleanor? For a moment, I–' Ben's eyes were wide and distant. 'How could I have forgotten?'

Ben sat alone in the empty house listening to the sounds of hot water gurgling through the pipes and somewhere out on the street, traffic. Slowly he got to his feet and left the room, taking the stairs down to his bedroom where he stood in the doorway. He stared at his rucksack, which lay on the floor in the corner of the room.

On the floor above, silence pressed heavily on the empty hallway, broken suddenly and sharply by the sound of a key twisting in the lock and the front door being opened. Hanna crossed the hallway and called out her greeting. No answer. She called again, moving quickly through the dining room and into the kitchen.

'Ben!' she called.

No response. Hanna felt the stillness and it disturbed her. She tore across the room and down the stairs, calling out to her cousin. She stumbled to a halt in the doorway to the bedroom.

Ben looked up at his cousin, where she stood in the doorway watching him as he pulled a couple more shirts from a drawer and stuffed them into his rucksack. His manner of packing was fast and careless.

'What are you doing?' Hanna asked.

Despite the overpowering pressure of his cousin's presence, Ben refused to answer. He stepped past her and gathered up a collection of books and maps with his phone and a first aid kit, sweeping them into his day sack.

'Don't try and stop me, Hanna,' he told her whilst avoiding eye contact.

Hanna approached her cousin, eyeing him carefully.

'I thought,' she began, 'You and Guðni – I thought he'd talked to you?'

'He did, yeah.' Ben answered. 'I've tried Hanna, but – I'm not like my father. I can't sit back and be patient. I have to be doing something – anything – helping to get the job done.'

'So when are you leaving?'

'As soon as I've packed.' He pushed a torch into the top of his day sack, 'There's a bus north – leaves at two-thirty. I'll have to break for the night at Akureyri, but that's okay – I'll be on my way. I'll be *doing* something.'

'So, you're leaving? Just like that?' Hanna questioned his intentions although she was unsurprised by his actions, 'When were you planning on telling us? You *were* going to tell us?'

Ben chose not to respond. He took up his water bottle in his hands and headed out of the room.

Hanna pursued her cousin, 'I can't let you do this.' She followed him upstairs.

'I have to. You can't stop me.'

He looked up at Hanna, who stood still and silent, arms crossed, mouth set, staring at him. Pushing the stopper firmly home into the neck of his water bottle, Ben turned to face her. She bit her lip, staying silent for a moment or two more.

'I'm going,' he told her again, 'I'm going to find her.' He turned his back on his cousin, and opened the fridge door to search for things to take with him.

Hanna stepped towards him. 'I see. So,' She folded her arms. 'When do we leave?'

Ben stopped. Slowly he turned round...

'When do *we* leave?' Hanna repeated firmly.

4

Finnur scanned the farthest ridge through binoculars. All around him, steam rose from natural vents in the ground; the landscape a smudge of muted red and brown ochre with vibrant yellows and greens. Mud boiled and glubbed out of the ground. He lowered his binoculars and turned to where Aðli had a map spread out on the bonnet of their van. Together they peered at the map and Finnur pointed out a line across the mountains.

'If she came off down the mountain here, she would be in this valley,' he said.

'That's some guesswork.' Aðli shrugged. 'For sure there was a storm – zero visibility – but she would still have to have wandered far from our path.'

'But it *is* possible.' Finnur nodded.

Aðli glanced at the map and again shrugged.

Hanna Katla and Ben sat at the front of the bus. Ben leaned against the window. He glanced back down the length of the bus as it filled up with other passengers. He felt the vibrations from the glass as the driver slammed shut the storage lockers.

Ben fidgeted impatiently. He scanned the car park for his father or uncle. There was no sign of them and he felt relieved. Hanna Katla pulled out a book to read. She glanced up at him.

'It's seven hours, Ben. Sit back, chill—' She pushed her small rucksack down between her legs. Propping her feet up on it, she rested her book on her knees.

Hanna looked up and glanced out at the view through ash-stained glass. Driving northwards through the last suburbs of Reykjavik, lush vegetation gave way after only a field or two to volcanic slopes of scree and craggy brown cliffs. She turned her head and observed her cousin for a moment, staring out of the window hypnotized by the view as it blurred past.

She frowned and returned to her book.

'What you reading?' asked Ben.

Hanna Katla looked up at Ben, framed by the window in a blur of lush meadows and grim but spectacular lava cliffs.

'It's by a friend's father. You know Elva? Her Pabbi is this art historian at the museum – well now he's written this novel. Well I say novel, but it's based around the whole museum/university art scene which of course he knows everything about,' explained Hanna, 'It's an odd read. Like *The DaVinci Code* – except better written – and there's various re-imaginings of the old sagas.'

'Sounds intriguing,' responded Ben.

'Certainly is that!' Hanna laughed. 'The author is adamant that it shouldn't be described as fantasy but there's a definite element of magic realism to it. It's like Angela Carter – you know *The Magic Toyshop?*'

'You should let Ellie read it.' Ben said, 'It's the kind of thing she'd love.' Ben stopped and fell into a preoccupied silence. Hanna frowned. His words, and the mention of Eleanor's name, brought home to the both of them where they were going and why.

Ben kicked a stone around the service station forecourt. A clear northern sun had broken through the clouds and the landscape was crisscrossed with shards of sunlight. He swung round and took in the view down the valley to the sea and round again to take in the mountain range. He turned again and again, faster and faster until he was giddy. Collapsing in laughter on the ground, he looked up, across to the middle of the forecourt, to where the bus stood alone, and beyond that to the far side, where a handful of cars were parked by the pumps.

Ben's sight was still dancing-dizzy, focused on his cousin as she walked back towards him. For the first time in days Ben felt alive and excited. He was on the road and was doing something. Hanna stooped to hand her cousin a hot dog and a bottle of cola.

'So this guy you called. The one at Hólar.' Ben was curious. 'You know him, how?'

'School.' Hanna answered, 'Bjäkk. He was drummer in my first band – crazy guy – real quick sense of humour.'

'So, what was it? Rock music to ... fish?'

'He was a real environmentalist. He used to pass up gigs to go on demos and research trips.'

Hanna and Ben made their way back to the bus.

'One of the reasons why the band split–' Hanna climbed the steps onto the bus, followed by Ben. Back in their seats, their conversation continued, shifting between the relative success and failures of her past and present bands and the details of

Bjäkk's aquaculture research into – Hanna grinned as she said it – the secret life of the arctic char.

Open your eyes–

Hanna sung softly to herself, the words coming to her in response to the view that she found herself drawn to as the bus swung out of the services and back onto Route One. She caught the beat of the music behind the words, humming the next line of the tune, as she tried to figure out the continuation of the lyric.

Ben looked across at his cousin. New song. He knew better than to interrupt Hanna when she was composing. Instead, he turned the other way and watched the view, slowly losing himself in the ever-changing, intricately bewitching scenery. He played a game in his mind of counting each yellow snow stick down the side of the road that they passed. As the bus rounded a bend, a waterfall tumbled into view; white and foaming out of a hanging valley.

Heading out along the road as it descended down through the valley, they passed through a farming community. The sides of the road were dotted with fields of cows and ponies, a main street consisting of a gas station, general store and a collection of houses of whitewashed concrete and arched corrugated iron roofs, brightly coloured but leaching streaks of rust that stained the walls. A group of children played in the yard on a swing made from tyres.

Beside him Hanna pulled a spiral-bound notebook from her bag and began putting down lines of a song.

Open your eyes
Listen to your senses
See. The journey you take.

She looked up and chewed on the end of her pen, gazing out though the front window at the road as it snaked ahead, crossing tumbling, churning rivers from one side of the valley floor to the other.

Ahead of them the road curved round and down through a suddenly steep-sided chasm through the hills that opened out again almost immediately into a gently rolling pasture. The grass was lush and the road took them down into the lowlands, a town spread out above a river and the beginnings of an estuary.

At a gas station at the edge of town Hanna and Ben stood on the tarmac with their day-sacks between their feet. More passengers disembarked after them, with some either heading straight for the shop, or making for their cars across the forecourt. Most remained near the bus, milling around and waiting. The driver soon climbed down and walked the length of the bus, slinging up the doors of the luggage lockers.

As the evening sun began to fade, the landscape was cast in a washed-out light. A chill wind blew in from the sea and a stillness surrounded Hanna and Ben as they waited. Across the forecourt they could see the town spread out across the sloping pastures with their painted roofs.

They turned and looked at every pair of headlights that swept up the road beside them. But all the cars passed by as the chill wind blew stronger and the light faded further. Ben frowned at his cousin and she shrugged a response, she shrugged. Where was he? She cursed Bjäkk under her breath.

The thumping sound of Icelandic rock reverberated around Bjäkk – he nodded to the beat and drummed the wheel with his hands. He sang occasional lines and grinned. In the cab next to him, Hanna and Ben were squeezed into the two passenger seats of the pickup truck. The road took them first down towards the

54

water and then cut back up into the mountains.

Ben sat quietly in the cab listening to Bjäkk's thick, gravelly voice as he questioned Hanna on life since school and she played out to him the specifics of her degree, the placement in Italy and of her new band – the recent gig and the rep from the record company who was handling their imminent signing.

'You never told me that!' Ben broke into the conversation.

Hanna cast her head round swiftly.

'You sure? Sorry, I forget who knows,' she apologised, 'Yeah. He saw us about three months ago now. He's been playing our demo to some producers, but of course he needs to sell us to his bosses.'

Ben could tell that Bjäkk was jealous of Hanna's success. Bjäkk nodded and swung the car round a last bend and leaned on the accelerator, driving up past the cathedral tower and round into a small car park, braking with a scrunch of gravel. With a flick of the wrist he cut the ignition and turned to his passengers, grinning broadly.

'Welcome home to Hólar.'

'Welcome home to Hólar?' Ben repeated Bjäkk's words. He stood fiddling with the straps of his rucksack in a classroom presided over by portraits of previous tutors, scientists and academics. Hanna pushed tables aside and moved to stack chairs.

'It's tradition,' Hanna explained, 'It's said that wherever we come from and no matter wherever we're headed, this place, Hólar – it's home to everyone.'

Ben nodded. 'It's a nice idea.'

'It's – welcoming,' said Hanna. She was about to say more when she was distracted by Bjäkk clattering backwards through the door, dragging two mattresses with him. The two cousins rushed to help, taking a mattress each and slung them down on the floor between the rows of school desks.

Bjäkk sidled around the mattresses, coming alongside Hanna to help her with the straps of her rucksack. Ben watched the two of them as he aired his sleeping bag and unpacked his towel and washing kit.

Bjäkk and Hanna shared a joke and a laugh. Bjäkk drew Hanna into a conversation of lowered voices.

Ben was only able to guess at the nature of their talk. They were close friends at school, he knew that, but he had never suspected – till now – how close they may have been. He looked away, as Bjäkk noticed Ben's watchful gaze and leaned his head closer to Hanna's, drawing her further into privacy.

'Just going to find the bathroom,' Ben said. Grabbing his wash kit, he left the classroom.

Hanna glanced briefly after him, offering her cousin a slight wave as he left the room. She returned her gaze to Bjäkk, taking in the rough lines of his jaw and his uneven fringe of black hair.

Under the portrait of a former headmaster, Eleanor found herself looking up, into Andy's hazel eyes. She giggled flirtatiously. He reached out towards her and fingered the collar of her shirt.

'Andy!' She grinned wryly. 'Don't!'

Eleanor took a step back, removing Andy's hand from her clothing. She smiled coyly. He was tall, slender and gorgeous, but she couldn't think like this. She found herself gazing into his eyes and knew that she mustn't think like this. Unconsciously she tugged at his sleeve, twisting her fingers in his cuff and pulled away as she turned her back on him.

'Eleanor!'

Hanna started. She pulled back, drawing her fleece tightly around her.

'What? Hanna, are you okay?' Bjäkk asked, frowning at her, his expression filled with concern.

'It's nothing.' Even so, Hanna shivered. 'It's just, I felt her here – with us.'

Bjäkk shook his head slowly. He remembered the events of only a few weeks ago.

'She stayed here, didn't she? You saw her?'

Bjäkk nodded. 'Just in the morning. The group she was with – I gave them the tour.' He grinned. 'You know – the aquarium, cathedral, the gruesome stories of beheaded bishops.'

'How was she? Ellie?'

'Quite the tour guide.' He grinned again. 'She knows the country, definitely. We made a good double act. I was the sombre professional and she – spirited–' Bjäkk gave Hanna a gentle smile, remembering how the group had stood before him, gathered ready for his tour. 'I think there was one that Eleanor – she was sweet on.'

Eleanor ran from the school and across the grass outside the front entrance to where the dozen other people in her party were gathered under the trees. She launched herself at Andy, thrusting her arms around him, her fingers entwining with his.

The three of them sat alone in the canteen at Hólar, whilst somewhere beyond kitchen staff could be heard clattering plates, bowls, pots and pans. Ben spooned up hot meat soup, savouring the warmth as it travelled down his gullet.

Bjäkk slid into the seat next to him pushing cans of Egils beer towards Hanna and Ben. He lifted a third can to his lips and nodded.

'Salut!'

*

Eleanor swigged down a mouthful of water whilst gazing out of the window, across the grounds to the square, white cathedral tower with its black spire, almost a silhouette against the darkening sunset. Drawn suddenly back to the group by a question aimed in her direction, she returned to her party of friends enjoying a late meal of soup and cold meat salad.

'Yeah, Ben, my brother, and I – we have dual nationality. Our dad – he wanted to make sure we grew to love this country. I don't think there's been one year I haven't visited.'

Kirsten Ball, a fair-haired, twenty-nine year old, fired friendly interrogation across the room. 'But you've never done one of these holidays before?' She paused to fork up more smoked fish.

Eleanor shook her head. 'It was Andy who suggested it.' She glanced across at her friend. 'We go fell running together at uni. He had done some of this kind of thing back home – and when I said what Iceland was like...'

Kirsten nodded. She glanced at Alice by her side. 'Kind of similar. We first met on a conservation holiday in Yorkshire – you know, dry-stone walling – rhodie bashing. This kind of deal seemed like the next step.'

'That's kind of similar to what Ben's been working on,' said Hanna.

'Yeah?' Bjäkk swigged back more beer.

Ben glared at Hanna with annoyance. 'Well, in a way. Hanna hasn't got it quite right. You're very marine-based,' he said cautiously, 'I look much more at the atmospheric and terrestrial models. I think I may have found a new way of measuring the subtle differences in temperature change, season by season, year by year.'

Ben smiled with satisfaction, yet acknowledged Hanna's eyes glaze over at his explanation. Turning to Bjäkk he was encouraged to see a spark of interest. It was enough for him to feel confident in further elaborating his theories. Soon the two men were exploring complex algorithms of sea ice formation against tidal reach and jotting down calculations and explanatory diagrams on paper napkins.

Hanna sat on the outside of the discussion, enjoying just watching her two closest confidants becoming friends. Slowly though, she tired of that amusement and her interest waned. Unnoticed, she slipped away from the table with her can of beer and was soon stepping quickly across the tiled and deserted corridors.

Eleanor padded barefoot along the silent vestibule, the slap-slap of skin on cold ceramic echoing throughout the unearthly quiet.

Hanna pushed through the doors and stepped out into the open. She wandered aimlessly in the grounds, smelling the fresh Icelandic night air. She quickened her pace and strode up the slope at the back of the main school building.

Laughter. Hanna stopped and listened. Nothing but the wind in the trees, so she moved off again, climbing the slope and approached the old farmhouse. A chill swept across her; she felt the spirits of those who had trod these steps before her. Giggling and joking penetrated the night.

A fumbling at the lock. Eleanor tumbled out of the historic, turf-roofed farmhouse at Hólar with Kirsten and Alice, all in a fit of mirth.

'No really,' Alice affirmed, 'At it like rabbits they were.'

'And they still don't know? That you all – you–' Her eyes bulged with disbelief. Eleanor mouthed the word 'know'. Kirsten smiled wryly, confirming the validity of the story. Eleanor could hold back no longer and she collapsed in hysterics and was joined by the other two girls.

A mobile rang, cutting across the still night and midnight hysterics.

*

Hanna pulled her phone from her pocket and glanced down at the number. The phone continued to ring. She bit at her lip and stared at the number illuminated on the screen, listening to the ringtone, unable to answer. Eventually it stopped and she was left standing in the night, on the side of the hill, her ears still ringing with the sound of her mobile.

Hanna looked down the hill and saw a man crossing the car park. She stuffed her phone back in her pocket and ran headlong down the hill.

'Bjäkk!'

He stopped and swung round on his feet. Hanna quickened her pace to join him, bounding down the slope and slowing up in the last few steps.

'Hanna?' I thought you'd gone to bed.'

She shook her head.

'You okay? You look troubled.'

It was silly. She couldn't tell Bjäkk about seeing-sensing-feeling Eleanor's presence. It was nothing but her own fears. But the phone call?

'Pabbi phoned.'

Bjäkk watched her. He waited for more.

'I couldn't speak to him. What would I say, Bjäkk? I'd have to admit what stupid, crazy thing Ben and I are doing—'

Her words stumbled to an end. Hanna looked searchingly in Bjäkk for help and reassurance. He took her in an embrace of comfort and warmth.

5

A clear, northern sun cast strong shadows over the rural city of Hólar. The simple whitewashed buildings were bleached in the light; their red roofs the only splash of colour in an otherwise green valley. Bjäkk led the party of twelve young men and women down through the grounds at the front of the school. Eleanor rushed down the slope ahead of the rest of her friends, pointing down into a ditch with a babbling, gurgling stream.

'You see that ditch down there?' said Eleanor, 'That's where the bishop was beheaded!'

'We'll come to that story,' Bjäkk told Eleanor, and then addressed the rest of the group. 'There are many gruesome tales from this part of Iceland. But first I think we should see the cathedral!' He slotted a key into the padlock and opened the gate to the church yard.

'Some cathedral,' Alice whispered to Kirsten. 'The parish church back home is bigger than this—'

'You are right, of course.' Bjäkk interrupted Alice's scoffing, 'You should remember that in the whole of Iceland we have a population only equal to your Norwich – I think. Hólar was, monastically, a very important community, but as you can see our community is only a few farms, houses and the agricultural school. As such we have a population of maybe just one hundred.'

As Bjäkk talked, he fiddled with a bunch of keys. Having found the right one, he unlocked the door to the church and beckoned his group to enter. He followed them in through the base of the tower and into the nave of the church with its slate floors and dark-wood pews. At the far end was a finely painted altarpiece and a large font of polished soapstone. The morning light filtered into the church through large windows.

Ben stirred from his sleep. He lay half in and half out of his sleeping bag on the mattress on the floor of the classroom. Blinking, he adjusted to the light that seeped in through the curtains. Rolling over, he looked across to his cousin's mattress, and peered closer. No one there. He flopped back onto his pillow, exhausted already – nights were never long enough.

Further up the hill, in the little single-storey accommodation block with the rust stains down the walls, Hanna woke in Bjäkk's arms, curled on the sofa. She untangled herself from him, as she remembered dimly the events of last night. Or was it early this morning? The bottle of Brennivin stood as a reminder to the shot drinking and late-night talk. How late did they stay up talking? And at what point did conversation fall to sleeping? She picked up a shot glass from the chair and placed it on top of the desk. She crossed to the window and pulled back the curtains.

The clouds had cleared, replaced by a clear, blue sky and bright sunshine in the valley all the way down to the fjord and the sea beyond. Hanna slipped the catch and opened the window, flaking the paintwork from the rusty frame between her fingers. She leaned out and took in a deep breath of fresh, morning air, her head still groggy from the night before. Out over the mountains, mist and low cloud still hung heavy.

A few minutes later, Hanna was walking briskly down the roadway before cutting back across the grass to the courtyard at the back of the main building. She slipped in through the entrance hall and skipped lightly upstairs, round corners and down some more steps, and arrived at the canteen.

She poured out a mug of coffee and made up a bowl of muesli, topping it with sour milk, skyr and fresh fruits. Moving through the canteen she approached Ben, alone at a table, eating his breakfast.

He lifted his head and smiled. 'You got up early?'

She sighed, hoping her relief wasn't too obvious. *Good; he hadn't noticed her stop-out last night.*

'Sleep well?' Ben paused over a spoonful of cereal.

Hanna nodded. *And it was honest.* She had had the best night's sleep since all of this began. With Eleanor going missing and the storms, for the first time in days she had felt safe and secure in Bjäkk's company.

Hanna gazed across her mug of coffee at Ben. 'You?' she asked.

'Yeah,' Ben nodded, surprising himself. 'It was okay.'

She nodded; pleased that she didn't have to report what she had seen and felt last night. The echoes of Eleanor's stay here scared her.

Hanna eased herself down into the water, revelling in the warmth that trickled up her legs and through her body. She launched out across the pool and joined Ben where he was already resting against the side. For a moment she treaded water in front of him before lounging back onto the ledge around the edge of the pool.

This is amazing–

The call came from some English tourists down the far end. Both Hanna and Ben glanced in the direction of the excited shrieking.

Look! There's the cathedral tower!

And there – can you see the snow up there on the ridge?

The repartee went back and forth around the group.

It's good here isn't it?

Hanna and Ben turned their heads in the direction from which the voice came; it was clear and unmistakably that of Eleanor. Both realised instinctively that they were sharing the same vision of Eleanor with her group of friends as they had been just a few weeks before. So real was it that they found themselves in amongst the laughter and the joking.

Hanna backed away and bumped into Andy, recognising him from their brief meeting at the airport, and the two girls also, Alice and Kirsten who were probing Eleanor with questions about Iceland. Hanna kept half an eye on Ben who was trying to intervene in his sister's conversation.

'Ben!' she hissed. 'They can't see you. You do know that...?'

Ben nodded. 'Then why are you whispering? Why am *I* whispering?'

Hanna frowned. He had a point of course. She shook her head and shrugged.

A splash; and waves washed over them. Bjäkk surfaced near to them and suddenly the three of them were alone once more in the pool.

'I heard the news earlier – on the radio,' said Bjäkk. Ben glanced up in interest.

'I'm sorry.' Bjäkk's tone answered all of Ben's questions without the need for words. 'They say they are going to scale back the search tomorrow. Review it even–'

Ben shook his head, his expression grim. It was hard to be honest with himself. 'They have to think of their budgets – and I guess Ellie – she's just one girl...'

One girl. His sister.

'They can't!' Ben snapped. 'They can't give up until they've found her. We have to help them look. We need to get going. Now!' His face was screwed up, his lips stretched over his bared teeth, as he spat out the words.

Hanna turned to Bjäkk. 'Doesn't one of the buses stop here for Akureyri?'

Bjäkk nodded. 'Já. But Akureyri – I have to go either tomorrow, today, it makes no difference. Why put you on the bus...?'

An hour or so later, Ben was helping Bjäkk stow rucksacks in the back of the jeep, tucking them beneath tools and buckets that reeked of fish. Bjäkk tied back the tarpaulin before climbing up into the jeep alongside the cousins and driving off down the single-track road down to where it turned sharply off back up the side of the estuary.

Bjäkk pulled the jeep to a stop at the junction with Route One. With the spin of tyres on tarmac, he swung the vehicle left and accelerated away. In clear summer daylight, the road stretched ahead, long and straight, flanked by yellow snow posts. Bjäkk cranked down the window and Ben did the same on his side.

Cast out your inhibitions
See what you're meant to see

Bjäkk's singing was angry and heartfelt, rasping over the low notes. An exchange of looks with Hanna and they came in together on the next line—

Open your eyes
Listen to the inner you

Bjäkk's fingers drummed out the rhythm on the steering wheel. He chuckled and revealed his pleasure at remembering past days.

'You've still got it, Hanna.' He glanced across at his friend and then back to the road ahead. 'Your words take me to that place. It's like magic.'

'You should come to one of our gigs.'

Bjäkk's mouth opened out to one side into a grin, 'Já. Next time I'm in Reykjavik. Definitely—'

He laughed. 'Though, you should play Hólar. In front of the cathedral. I can see it now—'

A tumbling, babbling river descended down the valley floor alongside the road, long and straight. It cut back under a bridge. Bjäkk aimed the pickup truck for the middle of the road and took the single-track bridge, accelerating over the surface. Inside, the cab resonated with the sound of singing.

I'm going to write it all down
In the back of the bus.
Oh oh I feel the heat
Oh oh I feel the rush.
Oh oh I feel the heat
I'm gonna move on down
To the back of the bus.

Alice led the vocals to the Iain Matthews song, but they needed little encouragement as the others in her group, fast becoming friends, sang along with the crackling, slurring tape. Eleanor sang along too from her seat in the far back corner of the bus. She looked to her right, sharing the moment with Andy and exchanged grins.

The bus drove the long, single lane bridge, that crossed the tumbling, frothing river on its way and chased the valley.

*

Ben chewed on his lip, as he lost himself in thought. Hanna noticed her cousin's silence and halted her singing. Quickly she hushed Bjäkk's words.

'You all right, Ben?' Bjäkk said in his thick, gruff voice.

Ben lifted his hand to silence any interruption. Hanna and Bjäkk exchanged looks of concern but nonetheless abided by his wish. Ben continued to run through his thoughts, holding the anticipation of his companions a few moments longer, he waited until he was sure of himself and ready. Finally, grinning broadly—

Open your eyes.

He spoke the words of the song like poetry—

See the truth around you

See the lives, See the loves

That touch you.

Open yourself

To the world out there—

Ben allowed space after the end of the words for them to settle before turning his head slowly and looking pleased with himself. Back to the road and it stretched down a steep-sided valley. For more than a few moments, silence lingered within the cab.

After a while Hanna nodded. 'Yeah. It's perfect, Ben.'

'Benjamin,' Bjäkk said, 'You're bloody brilliant!'

'Cheat!' Kirsten's call came quickly on the heels of Eleanor's turn. She looked up from her cards, appealing to Kirsten with big, wide, dolefully innocent eyes.

Kirsten was intense in her conviction of Eleanor's guilt. Looking at the card, she slowly moved to gather up the rest of the pile, shaking her head.

Eleanor laughed. 'What? Moi?'

'You have so been cheating.' She looked though the cards and then up at Andy, *'And you!'* She thrust a handful of cards in his face. *'Have you played honestly once this entire game?!'*

Andy made a shrug his only reply.

The minibus skidded to a halt, kicking gravel surface from the road beneath. After a murmuring of confusion, soon the whole bus was talking about the arctic fox that some saw and some didn't.

At the outskirts of Akureyri, Bjäkk parked the jeep in the ill-defined car park tucked away between a storage depot and a block of flats. He got down from the cab and began unclipping the catches to release the tarpaulin cover. All too soon, he found himself standing opposite Ben and Hanna with their rucksacks mounted, saying farewell and wishing them good luck. Last lyrics were exchanged with grinning enthusiasm to Hanna, and good wishes to Ben.

On a lonely hillside, Eleanor scrambled down through rocks and scrub. Her face was dirty and her hair tangled. She was weary from her nights in the wild, yet she walked on and finally reached the crest of a ridge. Pausing for a moment she looked out. What's that? Her face screwed up with curiosity and she reached for her binoculars. Headlights snaked their way along a track in the far distance. Her mood brightened at the first, welcome sign of civilisation. It was not much, but her trek was nearing an end.

A gust of cold wind suddenly blew down the valley from the mountain and almost knocked Eleanor from her feet. She staggered to steady herself. No, she decided; it was not over yet. Squatting near to the ground, she sheltered from the wind and once more scanned the horizon. Finding the headlights again, she saw that they had stopped on the road.

*

Down in the valley, Finnur sat in the cab of his van, discussing the situation through the crackle of his radio. His mood was despondent, as the weather, dark and foreboding, closed in on them again. Clouds that had built over the mountains now sunk lower into the valley and the wind whipped up stones from the floor. Finnur glanced nervously over his shoulder as the back window shattered from the stones striking the glass. He swore and barked the decision into the radio. He stuffed the handset back into its cradle, angry that Eleanor must soon be considered dead. She had been so spirited and full of life, and she had been lost on his watch. He flicked the switch on his radio again and called up Aðli. He recalled his colleague for the day.

Up on the hillside, Eleanor pulled her coat closer about her, as the wind swept her hair across her face. She pushed it back and watched, helpless, as the lights on the track down below moved off again and drove off further down the valley.

A thick, damp mist clung to the air, darkening the already grey concrete buildings. Water dripped from the corrugated iron roofs. The bus pulled into the lonely depot, deserted were it not for two men a mother and a small boy sheltering in the doorway of a roadside bar. A dog, keeping low to the ground, skulked out from around the back of some bins scrounging for scraps. After a brief announcement the driver and several passengers disembarked, running for the dry of the bar beyond.

'Twenty minutes.' Squashed into seats on the bus, Hanna turned her head towards Ben. 'You want a coffee? Chips?'

Leaving the bus they ran across the forecourt, avoiding the biggest of puddles and dived for cover inside the bar with its erratically blinking neon sign and steamed up windows. Inside, Ben sat, hands cupped round his chin and elbows pressed to the Formica table. Hanna pushed a cup of coffee in front of him and deposited a bowl of chips in the centre of the table. She took a seat opposite, turning her steaming mug of chocolate in her hands, and filched a chip.

Up on the wall a television flickered amongst a background hum of people chatting, the clattering of crockery and the hissing of coffee machines and deep-fat fryers; all merging into a cacophonous drone. Hanna drank chocolate, drawing chips from the bowl and enjoying the salty crispiness. She looked at Ben, who hadn't touched his coffee; hadn't begun on the chips, but stared intently up over her shoulder.

'What've you seen?'

Ben shushed her questioning. She turned in her seat. The television, tuned to CNN, showed aerial shots of a lava strewn hillside and the white expanse of the icecap; cutting to some archive footage of an erupting volcano.

She listened, engrossed, as the reporter rattled off the known facts of the story. A small party of hikers under the instruction of experienced mountain guides, descended the slopes from Krafla. It detailed the story of the twenty-one-year-old Eleanor Ármannsson, a student of Manchester Metropolitan University, now lost for seven days in what had been extreme weather conditions.

Finnur, the twenty-eight-year-old guide appeared on screen to explain the rescue efforts and gave details of the footprints and other tracks believed to have been left by the young woman. He went on to explain how worsening weather conditions and an evaluation of probabilities had led to the scaling down of operations. It was not said but it was immediately implied that it was no longer a Search and Rescue mission but one of body recovery.

Hanna glanced back at Ben, looking to him for a response which never came. Slowly, without averting his eyes from the television, he reached into the bowl for some chips.

The wipers swept rain from the windscreen. The bus steered the course of the road, marked out on either side by snow posts – their bright yellow the only colour amongst the volcanic ash. It was a road drawn out across a bleak landscape scattered with lava and the detritus of past eruptions – it meandered through the haunting cloud-laden slopes with a cold wind whipping up black sand and hurling it at the bus so that it stained the windows.

Ben nudged his cousin and pointed at the view through the windows opposite. 'She's out there, somewhere.'

Ben pulled another rucksack from within the hold and edged himself and the two bags away from the bus, pulling his waterproof hood around his ears. He looked about at the swarm of people stuck between the two buses and scattered out around the campsite. He spied Hanna returning across the stony ground and signalled to her with a wave.

'We're in luck,' Hanna told Ben as she got near him, 'Two places, only tonight though. Tomorrow we *have* to pitch our tents.'

'Whatever the weather,' Ben grimaced, flicking his eyes skywards. Hanna frowned; she shared his feelings.

For a moment they just stood in the car park as the rain fell on them, relieved that they were finally at their destination. Hanna hugged him, encouragingly. 'Come on. Let's go claim our bunks.'

Ben pushed the whitewashed door open and stepped into the dimly lit interior of the hut. A staircase rose above him away from the wood floorboards and pine panelled walls, up into the slatted roof space. Instinctively he moved to one side, pulling off his boots and leaving them on one of the many shelves as was the custom. He asked Hanna where their bunks were and after she gestured upstairs he ascended.

Inside one of the main dormitories, a single space under the sloping roof, Ben moved through it to the window at the far end. He looked out at the twisted, unnatural shapes of lava that had been frozen in the midst of its rush down from the crater centuries ago.

Images entered Ben's mind of Eleanor crawling between two towering columns of lava, arranging plastic sheeting over her and sheltering from ever-worsening weather. Huddled for warmth, she was tearing shreds of dried fish from a packet and chewing on its dry saltiness for nourishment.

Ben flinched and turned away. He couldn't bear to think of where his sister was now. Further back in the room Hanna lay out her sleeping bag onto a small strip of one of the large sleeping mattresses that took up each side of the room. Ben joined her, extracting his sleeping bag from his rucksack and throwing it out next to his cousin's to claim his spot.

'The rescue teams are staying here, you know,' said Hanna, 'That's why there's so little room.'

Ben grabbed a few belongings – his book and a notebook – before heading downstairs after his cousin. Soon, a kettle was boiling and condensation formed on the window. Hanna spooned heaped quantities of chocolate into a couple of mugs. She looked across the room to where Ben stood, framed by the doorway to the deck outside, talking on his mobile. She frowned, as she carried the steaming mug out to Ben.

'Here.' Hanna pushed the mug into her cousin's hand. He took it and in a few painful words ended his call.

The two cousins eased themselves into seats opposite one another at the picnic table. A now-familiar pause lasted between them. Hanna rolled her eyes and laughed. Ben raised his eyebrows, questioningly.

'Nothing,' she apologised, 'They are forecasting better weather tomorrow.'

Silence. Ben's thoughts were elsewhere, churning over thoughts in his mind.

'So, any more ideas for your project?' Hanna asked. 'Or are you firmly into song writing now?' She laughed. Then, seeing the way that he looked at her with disbelief, she added, unapologetically, 'There's nothing we can do till morning. And it's not healthy to brood.'

'So,' she said, 'Climate change?'

Ben returned a wry smile. 'You really want to know?'

Hanna closed her hands round her mug, clasping its warmth against the chill of the Icelandic night. Ben drank from his chocolate whilst musing over Hanna's request. She was right; there was nothing more that could be done until morning. And he had been wanting to talk about his research since he got off that plane six days ago.

Handing over money to the cashier, Ben took the bottle of brandy in the duty-free carrier bag. He left the store and made his way through Terminal One passing a departure board as it flashed final boarding for flight FI451, the 12:15 Icelandair to Reykjavik. He rummaged in his fleece pocket to retrieve his passport and boarding card, imagining the greeting when he stepped off the plane at Keflavik from his sister Eleanor, Hanna Katla ... and maybe his Aunt too? Just wait until he told them what he had discovered – his theories, his research – the paper he was planning even now; running the sections through his mind, indexing the main points, cross-referencing the arguments with established fact.

*

Hanna sat in front of Ben, waiting. Ben looked up and spoke, tentatively at first, until he found his voice. He outlined the first premise, and explained, in case she had forgotten, the complex variables involved in measuring sea level and sea surface pressure.

A cold wind blew in from the north; the clouds shifted and broke apart. A star blinked in the far off heavens. Eleanor watched, standing alone on the outcrop of lava. She pulled her jacket about her, her hands numbed by the cold night. She felt her matted, unwashed hair. Behind her she heard footsteps. She sensed them stop a few yards off.

Eleanor fixed on the star ahead, speaking softly, 'Is it time?'

Headlights criss-crossed the car park and tyres crunched on the gravel. An assortment of vans, trucks and jeeps drove up to the mountain hut in convoy. One by one the beams of headlights faded, leaving the valley plunged into darkness once more. Finnur climbed down from his van, exhausted and exchanged sporadic conversation with his friends and colleagues as they made their way indoors.

'Karl!' Finnur called to a tall, wiry, dark-haired man with a thin goatee, as he headed off away from the hut. 'You not coming for a—?' He mimed drinking.

Karl called back, declining, and then after few more steps, added, 'Shattered. Need my bed!'

Finnur understood and nodded, before calling out goodnight. Entering the hut, he found himself amongst his colleagues as they pulled boots off aching feet and stripped off their wet jackets before peeling away layers of sweaty fleece. They made for the kitchen and began to unwind from the stress of the day with trivial banter.

Aðli pulled a beer from the ice box. He called to Finnur and pulled out another to toss across the room.

'What do we have that doesn't need cooking?' Finnur asked, approaching the food box and began sorting through it.

'We have some trout, I think, some flatbrauð – maybe some hangikjöt too,' replied Aðli. Putting down his beer, he reached for another crate, emptying out packets of smoked trout, bread and dried fish onto the table.

'And skyr,' Finnur produced the tub with glee. 'To finish.'

Ben and Hanna were sitting out on the deck, under the darkening night sky. Distracted for a moment by the commotion within the hut, Ben continued.

'You see? And if I can just balance those equations and map the result in my programme...' he faltered. He could tell that Hanna's interest was waning by the way that she kept ducking her head round, peering back through the open door. He continued, 'Then I should be able to predict ... what?' He had now completely lost his cousin's interest.

'Sorry,' Hanna apologised, 'I think – the guides – they're back, shall we go in?'

Cards flew across the table as drinks were downed and crisps and nuts consumed. Laughter and chat continued into the night. With grey daylight still filtering through the windows at midnight, the wooden interior darkened the light to gloomy shadows. Finnur opened another can of beer with a reassuring fizz from the ring-pull. Action around the table subsided and one by one eyes turned to Hanna Katla. She tapped and fidgeted with her cards as she eyed the pile on the table and chewed on her lip.

'Okay, okay,' Hanna excused herself. She pulled at three cards, then changed her mind. Finally she lay down five cards in a row, 'Pick up two,' she reminded Ben.

Ben cursed and reached for the pile. He looked up, catching sight of the glint in Finnur's eyes as he laughed.

'Poor luck, Benjamin,' Finnur taunted, turning now to a colleague and playing word games in Icelandic. Ben fumbled with his growing hand of cards, and cursed his bad luck.

Hanna reached for the crisps. She stopped, catching Ben's gaze. She saw in his hands a tangle of twenty or more cards. She grinned.

'Crisp, Ben?'

Ben opened his mouth.

Hanna gently fed crisp after crisp into Ben's mouth. She grinned again and enjoyed watching Ben struggle with both a full mouth and full hands.

'Not funny,' Ben barely spoke the words with half consumed crisps lingering around the teeth and roof of his mouth, sticking to his gums.

'Last card,' Hanna declared her hand. She took a drink from her glass of gin.

'Ah!' Ben whooped excitedly, 'Bear with me,' and he began laying down cards, explaining his moves partly for the others, but mostly for the benefit of his own thinking. Runs were followed by duplicates and runs of duplicates, he changed suit, reversed order, forced one, two, three, four others to miss a go and he himself played another card and another, going out himself with a flourish of aces.

'Asni!' Aðli swore, as he reached forward and scooped up the whole pile.

Ben stood in the cold, Icelandic night, out on the deck. Finnur closed the door behind him, and approached Ben's side. He sipped from his can of beer.

'I'm sorry about your sister,' said Finnur in English tinged with a thick Icelandic accent, 'We've scaled down the search, you know.'

Ben turned and looked at him. He shook his head.

'Not my decision – my superiors, you know.'

'Does that mean Eleanor? That she's...?'

'Every day, chances are – she's fallen into a canyon, the river and–'

'Don't,' Ben stopped him; he could full well imagine the horror behind the explanation.

Finnur sucked on his cigarette as he eyed the brother of the lost girl standing next to him. 'I'm not giving up.'

Ben turned and looked at him, confused and bewildered, 'You said...'

'I know.' Finnur nodded. 'But I know your sister. She's smart. She knows her stuff. If anyone can survive out there, she can.'

'Can I come with you?'

Finnur stared at Ben, and frowned. He shook his head. 'Maybe in a few days. Let's get tomorrow out the way first.'

Beneath the resonating blue light of night, Eleanor stepped on. Cautiously, she flashed her torchlight ahead of her occasionally, confirming her direction, feeling the rock beneath her fingers.

Ben stirred in his sleeping bag. The interior of the dormitory was dark and gloomy. Snoring reverberated around the wood panelling. Someone muttered in their sleep.

6

Ben woke, and blinking his eyes open, he squinted out through the gloom of the dormitory. Above his head, rain hammered angrily on the roof and wind rattled at the window. He pulled himself from his sleeping bag and staggered around the table to peer out of the window. The mountains were barely visible behind dense clouds. A gust of wind threw rain at the glass and the clouds flared with light. Thunder followed immediately.

He found his clothes and pulled them on before padding downstairs in his socks, slipping slightly on a couple of the boarded steps. He was greeted in the hall by the stale air of damp clothes and boots.

Entering the kitchen, Ben found a boiling kettle pouring steam into the room and the air thick with condensation; the smell of drying towels and coats draped across chairs. He looked around the room and found Hanna hunched up on a bench, engrossed in a book. She looked up only as Ben approached. Spread out on the table were maps of the highlands, various geological and hiking charts and computer print-outs of weather forecasts and progress reports for the search.

Hanna smiled, 'Morning Ben, you sleep good?'

Ben nodded, distracted by the paperwork on the table, 'Yeah. Where is...'

'Finnur - everybody? Gone to check something at the site office, I think.'

'They haven't left yet?' Ben asked.

Hanna closed her book, 'Weather's turned too dangerous. As you can see.' She gestured to the windows and as if on cue, the door to the deck rattled in the wind.

'You want a drink? Breakfast?' asked Hanna, 'Aðli said we can help ourselves to any of their food.'

Ben shrugged. 'I guess.'

Hanna got up and went about making a couple of cups of coffee and sorting out some cereal for her cousin. As she busied herself, Ben turned his attention to the map; studying the contours of the area carefully, before noting the various trails and emergency shelters.

'Ellie was on her way down from here.' Ben pointed. 'But they searched that extensively. Why haven't they found her?'

Hanna Katla looked across from the kitchen and frowned; there was nothing useful that she could say. She dolloped some of Aðli's skyr into the bowl on top of the cereal and carried it across to Ben with a mug of coffee. Returning for her own mug, she took a seat opposite him.

'I guess we just wait. The weather—' Hanna said.

'I feel so useless.' Ben pulled his mobile from his pocket. 'And three missed calls from my dad. I guess I should respond.'

He dropped the phone down onto the map and picked up his bowl to begin scooping up cereal.

Light refracted around the cut surfaces. Shafts of sunlight twisted through a long fissure of volcanic rock ending in a deep cavern. Eleanor approached. She reached out with her left hand, and stroked the clean edge of obsidian. She stared into the translucent blackness, lost in the wonderment of the refracted colours. She saw her brother's face staring back at her. He spoke to her, asking her – pleading with her to let him know she was safe.

'I'm coming Ben, coming.' Her head turned sharply into the darkness ahead. 'Just give me a few more days.'

'Eleanor?' Ben stood in front of the safety notice that was fixed to the wall. In the glass he could see his own reflection. 'I thought for a minute - Ellie's face - it was there.' He pointed at his own reflection. 'I could see her! She was on her way back to us...'

The door crashed open and a cold draught blew through the hut, followed by Finnur and Aðli. Finnur stopped upon seeing Ben.

'Oh, you're up,' he said, 'Dreadful conditions out there.'

'She's out there,' said Ben.

'I know. And I really wish that we could go out there and and bring her home,' Finnur responded gravely, 'But this weather, it's intense.'

'So what's the plan for today?' Ben asked, 'We do have a plan, don't we?'

'Plan?' Aðli looked to his colleague.

Finnur shrugged. '*Tsjilla* – we take it easy, Ben.'

Ben stared back at Finnur, shocked and surprised, angered even by the response.

'We've been out there every day – long days,' Finnur continued, 'And we would be out there today if we could. The weather – it's unfortunate, but it's bought us some rest time.'

'You can't do anything?' Ben shook his head.

'We've gone over the reports and talked to the guys at the other sites this morning. They're out there still; it's not so bad. Plus, we're spent, Ben. And if we are tired one of us could make a mistake. Trust me, its better that we take it easy and rest than end up searching for two or more people tomorrow.'

'And the geothermal pool here looks inviting on a day like today,' added Aðli.

Ben's mouth gaped. 'You're not serious?' He looked from Aðli to Finnur and then to Hanna, as if for backup.

Hanna answered Ben's concern with a kindly smile. 'If I'm honest, Ben, a dip in a hot pool is exactly what this kind of weather calls for.'

Eleanor clambered onward, clinging to the ice walls, her feet stepping cautiously along the ledge, below which gushing cold melt water tumbled and flowed. She rounded a corner, light blinding her from ahead. A small spasm of hope surged through her as she considered that maybe this was the exit to the cave.

She stepped forward, suddenly quickening her step. The ground beneath her feet gave way and she was thrown away from the wall. The fingers of one hand clung to the rock cutting lines into her skin, whilst the other clutched the pickaxe lodged into the rock. Breathless, she hung for a moment from the cave wall. Not meaning to, she glanced down into the emptiness beneath. Slowly, as she eased her breath, she composed herself and lifted one foot to the ledge, then the other and straightened up on quaking legs. She sighed with relief.

Eleanor emerged from the cave and sunk to the floor, exhausted. Fine drizzle pricked at her face and above, the clouds began to break – small patches of clear sky appearing beyond. She reached for her water bottle, freed the stopper and took a swig. Looking out down the valley she can could see it; where the unmistakable blue, white and orange livery of the guides' van with the insanely big wheels was driving away down the mountain road.

The tops of the surrounding mountains were dissolved in a lowering shroud of thickening cloud. A blustery wind circled the valley and the rain drove horizontally across the marshland. Ben walked briskly, head down against the rain, along the boardwalk to the platform over the hot pool. Hanna followed behind, her face poking out from under the hood of her waterproof jacket. They disrobed from their Gortex and, as goose bumps rose quickly on exposed skin, they climbed down into the hot pool, joining – amongst others in the rescue teams – Finnur and Aðli. Ben lay back in steaming sulphurous water until he was almost completely submerged.

'You know what?' joked Ben, 'I think I prefer it when it's raining! There's something so refreshing about pricks of cold on your face, whilst–'

'The rest of you is gorgeously warm?!' Hanna Katla laughed, agreeing with the odd statement.

Ben slid back, allowing his hair to overlap with thick throngs of river weed. He poked his toes out of the water, retracted them, poked them out again; playing with them on the surface of the water. Thinking back he could vividly remember an earlier occasion in a pool very much like this one. Eleanor was there and so was his father. Not his mother though. *Where was Mum on that occasion?* He scanned the pool as he remembered it;

Uncle Baldur, and Aunt Lára and Hanna Katla of course – they were all there.

Guðni cracked a joke and everyone laughed. Ben found himself laughing too, but not because it was funny, but because it was an Icelandic joke told in his father's own inimitable style and he just did not get it. He laughed because everyone else was laughing – and he couldn't admit his ignorance.

And the vision was gone. Ripples of water spread outwards from a splash and Ben was back in the pool at Kisilverksmidja, with his cousin opposite splashing water towards him. He splashed water back at her. For a moment they forgot why they were here and they laughed and joked, losing their preoccupations in the water.

Ben saw Finnur across the pool, his untidy blond fringe flattened against his forehead. 'So what happened?'

Finnur frowned at Ben.

'To Eleanor – out there – that day,' explained Ben, 'I mean, I know what the press say, but you were there...'

Finnur frowned gravely and began to explain. He detailed what happened from his perspective; of how they were coming down off the mountain and how the weather suddenly closed in on them, far worse than they could ever have anticipated. He told Ben and Hanna of the snow storm and the white-out and of how he was right behind Eleanor yet suddenly wasn't.

'Last night I was thinking,' Finnur said, 'I distinctly remember stopping with Eleanor, she fastened her boot. That was at the time of the snow-storm and the white-out. Now if she had gone straight on, where we turned to come down the ridge, she would have come down to the glacier and then from there to the lava field above where we are now. It would be a long walk – five days – but she would arrive here.'

Aðli nodded. 'Five days without food, water and shelter.'

'It's true,' agreed Finnur, 'But there are also caves. I remember seeing them last summer. She could have sheltered in one of those.'

Again Aðli nodded.

Ben fingered the surface idly, watching the intricacies of the water, 'Would Eleanor have known she was going to die?'

Hanna Katla swung round to face Ben, with obvious perplexity as to his sudden change in attitude.

'If she is dead,' Ben continued, 'Do you think she would have known?'

Hanna struggled to answer the enormity of the question. 'How do you mean?'

'Well if she fell, the end could have been instantaneous, no chance, but if she was lost – she could have been out there night after night, slowly freezing...'

'Ben, you can't think like this. Eleanor's a good climber and you heard it from Finnur, the weather closed in. She wouldn't stumble around and fall. She would find shelter, keep warm. She knows the rules – how long have you guys been doing this – people do survive!'

'People die too.' Ben stated dispassionately.

Hanna watched her cousin with concern. 'Ben?' she began, 'this whole mess – Ellie, she will return to us.'

Steam rose from the water around them.

'If this whole thing ... if it wasn't so tragic—' Hanna looked appalled by what she was saying. 'It could be a film, a novel. Hell, I've probably read a saga or two with the same story!'

Ben looked at her; curious yet comprehending. In some weird way he got what she was saying.

'And the thing about sagas, they have this habit for being based on truth.' She hit the water angrily. '*Helvitis*! Ben, I've read this story and I enjoyed it!'

Ben looked at her. He reached out towards her. 'We read stories. We enjoy them, Cous. Tragedies happen.'

Hanna smiled weakly, 'Suppose,' she shrugged, 'and I guess the thing with sagas is that they go on longer than this. Eleanor can't be dead – the story's only just begun.'

Ben laughed. 'Eleanor would have enjoyed that. 'She'd have wanted to write it herself, most likely.'

Guðni Ármannsson erected the fifteen year old ridge tent in the grassy flatlands beside the Þjórsá river. Nearby, his children Eleanor and Ben, twelve and eleven respectively, were playing with his niece; Hanna Katla caught her uncle's eye. She turned and ran, chasing her cousins up the turf roof of an old hut. She caught hold of Ben's sleeve, using it to pull herself up onto the ridge. The giggling subsided as all three children became entranced by the impressive slopes of the Þjórsájökull and Hofsjökull icecaps beyond.

'Watcha thinking?' Ben reached for his can of beer wedged into the grassy bank beside the pool.

Hanna looked at him. 'Eleanor.'

Ben paused with the can to his lips. 'And...?'

'Do you remember?' she said, 'It was a summer holiday. You must have been about eleven. Your Pabbi brought the three of us out here.'

Ben thought back, ferreting deep into his memories. He remembered – his dad looked so young in those days. He remembered the yellow canvas ridge tent. What did happen to that tent?

'Guðni – your Pabbi – he slept in a tent, but we didn't want to,' Hanna gently prodded at the back of Ben's memory, stirring what he had half-forgotten, 'There was the old house there—'

'With the turf roof, yeah.' He grinned, remembering.

'Which we used to run up the side of – sit on the ridge.'

'And look at the view.' He sighed. His eyes widened as the memories came flooding back. He could scarcely believe it.

'The shepherd's hut, by the lake. Of course—'

Hanna Katla nodded. She saw in Ben's eyes that he understood where her trail of thought, her reminiscing, was leading.

'You have an idea where she is? Your sister?' asked Finnur.

Ben frowned at Finnur. 'Maybe. It's a place we used to go - as kids - with my father. If Ellie, if she got down off the mountain, I think she might have gone there.'

'You can show me,' said Finnur.

'It's easy walking. If you can give us a lift to the next valley,' Ben glanced across at his cousin.

Hanna looked from Ben to Finnur. 'The gas station down by Lundarbrekka'

Finnur nodded.

'Sure. The ranger should be able to take you. I'll arrange it.'

Eleanor climbed down the last steep section of path, her wet fingers stung in the rain. Her feet slipped and slid over the wet rocks and muddy ground. She turned and began to descend the last gentle slope off the mountain. It broadened out with grass on both sides and scrubby birch trees twisted around each other off to the right. She couldn't help herself - as her legs quickened their pace she found herself almost running the last few hundred metres, with rain forced horizontally into her face.

She found herself in long meadow grass - low cloud sinking lower onto the landscape. A narrow stream gurgled through the valley floor, on the far side of which Eleanor could see an old house with its turf roof. She strode out across the meadow, crossing the stream at some stepping stones and approached the house. Standing at the door, she slid back the wooden latch and pushed it open. Stepping inside, she slammed the door shut against the wind and the rain and turned to face the gloomy interior. A hazy light filtered in from the one window set high in the wall at the far end. She slipped off her rucksack, letting it down onto the dry, dusty floor and stretched her muscles. She smelled the mustiness of the room.

Eleanor heard a rustling in the corner. Her eyes darted to the left – the fair headed, sleeping bodies of three children, just pre-teen. Eleanor stepped closer, observing them carefully. She saw herself tucked up in the bright orange sleeping bag. She smiled; fondly remembering those days as they came back to her. Crouching down beside those little heads she looked from Eleanor – to Hanna Katla – to Ben. She reached out to stroke his tufty fair hair.

'Ben,' Eleanor said as tears filled her eyes. 'Don't give up on me, Ben.'

Yesterday's storm had passed, leaving a day that was clear and bright. Dirt was kicked up from under the wheels of the white saloon car as it drove off, streaked in dirt and discoloured with years of volcanic sand ingrained into the paintwork. Hanna and Ben were left standing in the road with their rucksacks.

Hanna smiled at her cousin. 'All set?'

Ben nodded. He held up the radio that Finnur had given him. 'Ready to find her.' He grinned and glanced out down the side valley.

Hinges creaked and grated and the dull thud of wood banged against rock. Eleanor crept out of the old house in T-shirt and trousers. Blinking in the clear and bright sunshine, she stretched, reaching out to both sides and yawned. She returned inside, ducking low under doorway. A few seconds later and she emerged again with water bottle and a slab of *mjölkurkex*. She stepped away from the house and walked round the side, climbing up a grassy mound and onto rocks to get up onto the roof. Soon she sat perched on the grassy ridge, surveying the valley beyond.

Striding out along the valley, Ben and Hanna followed the river. Side by side, they walked in silence through the lush meadow grass beside the fast flowing glacial river. Beyond, the meadow to a stony tundra and ridges behind ridges and the grey, mournful cliffs ahead and the ice cap further on.

Ben laughed and Hanna turned to look. He shrugged. 'This landscape; this country; it's beautiful yet harsh and bleak, but the bleakness is offset against this lush paradise.' He gestured to the meadow around them, peppered with yellow flowers.

Hanna smiled thinly. She looked across the valley and saw the clouds building over Krafla and the threat of looming rain against brilliant sun and blue skies.

'It's dangerous.'

Eleanor slid the wooden bolt across with a reassuring thud and fastened the door. She shouldered her pack and set off, following the stream by the house down through birch scrub and meadow to the main glacial river. Still fast flowing, it was a pale imitation of its winter glory. Eleanor climbed down the bank to the shore and followed it, buoyed up by the thought of the road farther down the valley.

Ben and Hanna sat back to back on a rock. Ben pulled a bag of biscuits from his rucksack and turned to offer them to his cousin.

'I have a good feeling about today.'

Hanna Katla remained quiet. She wished to share Ben's optimism, but found herself unable to voice her thoughts. *Eleanor's been lost for eight days now. What hope?* Hanna sighed, swigged water from her bottle and bit into the biscuit.

'It's a good walk, this. Beautiful,' hesitantly Ben attempted to continue the conversation, 'It's the kind of walk I thought I'd be doing this far into the holiday. You know, acclimatising myself for the big one...'

Hanna frowned. Yes, she knew what Ben's plans were. If they'd gone as planned then he would've been here with her now, yes, but with Eleanor. All the time cutting across her thoughts, she could hear the sound of the river farther down there in the valley floor somewhere; she peered out across the valley more intently.

Ben turned and waited for Hanna. 'It's funny,' he said, 'How all the time you can hear it, the river. Almost like a motorway. But – but it's just hidden, down there under a rise in the bank.'

Eleanor continued walking through the day, determined not to spend another night in the wild. Pulling down the zip of her jacket and her fleece, she let in the breeze to cool her. She considered her brother as she walked, briskly now and with a new burst of energy after her night's sleep in the hut. Had he heard yet? Of course he had. And her parents, where were they now? She imagined walking up the drive to her cousin's house in Reykjavik, letting herself in and seeing them all there in the living room...

In front of her, further down a valley, a plane circled and descended. There must be an airstrip close by. In her mind she imagined the narrow strip of tundra cleared of the larger rocks and vegetation and a plane landing, with sheep looking up from their grazing to watch the aircraft. In her mind, the scene was clear; the pilot jumped down across the wing and headed back across the airstrip to the small grey rendered hut with red corrugated roof.

Eleanor picked up speed. If she could just get there before the plane left, she could be back in Reykjavik by tonight!

Hanna and Ben continued their walk, following the scrub line up the side of the valley. She glanced at her cousin. 'I wonder,' Hanna Katla mused, 'Why did your Mum – Diana – never come on those camping trips?'

'Don't know.' Ben shrugged,

'Something I never thought of – back then,' continued Hanna, 'But she didn't. Nor did Mamma and Pabbi.'

'Dad said he always missed Iceland. I guess he wanted us – Eleanor and I – and you – to feel the same.'

The conversation faltered and they continued on in silence. Climbing out of a dip in the landscape, they reached the top of a slight incline. Ben halted, with Hanna stopping at his side.

'Look,' Ben pointed. Hanna followed her cousin's gaze, to the small, turf-roofed house a few hundred metres farther on.

'It's like it's always been,' Hanna said.

Guðni adjusted the small camping stove, pumping parafin furiously and flicking a lighter over the gas. He called to Eleanor and Ben, where they were walking back up from the river carrying between them a heavy container full of water. He joked with them and encouraged them to be quicker. Glancing the other way he spied his niece, curled in the grass, reading, leaning against the wall of the old hut.

'You seen this?'

Ben approached his cousin, curious about the way she was studying the ground. He saw a flattening to the grass. He squinted up towards the hut, where the grass was pushed flat around by the door in the same way.

'Someone's been here,' said Ben. He stepped towards the hut to inspect.

'Or something,' cautioned Hanna.

Ben frowned. He knew that the chances that this was evidence of Eleanor's survival were remote, but he had to hope. He shrugged optimistically and returned his attention to the hut.

Eleanor slid her backpack off her shoulders and carefully approached one of the roaring tributaries to the Þjórsá. Crouching down she splashed icy cold, yet refreshing water onto her face. She roused aching limbs back to life in the cold water and returned to her pack. Pausing for a moment she scanned the horizon, glimpsing a splash of red – the roof to a hut - near to where the various tributaries were pulled together into a wider river.

She followed the river, crossing one stream after another, taking each ford via one of the tiny footbridges until she had zigzagged across the flood plain and to the isolated airstrip. A single, weather-worn aircraft hangar with a red corrugated curved roof stood alone in the whole valley. The walls were stained with dirt beaten into the render with every storm, and there was streaking on the walls from where the roof had leached its rust. She rounded the corner and approached the office door that stood open.

The pilot sat inside, feet up on the table, hand clasped round a mug of coffee, reading yesterday's paper. Next to him, his mate dealt out cards. Eleanor's shadow crossed over them and the the two men looked up. Drawing on a cigarette, the pilot looked at her and beckoned her to step nearer.

Eleanor stepped into the room and she could tell by the way that the men looked at her that she was no longer a silhouette against the airstrip.

'You don't know how long I have dreamt of this, of being here – somewhere—' her voice stumbled over relief and thanks.

'Eleanor Ármannsson?' The pilot nodded to her.

'How do you...?' asked Eleanor.

The pilot didn't answer. He just looked at her and slowly closed the newspaper, turning it to face her and slid it across the table. Eleanor glanced down and saw her own face in the grainy print.

Eleanor choked. Her tongue felt the dryness in her mouth as she eyed the water cooler in the corner of the room. The pilot glanced behind him, before moving fast to fetch a cup of water; he passed it to Eleanor quickly. She gulped down the cold water and quenched her thirst. Then, laying down her pack inside the door, she pulled her sweating feet from her boots, extracted herself from her jacket and, invited by the pilot, she eased herself down into the comfort of a proper chair.

Ben pulled back the wooden bolt from the door aggressively and pushed it inward. He stooped and entered the dim interior. Instinctively, he called out his sister's name. His voice rebounded back at him on the wave of an echo and he sunk to the dusty floor where he could not help but cry. With his face in his hands he pushed the tears defiantly from his eyes.

Hanna approached him, laying a hand on her cousin's head. He turned and looked up at her, seeing the concern on her face.

'I know,' Ben said, 'The door was fastened – there was no way. But I just felt I had to.'

'It's okay,' comforted Hanna, 'We'll pitch our tents and stay here for the night just like we said. If she comes we'll be here.'

Eleanor stretched her head back in her chair, wincing uneasily at her aching limbs. Out of the corner of her eye she watched the pilot carefully; as he kicked his feet back onto the desk, he lit another cigarette. She glanced across the room to where the radio receiver sat against the wall.

'You're not going to radio me in, then?' Eleanor asked, 'That I'm okay. That I'm not dead.'

The pilot grunted and looked up. 'Nei. It don't work.'

'You'll take me back though?' Eleanor's hopes began to sink. 'To Akureyri, maybe?'

The pilot looked up again. He exhaled smoke from between his lips. He shrugged. 'Later, ja. Cigarette first. Then fly you – an airstrip. You get bus. But you promise; my plane – you not mention.'

Silence. Eleanor watched the pilot. He fixed her in his gaze until she nodded and cautiously agreed to his terms.

Ben sat on the doorstep of the old house, eating the last of his supper, spooning it from his aluminium mess tin; he looked out across the valley to where the sun sank beneath the farthest ridge. Though still not dark, it was sufficiently late in the season that the familiar washed out light of midnight was now an ever-darkening gloom.

A swishing through the grasses and Ben's head turned. Hanna approached him from the hill, brushing her teeth as she walked.

'This hut must be used by loads of people. And every kid who comes down here will go and look inside,' Ben snapped irritably, 'Ellie was never here. I'm kidding myself to think that she's still alive.'

Hanna ducked to one side and spat out the toothpaste. Wiping her mouth clean, she stepped closer and shuffled in next to Ben on the step. He continued to stare at her.

'We'll give it till the morning. Then go down, meet with Finnur – see what else is to be done.'

A bus pulled up in the deserted forecourt of an isolated service station on the outskirts of town. Beyond the corrugated iron roof were the looming slopes of Krafla. Amongst the passengers disembarking were Ben and Hanna. Pausing to stretch their tired limbs, they headed across the forecourt to the burger bar with its offerings of cheap hot dogs and soda drinks.

Inside, whilst Hanna queued for food, she watched as Ben found a table and sat, resting his head in his hands. He had finally come to terms with the truth and she felt his pain; she felt it too. Ordering her food instictively, she looked around the American-style interior as she waited, watching the people at tables and those queuing behind her; all of them going about their everyday business.

She handed over cash and began to weave her way with the tray to Ben's table. As she approached, she noticed a girl, seated, her back to the room, at a table furthest from them at the rear of the diner. Hanna was curious and suspicious. She set down the tray in front of Ben and continued past him, trepidation losing out to curiosity at the final approach.

'Eleanor?' said Hanna. Ben turned his head at Hanna's voice. The girl turned, pushing her unwashed mousy-hair behind her ears. Eleanor looked up into her cousin's eyes.

PART TWO

Stranger in the Hills

1

Beyond the sizzle and bubble of chips in the fryer and the steaming water from hot dog pans, Eleanor sat in the roadside diner with her brother and cousin. With her elbows pressed to the Formica top, she cupped her hands round the mug of chocolate, inhaling the sweet, revitalising aroma. Ben reached out to her across the table and gently squeezed his sister's arm.

'Benjamin.' Eleanor said sharply. He took his hand back swiftly and she relented.

'Sorry. Just, I can't believe you are really here. I'd begun to convince myself you had—' He began to babble.

Eleanor frowned. She saw her brother's concern was still heavy on his shoulders. 'There were times when I thought the same.' She attempted to make light of the situation. 'Then I remembered that you still owe me fifty quid...' She grinned.

Ben's response was quiet and subdued. He stared at his sister and Eleanor felt guilt for her choice of words.

'Ben, I'm sorry – but – after what's happened and I'm here now, so,' she justified.

'Ellie, you can't make light of what's happened! Do you understand what you've put our family through?'

Eleanor jumped suddenly. 'I should call Dad.' She pulled herself away from the table. Hanna Katla reached across and stopped her cousin.

'Just have,' said Hanna, 'Spoke to Diana. She and Guðni – I said you'd call them again when we are on the bus to Reykjavik.'

Eleanor looked up and said in a detached voice, 'I'm not going back to Reykjavik.'

The man placed an ancient text with words that were hand-printed on thick vellum down on the ice between Eleanor and himself. He also fetched a finely decorated bowl carved from whalebone and some implements and seated himself opposite her. He lay the tools out on the ice next to him and cupped the bowl in both hands before enchanting a few words of old Icelandic. A blue flame flared into life.

Eleanor watched as Ben and Hanna lifted their heads and stared questioningly at hers.

'Of course I'll go back,' said Eleanor, 'Just not yet.'

'Eleanor.' Ben's voice was incredulous with anger. 'We all thought you'd died – that we had lost you. You can't not come back with us to Reykjavik. Our whole family is waiting to see you agan!'

'It's not that simple, Ben. I have something I have to do first.' Eleanor bit her lip. 'I promised.'

Silence. Ben and Hanna Katla sat stunned by Eleanor's determination. In unison they voiced their objections and their bewilderment, only to stop again in a tangled mess of sentences.

'Sis, you're not making any sense,' Ben said forcefully, 'What happened to you out there? Who did you meet? And what did you promise...?'

Eleanor remained quiet. Ben's questioning pressed heavily on her conscience and stirred memories in her mind.

Eleanor gazed up at the blue sky, with the jagged, vertical cliffs of the canyon walls looming over her. She squinted against the sun and virulent kaleidoscopes of colours against the almost-black of her eye-lids. With a chill bite to the air, the sun was still warm on her face. From where she lay, listening in to her friends' laughter and conversation, she blinked open her eyes and turned her head to one side to see Alice and Kirsten from beneath.

'Looks like you've got yourself a new neighbour Ellie.' Andy's voice cut into the conversation.

Eleanor propped herself up onto her elbows on the rug, spread out on the grass, in front of their tents. She followed the direction of Andy's gaze over in the direction of her own tent to where a tall man – taller even then Andy – was erecting his tent; an old two-man ridge tent with A-frames and a heavy canvas fly.

'I remember my dad used to have one like that,' said Eleanor, 'Think he still does, in the garage somewhere–'

Andy laughed. 'He's safe from any storm that comes through. Storm force ten? The world will be ripped apart and that tent will still stand!'

Eleanor continued to stare across the field at the tall man with a shock of silver running through his hair. She couldn't stop watching. The man looked up and returned her gaze. Still her eyesight was fixed on him.

'Of course. He was watching me for days,' Eleanor mused. She drifted out of her memories to see Ben and Hanna again, opposite her in the diner.

'Who?' asked Ben, 'Who was watching you?'

'I don't know his name,' said Eleanor, 'I didn't know it then. I didn't realise till now how long he was watching me. All that time back at the campsite and...' Eleanor worked through her memories, forgetting that they were making little sense to either Ben or Hanna.

'Who did you see?' Ben asked again, 'Ellie, I don't understand?'

Briefly Eleanor glanced up and her eyes focused on her brother. She shook her head and looked away.

A mist of water rose up out of the canyon, mixing with spray from the deafening, churning rage of Dettifoss as it cascaded through the canyon. Eleanor, with the assistance of Alice, carried a bucket-full of rocks slung between two poles, like a sedan chair. They slipped and slid through the sticky mud at the edge of the canyon. Setting down their load for a moment they looked out from under the dripping hoods of their waterproofs. Up above on the cliffs they could see that the others had stopped for a break and leaving the rocks where they were, they cut across the grass and deteriorating path and climbed up to join their friends.

Clambering up onto the top of the cliff, Eleanor found herself out of the spray. She laughed. 'It's like turning off the rain!'

Alice grinned as she pushed back her hood and unzipped her jacket.

'Biscuit?' asked Mike Potter, 'It's tough going down there isn't it?'

Eleanor smiled thinly. She took the packet and pushed a slab of mjölkurkex out of the plastic and passed the rest on to Alice. She looked up and out across the canyon. She looked again. There, further along the cliff, a man was standing tall, gazing out across the waterfall. He turned and Eleanor felt his gaze on her.

'No!' Eleanor lowered her head into her hands.

Ben watched his sister carefully, studying her every move and expression and tried to figure out where she was going with this crazy talk. He turned briefly to Hanna for support.

'You're not making any sense, Eleanor—' said Ben.

'I'm trying,' Eleanor said weakly, 'I need to tell you what happened, Ben.'

Ben frowned and reached across the table for his sister's hand, offering reassurance to her.

'It's okay. We'll get the bus, Ellie. We'll get you home. We can talk.'

She smiled thinly. 'I'd like that,' she said, 'I'm so tired, you wouldn't believe. But I told you, I can't go home. Not yet.'

The man returned her gaze with a simple and honest expression. His face was marked with the lines of age, his skin, weathered against the cold. A line of silver ran through his hair. Light glistened on the ice walls around him. A refraction of every colour swirled up through fissures in the ice ceiling. He nodded. Eleanor took the flame in both hands and held it.

'I promised,' Eleanor said, but her resolve was weakening.

Ben shook his head slowly. 'You've been missing for nine days and nights, Ellie! You've got to give me more than that!'

Eleanor remained silent, struggling to separate thoughts and dreams and memories from one another. Nine days. *Was it really that long? It didn't seem that long but who knows how long she was there – in that place...*

Hanna Katla reached across the table and took Eleanor's hand. 'What is it, Ellie? Who did you promise what to?'

Eleanor lifted her head and looked into her cousin's eyes and saw the kindness and the friendliness behind the words.

'We don't want to break your confidences, but you have to tell us. You do see that—' said Hanna.

*

Beyond a low babble of voices in the dimly lit interior of the mess tent and the hard, rhythmic drumming of rain on canvass, Eleanor got up from the bench and dived around a pole to the large pan of water, now steaming enthusiastically by the entrance.

'Who's for a bit of Swiss Miss then?' Eleanor grinned as she reached for the tin of hot chocolate. 'Hey and this time it's got added marshmallows.'

'Woo!' exclaimed Alice, 'You can count me in.'

As other cries of agreement came from the group, Eleanor fetched out more cups from the shelving around the tent and began spooning heaps of chocolate into them.

A breeze gusted into the tent setting the flames under the gas growling as Mike burst through the flap of the door. He ducked round Eleanor, apologising profusely for knocking into her.

'It's hell out there,' Mike said, 'Can you imagine if we were still up at Dettifoss now? Miserable...'

Shortly afterwards, Eleanor was back at the table holding her mug of hot chocolate close. She looked down the table to where Andy was shuffling a pack of cards. As he sorted through them, Alice leaned in closer to him, peering at the illustrated novelty deck. Suddenly, she laughed and pulled one from the pack.

'Hey, have you seen this one?' She held up the Queen of Spades to the group. 'Isn't that the splitting image of that old man? You know the one who's pitched up next to your tent, Ellie?'

Andy glanced at the card. 'Looks more like an old drag queen to me!' The others laughed, and Eleanor reached forward and took the card between finger and thumb. The card was creased and well-used with dirty, slightly splayed edges. Between the usual design of a playing card the picture of the queen was dark and brooding and painted with oils. With a staff clasped in his hand, he stood on a mountainside, his face thin and stretched. But it was the streak of silver that ran through his hair that Eleanor found distinctly reminiscent. She laughed.

'It is,' Eleanor said, 'It's him. It really is.'

She passed the card back to Andy and watched as the Queen of Spades slipped back into the middle of the pack. Andy shuffled through the cards. Where was the old lady now?

Eleanor looked from brother to cousin and back. She glanced at her watch. 'If I tell you. You've got to promise you won't tell Dad.' Eleanor was firm. 'Promise?'

Eleanor dropped her gaze to her hot chocolate. She tilted it between her fingers, rocking it from side to side and peered down at the dregs of her drink and watched them slide and curl around the bottom. She lifted her head in time to see Hanna glance briefly at Ben.

'Yeah, okay. Tell us your story,' Hanna Katla agreed.

'Ben?' asked Eleanor.

Ben nodded.

Eleanor lay in her sleeping bag, propped up on her elbows on the, giant bunk that filled one side of the dormitory. The air smelt thickly of seasoned wood from the panelled interior. Next to her was Andy and beyond him, Mike. Opposite her, in sleeping bags on the other bunk, were Alice and Kirsten. Eleanor peered down the room, past the rows of sleeping bodies to where Finnur could be seen sitting with Aðli, drinking from their cans of beer.

Finnur turned and looked back down the length of the dormitory towards Eleanor. 'It's a sad story – very Romeo and Juliet.'

'Kind of R and J, já.' Eleanor laughed. 'But where instead of families it's the environment that separates them.'

Finnur nodded. 'And you do this professionally.'

'I dream,' said Eleanor, 'History at University – but I've always written.' She laughed. 'I've got my notebook with me now.' She reached down to her side and took up a Moleskine notebook and waved it forward.

Finnur walked down the dormitory and, can of beer in one hand, reached out with the other. Eleanor snatched the book away.

'Steady on.' She grinned, then chewed on her lip. 'I can't let you read my work in progress.'

She found Finnur's stare on her across the rim of his beer can. 'You must tell me when it's published, then. When I'm in Reykjavik I will buy a copy. And I don't buy books often.'

'I'll send you a signed copy.' Her face reddened, and through her hand she felt her cheeks burn.

Eleanor lifted her head and staring past Finnur, as he drained the last of his beer, she imagined the grey peak of Krafla in front of her. Finnur crushed the can in his hand and glanced down at Eleanor.

'Bed, I think.'

Eleanor nodded, turning onto her side and tugging the sleeping bag up round her neck. 'You think we can make it tomorrow?' She turned her head and caught a glimpse of Finnur's bare muscular chest as he pulled off his fleece and sweater.

Finnur shrugged. 'We'll go up on the ridge. From there we can assess the weather. If it looks good – we'll go up – if not, then we can go down the other side to the canyon and, from there, home.'

Eleanor glanced back over her shoulder and watched as Finnur unfastened his trousers to reveal his long, thermal underwear beneath.

Ben stared at his sister. 'We know about the hike you were going on. Do we really need to know about the affair you were having with one of the guides?'

Eleanor kicked him under the table, glaring at him above. 'It's my story,' she said impetuously.

Gunnlaugr stood on the hillside opposite the small rescue hut, scanning the slopes between. A mountain river of tumbling melt water cut the landscape between him and the hikers that he had been following. A single lamp within the hut was extinguished and Gunnlaugr took this signal as his opportunity to stride forward.

His fingers clasped around his staff firmly. He stood tall and strode down the mountainside taking stepping stones across the mountain river without pausing and stepped up to the hut. He lay the palm of his hand against the wood and sensed the people within.

Eleanor lay on her bunk within, awake, listening keenly. She could hear the mournful wail of wind outside – and there – a crunch of gravel. And there again – a sound of hands on the wood. And nothing. She listened harder, closer, but heard nothing more. Eleanor shivered and pulled her sleeping bag tighter around herself. She relaxed and subsided into sleep.

2

'Last night. Did you hear anything – strange?' Eleanor lifted her head from her pillow of micro-fleece. She peered out into the room. Finnur was packing his sleeping bag away into his rucksack. He turned towards her and shrugged.

'Probably an artic fox.'

Eleanor frowned. She remembered what she had heard last night during her ebbing consciousness before sleep, and those sounds now reverberated back through her mind. It could've been an arctic fox, she guessed. Most likely though Finnur was right. Night sounds did, after all, get amplified. Even so, those weren't animal footsteps.

'But it wasn't?' Hanna questioned.

Eleanor shook her head to Hanna's enquiry. 'Didn't know it then – but it was no fox...'

'Of course it was,' snapped Ben. 'It's just to do with the air pressure outside relative to that in the hut. It caused the sound to travel at a different frequency and distort the effect of—'

'I know about the flaming Doppler effect, Ben!' She stared at her brother.

Eleanor only lifted her gaze from Ben after a long, hard stare and looked again to her cousin. She smiled kindly at Hanna.

'So if it wasn't a fox?' Hanna pursued her question.

Eleanor laughed. 'I forgot all about what I thought I heard. Until...'

'Until what?' Hanna probed.

'I'm sure you know already. The weather closed in. Thick cloud, that sunk lower and lower. Over lunch we thought it might lift again, there was brightness down over the southwest. Finnur radioed out for a forecast. We had a choice between going down into the valley and sheltering overnight to hope for better weather in the morning – or turning back there and then to get down off the mountain.' She looked across at her brother, regretfully. 'You were flying out to join me. We decided to come off the mountain.'

Eleanor lifted her head and watched for a reaction from her brother. She saw puzzlement on his face.

Ben shook his head. 'We know this. Finnur's told us – hell it's been all over the news.'

'Then I guess you know that whilst coming down off the ridge the cloud closed in around us so thick and then the rain and snow – you know what Iceland's like but this year it's been mental – I swear I couldn't even see the end of my arm—' She held out her hand to demonstrate. 'Finnur was behind me. And there was this steep section – we had to leave a little more gap, I must have stumbled off the path at the end of that section and by the time Finnur realised—'

'You were already too far separated,' said Hanna.

Eleanor nodded. Hanna pushed a refill of coffee across the table towards her and Eleanor placed her hands around the mug, feeling the heat through the china. In her memory she could still feel her face stinging from the cold, wet wind and the driving snow that had enveloped her and seeped beneath her clothing.

Eleanor called out to Finnur – and to Aðli. She called to her friends and cursed and swore when they didn't answer; she muttered about her foolishness then and of her actions now. She kicked her feet into the dirt.

Gunnlaugr observed the girl with keen sight that pierced through the fog. Moving as she moved, halting as she halted, he kept himself back behind rocks and bided his time. Observing her and studying her movements, he learnt from her actions.

His boots slipped on the rock and crunched into the gravel.

'Finnur!' Eleanor called, staring this way and that out into the grey fog.

No reply. Fear seeped into the pores of her skin.

'I stumbled around that hillside for an hour or more calling for the others.'

'You should have stayed where you were - on the path,' Ben said crossly, 'You know the drill!'

'You think I don't know the theory?' Eleanor snapped. 'Benjamin, it's a whole different story when you are out there in the cold and the fog - and the snow. When you don't even know where the path is—' She stopped, remembering suddenly that weekend in The Fells back home. From Ben's reaction she saw that he too remembered. A stillness subsumed the conversation.

Finally, Hanna Katla turned to her cousin. 'So you were lost on the hillside - somewhere on the slopes beneath Krafla - but you still found shelter?'

Eleanor stopped her aimless wandering and began a more purposeful route. Climbing down through the rocks she made her way across the slope. Gunnlaugr followed, surefooted and stealthily. He kept his distance; keeping the girl only just in sight.

'I knew that I'd stumbled well away from the path and in those conditions – even if Finnur and Aðli had returned what were the chances of them finding me that night?' Eleanor paused for a moment. 'I knew I had to find shelter. And the only shelter I knew about for certain was down.'

'Stumbling about on exposed mountains in adverse weather conditions? It's pretty stupid–' Ben stated thoughtlessly.

Eleanor scowled at her brother. *Why was he taunting her like this?* It made her wonder if he really wanted her to continue with her story. She caught sight of Hanna's compassionate smile out the corner of her eye and turned to her cousin.

'But you did find shelter?' Hanna asked.

'Yeah.' Eleanor nodded. She felt the weight of her cousin's probing gaze and tried to remember but found it difficult to put what happened next into words.

'I found myself in a cave.' She bit her lip, agonising over the memories. 'Though how, I don't remember. Must have been *that* sick with delirium...'

She looked up to see Ben and Hanna observing her intently now, as she struggled to recount her story.

'The next thing that I remember I guess, was–' Eleanor shivered.

A draft swirled across the gravel floor, tickling Eleanor where she lay half sleeping, half awake, huddled in her sleeping bag. She blinked her eyes open, and peered out into the gloom beyond the cave entrance. From where she lay it was impossible to tell if the wall of grey was fog or glacier. She began to pull herself from her bag and reached for her boots. She stopped. The crackle of flames and the hissing pops of spitting fat punctuated the silence. The smell of cooking food wafted over—

'Fire!' Eleanor swung round to face the back of the cave. A small fire had been made underneath a simmering pitcher of water and pan of frying food. Eleanor stood up and approached cautiously.

'How?' She looked around, peering further into the gloom. 'Who's done this?' Eleanor returned to her rucksack and retrieved her torch. She flashed it into the dark. Nothing and nobody.

'Show yourself. Who are you?' She spoke to the emptiness, demanding answers. Then, chancing on a thought, she added. 'Finnur?'

No reply. Eleanor frowned with resignation. *It was always going to be unlikely*. She returned to her camp and tucked her legs into her sleeping bag for warmth whilst she breakfasted on dried dates and a slab of *mjölkurkex* washed down with a swig of water from her bottle. All the time she watched the fire, pondering its maker and more importantly its maker's whereabouts.

He watched her watching him. If she had eyes as keen as his she would have seen him. Eat, he willed her. He cursed the girl and her suspicions as the pitcher boiled and the food blackened and burned. And now she was off again. Slipping into her boots again, he waited for her to leave. But no, she had left her pack as she just stepped out towards the cave mouth. In the dark he moved forward, closer, staying to the shadows. It was almost time.

He listened to Eleanor talking to herself and stepped from the shadows. He took the frying pan and removed it from the heat, scraping away at the charred and inedible food. He took the pitcher and crushed some herbs into the liquid, before pouring it out into a aluminium cup and approached the girl.

Although the air was clear of the penetrating fog from yesterday, the sky was grey and leaden. Eleanor looked out from the cave mouth at the ridges and escarpments that stretched out for miles in every direction.

'Which way now Ellie?' she asked herself, 'Up to the ridge and try and find the path? Or down into the valley?'

The wind turned and a howling icy blast rounded a rocky outcrop. And then silence except for the crunching of boots on gravel. Eleanor swung round as a man, tall and weather-beaten stepped out from the dark inside of the cave and approached her.

'Who are you?' Her voice was unsympathetic.

The man remained silent. He simply pushed the cup towards her.

'He just approached you, like that?' Ben's face was twisted with disbelief.

Eleanor nodded. *It's all true.* She sensed immediately Ben's suspicions and turned to Hanna for support. From her cousin she found a reaction that, whilst still obviously doubtful, was more openly curious. Eleanor smiled.

'You said, I think, that he'd been watching you?' asked Hanna.

Eleanor frowned. *Yes. Maybe. But no.* She sighed and sipped her coffee and stared out across the rim of the mug at Ben and Hanna. 'He just stood there in the cave entrance, staring at me and offering me his food. 'Of course I didn't take it—'

'The weather.' Eleanor pulled her coat closer about her. 'You got lost too?'

'You need more than biscuits and dried fruit. Drink. It's better than food.'

'What do you want?' she asked, pronouncing the words with strong, hard edged accents.

The man's smile stretched over his lined and weathered face, etched deep with the traces of many years. Slowly he stood the cup on a flat-topped rock at Eleanor's feet and stepped away. Eleanor watched him and glanced at the cup. Her stomach ached for nourishment. But to take food from this man?

'You are so like my niece.' His voice, thick with an Icelandic accent was beguiling and friendly. 'She wouldn't touch food from a stranger like me.'

'Your niece has sense.'

The man nodded.

'It's going to be a full day at least. To get back to the road,' said Eleanor.

Again the man nodded. He stepped back into the cave and into the shadows. Eleanor continued to watch him as far as she could before she returned to the cave and moved again into the dim interior. She listened to the man rummaging through his belongings. She glanced back at the food. Her stomach ached again.

'I suppose,' she said, 'If you did wish me harm – you've been here all the time I was asleep.' Silence greeted her reasoning. 'So much easier to kill me – or whatever – in my sleep.'

Eleanor crouched and cautiously sniffed the concoction; and took a sip. The taste lingered in her mouth and melted into her senses. It was good – warming, refreshing and incredibly sustaining. Finally she put down the cup and glanced towards the mouth of the cave. Cloud had sunk again around them – thick and impenetrable.

'I knew you were there, of course.' Eleanor approached the stranger where he was inspecting the rock face at the back of the cave. 'From the moment I woke up, I knew you there, skulking–'

'Skulking,' the man hissed sharply, 'No! Not skulking.'

'Whatever.' Eleanor shrugged. She saw the remaining liquid in the pitcher and quickly decanted some into her waterbottle. 'So you got lost in that storm as well. We didn't see you on the path yesterday?'

'I like to keep my distance,' said the man, dispassionately, 'You needed help to find shelter though. Or you would have died out there.'

Eleanor swung round sharply and stared at the man. 'You brought me here? How – I don't remember...?'

The man remained silent but stared intently at her from his pale eyes. She blinked and looked away; down at her feet she kicked at the ground and knocked stones around the floor. Eleanor wandered aimlessly and found herself reaching out to stroke the smooth ice-hewn rock surfaces. Suddenly she remembered her brother and wished he was here. He would be able to tell her what particular variety of volcanic rock this was. Ben? She pulled at her wrist, reading the time. He would be at Heathrow, selecting some Duty Free no doubt.

She glanced across the cave towards the man and to where he was feeling the rock, almost in a sensual way. She laughed.

'You're a geologist?' asked Eleanor, 'Or are you looking for something?'

She continued to watch the man and awaited his response. He remained silent. Sparks flew and shocked his hand. She pulled it away from the rock.

'What the hell?' Eleanor reached out again, curious to touch the rock. Beneath her palm a flare of light blazed from the rock: an effervescent burning of reds, browns, greens and blues.

'You've done it!' The man was now at her side and excited. 'See how the cave opens for us.'

'Magic,' said Hanna.

'Magic?' Ben said blankly, his face convulsed with incomprehension.

'Certainly a trick,' Eleanor said, 'or so I thought then.'

'What was it? Alfar magic? The huldufolk?'

'Hanna don't encourage her,' Ben said adamantly, 'The ordeal, lack of sleep and hunger – it was all playing tricks on my sister.'

'In dark places, untold secrets reveal themselves,' Hanna spoke the words calmly.

'Icelandic fairy-tale,' reasoned Ben.

Eleanor chewed on her lip as she watched her brother and her cousin tussle with their beliefs. 'I don't know what it was. Not then. It was beautiful though. Ben, if you'd been there, you could not have not believed...'

Ben looked up. He fixed his sister with his gaze. 'Go on.'

Eleanor felt a tingling coursed through her fingers. She reached out with both hands and pulses of light flared from her fingertips to connect with the rock. She glanced over her shoulder as the man watched her.

'What's happening?' Eleanor's tone was forceful. 'You know, don't you?'

The man smiled, thinly. 'You asked Eleanor, what I was doing.'

'You were looking for this.' The flares of light intensified.

'I was walking, climbing, just like you, yes. Exploring and searching, most definitely. And you, you have found it.'

'You were looking for me?'

'In part,' the man responded. 'Draw from a rock the greenest of green of the light – let the blaze strengthen. This is just the beginning – the first steps.'

'First steps?' snorted Eleanor, 'Steps to what?'

'Understanding.'

Eleanor's eyes widened. She heard the word spoken calmly and reverently and realised that this man treated what he told her as if it were a religion.

'The lore of Bláfell. It's here, deep in the rock, the very fabric of this land.'

Eleanor nodded. This man, he's crazy – too many days in the wilderness.

*'You weren't lost then?' she said, 'You've come here for a purpose
and now I've stumbled in and got involved.'*

'Careful,' he cautioned her, nodding towards the rock.

*Eleanor looked again. Her jaw dropped. In front of her very eyes,
amongst the swirling, shimmering light, the rock was melting away
revealing a doorway through into the mountain. She shook her head
incredulously.*

*'Enough now.' He pulled her hands away and the light faded, but
the door remained. He barked the order. 'Get your stuff! We're going in.'*

'You,' Ben interrupted, 'You followed him?'

Eleanor looked at her brother crossly. 'You didn't see it. The
door. If you had, you would've too.'

'Where did it go?,' asked Hanna, 'What was it like?'

Eleanor turned to face her cousin, as she remembered. 'It was
amazing.' She recalled every moment and every memory as if it
was then. The surging, flaming light that burnt from the rock
and seeped into her skin to fill her with the same illumination.

*Eleanor stepped further in, hearing her guide follow her. Suddenly
the light was gone and Eleanor knew without turning that the doorway
had closed behind them. Reaching out to each side she trailed the rock
beneath her fingers and moved on further down the passage.*

'Where are we?' asked Eleanor.

'Deep in the mountain. Far beyond the reach of mortal men.'

*Eleanor found herself for the first time in ages feeling fearful. 'Where
are we heading?'*

*Silence. She could hear the man's breathing behind her. Presently, in
a low reverent voice he said, 'To find learning.'*

*'Here.' The man held Eleanor back and stepped ahead of her into a
wider space. The floor was still of rock, but broken and pitted. Above, the
ceiling was carved out of basalt through years of glacial and volcanic activity.*

Eleanor reached out and touched it; smooth grooves between sharp and twisted rock. It is warm to the touch.

'Where are we?'

The man nodded. 'The stair we've just descended is centuries old. In the old texts scribed by Bláfell he talks of this stair in the days before the great fire storms and the ice that carved out our land.'

Eleanor looked to her companion. A stair that descended down – to what?

'It's an alfar stair – that's why the entrance was so well hidden. It would once have descended into the very heart of the mountains.'

'And where are the alfar now?' Eleanor imagined a community of the ancient people living in caverns deep beneath the mountain.

'Cast out. Twice,' the man told her, 'Firstly at the end of the great war with the Purs and then later by the most deadly of foes.' He stopped. Eleanor found so many thoughts coming into her mind. What was deadly about the foe? How?

'Where do the alfar live now?'

'Scattered,' he said bluntly, 'In our age, they have forever been pushed to the surface, living where they can amongst people, moving from vale to ridge. Such are the stories. Gone are the great halls, the Alf cities beneath the mountain.'

'But what was the second foe that drove them out?'

The man shook his head slightly and led her on through the lava tunnels until finally they arrived at a larger cavern lit by the shimmering orange iridescent glow of fire, emanating through a fissure in the floor from a deeper cavern far beneath.

'We stop here.'

Eleanor slipped her pack to the floor and quenched her thirst from her water bottle. She quickly swallowed a small handful of dates, before exploring the chamber. A central column of twisted rock – black obsidian – rose up through the ceiling. She stroked its smooth edges and considered the curves of light reflecting within it. Light from the chasm beneath reflected and refracted colours across the iridescence of the surface.

For the first time in what seemed to her like an age her mind turned to Ben. Where was he now? What was he thinking? Did he even know of her disappearance yet? Is he, even now, planning her funeral with mum and dad? In her slowing, dreamlike awakening she saw her brother's face in colours reflected in the ice. And then he was gone.

3

A cold wind gusted in from the north, slamming sheets of rain across a grey and dismal forecourt. Eleanor, Hanna and Ben ran across the flooded concourse towards the lonely bus. They dived towards the luggage hold and stowed their bags hurriedly before rushing to board the bus and bounding up the steps to take their seats.

Dark clouds gathered overhead, enveloping the sky. Rain lashed out at the bus, at the scattered farms that it passed, and at the windswept ponies in the fields. The mountain loomed close again. To the right the bus passed Mývatn – the lake was not so beautiful in this weather but bleak and haunting. Eleanor watched the scenery pass with her face pressed to the cold glass. She saw the scene through the blurred outline of rain drops and thought for a moment that she saw shadowy figures move along the shore.

Lake-trolls moved in the half-light, cautiously, for fear of the sudden re-emergence of the sun. They sought out food of small mammals and birds and fish from the lake. They spoke little as they moved, keeping low to the ground. Sheltering behind boulders, they blended themselves into the environment around them.

Eleanor watched them, her eyesight quickly picking them out from the rocks on the shore. For a moment she was almost lost in their world; gathering food and strengthening the defences of their world in readiness for some great siege.

'Eleanor!'

Eleanor murmured as she stirred herself awake. She was vaguely aware of an arm reaching across the headrest and prodding her gently.

'Eleanor.' Hanna pushed and shook her cousin again.

'Your story? What happened? And–' Hanna paused, unsure of whether she had Eleanor's full attention. 'How did you get out from those caves?'

Eleanor blinked. She stared back through the gap between the two headrests at her cousin's face. Eleanor glanced to her left. Ben too was waiting for more of her story. She stumbled for a moment over her words, as she searched for clarity.

'The chamber where we stopped, it was more than just a resting place. My guide, he – or someone – they had fashioned that place for – a purpose. He had all these strange tools and old books – implements of great – magic, I guess.'

'Who are you?' demanded Eleanor. The man looked up at her with those piercing bright eyes of his.

'If by that, you mean my name,' he answered, 'You may call me Gunnlaugr Ólafsson.'

Eleanor shook her head dismissively. 'But who are you? What are you doing out here?'

Gunnlaugr chose silence as answer to her question, and instead offered her his hand. She stared at him. What? She thought she understood and slowly lifted her hand to his. He nodded and slowly, fixing his gaze to hers, he crumbled a mixture of powders and granules through his fingers. He enchanted words in Old Norse and Eleanor felt the surge of power through every bone of her body.

Eleanor twitched herself awake. Her fingers clawed at the gravel beneath her. She blinked her eyes open and sat up almost immediately. She was in a new chamber, darkly lit and hewn from stone. She picked herself up, and began to explore the room in which she found herself.

'Gunnlaugr?' she said quietly.

No answer. Her hand traced the shape of the designs etched into the walls. Where had the man gone and how did she get here? Dimly she remembered magic spoken.

'Eleanor.'

She turned sharply upon hearing the old man's voice. 'Where are you?' she said sternly.

'Eleanor.' Gunnlaugr's voice resonated inside her head. She stopped. Hand on the stone walls she found her sight settling on a tablet of runes carved into the mountain.

'Speak the words, Eleanor.'

Eleanor's face twitched with the confusion and uncertainty within her. She reached out and traced the markings in front of her on the wall. The words burned at her mind and almost uncontrollably she voiced the scripture, and intoned the words.

She said them over and over again, enunciating every nuance and inflection of the words, instinctive to the pronunciation whilst remaining consciously oblivious as to their meaning.

*

'Consciously?!' scoffed Ben. His mind attempted to process how one could be consciously unaware of something and yet still act upon it.

Eleanor regarded her brother strongly. 'I think it's true – deep down, subconsciously I did understand. I think I still do.'

Ben shook his head. Refusing with equal determination to accept the fantasy that he was being told.

Eleanor shivered. A draught swept across her and she pulled her coat in closer around her. She was not alone; she could feel it. She turned in time to see a shadow disappear out of sight down the hall. Impulsively she followed, slowly at first before hurrying to catch up.

Around a corner and she saw him for the first time. He stood facing her. A creature straight out of mythology, he was short and stoutly built, with a coarse beard of black and shaggy hair over a podgy face. With layers of fat for a neck it was unmistakably a man. But could it really be a troll? Eleanor narrowed her gaze and was about to speak – to introduce herself – when she remembered that she did not know the language.

The man turned and lumbered off, taking a narrow stair up through the rock. Eleanor moved to follow, slowly at first, she lay her hand on the door frame and held herself back. This was silly, she mused.

'Too right it is,' Ben told her. 'Going off after trolls? Pretty bloody silly!'

'What would you rather have had me do?' Eleanor countered, 'Stay forever who knows where? And besides, it's not like he attacked me before, when he had the chance.'

'So these þursar?' Hanna breathed the name out of her country's legends. 'Were there others?'

Eleanor nodded fervently. 'They're incredible Hanna and they do resemble rock formations – you can really see how the legends have begun. When I saw him again I could see that his skin was as hard as old leather and his eyes, they stared out at me big and wide, from these huge, bony eye sockets...' She laughed. 'There were these large tufts of hair sprouting out of his flared nostrils!'

Eleanor climbed the spiral stair, constantly adjusting her speed as she pursued the large shadow of the þursar man. A murmur of conversation punctuated with the clattering of wood and metal and the neigh of horses grew louder the higher she climbed. Then suddenly she reached the top step and emerged out into a busy subterranean street.

She jumped back into the stairwell as a cart crashed past in front of her, pots and baskets swinging from the back. Stepping out again, more cautiously she looked up and down the street, scouring the faces and figures of the crowd – and there – she saw him. The þursar man who she had been following was already at the far end of the street.

Eleanor pushed out into the crowd; worried at first that she was going to be accosted by these strange people but soon found that they ignored her. Dodging in and out of the crowds she weaved her way through market stalls. Trays of meat, fish, and vegetables were cheek by jowl with earthenware pots and utensils carved out of whalebone and roughly hewn driftwood.

Ahead of her she tried to keep the þursar man within sight as he weaved his way on through the crowds. She dodged out from under the wheels of a cart, tripped and stumbled sideways into the wall. A large hand reached out gripped her firmly and pulled her back. Eleanor turned to see her saviour and found herself staring into the eyes of a þursar woman.

'Thank you,' said Eleanor.

'Þú ert velkominn,' the þursar woman replied.

For a few moments longer the þursar woman kept hold of Eleanor's arm as she stared at her sternly. Slowly her grip relented and Eleanor slipped herself free, all the while under the watchful gaze of the woman from her big, wide, searching blue eyes. Eleanor turned and stepped back to scan the street, fixing her eyes once more on the þursar man and pursued him, this time faster.

Having taken a turning down a side passage Eleanor found herself once more away from the crowds and following the man down dimly lit halls past entrances to smaller caves and chambers, many of them smithies that resounded to the thud of tools on molten metal.

And then she was alone, walking deserted passages. The man had vanished. She cursed herself for not having caught up – and wondered why she pursued this þurs in the first place. She walked further on, dispirited, trailing her fingers across the stone walls.

Turning aimlessly down further passages, Eleanor stepped on, listening to her own quiet footsteps and the gentle patter of water dripping from the roof. She stopped, considering the stupidity of wandering around caves with no idea of where she was going. Which way now, exactly, where was the main street that she had left? She looked up and froze. Opposite where she had stopped was a chamber, at a slightly lower level to where she currently stood, in which the þursar man was working.

Cautiously, Eleanor stepped down into the chamber; a naturally vaulted cave of twisted basalt and obsidian.

'Finally.'

Eleanor looked up as the man spoke. 'What do you mean?'

'No matter. You have come.'

'I had to,' began Eleanor. She stared at the man where he worked, standing over a long table working at manuscripts with a careful hand. 'You were watching me. Why?'

The man continued to write, transcribing the text from a further volume. Without turning, he answered the question. 'It is not everyday that a child of the overworld finds their way into our halls. How, may I ask, did you achieve it?'

'I–' Eleanor stumbled from the first word, to continue her story. How could she explain how she got here – when she didn't understand herself – and – and could she should she, reveal the magic that Gunnlaugr revealed? She bit her lip and considered her choice of words.

'I've been studying some of the old legends and–' Thinking back to her university course and her recently finished dissertation, Eleanor considered this to be only a half lie. 'And when I got lost in the mountains I was going over the texts in my mind. It's weird but it stopped me thinking about the cold.'

'And there was no one else with you? No one who helped you?'

Eleanor was about to reply when she stopped herself. Better, she decided to say nothing.

'It's powerful magic that you have used. To cross between your world and this – you should be careful.'

'I am–'

'And yet you seem to trust me.' The man stepped towards Eleanor. For a moment she feared what he might do. 'Why is that do you think?' The þursar man reached out past Eleanor and took an old, leather bound book from a ledge in the rock.

'Who are you?' asked Eleanor. 'What's your name, I mean?'

'Erik,' the þursar man replied, 'And you. You are Eleanor Ármannson, a daughter of Guðni Ármannson.'

'How do you...?'

'Your lineage has long been told of in our stories. See.' Erik opened the book and pointed to the text. Eleanor pulled herself closer and scanned the text. Amongst the flowing handwriting of Icelandic she could clearly see her own name.

'You see? You really were expecting me!' Eleanor stopped. She clutched at her head. She felt suddenly dizzy as she stared at the page of text, and the words faded into a fog of incomprehension in front of her. She swayed on her heels and–

Eleanor blinked her eyes open and adjusted to her new surroundings. She was sat in a great hall, lit by torches and adorned with tapestries and weaponry. At a large piece of lava hewn from the rock sat a council chamber of þursar elders.

Every þursar eye was observing her. It slowly dawned on her that they were awaiting a response from her. She stumbled and stuttered over excuses and she even considered making a run for it. Think Eleanor, where would you run. You need magic to leave this place. She retreated into her shyness and her uncertainty. Eleanor found her feelings both silly and stupid and reminded herself just how ridiculous she could be.

She remembered another set of eyes staring back at her from the group of volunteers gathered under the fluorescent lights of Heathrow's Terminal One. Eleanor remembered glancing around for support but Andy was still busy at the bureau de change. She garbled a hello tentatively.

Hanna sat hanging on her cousin's every word with pictures forming in her own mind to illustrate the scene that Eleanor set. Her own heart ached with the possibility that she too might, one day, meet with the þursar. Memories came back to her of standing on the shore of a river beneath towering canyon walls imagining the þurs people fishing in the river under moonlight. Then, trapped by the strong currents, Hanna could see the panic as the sunrise picked them out from over the cliffs that set them to stone. She remembered all the stories that have grown up over the years.

'What did they want from you?' asked Hanna, 'They weren't hostile towards you, were they?'

Eleanor grinned, divining pleasure from her cousin's reaction to the story. She knew that she was enjoying her role of storyteller too much, but even so, couldn't stop herself enriching it with every sight, sound and detail of what she experienced.

'It was a counsel of elders,' Eleanor explained, 'I didn't understand most of it to be honest. The whole debate – an emergency meeting I believe – was to decide upon action against some threat to their mountain halls'

'That doesn't explain why they needed you,' interrupted Ben.

Eleanor shot Ben with a withering glare and ignored his dismissive words. 'They've been sending scouts into our world to try and find out what's happening. Since I was around they wanted to find out what I knew too.'

'You were able to tell them how we're wrecking the planet then,' snorted Ben.

Eleanor eyed her brother. She knew him and knew that those words were spoken far from as contemptuously as they sounded.

'You did at least mention the melting ice caps, the levels of carbon dioxide in the atmosphere and the increasingly erratic nature of the Gulf Stream.'

Eleanor smiled thinly. 'Of course, Benjamin.'

'And?'

'And nothing,' she replied simply. 'They are more interested in what was happening in the Highlands. It seems that is where the worlds are fracturing.'

Ben nodded. 'Makes sense I guess. If the environment is going through cataclysmic change of historic proportions then it's going to be at the weak points of the Earth's crust that the change is going to be at its greatest.'

'The mid-Atlantic ridge,' said Hanna.

Eleanor was suddenly quiet. 'I don't know,' she said eventually, 'I don't think that's what the þursar meant.'

She turned to her brother, looking to him for a response and a reaction to her story. 'Ben?'

Ben remained silent as he worked through his thoughts.

'So – if I'm understanding this, sis,' he said eventually, 'You get lost from the party you're with and you stumble into this cave where you meet this spiritual Gunnlaugr man and he leads you into the mountain, performs some magic on you and you end up in the company of trolls sat round in council discussing some great evil. Is that right?'

Eleanor stared back at him with obvious disappointment towards his reaction. Slowly Ben found himself relent. 'Ellie, you've got to give us more,' he told her, 'Why were you there? And what did they want from you?'

4

'Help us.'

Eleanor stood at the edge of the council table having retold her story as best she could and heard of the plight of the pursar people.

The bus descended through a lowering gloom as it took the narrow road between two oppressive cliffs. From her seat Eleanor looked up at the 'faces' in the clefts of rock that seemed to follow them as they passed. They followed her. Almost as if they were listening to her story. Ben's ultimatum rang in her ears and his words lingered in her mind.

'Their world is dying,' said Eleanor, 'You of all people should know that, Ben.'

Ben's face convulsed – *what?* Now his sister was lecturing *him* on climate change?

'Thermo glacial dynamics, the gulf stream conveyor. It's killing their world, breaking it apart.'

Eleanor found that she enjoyed telling him this - regurgitating his own theories at him. *She was enjoying this probably way too much*, she thought.

'Hanna, you know the old legends - þursar that have stayed above-ground too long...'

'Left only now as stone,' breathed Hanna.

'They're inexorably linked to the environment - to the world out there.' She flung back her hand enthusiastically and smacked her knuckles into the window. Ben watched his sister pull back and rub her hands. *That's got to have hurt*, he considered.

'And the þursar. They want your help?' Hanna followed up on Eleanor's words. 'But Eleanor, why you? What can you do?'

Bergur lifted himself from his throne-like chair of twisted basalt. Eleanor found it hard not to laugh at just how similar in complexion the þurs elder was to the rock; as he moved she could hear his limbs creak and groan like rock grating against itself.

'You should go with Erik.' He nodded towards the younger þursar and Eleanor followed the gaze to the þurs scholar who had brought her here. 'And if he thinks that you still have anything useful to report...'

Bergur's voice trailed away as he sat once more, settling back in his throne. Eleanor waited, and she guessed so did Erik, for something more from the elder but there was nothing more coming other than a thin, tired breathing and a pale, rested expression.

Erik rose from his seat at the counsel table and led Eleanor away back down the passageway through which they had come. Passing through the room in which she had first met Erik, he took her up some more steps and into a smaller book-lined anti-chamber.

The familiar smell of the musty-warmth from old papers and leather bindings filled Eleanor's nostrils and took her back to those dark, winter nights when her father would sneak her into the labyrinthine stacks beneath the Bodleian Library.

Almost immediately Erik began fetching out books, scrolls and parchments; laying them out onto table tops and cabinets.

'Here.' He pointed to the page. 'You see our history.'

Eleanor stepped round the table to join Erik and read through the text. Words and phrases jumped out of the page and forced to the front of her mind the sagas that her father used to read to her.

In an oak-beamed bedroom, Eleanor, then aged nine, cuddled up to Big Ted. Her father sat at her side and in front of the both of them was an old, leather bound book, but from which Guðni did not read from, for the story he told was only based on the sagas and not written down. He told the story of his family, long ago, when they first arrived on the Icelandic shore.

Eleanor's small fingers reached out and stroked the pages of the book. Her eyes turned upward, big and wide, looking searchingly up into the rich blue eyes of her father that were set into that warm, kind face.

'Here.' Eleanor pointed to the text. 'The great bridge. Until it crumbles—' Out of the corner of her eye she could see Erik watching her with large, round, podgy þursar eyes.

'It's true. The Bifrost has been failing us. Several of our people have been unable to return after going to the overland for food.'

'And you want me to find out why—' confirmed Eleanor, 'Why this bridge – the Bifrost is failing?'

Þursar Erik nodded as he pulled another scroll across the table and unrolled it to reveal a map of the over-land. 'We think the disturbance is happening in this area.' He pointed with stubby fingers to an area of the highlands.

'So you want me to go there and find out what's causing this?' She laughed. 'You had this planned didn't you—?'

The troll chose to remain silent.

'All along – I thought it was me, that stumbled here, but no – you've brought me here to go off and do your work.'

The troll gathered up the papers and documents, moving to put them away in the storage chest.

'You need me.'

'Come, girl.' The troll instructed her dispassionately, 'I must show you to the bridge.'

'The Bifrost?' Hanna interjected, an aura of jealousy lingering in her voice.

'What's the Bifrost?' asked Alice. She and Eleanor heaved on their rock bars one last time and sent the boulder that was almost half their size sliding into the scrub with a resounding thud.

'Huh?' Eleanor panted for breath.

'Last night at the ranger's hut. You were talking about Bifrost.' Alice laughed. 'I got the feeling we weren't talking Jack Frost!'

Eleanor shook her head. 'It's a rainbow, Alice. Really simple.'

Alice watched Eleanor, rolling her eyes to show her distain for the perfunctory response.

'Here – can you get that other rock bar under here,' Eleanor gestured to a gap that had been prized open under another rock and leaned down on the bar. 'Then maybe I can...?'

Alice jammed her bar down into the gap, careful to mind Eleanor's fingers. 'We just levelled this one?'

Eleanor nodded.

'So is that Icelandic then? Bifrost?'

The rock creaked and groaned from beneath.

'That'll be the elf then. Unhappy about his home being relocated!' Eleanor joked. 'No. I mean – kind of, I guess. It's an old legend that the Bifrost is this bridge between this world – the world of men – and the world of the gods.'

'According to legend the bridge is always there but we can only see it if the sun and rain are in the sky together.'

'So, a rainbow?'

'And even then only the chosen few are ever able to reach its gate and cross between the worlds.'

'Cool,' said Alice.

'Twist, Alice!' Eleanor was sudden and sharp. She accompanied her words with a sweeping hand gesture as to what to do with the rock bar. Seconds later and the rock gave way and swung, almost exactly into position. The two girls took a step back to admire their work. Looking from the path to each other they nodded and grinned.

'That about right?' asked Eleanor.

'I'd say so.'

They stood on the path, resting and admiring their work.

'I remember chasing rainbows,' Eleanor said eventually, 'It used to be such great fun.'

'I was once, this far from the base of a rainbow.' Alice gestured a six foot distance.

'Yeah?'

Alice nodded. 'I was with my folks. We were staying in upstate New York. We were just eating our bagels down by the Hudson. I swear to you, the rainbow came down right on the shoreline in front of us. Couldn't have been any further than–'

As Eleanor climbed, her fingers clasped around clefts in the rock to either side of the shaft in the rock. Somewhere ahead of her, Erik moved swiftly, at one with the rock. Beneath the sound of her own breath, she heard her own words echo back at her–

Only the chosen few are ever able to cross between the worlds.

Eleanor smiled smugly to herself at this thought. *I'm going to cross over.*

Under a heavy night sky with rain lashing at the window of the bus, the driver slowed and turned off the highway into a driveway, curbed against rock and lava, of ice-fractured tarmac. Eleanor, Ben and Hanna were the only people to disembark here, in a lonely car park where a few isolated tents remained, bravely buffeted against the wind.

'I have crossed over,' Eleanor said to Hanna as they stood near the bus with water running round their hoods and dripping down their jackets. Ben fetched their bags from the storage lockers under the bus to them, dumping them at their feet. He shook his head at the smugness on his sister's face.

'It was everything that you've ever read, or dreamed of,' explained Eleanor, 'And more.'

Ben raised his eyebrows at his sister's comment. He shook his head to the eagerness and the sense of awe with which his cousin responded to the story.

Eleanor glanced behind her, back down the passageway. Her guide, in the dim light, was merging back into the stone. Ahead, she stood at the threshold of the bridge back home. Two huge columns of lava etched with centuries-old designs flanked a stair shimmering in light.

She took a step forward, onto the first stair. A rush of exhilaration flowed through her. Has any other man or woman from her world ever stood where she stood now? She felt the magic that contained the Bifrost seep into her every bone, every muscle. As she proceeded she allowed her fingers to trail against the walls of the passage. They were damp to the touch and in places dripping water, but in no way were they slippery or slimy.

A shaft of sunlight broke through the clouds, and sliced through the rain to cast a glare across the hillside. Finnur stopped his climb; and stood hawk-like on the ridge, silhouetted against the drama unfolding amongst the canopy of clouds above. Aðli stopped too, and looked back at his colleague.

'You've seen something?'

Finnur paused, considering for a moment what he thought he had seen. He shook his head and moved on.

Water seemed to seep from the rock and flow down the roof, the walls and on to the stairs. Eleanor climbed further and the higher and as she ascended the walls seemed to become more translucent. Reaching out to touch them, the water flowed around her fingers; and with the texture of rock beneath her fingertips, Eleanor imagined that if she could just push a bit further she could touch the swirling, tumbling clouds as they built over the valley beyond.

She paused, taking a moment to rest. Eleanor examined the rock wall, staring into every scratch and formation in it. Beyond she seemed to see a mountain landscape dowsed in a storm, and making their ascent up a narrow ridge she saw a party and recognised a face.

Eleanor threw herself forward, the palms of her hands lying still on cold rock. 'Finnur!' she called his name.

Finnur stopped. Across the hillside his name echoed around him. A rainbow faded into view and for a moment he thought he saw her face.

'Eleanor?' he uttered her name softly and with confusion.

'It's just the wind,' said Aðli, 'Come. We still have a way to go.'

Eleanor stood, staring at the cold stone wall of the bridge. She dried her face and stopped. How? She never pushed her face into the water as it flowed off the walls and for all the water here there were no drips, so – rain? She was on the – she was on the bridge. It was raining out there and she was in the rainbow. Glancing back down the steps, she turned and looked on, up the slowly arcing stair and recalled.

'I wonder what it's like?' asked Alice, 'To be in a rainbow?'

She was sitting alongside Eleanor in the minibus. Behind them, came a spontaneous and rousing chorus of Somewhere Over the Rainbow, led mockingly by Andy from the back seat. Alice glared at him sternly and the singing quickly faded and stumbled away.

Eleanor laughed. 'Inside a rainbow? Dunno. I guess if it was a bridge it would have to be paved in some way–'

'Gold, maybe?' Kirsten suggested with a shrug of her shoulders.

Eleanor sat on the step – a hexagonal column of basalt that projected above the flowing water. She bit into a biscuit, savouring the crumbling, milky taste on her tongue as she remembered the conversation in the back of the bus. A smile stretched across her face as she remembered with amusement the single, twisted, slurring tape of eclectic pop. The bus seemed to be a character in its own right on the holiday.

Eleanor sat on the edge of her bunk as she pushed the brush slowly through her hair. She gazed idly across the room and spied the orange and black markings of a rucksack. The frayed nylon cords and battered fabric hit her memories.

'No, it can't be!' Eleanor slammed the hairbrush down on her sleeping bag and rushed from the room. She bounded down the wooden stairs and swung round the hall and into the kitchen. He sat there, hand round the can of Egils beer, laughing and joking with Aðli, Hanna and Ben. In the doorway Eleanor stopped and stared. Finnur turned his head and looked and they exchanged glances.

'Eleanor?' The guide could only now, on seeing her, believe in her safety.

Eleanor was breathless with agitation.

'Eleanor?' Hanna nudged her cousin gently, rousing her from her sleep. 'Eleanor?' she said again. 'Ben's made some dinner. You coming?'

'Finnur?' Eleanor stirred from her sleep. 'He's here.'

Hanna shook her head.

Eleanor dropped her gaze and frowned. 'Must have dreamt it.' She nodded and picked herself up. 'Just give me a few minutes. I need to—' Her voice, husky and tired, trailed off as she pulled a wash kit from her rucksack.

Hanna smiled and left, taking a last, slightly anxious look back before she closed the door.

Eleanor continued her ascent up the the stair, flanked sometimes in impenetrable rock and at other times by the shimmering light of the Bifrost cast out across an open landscape. In time the path began to level off and she could see the way down.

At the foot of a rock face, Finnur slipped ropes through shackles, locking them into place. He looked up at the ledge which Aðli had already reached; and then back. He studied the worsening weather looming over the far side of the valley. A helicopter circled above, and headed for home down the valley, Finnur felt stressed and punched the air angrily. *Why? Why did he get talking to Andy and Eleanor and suggest the hike?* He stared up at the mountain and remembered clearly how he had encouraged the fated journey.

Reflected in the stream edged by lush and broad-leafed grass, the canyon walls were tinged in the red-ochre hue of sunset. Finnur ran along the side of the stream, his silhouette mirrored in the water, and pulled back the heavy canvass door to the mess tent and dived inside. The dozen volunteers, their leader, a couple of rangers and Finnur's colleague Aðli sat around the trestle table with their mugs of coffee and hot chocolate cupped between their hands were.

Finnur pulled a chair forward and settled once more at the head of the table. He spread out his map and began to point enthusiastically. 'The trip. It's three days walk – not hard but long I think.' He lifted his head and scanned the group of young adults. Some, he could see, were already balking at the idea.

Kirsten lifted her hand tentatively. Finnur nodded towards her.

'Three days? Where will we be sleeping?' Kirsten chewed on her lip cautiously. 'Would we have to carry tents as well as all our gear?'

Finnur laughed. 'Yes, I have slept out there with nothing but my sleeping bag – damn cold though.' His tone became more serious. 'No. There are huts. We will walk between them and then at the end – at Mývatn there is a thermo pool. It's very nice.'

Finnur watched Kirsten. She smiled, relaxed and became more enthusiastic and excited by the idea. She glanced across at Alice and grinned.

'I would recommend tents, if at least some to share. The forecast is okay but in Iceland, nobody can tell. If we take longer then – we need to be prepared.'

A cold wind stung Finnur's face. He stepped up to the rock face and placed his fingers carefully around the fractures in the rock. Glancing up he could see Aðli making good progress. Why had he not been prepared? Why had he allowed Eleanor to get lost? He was a guide – he should have stopped it. He cursed his folly and hated the feelings that rose up within him to punish him. He hated himself more.

'It wasn't his fault, you know,' said Eleanor, sitting opposite Hanna and her brother at the table. She frowned and forked up food idly, preoccupied with the mixed up mess of thoughts and feelings.

'I don't think anyone is blaming him,' Hanna said, 'The weather conditions, they were unique.'

They continued to eat in silence but Eleanor felt her brother's gaze was always on her.

'So tomorrow,' Ben said eventually. He pushed a map of the highlands across the table. 'You are going to tell us where we are heading?'

Eleanor remained silent.

'Do we need anything?' He was adamant. 'Is this a day trip or do we need our tents?'

'We?' Eleanor shrugged. 'What's with the *we*? Ben, this is something for me alone.'

Ben's mouth dropped. 'No.'

Eleanor shook her head.

'If you think I'm going to allow you to go off again alone after what's happened—'

'Of course I don't.' Eleanor admitted. 'But we've got no choice. What I have to do, I have to do alone. I wish you could, but you can't help me in this.'

'You can't leave it like that!' Ben was angry. 'You can't honestly expect me to accept this?' He hit the table. 'What's so important?'

'You've not been listening to my story…?' countered Eleanor.

Hanna shook her head and stepped up quickly from the table. She cleared away her plate and edged towards the door. 'I'm going to leave you to argue this one out. I'm tired and I need to, just be. When you're sorted, come and find me.' She smiled. 'I'll be enjoying the night air in the hot pool.'

Hanna slipped quietly from the room. Ben watched his cousin leave before returning his attention onto his sister.

'I'm serious—'

Eleanor shook her head and silenced her brother. She unfolded the map in front of them and began to trace the valleys with her finger.

'Here.' She tapped the map. 'I have to go here. It looks as if there's a hut too, so – you and Hanna could stay there.'

Ben looked from the map to his sister. He was not sure – not sure at all.

5

Highland, Dark
A light in the night
The wind that blows
Standing; cold on your face.
Sensing—
Seeking; The warmth of home

Hanna sung the words softly in the grey dusk of the Icelandic night. Natural hot spring water lapped around her shoulder as she worked the tune in her head. Around her, hollows in the ground filled with thick gloopy mud and sulphurous water that boiled and gurgled. A surge of hot water flowed from the pipe and Hanna felt heat rush through her body. She stretched her arms into the warm current and flexed her muscles.

*

A cold wind blew across the open landscape between the mountains. From inside one of the huts, Gunnlaugr stood at a window watching Hanna singing through the words of the ballad with an undercurrent of pop-rock. After some minutes he eventually moved away, and slipped into his coat before heading out into the night.

A sliver of light cut into the night from an opening door. Ben stepped from the hut followed by his sister as they began to make their way across the car park between the two isolated huts. Standing on its own, raised up on stilts over an outcrop of rock were the frontier-town-like toilet cubicles and sinks that were open to the elements. Eleanor stopped. There, across the car park, just beyond the washing area stood the solitary figure of a man.

Eleanor held back suddenly and listened. The wind blew across the empty landscape and in it she picked out her name.

Ben was staring at her. 'Ellie?'

So Ben didn't hear the voice; he hasn't noticed the man. Why would he? Eleanor frowned. 'You go on,' she said, 'I've just remembered – there's something – before I forget.'

Eleanor waited until Ben had rounded the side of the furthest hut before running back to her hut and bursting into the dormitory. She slammed the door shut so violently that the panelled wooden walls vibrated in echoes. Diving towards her bed she stuffed her hand into her rucksack to retrieve a small leather bag and emptied out the contents onto the bunk. The six small whalebone rune stones tumbled out with the delicate silver cup and the book onto her sleeping bag.

She sat on the edge of her bed and looked at the objects. Taking the book in her hands she flicked through its pages and examined the words. *This is what he wanted – Gunnlaugr.* She was sure of it. She must go now and give these objects to him and then she could go, back to Reykjavik, re-join her family and get on with her life.

The Bifrost has been failing us ... several of our people have been unable to return after going to the overland for food. Erik's words echoed back at her, and she felt the loyalty to the huldufolk; stronger than any loyalty to the stranger in the hills. She stared at the objects and decided. She couldn't do it. She couldn't hand over the entrusted secrets of the þursar people to a man she did not know. But if she had to take him something, could she dare take him something worthless?

Eleanor reached for her journal and opened it to the blank middle pages. She tore them, ripping them from the spine, before arming herself with a 2B pencil and began rubbing the rune stones, quickly but carefully, insuring to get a good impression of every size, shape and orientation. In the back of her mind was the constant thought that she mustn't be too long. She had to finish this and join her brother in the hot pool before he came looking.

Drawing done, Eleanor folded the sheets of paper in half and tucked them inside the back cover of her journal. She then stuffed the journal deep down inside her rucksack alongside the small silver cup and the þursar book. Lastly she returned the rune stones to the leather pouch and it was that that she took with her.

Venturing out again into the cold night, the wind continued to howl across the car park. Eleanor strode purposefully towards the toilet block before veering off at the last minute to take a narrow path to a further outcrop of rock where the tall, unmistakable silhouette of Gunnlaugr stood waiting. As she approached him, he turned to face her and Eleanor looked again at Gunnlaugr and that distinctive streak of silver that ran through his hair. *What was he? Not þursar certainly, and too tall to be of alfar kind. Could he really be human, like her?*

'You called,' said Eleanor. She stepped closer to Gunnlaugr.

Gunnlaugr stood in silence. He turned his head and gazed out across the plain to the glacier beyond.

'What did you see?' he said eventually.

See? For a moment Eleanor was unsure what he meant. 'You mean where you sent me? It was incredible.'

'You know the writing that you carved out into the circle when you worked that magic? It was repeated into the stone walls of the cavern that I found myself in—' As the memories flooded back she recounted the details as they came and in jumbled sense. 'There was a kind of gate keeper troll, waiting for me. No - we linked in our minds, read the words and you sent me further back. It was in that further chamber that the troll came for me.'

Gunnlaugr volunteered nothing to Eleanor, as he stood emotionless, listening to her.

'They were having a council. Something is destroying their world, killing their people and they are determined to find out what.' Eleanor tried to figure out how much she should tell him. 'They are going to stop it.'

She looked up at the stern face of Gunnlaugr, at the lines on his cheeks which had been etched deeper by the wind and the cold.

'Did you find it?' He was insistent.

Eleanor was unsure how to answer the man. Keeping in her mind her memories of Erik and other þursar, she now began to question his motives.

'You couldn't cross into the troll world yourself could you?' accused Eleanor, 'You were waiting for me, or someone like me, who could make the crossing for you.'

'Do you have them?' Gunnlaugr remained impassionate and his stance only served to annoy Eleanor further.

In the cold of night, Eleanor dipped her fingers into the leather pouch and felt the smoothness of the whale bone and the pattern of the carving beneath her fingers.

Eleanor stood alone in the troll's chamber, her gaze darting back and forth across the room as she tried to take in the studious, archival nature of the place. She saw something and felt herself drawn to it and crossed the room. On the top of the chest, alongside a book of bound parchments within vellum casing, was a cup. She reached out and stroked the intricately carved surface; silver. Standing by the chest she looked down at the cup and dipped her fingers inside. She pulled out a small leather pouch within which were similarly carved whale bone tablets – rune stones – a half dozen of them. She lifted one out and felt the pattern between her fingers. This was it – what Gunnlaugr was looking for – what he had talked about – she knew it. Eleanor bit her lip and quickly dropped the tablet back into the pouch and stuffed it back into the cup. Quickly, she swung her rucksack off her shoulder and stuffed the box down the side and shouldered her pack once more before the troll returned.

Eleanor pulled from her fleece pocket the leather pouch and offered it to Gunnlaugr. He took it in his large weathered hands. His gaze narrowed onto hers. 'Is this all? There was nothing more?'

Eleanor felt instant regret for handing over the runes, suddenly sure that it would have been better to fail completely than to attempt to hide something from the man. She shook her head. She could tell from the way that he reacted to her definitive response that he did not believe her for a second and she felt her heart beat faster because of it, scared now for what he may do.

He held her in his gaze, almost as if he were attempting to probe her with his mind. Then, suddenly, he snapped his fist shut swiftly on the leather pouch and stepped away. He turned again and looked back at Eleanor with his piercing, penetrating eyes. She flinched.

'You have done this country a great service. Thank you.'

Eleanor remained for a few minutes longer after Gunnlaugr had departed. Alone, and cold in the bleak landscape, eventually she crossed the yard, rounded the side of the hut to where the hot pool was carved out of the rocks. She dropped her fleece to the decking and kicked away her boots before stepping down into the hot pool and joining her cousin and brother. She thought of Gunnlaugr's last words and pondered over what he had really meant. Why then, did it feel like a betrayal? What had she done? It felt right, so why did she feel so wrong?

Water splashed across her face. She looked up, to find Hanna opposite her, full of child-like playfulness with Ben. Eleanor knocked back the water at Hanna.

Eleanor laughed. 'All we need now is a nice cold beer!'

Hanna grinned. 'It's funny you should say that—' She reached one arm out of the pool and pulled her bag closer, from which she produced three cans of Egils.

The water steamed under the cold night sky. Andy pulled back the ring pull of his can and swigged down cold beer whilst lounging in the hot, sulphurous, waters. He laughed at Alice's joke and she manoeuvred herself closer to his tanned, muscular physique. Empty cans of beer were lined up along the decking behind them. Eleanor observed the chemistry of her two friends; the way that Alice was reflecting Andy's every mannerism and gesture; and the way that Andy was lapping up the attention. Clutching their beers, their lips came together in a kiss.

'Are we coming to the pool tomorrow,' asked Andy, louder and this time to the whole group. 'It's our last day of work? Surely we can't not come here...?'

Eleanor nodded; the last day before she finally got to climb Krafla.

She stared up, past Alice and Andy in the pool, past the corrugated hut, to the grey-brown peak of Krafla shrouded in cloud and dreams.

Eleanor lay on her bunk; her limbs tucked up and folded within her sleeping bag, cocoon-like. From where she lay she could just about make out her brother on the opposite bunk, and somewhere on the top bunk, Hanna.

Thoughts preyed on her mind. Somewhere, the man Gunnlaugr was out there. She recalled the stance he took earlier that night, and the image of his weather-worn face haunted her mind. There was something that she now saw in his behaviour that she distrusted and with him so close, it made her fear sleep. She reached out a bare arm from her sleeping bag and felt in her rucksack for the book and the silver cup.

Did he know that she had cheated him, she wondered. She allowed her fingers to stroke the edges of the etched silver as she wondered to herself why she felt she must keep this. *I just had to* – she considered. *I don't know for what yet but there was a reason.*

Her head ached with tiredness and she pushed the box back into her rucksack, burying it deep beneath her clothes before she pulled her sleeping bag close around her. Curling up into a foetal position, she squeezed shut her eyes and thought of sleep.

Dawn broke over the mountains; shafts of clear light were cast across the floorboards through the curtainless windows. Ben woke, lifted his head from the pillow and blinked. He looked across at Eleanor's and sat up sharply. No! It can't be all a dream? My sister? Where is she? He relaxed again after seeing Eleanor's rucksack neatly repacked and leaning against the end of her bunk.

He stretched out the aches of night and sleep and reached for his clothes. A little later he padded out of the room in his hiking socks to find his sister. Snooping his head around the kitchen door, and then the ranger's office, he continued out across the hall and pulled open the door to the outside.

After the icy wind that had blown across the tundra the previous night, the morning air was still and filled with bright sun. Ben stood in the doorway to the hut and looked out across the camp with its rows of jeeps, trucks, and vans, its two sleeping huts, and the washrooms. This was a community of tourists and rangers on the frontier of the wilderness.

Ahead of him, Eleanor was standing by a pickup truck chatting with the driver. Ducking back into the hut to slip on his boots he crossed the car park to join his sister, and nodded to Ásta, the student biologist they met last night and who was ranger here for the summer.

'Ásta was just telling me,' explained Eleanor, 'That the forecast is good for the next few days.'

'So?' Ben tried to imagine where this might lead.

'I'm thinking we head off now, after breakfast, and get to the high hut. Ásta's going to show us on the map,' said Eleanor, 'I go do my thing and we head back here. Then, by the time the weather worsens next we will be on the bus back to Reykjavik.'

Eleanor knelt on the floor beside her bunk; maps, sketchpad and loose sheets of paper spread out before her. She traced her hand over the pencil rubbings she had made of the whale bone rune stones, puzzling over the ancient scripture. She sucked in air through her teeth and wrote notes in her journal.

'Watcha doing?'

Eleanor jumped, startled. Her hands instinctively moved to sweep her map over the top of the other papers. She traced her thumb along a ridge and turned to look up at her brother.

'Just planning the route.' She grinned.

'Yeah?' Ben squatted next to her and reached out to look at the map. For a moment Eleanor observed him closely but he appeared not to have noticed the papers that lay beneath.

'Well?' he asked.

Eleanor pointed to the map and began to outline her plan.

Eleanor pushed her hair back behind her ear as the wind tried to blow it across her face. Leaning her chin on her forearm, she looked across the roof of the truck. She glanced across at her brother, where he too, sat hunched, in the other corner, amongst the tools, rope and the can of kerosene. She followed her gaze back down the truck and beyond to the road they had travelled, to the solitary yellow signpost at the crossroads between two tracks.

She turned again to the road ahead. The iron-rich slopes tumbled down the valley to either side of the track. Winding round the end of the ridge, Ásta pulled the truck to a halt in the road as the landscape plateaued out into a rolling lava field, bordered at its horizon by mountains topped with glaciers.

A little later and Hanna was looking back from the first cleft in the broken, ice-scratched lava as Ásta's pickup truck was driving away down the track. She turned and fell into line again with at her cousins' steps. The three of them were alone again in the mountains.

Kirsten Ball, one hand to the polished metal of the Viking ship sculpture on Reykjavik harbour, glanced across at Alice and shrugged a response to her friend's questioning, almost despairing, expression.

'He said he'd be here,' said Kirsten, 'by the Viking ship on Saturday afternoon.'

'He said he would be back for the flight tomorrow,' offered Alice.

Kirsten glanced around her, staring into the crowds and searching out familiar faces. 'He does know, doesn't he? You know—'

Kirsten stopped. Alice was kneeling by her daypack; rummaging through paperwork until she found the participant list for the holiday. Alice passed it to Kirsten.

Andy rolled a cigarette whilst gazing out through the condensation-smeared windows of the lakeside bar. From where he sat, with a large beer on the table in front of him, he could see his tent pitched by the shore of Mývatn. He looked down at his mobile phone and the scratched and battered screen. He thumbed through the address book. Eleanor.

'I wonder.' He hit send and the dialling tone cycled through the series of tones. The answering service cut in almost immediately with an announcement that the mailbox was full. Andy frowned and allowed the phone to slide from his fingers and clunk onto the table. He turned his head and stared blankly again, out to his tent near to the shore, and to the blue-grey water punctuated by grassy islands.

The phone rang.

Andy glanced down at the mobile. Anonymous call. He thumbed to answer it, and barked a hello. Kirsten's voice came back at him into his ear, 'Hi Andy, I thought you should know. Eleanor, she's safe.'

Ben stooped to pick up another piece of rock and studied it to compare it with others that he had gathered. He dismissed its worth and discarded it with a flick of the wrist that sent it scattering across the lava field.

Hanna quickened her step and pulled into line with Eleanor. 'So Ellie, so far you have avoided the subject. But tell me – how did it go? Going on holiday with Andy?'

'He's cool.' Eleanor shrugged. 'He's a good mate. I'm glad I've got him.'

Hanna grinned suspiciously. 'You sure he's nothing more?'

Eleanor swung round and fixed Hanna with a sharp stare. She laughed.

Light from the slow-blinking neon sign filtered in from the forecourt in the roadside diner that was otherwise dimly lit. In another part of the shop, people moved along the aisles of tinned fruit and vegetables, boxes of cereal and bottles of engine oil. Andy laughed a loud guffaw that broke through the whistles and steaming of the cappuccino machine. Andy shared his joke with his new friends, all gathered around the dining cubicle. Wrapped in their fleeces, they hugged their mugs of hot chocolate and breathed in the sweet vapours.

Eleanor poured out the themes and plotlines of her novel to Kirsten, enjoying the opportunity to talk it through. Suddenly, she stopped. A glance down the length of the table and she saw Andy, darkly attractive and enjoying the attention of friends. Eleanor looked away, annoyed that a glance from Andy had caused her to lose the thread of what she was saying.

'Everyone seems to ask me that!' Eleanor sighed. 'Think that–' She looked out across the valley. 'Why does everyone think there's some relationship there?'

'Maybe because you are always with him?' spluttered Ben. 'May Ball, your room in halls, our house last Easter – and Christmas – the summer before it–' Ben shook his head. 'You two are such flirts.'

Eleanor glared at her brother. 'Ben! We are just friends, honestly.'

'There is way more than friendship going on there,' declared Alice.

'We're mates.' Eleanor shook her head. 'We have a laugh. We go fell running together.' She noticed Alice's mischievous response. 'Hell, Alice, we're such good mates we can shower together, or share a bed and it means nothing. Completely platonic.'

Alice and Kirsten did double-takes to this revelation before collapsing in fits of giggles. Contagiously, Eleanor joined them.

Reaching the top of the ridge, Eleanor swung her rucksack to the ground and collapsed. She clutched her water bottle to her and swigged great gulps of fresh spring water into her mouth.

'Is that it?' Ben removed the binoculars and pointed across the valley to where, away in the distance and clinging to the foot of the mountain, was a hut.

Eleanor followed her brother's gaze. 'I guess so.' She pulled her map from her bag and traced their route. She glanced back up at the distant hut. 'Yeah. It's not so far.'

As the light faded, Eleanor climbed with Ben and Hanna up the last section of path to a narrow escarpment between two ridges. Set back close to the cliffs was the small, battered emergency hut with peeling orange paintwork. Eleanor slid the bolt across and stepped into an antechamber stacked full of old climbing ropes, poles and fluorescent jackets. Further in and the main room was lit by one storm-smeared window to the front with a table beneath and four bunk beds squeezed against the back wall.

'No lights,' said Eleanor.

Hanna shook her head. 'Ásta mentioned there was a radio for emergencies but it's battery charged I think.'

Ben swung his bag down onto the bunk. 'It's kind of cosy—'

'Yeah.' Eleanor grinned. 'I'm sure we can make it like home, Benjamin.'

A sun was split into shattered shards by clouds; a fragmentation of colours across the Reykjavik skyline. A cold breeze blew in off the harbour into the sidestreets of downtown 101 Reykjavik. Hanna and Alice stood near to the hot dog van, munching on their dinner as the rest of the group continued to queue for theirs.

'I'm going to miss these after tomorrow,' Kirsten said between bites.

Alice nodded. 'Too right. You remember the first one – seems so long ago now.'

With only the flickering light of a paraffin lamp to see by, the three cousins sat around the table in the dark of the mountain hut playing whist. Between turns, Eleanor watched her brother across the table. Finally he seemed to have accepted the events of the last few days – and maybe this – this game of cards was the resumption of normality for them.

'Ellie?' said Ben.

Eleanor jumped, woken from her daydream. She saw her brother's gaze upon her. *What now?*

'It's your go,' he prompted.

Eleanor felt her face redden and she looked down at the game, hiding herself behind her cards. Out of the corner of her eye she watched Ben focus now on their cousin who was keeping score in her notebook. *Score? No – what then is she writing?*

'Han?' asked Ben.

Hanna continued to write, occasionally going back over a line and augmenting it. Ben repeated his question. She looked up.

'Got it.' Hanna pointed her pen to the score, allowing it to drift back to her songbook full of half completed lines and crossings out. 'I've got the tune in my head.'

Ben nodded as Eleanor placed down her cards. 'And it's still your turn...' she said.

Hanna picked up her cards and looked through them and quickly played her go almost without thinking and returning to her notebook.

Beneath my feet
Stillness; moonrise.

Outside, the wind drifted around the hillside, gently swirling, occasionally gusting forwards and pushing itself onto the tiny hut. Eyes, bright as stars, flashed to life in the dark. Small, sprightly creatures emerged from behind and beneath rocks, all watching the hut. Creeping forwards towards the window they keenly observed the people enjoying their human games. They moved quickly on, always whispering to each other.

'You sure you don't want company?'

Eleanor shook her head to Ben's offer, 'Of course I do,' she admitted, 'But this is something that I *do* have to do alone.'

Ben looked at his sister with despair. He had come to accept, if not fully understand, her reasoning. He headed back inside the hut for a minute, returning with a handset from the radio unit.

'Here. Take this,' he said, 'Any problems, just radio us.'

Eleanor set off, taking the path up behind the hut. Ben watched until she had rounded the bend and was out of sight. And even after that, he remained, hoping without hope to see her coming back round the curve in the path having had a change of heart.

*

During the course of the day, clouds gathered over the distant peaks while the sun bathed the valley in light. Hanna sat, in a moss-upholstered seat between two clefts of basalt below where the mountain hut was nestled in the foothills. She had her pen and notebook to hand as she gazed out across the landscape watching the hikers on the mountain trails. She dropped her gaze and focused again on the pad and on the words.

Inside the hut Ben turned dials and fiddled with switches on the radio, tuning into an orchestration of fizzes and crackles interspersed with short-wave broadcasts.

'What are you up to?'

Ben swung round to find Hanna at his side. She fiddled with the zip of a cool bag.

'Lunch?' she asked. And then. 'Found any cool tunes on that thing yet?'

'Short-wave radio.' Ben offered by way of explanation, 'Should be used just for emergencies but I've discovered that climate seismologists use it round here for discussing environmental changes – anomalies – you know?'

'Yeah?' replied Hanna, 'There much going on?'

Ben joined her at the table and began picking at the smoked fish. 'Funny you should ask, but there are some interesting irregularities.'

'What do you mean, irregularities?'

'They've measured some distinct seismic differences in areas across Iceland.'

'You mean earthquakes, volcanoes?' Hanna interupted. She stepped towards the door and looked up to the mountains before turning again towards Ben. 'Are we safe? And what about Ellie?'

Ben frowned. 'You know what *significant* is for scientists. We are talking years maybe.' He scooped up a handful of peanuts.

'It is interesting though. There are some interesting thermo-dynamic variations I'm going to have to look up when we get back to Reykjavik.'

'Your studies?' Hanna asked.

Ben nodded. 'I only got a bit just now but if these variances prove to be true—'

Eleanor sat on an outcrop of rock eating from her bag of crisps and took the occasional swig of water. Her brain absorbed the view in front of her. Where the sun broke through the heavy-grey layers of cloud it picked out patches of landscape with iridescent colours. She sat, listening contentedly to the rich orchestration of nature. She heard the murmuring of the wind; a whistling as it passed through sparse vegetation; geese taking flight from the surface of a grey lake—

The thunder of heavy machinery. The clanking of steel on steel; and of tyres on gravel tracks. The noise cut through into her mind intrusively and she was brought crashing back into the here and now, suddenly acutely aware of the wide roadway of gravel carved out of the slope beneath her and found herself instinctively slipping off her rock and hiding herself into a hollow as a rust-stained construction truck thundered past.

Thoughts of Erik and Bergur and the mission that they had entrusted her with came back to her, jolted into the forefront of her mind by the ugly, man-made sound of heavy industry. She knew instinctively that she must follow the haulage truck and realised that it must be now. Climbing out of her hollow, she shouldered her rucksack again and took a higher path that ran parallel with the road.

6

Hanna sat at the front of the stage, legs astride in tight leather trousers, shoulders back, holding the audience with her voice. Looking out she saw a sea of heads moving to the beat of her song. Behind her the guitar played softly to a gentle, soothing percussion beat. Hanna brought the microphone back to her mouth and sung the ballad to the intimate gig. Hanna's voice resonated across the room, and through people's hearts and minds. She took them across the fjords, over the hillside, and into the mountains. She cupped her hands around the mic and almost breathed out the words. She glanced behind her, at the band. They could rock, but they could also totally capture a room like this.

Hanna scribbled down the lyrics. Around her, black clouds continued to gather. A splodge of rain hit the page and the ink spidered out into the surrounding words. Hanna blotted it with a thumb and continued to write, finishing the song as more raindrops fell. Finally, as the wind gusted in across the mountain slopes and the dark clouds overshadowed the land, the rain broke and fell fast and heavy. Hanna grabbed her book, her water bottle and her jacket and ran up the slope to dive into the rescue hut just as thunder exploded and echoed across the hillside.

Eleanor climbed along the side of a ridge until she bridged an outcrop of rock carved into fingers by wind and weather, where she stopped. Beneath her, the roadway was barred by three-metre high security fencing and guards sat in their truck by the gate. From beyond the gate, came the sound of grinding and clanking on the construction site. Eleanor sunk to the ground and looked out at the heavy machinery and the tracts of carved out land and spoil heaps. She found the noise oppressive and jarring. It penetrated her mind and she pressed her head into her hands and tried to shut out the sound.

Inside her mind she felt the pain of a thousand or more cave dwellers; old people of the ancient world. She heard the council above it all, in urgent and fraught dialogue. She collapsed back onto the rock and clutched at her head. It span with images and arguments and people and pain.

An explosion. The ground shook. Eleanor looked up long enough to see a dust cloud rising from a shower of rock that had been blasted out of the hillside. She heard a screech of pain again, deep from within.

'What was that?' asked Hanna. She was standing in the doorway, looking out at the rain and the sinking cloud. 'That wasn't thunder.'

'Sounds like explosives,' said Ben. 'They're not building a new road through here, are they?'

Hanna shrugged.

Eleanor scrambled back down the ridge, away from the construction site, putting distance between her and the deafening, thunderous noise. She found a small hollow in the ground, hidden from below, that led to a cave formed from the arcing, tessellating, honeycomb of basalt columns. She entered and climbed into the dim but not pitch black mid-cave.

Urgency took hold of her and she swung her rucksack off her shoulders, stripped off her waterproof and fleece and slung them to the ground. She dived into her bag, pulled out her notebook and quickly found the sketched runes. Studying the sketches as she went, Eleanor walked the cave looking and searching for pebbles, flat and worn smooth by the weather. Gathering up a dozen of these, she returned to her rucksack and found her penknife before setting about copying the designs from the runes, and scratching them into the stones.

Andy stood at the side of the road with Mývatn shimmering like a silver-grey mirror behind him. Rain began to fall as small spots of water in the air. He glanced down the road as the bus slid into view, the destination board flagged with Reykjavik. He shouldered his pack and prepared to board.

Kirsten Ball stood in the departure hall staring at the rain as it streaked down the glass, blurring the view across the lava field beyond. The queue to the check-in desks moved forward slowly and she pushed her rucksack along with the toe of her boot.

'It seems wrong doesn't it,' said Kirsten, 'I mean, I know Eleanor is safe now but to leave before we have a chance to see her again? It's not right.'

Alice shook her head.

'He's not going to make it in time is he?' Alice glanced up at Kirsten. 'Andy. He's going to miss the flight too.'

Kirsten shifted from side to side uncomfortably, relieved when she was able to push her rucksack further up the queue.

The mountain rumbled beneath her feet as another explosion blasted away at the rock. Eleanor knelt on the ground laying out the roughly fashioned rune stones, taking, as a guide, fragments of notes and sketches from the small book. Mostly though, she relied on instinct. With the stones arranged she sat cross-legged before them and lit two stubby candles that she wedged upright into the black volcanic dirt.

For a moment she sat in silence, cautious of what she was to do. Another explosion ripped through the ground and the candle flames wavered. *Now*, she decided. *It has to be now.* Not knowing where the words came from, Eleanor chanted the words in Old Icelandic.

A wind gusted across the mouth of the cave and whipped up dust clouds. From the shadows at the back of the cave and out from under rocks, the huldufolk approached to encircle Eleanor where she sat.

Eleanor tasted the magic on her tongue, and fed on it as it seeped into her blood and her bones. Music played in her mind, which danced with the spirits that were now here – were now gone – were here again. Visions were inter-cut with reality, sometimes discordantly, and Eleanor saw them all as she enchanted the words.

Raining hard now, water cascaded off cliffs and rocks and splashed into the dark, volcanic mud. Rivers of black snaked down from the cliffs, carving paths through the sand. Inside the cave, Eleanor was oblivious to the weather. The alfar and þursar people began to gather around her. She imagined the sun and spoke the words again. Outside the clouds fractured and a ray of sunlight sliced through into the world.

Birds circled, silhouetted against the dark sky. The air turned cold and the landscape was bleached of its colour. Raindrops landed, once, twice on the rocks in front of Hanna and Ben. Then more came, faster. Soon the rocks were peppered with wet splashes and the cousins were grabbing their stuff and running for cover in the hut as the heavens opened.

Hanna pulled her jacket around her, tugging its hood over her head and as she retreated to the open doorway. She pushed Ben's coat into his hands as she approached. Despite the weather, they felt compelled to stand in the open doorway and watch the war that raged in the sky.

'Look—' Hanna pointed.

Ben followed his cousin's gaze. A rainbow, every colour clear and strong, arched out of the next valley and over them into the distant sky.

'Don't think I've ever seen one so strong,' said Hanna. 'It's inspirational, don't you think?'

Ben nodded. He glanced up as another black cloud loomed over them and more rain continued to fall. As the hut once more echoed to the rhythmic percussion of the rain, Hanna began to sing softly.

Under the mountain
Inside of your soul
I see you; I feel you.
You're with me, You hear me...

A fork of light broke from the heavy clouds, followed immediately by a deafening crack of thunder that reverberated across mountain and through air. Opposed to the destruction, the sun lit the land in an iridescent, unearthly glow and the rainbow bridged the conflict.

Eleanor walked across the hillside in her combat trousers and shirt, oblivious to the driving rain that soaked her hair and dripped down her face. Around her, the storm raged. Another fork and flash of lightning preceded a resonant rumble of thunder. The sky blackened under the weight of cloud, lit only around the perimeter of the valley, where the sharp edges of mountains torn by fire and ice were burning in sun. In the middle distance the colours within the rainbow intensified.

Eleanor walked the last stretch of the road to the construction site. Beyond the security fencing, on a plain blasted out of the mountain, was a new factory. Rising out of the ground on stilts were platforms that bore a similarity to that of oil rigs. Four shafts of steel protruded out of its heart and descended deep into the mountain, out of which steam rose in thick clouds. Beyond the first platform Eleanor could see one, two – three more beyond in earlier stages of construction.

As Eleanor approached the main gates, the howling gale seemed to be attracted to the construction site. It threw walls of water at anything and everything in its path. Workmen in fluorescent jackets ran, heads down into the rain to secure the site. The bitter, unforgiving wind howled and wailed around the buildings, speaking with the voice of some terrible, evil monster. Panels of security fencing grated with the ear-piercing scrape of metal on metal and crashed open, broken by the wind.

Eleanor pushed onward up to the fence, her head held up, face into the driving rain and walked calmly through the gates. She moved steadily on to the heart of the construction site and to a bore hole beneath one of the platforms. Her eyes burned bright, the faces of þursar warriors reflected in her pupils.

Through the wind there was a shout and out of the corner of her eye the flash of a florescent jacket; a construction worker had seen her and was now closing in on her. Eleanor raised her hand and the wind knocked the man back, tripping him off his feet. Eleanor stepped up to the bore hole.

Alice stood, fingers to the glass walls, transfixed by the storm that was building outside. Behind her she could hear her friends discussing the second-by-second updates of cancelled and diverted flights. Forks of lightning illuminated the mountains. Clouds, dark and oppressive were heavy with rain. They blocked out the sun completely. Water flooded down the glass in front of her; inches from her nose.

'Eleanor.' Ben shivered in the doorway to the hut. He stared out at the oppressive landscape.

Hanna reached out to her cousin and gently massaged his arm. 'She'll have found herself shelter,' she said. Instinctively, they both turned and looked to the interior of the hut and the radio where a couple of its lights winked in the dark.

Eleanor stood at the mouth to the drill shaft that descended into the very heart of the earth. She pulled the torn out pages of her journal from her pocket and spoke the words aloud. The paper was already damp and it quickly became sodden, the pencil sketch bleeding under the weather. Eleanor stooped and placed it on the ground, weighting it down with rocks. Standing again, she walked around the shaft to the opposite side and repeated the process. Then again, twice more, to form a cross bridging the fissure. Lastly she stood back and finished intoning in the words.

Lightning flashed between the clouds above. A fork, bright and electric, struck the chasm in front of her. A deafening boom of thunder followed instantaneously and the sun broke through the clouds again, a flood of golden light spreading out across the valley floor, engulfing Eleanor. She gazed out into the sky, as a rainbow arc descended towards her into the chasm at her feet. From its base, the þursar lumbered out and Eleanor recognised some of the faces from around the council. As they filed past, Eleanor noticed one in particular. Erik, staring directly at her face, nodded gravely before continuing on to join his folk.

Lightning ripped through the sky with a deafening crash of thunder. The plate glass windows rattled in their frames and the lights of the terminal buildings flickered. Kirsten stared up at the departure board as it momentarily died before blinking back to life with fractured graphics.

'Christ, this is bad.' Kirsten shook her head. 'Alice, we're not getting on any plane anytime soon.'

Silence. Kirsten turned towards her friend to see her at the window, transfixed by something.

'Alice?' asked Kirsten, 'It's going to be alright.'

'No, it's not,' answered Alice.

Kirsten stepped up to her friend and followed her gaze. Beneath the blackest of clouds, a dark, writhing funnel was building and snaking closer to the ground. Puddles were swept up off the tarmac and thrown at the windows and baggage handlers were running, heads down into the wind, to shelter.

The ground throbbed and seemed to vibrate beneath their feet as the wind became louder and louder in their ears, slamming into the building and howling through the smallest of cracks. The funnel of wind tore through the long arm of the terminal and as glass, concrete and metal splintered the electricity exploded and plunged them into a darker gloom. Kirsten couldn't take her eyes off of the tornado; nor could Alice. The storm lifted a plane from the ground and dragged it effortlessly across the tarmac, scraping the wing towards them.

Kirsten closed her hand around Alice's wrist and began to back away from the vibrating window; she tugged her friend with her.

'Alice,' said Kirsten, 'We've got to move from here.'

The tornado grabbed hold of the plane and flipped it into the air and swung it towards the departure hall. Alice and Kirsten ran from the windows and dived across the wooden floor with their friends as the plate glass exploded inward and the fractured wing of the plane ripped through the building.

A light wind drifted across the mountains. The air was cold and fresh and the sky was clear. The wind circled; birds circled. Seconds blurred into minutes and minutes into the endless vista. Eleanor looked down on the aluminium smelter; she saw herself lying motionless in the dirt in the middle of the site. Nearer, she saw herself, splattered with dirt and rain, a breeze blowing at her hair.

She heard the scream; wailing through the wind, it penetrated and tore its way into her mind. Suddenly Eleanor was looking down on a bleak land of volcanoes erupting in a ring around the horizon. The sky seethed with rain and electrical storms. Down below was an island surrounded by sea; and an expanse of black sand that she now walked across. She stepped up to a solitary tree encircled by the stone remnants of þursar guards and reached out to touch the tree – an ash. She fingered the leaves. They were hot and even as she touched them she could feel them wither and shrivel. She stepped back hastily.

'The tree of life.'

Eleanor turned swiftly at the sound of her cousin's voice. She was there with Ben, but how? Eleanor looked around the mountain hut which was both so alike and different at the same time as the one that she had been in.

'How did you—' stuttered Eleanor, 'how did you know where I was?'

'You showed us on the map, remember?' said Ben. 'When the storm hit, we came as soon as we could.'

Hanna reached out to her cousin with a mug of coffee. 'You wait and see what it's like – the pylons have been taken out further down the valley and the roads are a mess.'

Eleanor stared back at her cousin, trying to make out the shape of her face, as the eyes, nose and mouth blurred and shifted in her vision. Colours and shapes swam and slid in her view until she was looking at the battered remains of Keflavik airport with the terminal buildings broken in and smouldering. Bits of plane littered the runway, with one smashed through the shattered glass front of the departure lounge. From somewhere within, Eleanor heard her name called out of desperation and anguish. Alice. And now Kirsten called out. And then Ben and Hanna Katla were calling...

'Eleanor!'

Vaguely she saw the blurred outline of figures moving towards her, closing in on her where she lay in the dirt. There, she could recognise faces and then... Nothing.

Eleanor woke; blinking her eyes open she found herself sat on the back seat of the pick-up truck. She lifted her head from her brother's shoulder.

'How?' she asked.

Ben frowned at his sister. 'You passed out in the middle of the storm.'

'The storm, yes.' Eleanor remembered. She turned over her hands and examined her palms for the grazes and indentations of gravel. 'I think I created it.'

Eleanor looked to Ben for reaction to this admission. He frowned.

'I had to open a bridge. Strong enough for the þursar to – to see what they are building here,' Eleanor told him. 'I don't know exactly what that factory is for but its ripping the world apart.'

Eleanor thrust out her hand to gesture at the construction site visible though the windscreen of the jeep. Ben shook his head.

'Well you're right there,' he said. 'Fuck knows how they got permission for that.'

Hanna looked round from the front seat, rubbing her fingers together. 'Money.'

Ben nodded despairingly.

'Anyway,' said Eleanor, 'you never said – how did you find me?'

Ben narrowed his gaze at his sister. 'You don't remember? You radioed out to us...?'

Eleanor shook her head. No, she couldn't remember.

'And Ásta,' Hanna added, pointing to the gate where the ranger was having an animated discussion with the construction workers, 'she called us up and said she was coming up to fetch us down off the mountain. They think it's not the last we've seen of these storms.'

Eleanor nodded slowly, uneasy about the likelihood of further destructive storms.

'So you succeeded then?' asked Ben.

'What?'

'The bridge allowing the þursar through, you achieved it?'

'I told you didn't I?' answered Eleanor. 'The storm...?' She wondered also about Gunnlaugr. Would he have worked out yet that she had lied to him? He must have done; he would have experienced the storm too and would know that it was not just a meteorological event.

'What?' Eleanor realised that Ben had asked her something.

'You ready then?' Ben repeated. 'To return home?'

Home. Of course. And her degree results – it all seemed like another lifetime away. She nodded and smiled at her brother.

Eleanor leaned on her hands, at the back of the bus. She stared out of the window and watched as the mountain receded into the distance. Beneath her the bus lurched and turned onto a metalled road. The gentle hum of conversation on the bus faded into the background as she allowed her thoughts to drift. She watched the view slide past the windows. The mountains sunk into gentle slopes and the craggy slopes into a cushion of rich, fertile fields. Scattered farms became hamlets and their gaudy-painted corrugated iron roofs blurred into a melange of colours. Hamlets gave way to villages and villages to suburbs. Pavements replaced grass verges and the roads became adorned with white lines and traffic lights. Ahead, the bird-like shape of Hallgrimskirkja cathedral rose above the Reykjavik skyline.

Eleanor's attention was snatched back to the here and now. In the seat in front of her Hanna was talking on the phone. She tuned into the voice and to the words; her mum? No, dad. Suddenly Eleanor was gripped with nerves at the reality of going home. She looked away, out of the windows at the streets, the cars, the people, and it all seemed so alien to her.

Images of þursar men loomed out of her memories. When she looked up, cloud formations twisted and changed in her mind and Eleanor saw broken hillsides and sweeping vistas. She saw caves and tunnels and underground halls and all of it—

Eleanor jolted forward and back. The bus lurched to a halt in traffic. *And it's all so much more real than this*, she mused. She sighed and leaned back on the window, watching the verge slide past as the bus descended down off the highway and slowly round into the forecourt of the coach station.

The sliding doors hissed open in front of Guðni. He walked out, a tall figure, laying his left hand across the curve of his wife's back as he stepped out onto the forecourt. There it was. The grime-stained, dark red number 14 bus from the Highlands. His heart quickened and he gulped down breath; he felt a churning queasiness in the pit of his stomach.

Passengers disembarked and began to make their way to friends and relatives. Guðni stepped forward and again stopped. Ben. He called out to his son and waved.

Across the forecourt, Ben waved back. And Hanna followed her cousin down the steps. *Where was Eleanor?* And then, a face he thought he had lost. Eleanor. For a moment their eyes met. Eleanor flinched and looked away.

'Look, Di,' enthused Guðni, 'it's Ellie.' He called across the forecourt, 'Eleanor!'

He broke into a run, charging across the forecourt and throwing his arms around his daughter. Diana watched, tentative and unsure. Alice and Kirsten stood alongside her.

'You not going?' asked Alice. 'Your daughter?'

Kirsten reached out towards Diana. 'Are you okay?'

PART THREE

Northern Capital

1

Ben stood amongst puddles on the bus station forecourt, surrounded by cracks and fissures in the concrete that resembled seismic charts in their complexity. They separated him from his family; his sister now being embraced by their father. He caught his father's gaze across his sister's shoulder and in his mind he pre-empted the criticism that would follow.

'It'll be okay,' said Hanna.

Ben turned. Hanna was at his side. He lay down his rucksack at his feet, and frowned.

'I guess so,' answered Ben, 'I just feel like I've gone against his every instruction.'

'You brought Ellie back. It'll be fine.'

They looked up, towards where Eleanor, now released from her father's grip, was facing Diana. Ben watched the way that both mother and daughter did not know how to react or how to behave. He knew what Ellie was wanting; she wanted to be welcomed home with the love and relief and not to be judged or told that what she did was wrong. He watched his mother's face and he knew she wanted to give that too, but was somehow unable to. Diana remained stern and silent. Ben could see that the dressing-down was imminent. Diana began to speak but stopped herself. Ben watched as his mother grabbed Eleanor into a sobbing embrace.

'Ben?'

Ben started. He looked around to find his father next to him.

'I'm sorry, Dad,' began Ben, 'I know you said to leave it, but I couldn't. I had to—'

Guðni was shaking his head. 'I know, Ben,' he said, 'You've done well – bringing Ellie back to us...'

Eleanor felt the warmth of her father's embrace. She looked up at his always-kindly smile and his bright, alert eyes. She wriggled closer and felt secure in his arms. She had missed this. This, of all things, she had missed the most. He was talking to her, welcoming her home but she didn't take it in. This was enough; to be held in her dad's strong arms.

'Eleanor?' said Guðni.

Eleanor felt her father ease out of their embrace. She tightened her grip.

'Eleanor.' Guðni fixed her with his gaze. 'Your mother...' He removed his daughter's arms from around his waist and pointed her in the direction of Diana.

Eleanor glanced back at her dad. He nodded to her and she turned and stepped up to Diana.

'Mum, I'm sorry.'

Diana said nothing. She pulled her daughter into a tight embrace and kissed her on the cheek, before releasing her. From around the back of her, Kirsten and Alice came into view. Eleanor's heartbeat skipped jubilantly.

'Kirsten? Alice!' called Eleanor, 'What are you still doing here? The flight home – I thought...?'

Kirsten and Alice leapt forward towards their friend and greeted Eleanor enthusiastically.

Ben watched his sister; heard the babbling conversation of friends reuniting; he saw his mother left alone on the forecourt, standing with obvious unease. She smoothed the lines of her dress with her palms and looked about her.

Guðni walked towards his son and Ben moved to meet him. The greeting was staid and difficult; an uneasy handshake, and a tentative hug. Guðni did not mention Ben's rash actions in taking off after Eleanor but even so Ben felt the tension that it had generated. He made his excuses and moved to help Hanna unload the rucksacks.

Ben paced the hallways and landings of his uncle's house. He lingered in the doorway to one room, then another. He heard his sister's voice; chatting with her friends from the holiday. Eleanor backed out of the room wrapped in a towel and passed him on the landing. He looked away and ambled towards the doorway of the room out of which she had come.

'Hi.' Alice looked up.

Ben felt awkward, and kicked at the air pathetically.

'Ben? Isn't it...' Alice offered by way of introduction, but he hadn't heard, or had chosen not to hear as he shuffled off across the landing. She tilted her head quizzically and began to blather again to Kirsten.

Ben reached the stairs. Hanna slid her arms into her leather jacket and pulled back her hair into a ponytail whilst crossing the landing.

'It's ironic,' Ben said, 'but after everything that's happened, I kind of feel lost.'

'Sorry Ben.' Hanna winced. 'I'm late already. Been away – and I've got band rehearsal...'

Ben felt his whole expression drop, and Hanna noticed it. She smiled. 'Later? Okay...' She squeezed her cousin's hand, fired him a last, friendly grin, and hurried down the stairs. Ben rolled his eyes and mooched his way downstairs.

Ben and Eleanor watched from the windows as the bus turned off the main road and swung round the terminus building and their parents slid into view. Ben nudged his sister. She looked up.

'So, you decided yet what story you're going to tell them?' he asked her.

Ben perched at a table in the living room as he worked though his notes. In his head was the cacophony of conversation of Eleanor telling her family what happened on the night she went missing. His brain tuned into and out of the adaptation of the truth. Questions continued to come, and explanations followed as echoes. The sound was layered over Ben's mind. He pressed his fingers at his temples and leaned closer to the paperwork but it was useless. He just could not concentrate.

Ben looked up. Across the room he saw Eleanor, his sister, silhouetted against the light from the window. He saw his father and mother, listening, and concerned. He saw Eleanor's two friends, Kirsten and Alice sitting at his sister's feet enraptured by the tale of her adventure. He sighed quietly and shook his head. It was not even the true story but some abstraction – just where did she get the ideas? And how did she make a fantastical tale of staying alive for nine days in the wild sound more credible than the true story that she now hid...?

Ben looked down at his paper, at the notes and the graphs in front of him. His eyesight was out of focus and his understanding blurred. The background noise intruded further into his brain. He wiped away sweat from his brow, and sighed loudly. He glanced up to see his whole family staring at him with concern, and he felt the heat as his whole face blushed.

'I'm fine.' He shook his head and pushed his papers together into a pile. Getting to his feet, the chair scraped back across the floor. He stacked his papers and books and pens into a pile, cradled them in his hands and shuffled from the room muttering his apologies.

Eleanor lifted her head and watched her brother leave. She had wondered about his quietness since their return from the mountains. She wanted to go after him and ask what was bothering him. Around her she felt the weight of her parents' gaze and the intrigue from Kirsten and Alice. She remained in her seat.

'The night I went missing,' said Eleanor, 'What happened to you guys?' She looked first to Alice; then to Kirsten.

Kirsten stared back apologetically. 'I'm so, so sorry Ellie,' Kirsten said, 'It wasn't till we were nearly back at the hut that we realised you weren't with us. The fog was that thick – you remember – and came right down into the valley.'

'Did anyone come back for me?' Eleanor asked.

'Not immediately.' Kirsten shook her head. 'No.'

Eleanor saw the image of that man in her mind again, a dark shape amongst the thick cloud. His call echoed back through her mind. *So it wasn't Finnur; and nor was it Aðli. Gunnlaugr then? How long had he been watching her?* She looked up at Kirsten.

The fog penetrated her skin, and water leached round the edges of her clothing, running in miniature streams beneath the layers. Kirsten stood near the foot of the hill amongst the rest of her party trying not to think about the coldness and the wet. Just outside the group, their guides, Finnur and Aðli were gesticulating fast and talking faster in their native Icelandic. She glanced round at Alice, peering out from beneath her hood and subdued from her normal boisterousness. Rushing from person to person was the tall and lean, almost wiry, Andy. He had just been to Alice to quiz and confirmed with them, urgently and impatiently about when they last saw Eleanor.

'Andy?' Eleanor's face went white. 'Is he still...?'

'Last we heard,' said Kirsten, 'He was on his way back to Reykjavik.'

'So he didn't come back with you guys then?' Eleanor asked.

Kirsten caught Alice looking at her. She nodded. 'Once Finnur had got us off the mountain, Andy – he wanted to stay and help...' She shook her head. 'He refused to get back on the bus.'

Kirsten leaned across Alice. They pushed both their faces to the window, wiping back the condensation and peered out into the gloom. Outside, Andy was confronting Finnur; arguing and gesticulating. Finnur pointed to the bus whilst Andy shook his head and backed off in the opposite direction to reclaim his bag from the trailer. Finnur pursued him, attempting to reason with Andy. He grabbed his rucksack from the trailer, and shouldered it in the driving rain. He shook his head at Finnur again and walked away, heading off down the road towards the lights of the gas station. Kirsten sat back in her seat, as Finnur leapt back into the bus. He leaned round to address the volunteers.

*

'That was the last we saw of him. Except for on TV.' Alice smiled coyly. 'He went off, to search for you. We came back to Reykjavik.'

'He should have gone with you guys. What was he thinking?' Eleanor shook her head.

'It was dangerous, yes, but Andy was worried about you,' Guðni told his daughter.

'But Andy, he knows the risks – Ben too!' Eleanor retorted, 'They shouldn't have risked their lives coming after me—'

Guðni nodded. 'True enough. But you can't be angry with them. You can't hate them for caring.'

Eleanor looked away, beyond the window, at the garden. 'I was fine.' She turned back to her family and friends, and shook her head. 'And if I wasn't, there wouldn't have been anything they could do.'

She raised her head to be caught by her mother's stern expression. Diana shook her head sadly.

'What?' asked Eleanor, 'I'm safe now. I went missing and I'm back. It's not my fault I got lost.'

As he watched his daughter, Guðni felt her pain, and went over to her. He knelt beside his daughter and held her in his arms. Eleanor's fingers clutched and clung to her father. She was home. She was safe.

The neon lights blinked in the pale dusk. It was night on Reykjavik High Street. Inside the club, lights swirled and music pumped. The air was sticky and reeked with the stale odour of beer and cigarettes. Halldór weaved between the crowds with his fingers entwined round several bottles of beer. He ducked across the room and descended the back stairs. He pushed through into a smaller room where Hanna Katla was sitting with her bandmates, strumming her guitar and singing a new song. She looked up as Halldór entered and handed round the bottles.

'Skull.' Hanna toasted, and with Halldór and the rest of the band they swigged down beer.

I put out my hand
I feel the pulse
The mountain stirs
Beneath my feet
Stillness; moonrise.

Hanna Katla's voice was impassioned, her fingers once more on the guitar. Halldór had fallen in behind his keyboard and lay down chords to Hanna's words. Brýn, finding the rhythm in his head, began to beat out the percussion on his kit.

The song progressed and faltered and they fell back on laughter and drinking. Noise from the bar above filtered in through the ceiling – the oscillating murmur of voices set to the thump-thump of the sound system vibrated through the walls. Again Hanna began her song – varying the words – feeling for an improved rhythm.

Again the song disintegrated into laughter, jokes and beer.

Ben stood in his bedroom, staring at the black and white photograph of the Leirhnijú volcano. It pulled him in and he stared at the grain of the picture. In his mind he plotted a mathematical graph. He saw thermo-climatic illustrations and the numbers behind them and his mind processed the data. He felt in his pocket for a stub of pencil and a scrap of paper. Without looking he wrote what was in his mind. Slowly, he raised the scrap of paper up at arm's length in front of him and focused his eyes off the grain of the photograph and onto his pencil-scrawled words. He nodded. Yes.

Eleanor stood in the doorway, and lingered for a moment before she tapped on the door and pushed it open. She crept into the room where Ben was lying on his bed staring up at the ceiling with the science book face down next to him.

She approached her brother slowly and perched on the end of the bed. She cocked her head to one side and took in the view of her brother – relaxed in body yet tense and preoccupied of mind.

Eleanor started at a sound from her brother. No conversation followed though and Eleanor supposed it to be nothing more than a grunt, or a sigh that she had mistaken for words. For a while longer she continued to look at her brother, arms crossed behind his head, staring out across the room. Eleanor turned – the picture. She looked back at Ben, then again at the picture and slowly she remembered.

Eleanor crossed the room to look more closely at the picture. She stared at it just as Ben had done a week or more ago. She found herself lost in the grain of the picture, but it was not mathematics and climate change modelling that she saw. Lost in the grains of black and white photography Eleanor saw the figures and faces of ancient people moving amongst the rocks. As she noticed one, so another þurs would come alongside, gathering around a stone table – the council chamber that she knew all too well.

'You see it too?' Ben was standing alongside his sister now, directing his hand at the picture like a weatherman on television explained his maps.

Eleanor turned to her brother, shocked and surprised. 'You too?'

Ben looked at her strangely. 'I don't know why I didn't think of it earlier.' He shrugged. 'A week ago I was looking at this picture and I saw the fractual beauty of it. The scientific mapping of it made me see what I had been missing for all my computer modelling and geo-thermic graphs.' His enthusiasm blinded him to his sister's confusion.

Eleanor smiled. It never ceased to amaze her how Ben's enthusiasm for his research could mask his awareness of her own confusion. She heard his scientific theorising and realised with disappointment, if not surprise, that where she had seen traces of other worlds he had seen none of it. She looked back at the picture – a black and white landscape photograph of a famous volcano. The þurs and the alfar that walked with her were gone.

Hanna grabbed the microphone towards her. She swept back her hair and lets go of her voice.

The Earth in me
The fire in my soul
Hanna turned towards her band mates—
The mountain it erupts.

Alongside her, Halldór's fingers moved across the guitar strings, his face stretching and contorting with the music. Behind her, Jon felt his fingers move across the keys and found the chords. He sung a backing to Hanna's melody.

Around the room lay the dregs of beer in bottles and glasses.

Alice and Kirsten leaned across the dining table, watching Guðni's fingers trace the road south on a map. They listened as he explained how the house was his great grandfather's - an old farm - and of its long history. Of how he and his sister inherited one of the oldest working farms in that region - maybe in the whole of Iceland.

'But you've never farmed?' Kirsten looked at the few dots on the map that indicated the 'town'.

'No. Nor my father,' Guðni said, 'He left my grandfather's house for University and never returned. As children, Lára and I, we remember a few holidays, Christmas - and maybe a couple of summers. My father was in love with the city. He was not a farmer.'

As he talked Guðni had been handling his empty whisky glass, moving it round between his fingers. He now stared into it, watching the light reflect across the surface. Thrusting it down onto the table with a reassuring clunk he stroked his finger around the rim.

'I love the old house. So do the kids, Eleanor, Ben – I made sure of it. You can lose yourself there.'

'I can't wait to see it,' enthused Alice.

Guðni smiled. 'Tomorrow evening.' He nodded 'It's two hours' drive. If I still have time to change my niece's mind.'

Kirsten looked up, surprised. 'Hanna's not coming?'

'She says she has to study and all this with Eleanor, she's missed so much work.' He shook his head.

Andy signed his name across the visitor book and slid the key off the counter. He shouldered his rucksack and stooped upstairs to find his accommodation within Snorri's Guesthouse.

2

Eleanor laughed. Alice played her cards; then Kirsten. She was followed by Guðni who laid down an ace. All too quickly it was Eleanor's turn again and she was silenced into staring at her cards. Slowly and deliberately she played an '8' and reversed play.

'Sjít!' Guðni flung down his cards. He lurched forward and pointed a finger at his daughter. 'I remember a day when you couldn't beat me.'

Eleanor laughed. 'Yeah, but you haven't been playing every night with a dozen conservation volunteers...'

'You could try your luck at *Pigs* if you prefer?' Alice grinned.

Guðni raised his eyebrows. 'Pigs?'

'You have these couple of plastic pigs – they are Kirsten's,' explained Alice, 'you roll them like dice and score according to how they fall. On their backs, all legs in the air – that's a double razorback – but if they're touching, they're making bacon and your score is zeroed.'

Guðni smiled, albeit cautiously.

Candles in baked bean cans cast flickering pools of light along the tables within the tent. The canvas sides were blown inward and out by the wind and the rain drummed on the roof. The air smelt of steam and damp towels. Conversation ceased for a moment as the door flapped open and blew free in the wind. A gust of wind surged in, forced back as Billy leapt out of his seat to pull down the zips and fastened together the clammy canvas. He quickly returned to the table and to the medley of conversations, jokes and games. Andy handed round the Frisbee containing the two little pigs.

The pigs were thrown again, and again another throw; and another. This time Billy trusted to take no more and the scores were calculated and so the pigs were passed on to the next player.

Kirsten pulled together the cards and began to shuffle them once again. She looked across the room at Ben.

'You going to join us this time, Ben?' she asked.

Ben continued to work, head bowed to his notes.

'Ben!' Kirsten called sharply.

He looked up. She repeated her question. He glanced down again, and then hesitantly across the room. He caught sight of Kirsten's smile and placed his notes back into the file. He was about to the cross the room with them, before pausing in his step and reconsidering. He laid the file down carefully on the table and joined the others around the coffee table. Glancing up from the bean bag, he smiled at Kirsten. She smiled back.

*

Bryn laughed; his voice was deep and resonating. He sat opposite Hanna Katla, his finger idly stroking the condensation from the side of his beer glass. She sat watching him through her glass which she cradled in front of her. Halldór pulled up a chair between them.

'So how was Bjäkk?' Halldór swigged from his bottle. 'Still counting fish?' Both he and Bryn laughed.

'Less of the fish, I think,' Kirsten answered, 'more concerned with climate change now. Everyone seems to be—'

Bryn nodded, and drank more beer. 'Climate change has been big news this summer. The storms that your cousin was caught in and that big one two nights ago - it's had all the scientists talking.'

'You should see the university,' said Bryn, 'it's crawling with scientists from across the world. And you know the North Bar? It's been taken over by these wild, grey-haired academics hooked up to the net on their laptops and cell-phones.'

Hanna laughed. 'I should tell Ben. He would be in his element.'

Bjäkk glanced up from a desk piled high with papers, files and books. He gazed out through grubby windows at the sun sinking low over the mountains. He returned to his papers and referred to some figures before scrawling a line of notes with a chewed black biro. He leafed through more pages, tapping the end of the biro on the pad. A thought occurred to him and he peered above his shoulder at the packed shelves to scan the length of them. Finding the book that he was looking for, he leaned back in his chair and retrieved it.

Several loose sheets of paper fell down with the book. Bjäkk sighed and slung them aside onto one of the already precarious piles. As he turned back to open the file in front of him, something about the paper caught his eye. He reached out again and snatched it back to study the message on its reverse. Slowly a smile drew across his face. He turned it over; a photograph of Hanna Katla smiling sweetly back at him.

After a few moments just looking at the photograph, he twisted in his seat and slipped it into the inside pocket of his leather jacket. He sat forward and delved into the new file. From notes, forms and data he extracted answers and more questions.

'Climate change and tourism, huh?' Kirsten nodded and leaned towards Ben.

Ben blushed. He hid his face behind his hands. He knew this was silly and dropped his arm, but he still felt awkward.

'I did a geography module myself,' said Kirsten.

'I thought you said you were – a vet?'

'Veterinary nurse, yeah.' She grinned. 'Not strictly relevant, but it was either that or doing some IT course for beginners.'

Ben nodded. He fidgeted and tried to compose the next lines of conversation in his head. He pulled his notebook closer and began to sketch out his project and explain it in enthusiastic detail to Kirsten. She leant over him and followed his every word. With increasing regularity, Ben glanced up to catch Kirsten's blue eyes, struck by the intensity with which they watched him. He drew diagrams and plotted his ideas. Kirsten asked questions that were both insightful and thoughtful. Ben mirrored her actions and her movements. He slipped into her ways of speech. He didn't want this conversation, this moment, to end.

'Eleanor!'

Eleanor jolted herself awake. She blinked herself out of her day-dreaming and glanced round. Alice waved her hand in front of Eleanor's face and grinned. Eleanor looked back across the room at the scene on which she was previously fixed, though not registering. Ben was on the far side of the room in close conversation with Kirsten. She stared again. Ben? And Kirsten? Ben and Kirsten?

'Eleanor?' asked Alice.

Eleanor sighed and turned towards her friend. 'What?'

'It sounds amazing,' said Alice, 'your uncle's summer house.'

Eleanor smiled modestly. 'Yeah.' She focused her attention onto Alice. 'Ben and I haven't been there for ages, though. Usually we come here, then go out hiking - staying in huts - camping.' She smiled; remembering fond childhood memories. 'We used to go to the farm all the time when we were kids.'

'She doesn't realise what we've been through,' Diana said, standing with Guðni in the doorway to the room.

'Does it matter?' asked Guðni. 'She's home. She's safe.'

'But like none of this has ever happened...?' Diana rounded on Guðni. 'You are too easy on her - on them. You always have been.'

Guðni reached out to his wife, and steered her out the room. He pulled back the doors to the lounge. She answered his concern with a steely gaze.

'Our son behaved recklessly. Against our wishes he put himself in danger when Eleanor - she could have been dead,' Diana said.

'I know.' He frowned. 'Diana, don't think I'm not cross. But we can't punish them. They're adults - and I think - they are strong.'

'They're not telling us anything!' Her breaths were short and heavy with frustration. 'You must have seen through it, too. Her story, it was just a story. There's more—'

'Of course.' Guðni took his wife's hands in his. 'Of course there's more. But I am sure it's nothing sinister.'

Diana rolled her eyes at her husband.

'I just want her, so much,' Diana said, 'to tell me the truth.'

Beneath the first floor window, Finnbjörn played in the garden. He was slender and dressed in a suit of velvet and lace. He conjured tricks from the stars and frolicked with the sprites and faerie folk. He climbed the wall of the house nimbly and perched on the windowsill where he could sit and stare in at where Ben and Eleanor were sleeping.

'She never said thank you.' His voice was light and lilting. 'She didn't give us credit for what we did.'

Inside the room, Eleanor turned over and tugged the covers in. Through the half-light of night she saw her brother in the bed opposite.

'Ben?' She repeated his name. 'Are you awake?'

Ben lay facing the wall. His eyes open. 'Yeah...?'

Eleanor sucked on her lip. 'I think she knows.'

Ben lifted his head from his pillow and rolled over to face his sister. 'She's sharp, our mother.'

Eleanor sighed and collapsed back onto her pillow. She stared up at the ceiling. 'She's going to find out.'

Ben's mind spun with other possible things to say. Silence lingered. Outside on the road, cars moved. Occasionally their headlights penetrated the gloom before sweeping back out into the night.

'So you and Kirsten then...' began Eleanor.

Ben was suddenly alert. 'Yeah?'

'Who'd have thought?' continued Eleanor, 'my little brother, all in love...' She grinned.

Ben bit his lip. *Love? Is that what it was?* He considered the evening and mapped out the possible futures. Again silence lingered in the air.

Finnbjörn looked along the glazed window to where his sister Johanna had joined him on the sill. Her fair hair glistened, her eyes the shiniest blue, and her face was angles of beauty and shining silver. She turned her head towards her brother.

'You remember the girl's friend? He has arrived back in the city?'

'Is this true?' asked Finnbjörn. 'Why has she neglected her boy?'

'This is true. Olà saw him arrive.' Johanna slipped the catches to the window and pranced down into the room. She stepped lightly across the floor in her satin gown, her jewellery glinting in the moonlight as small circles of light that reflected across the floor. She leapt over Eleanor's bed and ducked down close to listen to her breathing. She gazed upon the sleeping Eleanor. Finnbjörn's playful smile was close on her other side.

Two smaller alfar joined the brother and sister in their midnight vigil of Eleanor and Ben's room. Perched on the windowsill they played flute and fiddle, and conjured music out of the night. Johanna lifted herself from Eleanor's bed and swayed around the room singing softly and made her way over to Ben. She crouched close to where he lay and stroked her fingers through his hair, trailing her long, delicate fingers down his cheek. She sung to him; her voice lilting with the music. She drew out the sprites and the spirits, first as twinkling lights floating free in the air; they drifted in arcs through the air until finally settling on the shoulders of the alfar people.

Clouds that had built over the high peaks across from Reykjavik harbour now pushed in across the bay. The temperature of the air rose sharply; the night suddenly close. A fork of lightning split the horizon in two and thunder reverberated across the bay. Rain fell, sharply at first – big splashes of water on road. A downpour followed and soon the night smelt of rain.

The bar was almost deserted now and the music silenced. Hanna stood just inside the doorway listening to the howl of the wind and the driving rain. She watched the drops form, and drip down the window. The neon reflections of the shop signs outside and the lights were reflected within in the curvature of every drop. She pulled the zip up on her leather jacket and freed her hair from the collar before reaching decisively for the door handle.

It was quiet within Eleanor and Ben's room. The alfar had gone, their singing replaced by the drumming of the rain on the window and by the wind as it rushed around the corner of the building.

Professor William Tyndale pulled apart the louvre of the venetian blinds. He peered out from his office at the developing storm. Each flash and fork of lightning cast dramatic light and stark shadows across the Reykjavik skyline. Over the rooftops of the city, the looming spire of the Catholic cathedral stood sharply silhouetted against the storm clouds with every burst of electrical activity.

He let go of the blinds and returned to the dimly lit room. His two assistants – Níls, a young Viking-like Icelandic researcher and Kathryn, a student on sabbatical from her studies in Southampton – were working at their terminals, cross-checking data with other resources.

Níls pointed to his computer screen. 'Today's data is just wild.' He speculated over the data as William approached and Kathryn left off what she was doing to roll her chair towards them both.

'See here.' His finger traced the colour graphs on screen as he scrolled through the hours. 'Here and here. These temperature fluctuations are just not normal...'

'Not even for Iceland!' joked Kathryn.

William smiled; a thinly drawn show of emotion. He pulled a chart from the precariously balanced in-tray on his desk and shook his head. 'With the frequency of these storms and the intensity of the electrical activity recently I am fast coming to the conclusion that Iceland is now a significant thermo-dynamic conductor between the earth and the upper atmosphere.' He leafed through the charts. 'Here and here again.' He looked up. 'Kathryn, what are today's measurements on the glacial shift?'

Kathryn swung round in her chair and rolled it back up to to her desk. She tapped out the commands. 'Here.' She pointed to the screen. 'The ones that are blinking, they are showing growth every time we take readings...' Her voice trailed off as she stared at the screen. 'These two. I've not seen them before.'

'Let me see.' William leaned across her, and began to tap in some data. 'It's Skaftafell. The glacier has been in retreat here for years.'

A shuddering light ripped through the office. Thunder followed and almost instantaneously the building trembled and the lights flickered. Around the room, computer equipment droned away, and the screens went black.

William rushed to the windows flanked by his two assistants. Nils tugged on cords and pulled the blinds up. Black smoke poured from the top storey of an apartment building three blocks away. The flashing lights of emergency vehicles could be seen in the street below, swinging round the corner, sirens blaring.

'The storm,' William said flatly. 'This is getting worse.'

3

Eleanor pulled back her hair and dropped it over the collar of her shirt. She passed a mirror and lingered for a moment before pulling open the door and stepping out onto the landing. She stopped. Across the landing she could see her brother and Kirsten. Not kissing, not touching, but close.

'Morning, Ben,' she said as she passed by to descend the stairs. At the ground floor she wandered aimlessly and arrived in the sitting room. Her uncle and aunt are transfixed with horror by the television.

'What's happened?' asked Eleanor.

'The storm,' said Baldur.

Eleanor ventured further into the room. The television showed news coverage; aerial footage of a Reykjavik suburb destroyed by fire and storm.

'Looks like a bomb has gone off.' Eleanor sunk onto her chair, transfixed by the news reports.

'Three direct lightning strikes. Five blocks completely destroyed.' Baldur shook his head. 'I've never seen this before.'

'Ben!' Eleanor called out. 'You should see this!'

Ben lingered at the bottom of the stairs. His fingers trace the lines of Kirsten's palm and he glanced briefly at her eyes. They stepped forward, down the hall and through into the sitting room. He saw first, the pale faces of his family, and then the flickering light of the television screen. The commentary of journalists hit him.

'This was last night?'

Ben sat at his laptop, working fast as he input the data, taking the information from notes extracted from news websites. Finally, he finished the calibration and clicked the model into action. He sat back in his chair; and crossed his hands behind his head, to watch.

'Ben? How long is that going to take?' asked Eleanor.

'Depends. Half an hour – maybe an hour.'

Eleanor nodded. 'Don't forget we need to be packed for going to the old farm.'

Ben nodded. His gaze once more focused on the laptop. Eleanor drifted back out to the hall and passed Alice on the stairs. Ben screwed up his eyes in thought. He picked up a pen, and slid a pad across the table towards him.

Later, Ben gathered his sister and father alongside him and pulled open the newspaper. He spread it across the table before scanning down the left-hand page and pointing to the chart.

'See this front – and the depression.' He looked up at his father, 'That. It's coming straight for us. These storms aren't finished yet.'

Suddenly the front door was flung open and the noise of the traffic on the street emptied into the room, silenced again as the door slammed shut. Hanna hurried into the room and made straight for Ben's laptop. She swept her finger across the touch-pad to open the web-browser. Ben swung round to see what she was doing.

'Hanna...!' he protested, and dived towards the computer. His cousin looked round as her fingers keyed out the web address.

'My program.' Ben offered up resignation as he saw the task-bar icon blink a warning on the screen. He took control of the keyboard...

'Ben, I'm sorry,' Hanna apologised.

Ben turned away from the computer and glared at his cousin. 'It had five minutes left to run.'

'Ben. Really, I'm sorry,' implored Hanna, 'I was talking with the guys last night and they were telling me this stuff – it makes sense of what both you and Eleanor have been telling me...'

Ben didn't answer. Tabbing between windows he tried to work out what, if anything, he could save. Hanna edged closer before backing away.

Guðni pushed forward and laid a hand on his son's shoulder. 'You can run it again later. Hanna didn't mean—'

Ben pushed his away computer. 'I guess. I'm sorry, Hanna,' he said, 'You wanted to show us something?'

'It's probably nothing,' Hanna answered. She glanced across at the computer. 'Take a look.'

'What is it?' Eleanor moved to the computer and clicked through to the web browser. 'Alcon Corp?' She turned to her cousin.

Hanna nodded. She pulled up a chair in front of the computer and repositioned it to see the screen. Talking her way through the navigation she found the press release pages. Finding at last what she wanted, she pointed. 'Here. You see.'

Eleanor and Ben closed in to either side, looking over Hanna's shoulders.

'It's the new aluminium factory.' Eleanor read. 'The one that I saw being built.'

'Exactly. And see how they are proclaiming it as *a new kind of factory*.' Hanna clicked through the pages. 'It's an aluminium factory. How can it possibly be any better for the environment?'

Ben moved forward and took control of the computer from his cousin. He clicked through some links and found a page of technical specifications, 'How's it getting the power?' He read on, scrolling down the page, 'They keep on referring back to how this factory won't be driven by the damming of a glacial river.'

'Not a repeat of the Kárahnjúkar project, then–' Eleanor interjected.

'Must be geothermal, I guess?' Hanna offered.

Ben shook his head. 'Geothermal is a good domestic solution – some light industry even, but a smelter like this one...' Ben frowned. 'They are saying that it will take half Iceland's yearly aluminium production. Geothermal alone wouldn't be enough for that kind of operation.'

'It mentions here that new techniques have been employed to harness underground energy sources,' read Hanna, 'What else can it be?'

Ben shook his head. 'If I knew that?! There must be more here. Discussion boards maybe? Something like this doesn't happen without arousing the attention of conspiracy theorists.'

Sunlight broke through the stormy sky and illuminated the front garden of Hanna Katla's home with an iridescent light.

Guðni helped his brother-in-law stow bags into the back of the family jeep whilst Eleanor wandered out from the house and across the garden to where Alice was sitting on a large, weatherworn slab of lava that projected from the middle of the lawn. She looked intently at her mobile. Alongside her on the rock was Kirsten.

'Alice? You alright?' asked Eleanor.

'Yeah.' Alice flicked shut her mobile. 'It's fine.'

Eleanor squeezed in alongside Alice on the slab of lava as her friends shuffled up to make room. She frowned at Alice. 'It's not, you know.' Eleanor told her friend. 'What's up?'

Alice looked down at her mobile and glanced sideways at Kirsten. She spoke cautiously. 'It's Andy.'

Eleanor's face dropped on hearing her friend's name.

'Tell me. Where is he?'

Alice shook her head. 'He should be back in Reykjavik, but he's not answering his calls.'

'Maybe he's out of credit?' suggested Eleanor. She remembered, even as she spoke, Andy's obstinacy to stay on pay-as-you-go rather than contract.

A light wind whistled through the twisted birch branches of the trees that surrounded the garden's perimeter. The three girls were each left to inhabit their own thoughts.

Kirsten shook her head. 'It doesn't make sense.'

'When we phoned to say you'd been found,' said Alice, 'He said he was on his way back.'

'So where is he?' Eleanor asked again.

Kirsten shook her head. 'There's only one place he knows to stay here...'

'Snorri's.' Eleanor and Alice answered together.

'Why wouldn't he have phoned?' asked Alice.

Eleanor cut off her friends words. 'The storm, Alice.'

At that moment, Hanna Katla rounded the corner of the house with a box of food that she took over to the car.

'Hanna!' Eleanor called. 'Can we borrow you?'

Hanna Katla pulled at the steering wheel, and swung her jeep round the corner onto Snorrabraut, only to screech to a halt at the fluttering ribbons of police tape. She stared at the burnt out remains of Snorri's guesthouse. Kirsten and Alice leaned forward across the seats and gaped. Eleanor threw herself from the front passenger seat and ran forward, only to be pushed back by a police officer.

'Andy?' She repeated his name, again and again. Her cousin and her friends joined her on the street, transfixed by the burnt out shell of a whole block.

'We don't know that he was in there.' Eleanor turned to her friends. 'He wasn't was he?'

Kirsten shrugged and glanced sideways at Eleanor as she shook her head. She looked back at the ruins of the building. Firemen in smoked-stained suits brought out charred and smouldering remains in their search for survivors. Suddenly she noticed the red and blue stripes of nylon fabric. For a moment she was standing back in the north, in the trailer parked up beneath the canyon walls; rucksacks all around her.

Kirsten lifted a red and blue 80-litre rucksack and called out for its owner. Andy stepped up to the trailer and took it from her; and swung it onto his back in one effortless movement.

On the Reykjavik street, Kirsten grabbed Alice's arm and pointed. Alice recognised the charred remains of their friend's belongings. Diving under the security taping, they rushed forward to the scene and caught a glimpse of the UK Fell-Runners badge stitched to the front. They stopped, their worst fears of this day made real. A policeman led them back across the road. Eleanor gripped the tape, her nails cut into her skin as she heard her friends speak.

'It still doesn't mean anything.' Eleanor told herself more than anyone. 'Just because that's Andy's bag, he could've been out.'

Eleanor returned to the jeep with the others. Slowly and despondently, they climbed back up into their seats. In the front seats, both Eleanor and Hanna turned to face each other. Hanna Katla sat quietly for a moment before she fired the ignition, slipped the jeep into gear and slowly turned the car round. As Hanna drove back down the road Eleanor turned and looked back. In the back seat Kirsten and Alice were looking too. Behind them, the emergency vehicles around the devastation on the street corner were slowly becoming smaller and then, as Hanna steered another corner, the scene was gone.

Hours later and Eleanor sat on the sofa in her uncle's house, head in her hands. On either side, her mother and father comforted her. Ben stood in the doorway alongside Kirsten, whose hand he stroked with his fingers.

'You okay?' he asked her.

Valdís traced her long, slender fingers up the sides of Andy's face. Her long fingernails stroked him whilst he slept. She pulled the satin cloth from beside her and laid it over his naked body; under the flickering faery light within the underground cavern she sat with the human, watching him closely and working magic with the touch of her fingers.

William Tyndale leant over the desk, watching and waiting as the blue status bar edged across the computer screen; in another window, a DOS box scrolled through the data. His mind was already at work on future calculations and hypotheses.

'You should get some sleep.' Kathryn told him. 'Nils and I have got this covered. You go. Sleep.'

'I'm fine.' William removed his glasses and rubbed his eyes. He pushed his glasses back on, sat back and stretched. Getting up suddenly, he crossed the room to pour himself a coffee.

Kathryn answered his defiance with a stern gaze. Resigned to William's stubbornness, she returned to her work, taking some print-outs of storm data across to a map of Iceland that was spread out across a table top. She paused for a moment as she looked out through the window at the storm-destroyed suburb beyond. She felt the loss out there in the community and it stung her heart. Thinking again of work, she put emotion aside and focused on plotting details from last night's data.

Hanna Katla shouldered her bag and scooped up her car keys, before sweeping through the house to the lounge. Eleanor was staring at the live television news reports.

'We should be going.' she said.

Eleanor didn't answer. She stared out blankly, her face drained. Hanna approached her slowly.

'If we hear anything, I'll be back first thing tomorrow, after that, Pabbi can drive you home anytime you need. You need to get away from this...'

Eleanor looked up, sniffing away tears, she forced a smile.

'Just give me a few minutes, okay?'

Eleanor stood at the dressing table, holding the piece of alfar silverwork in her hands. Staring at the twists and curls of the patterning, she remembers how it was given to her.

She stood in a cavern, carved from the lava. Flaming torches reflected around the walls of cut obsidian. The þurs elder before whom she stood, pressed the small object of silver into her hands, nodding his vast head earnestly. Eleanor took the abstract patterning of silver, turning it over in the palm of her hand.

'What am I supposed to do with this?'

'You will know.' She heard the þursar voice and his gaze seemed to penetrate her head. He turned and ambled away.

In her bedroom, Eleanor looked again at the silver patterning, remembering the troll's words...

You will know.

She tossed the silverwork in the air and caught it in her hand. She slipped it into the coin compartment of her purse and pushed this into the pocket of her combats.

The indicators blinked at the stop line. Hanna accelerated and pulled the jeep out of the side road. Ben watched the scenery change, as the meadows of yellow flowers and the green of the grass and the iron-rich-red-ochre of the soil blurred into an impressionistic haze of colour set against a backdrop of steep cliffs rising up alongside the road. He became lost in the scene from his passenger side window, whilst behind him his sister chatted with her two friends.

Nils lifted the crate into the back of the jeep and slid it back with a grating noise that cut through his senses. Twisting round he moved to lift another crate, packing the jeep with scientific equipment. He heard Kathryn's voice behind him, chatting away with William as they brought down more boxes. She soon helped him stow the camping gear away in the back, as William settled himself in the driver's seat of the cab and connected up the GPS unit.

4

Under the light of a setting sun, fractured across the sky by storm clouds, Hanna drove the valley road. She turned off the metalled surface onto a solitary track that curved through lowland meadows to an old farm that was almost on the beach. She parked up at the front door.

Kirsten leapt down from the back seat, followed by Alice, and the two were immediately struck by the stillness of the air. There was nothing more than a slight breeze that stirred the surrounding grassland. They followed the three cousins across the gravel yard to the yellow-painted, corrugated iron house with the blue roof set back behind a small front garden and an old gate that swung open with the squeal of unoiled hinges.

'This,' Alice whispered to her friend, 'This is how I imagined Iceland.'

Kirsten nodded, pointing out the stains of rust from the corrugated roof down the peeling metal walls. They stepped in through the front door and followed the others through the small porch, passing a steep set of ladder-like stairs, into the wood-panelled back room of the house. The room smelt musty and the décor was a mismatch of styles and decades. The floors creaked as they crossed them, and the doorframes were twisted and warped through years of freezing temperatures and shrinking timberwork. Turning a corner into the back room, the girls found an archway where the room had once been knocked through to the front. Against the far wall was a battered upright piano. On the wall above, looking out across the room was the stern, penetrating stare of a fulsome dark-haired lady.

Hanna Katla stepped up behind Alice. 'That's grandmother.'

Alice turned and looked up again at the lady in the picture.

Hanna smiled. 'It's actually my great-grandmother. There's a picture of Pabbi's grandfather through here.' She led Alice through to the kitchen next door and to the dining room beyond. She pointed to the far wall and a second black and white photograph, this time of a man with thinning fair hair, against a backdrop of meadows, sea and mountains.

'He looks kind. Did you ever know him?'

Hanna Katla shook her head. 'Pabbi—' She took a backward glance at where her father was unpacking food from boxes into the large 1950s American-style refrigerator. 'He died when my father was still a little boy.'

Upstairs, Kirsten shook out her sleeping bag onto the bare mattress in the small half-timbered room in the eaves of the old house. 'And this is their house?' she asked.

'Já,' said Ben, 'Yes. It was my great-grandfather's farm. And his father's before that. My dad and my uncle were the first generation to really leave; to live in the city.'

Kirsten stepped towards the window and gazed through the small grubby panes, past the blanket of cobwebs and dead flies, to the view out across the bay.

'It's still farmed though? The land?'

Ben stepped up behind her. 'It's still owned by the family. Not sure which side though? They live up there somewhere.' He leaned close to her and pointed at the distant headland. He shrugged. 'I don't think I've ever met them.'

Kirsten felt Ben close to her. They stood at the window, catching the changing light as the sun crawled down the sky towards the horizon.

'It's a beautiful walk down to the sea.' Ben began. 'After dinner would you like to go? We might catch a fantastic midnight sunset.'

Kirsten smiled at the thought. 'That would be lovely.'

Headlights on the road; a single vehicle drove the main road south. It was a jeep, its bodywork etched by salty winds and harsh winters that sped through the icy wind blowing in from the southern sea. Inside the cab, the heaters blasted out warmth. Kathryn watched Níls, head down, working on his laptop in the seat next to her. She turned to William.

'Yeah, we were based down on the docks. Do you know Southampton at all?'

William nodded. 'A little. Been to a few lectures there when Dr Gore was teaching there. Don't remember much more than the route from the Holiday Inn to the lecture theatre though.'

'That's about all there is to Southampton!' Kathryn laughed.

William smiled too. They passed the sculptural remains of an old bridge before slowing down as they approached a junction.

'Here. I think.'

Níls looked up. 'Skaftafel. Já.'

A little later and Kathryn and Níls were making camp. William sat in the jeep, with the headlights casting beams of light across the tents, working through scientific models on his laptop. The stillness of the Icelandic night was broken only by the throaty purring of the engine as it ticked over.

Laughter ricocheted across the dining room. Baldur poured more wine as Guðni recounted the family history to an enraptured Alice and Kirsten. The three young cousins listened to stories that even they were hearing for the first time.

'The house has changed, yes.' Guðni leaned across and pointed through the window. 'The deck at the back, my uncle built three summers ago. His son owns this house jointly with myself and Baldur, but other than that the house has changed little.'

Guðni enjoyed telling his family's history. He explained how the lounge used to be two rooms, with the back half being grandmother's. Her parlour was kept for best with all her family mementoes. He recalled his own childhood here and the long summer days when he would help to work the farm. At times Baldur dryly interjected his own memories of family and events and Alice devoured the conversation with as much eagerness as she did the supper of smoked fish and delicious, earthy potatoes.

'Has Hanna or either of my two shown you the shop yet?' Guðni turned the question to Alice and Kirsten.

'Shop? No...' Alice answered.

Guðni smiled with wry pleasure. 'You saw the old extension out the side? The farm didn't do so well. And here, on this road we are very well placed between towns. My father opened a small store, petrol station and postal office. I think even, for a time, they operated a small bed and breakfast.'

Guðni looked across the table at his brother. Each knew what the other was remembering and they laughed. Presently Guðni turned to his guests again. 'During the holidays, if we weren't out on the farm, we were in the shop. That was a good job. You must go and have a look – a lot of it is still there – there were these shelves behind the counter lined with big jars full of sweets.' He grinned at the memories and poured out more beer. All the time he extolled his family's history to his guests. He passed glasses of Egil's beer to Alice and Kirsten and followed it up with dishes of food. Kirsten took a small wafer biscuit topped with what looked like pate. She frowned and pointed to the food.

'Súrsadir hrútspungar,' explained Guðni.

Kirsten and Alice exchanged confused expressions.

Hanna threw in a translation, 'It's pickled ram's testicles. It's nice.' She tried to allay their shock and suspicion. 'No really. That is delicious. But you see the plate Alice has got. Don't touch it.'

'Nei, don't listen to my niece. That too, is delicious,' said Guðni.

'What is it?' Alice lifted a cube of the pungent, yellowy-orange meat, 'Fish?'

'Hákarl,' said Eleanor, 'Rotted shark.'

Alice's face soured. She put down the dish and held her cube of rotted shark aloft and considered it.

'Seriously? It's disgusting,' repeated Hanna.

Kirsten laughed. 'I'm not sure which is worse, rotted fish or sheep's balls?!' She glanced around at Ben. 'These are Icelandic delicacies?'

Ben grinned. He took the biscuit of *súrasdir hrútspungar* and popped it in his mouth. Swallowing it quickly he approved of the choice. Kirsten glanced round at Alice in time to see her reach for the plate of pickled ram's testicles. She watched, somewhat aghast as Alice popped the biscuit in her mouth, chewed and swallowed. She awaited the verdict.

Alice nodded. 'It's good. Like pâté.'

Kirsten realised that all eyes were now on her. Still slightly cautious, she took a biscuit from the plate and slowly bit into it. A strong, coarse-paté taste swelled. It was good. Very good. She smiled and reached for another.

Ben and Kirsten stepped down through the garden away from the house, pulling their coats about them against the chill of the Icelandic night. They were followed through the long, lush grass by Eleanor and Alice. Ahead of them, Hanna sat on the dry stone wall playing chords on her guitar, a notebook and pencil by her side.

'You coming with us down to the beach?' Ben asked his cousin, as he and Kirsten hopped down off the wall into the field outside the garden.

Hanna Katla looked up, half her mind still turning over the words of a song. She shook her head. 'You go on,' she replied.

Her fingers tripped over the strings and out of the silence a tune emerged. Hanna gazed out over the bay, at the two pairs of figures striding out, some distance apart, across the meadow. The words emptied themselves into the world.

I didna know,
I didna know,
I didna know
that I love you.

Hanna felt for the chords on her guitar. Across the meadow, beyond the beach, the shore was cast in a shimmering golden light from the sun, now low in the sky. She watched Kirsten walk with her cousin through the meadows with arctic terns circling above protecting their nests. A little way behind was Eleanor, walking with Alice. Her mood found her voice again.

You went north
we moved on
And it wasn't for
two years or three?
I was on the road
And so were you—

—and instinctively she found the chorus waiting for her. Her fingers at the ready, the words repeated themselves with a subtle variation.

And I didna know,
I didna know,
I didna know
that you still loved me.

Ben walked alongside Kirsten and found, as they reached the beach, a new friend in this girl. Their conversation weaved through subjects that touched on both the serious and the inane. Often he glanced down at his side and saw the close proximity of his hand to hers. Desire fought in his mind with nervousness. They strolled onwards, along the shore, stopping occasionally in mid-step to reach for an interesting stone or shell. They turned each one over, reached a decision and either carried it with them, or tossed it aside into the sea.

*

Long way off across the sea
You're walking with a girl
that isn't me.

Hanna's fingers reached for the chords and her voice picked up the tempo of urgency and of intense feeling. No longer was she staring out across the meadow in the evening light, but into her soul and herself...

I'm sitting here waiting
I hear your voice
On every breath of wind.

Ben glanced behind him. Along the shore Alice was skimming stones into the sea. He looked back at Kirsten.

'So you and Alice – you came out here together.'

Kirsten nodded. 'Uh huh...'

'How do you know each other?'

Kirsten shrugged and smiled. 'Conservation holiday. A couple of years back. We both chose this one doing footpaths and dry stone walling up in Yorkshire,' She laughed. 'We stayed in touch.'

She stopped, and frowned. 'Why do you ask?'

'No reason.' Ben felt a need to reach out and take Kirsten's hands in his. He repressed the need. 'She's very spirited. Lots of life.'

'She is so funny. Outrageous sometimes–' Kirsten considered her words, contemplating how much to say. 'She really does care though. She has a clear passion for her career, but is so, so kind and caring to her friends.'

'Like you, I reckon,' Ben said the words almost before he could think about them, and reached out for Kirsten's hands.

*

I wanna know,
I wanna know,
I wanna know
what loving you is like

The notes hung in the air. Hanna pulled her notebook closer and readied her pen. She ran over the tune in her mind, hearing back the layers of song and imagining it in the studio; on the stage.

Eleanor tipped back her glass and swallowed a mouthful of Icelandic beer. U2 blasted from the sound system that was hooked up to a generator in the back of a battered jeep. She was gathered with her holiday friends, around a bonfire. The flames cast dancing shadows across the canyon walls around them.

Alongside Eleanor, Andy was talking – reminiscing about the holiday. Alice and Kirsten were there too. The so-called Gang of Four – the Crazy Gang – replaying the jokes and the anecdotes. They cast their gazes around the camp at their compatriots, laughing at shared jokes – still drawing on material gleaned from the first few days – hours even – of their first meeting at Heathrow and the flight out.

Eleanor turned to Andy. She stared up at his thin, angular face, and realised in this moment what she had learnt about her friend that she had not known previously. She remembered long evenings down the student union bar back at university. She reached out and pulled him to one side.

'Andy,' she said his name calmly.

He looked at her with those seductively dark eyes. She remembered how not that long ago she couldn't resist the power behind those eyes.

'I'm sorry.' Eleanor looked at him directly. 'What you asked – I can't.'

More fuel was thrown onto the fire and the flames leapt high. Shards of orange and yellow cast reflections across Andy's face and for a moment it looked as if he was burning.

A bolt of lightning came instantaneously with a deafening crack of thunder. The building burned. People stumbled out into the cold night in their pyjamas as smoke poured from the roof and fire raged within.

Eleanor sat bolt upright in her bed. In the dim light of night the edges were softened with the bleary eyesight that you only have on first awakening.

'Andy!' Eleanor called out involuntarily.

Upstairs, the music was felt through the walls, but the family lay sleeping, dreaming and unaware of the little people who shared their house.

Eirný laid her long, slender fingers around the door frame with its chipped, peeling paint and peered into the room where Eleanor sunk back onto her bed and tried to find sleep again. She turned swiftly and descended the steep staircase to where the alfar party was raging.

The alfar were dressed in suits and dresses of satin and fine lace. Around the edges of the room, a few alfar stood with goblets of wine and in the centre of the room they danced. Eirný entered into a room where the very air emanated light in a haze of colours. She was swept up into the dancing and soon had a partner in the form of Greipur, an alf who was tall for his kind.

The music played, on fiddle and flute, and the wine flowed. The night drew on.

Far away across the country, at the snout of a glacier, dark shapes moved amongst the rocks. The Þurs were out in the early hours scavenging for food. Their large, lumbering shapes reflected in the milky pools of meltwater. Further from the glacier, within the tents pitched up next to William's jeep, the three scientists slept...

Clouds lingered on the slopes that overshadowed Baldur Aðalsteinsson's farm. The first light of morning filtered through an overcast sky. Birds rose and fell over the meadow, picking out food. Snipes swooped low with the familiar whir-whir of their wings.

Alice woke in the small room under the eaves blinking open eyes that were not yet conditioned to the new day. Without her contact lenses the wall opposite, with its faded patterned wallpaper and the peeling skirting, was hazy and ill-defined. She lay still for a moment on her side listening to the creaking of the old house in the morning, wondering what time it was. Slowly she drifted in and out of consciousness, dozing and idly dreaming of the memories from the past few weeks.

In a state of half-wakefulness, and with her sleeping bag tucked up around her bare arms, a cold draught crept through the timberwork. In the doorless next room, she could hear the faint rumble of snoring – that grew louder in her mind the longer she laid still.

Time for action she declared, after a few more minutes. Yes, action...

A minute or so later Alice let herself down the steep stairs, treading lightly on the boards to minimise the creaking. On the ground floor, she stepped through the hall and lounge. Through the windows she saw the sun breaking the cloud cover highlighting patches of the dark green meadow.

'Hi.'

Alice turned swiftly. Hanna Katla was standing in the next room, a bowl of cereal in one hand and spoon in the other.

'Good morning,' said Hanna.

Alice stepped through into the kitchen. 'You're up early.'

Hanna smiled wryly. 'So are you.'

Alice nodded. 'Good point.' She poured herself a cup of coffee and breathed in the smell.

'So—' Alice stopped as her words stumbled into Hanna's own.

'I have to drive home. Work, you know?'

'You're definitely not staying then?' asked Alice. She cupped her hands round the roughly shaped stoneware cups, flecked with natural colours. She felt the warmth through her fingers and enjoyed the rich aroma rising into her face.

Hanna turned suddenly. 'Pabbi never showed you the shop did he?'

'Shop?' Alice was briefly surprised, before she remembered the evening before. Guðni's and Baldur's words came back to her. She wondered how come they never followed up the stories. 'No...'

'Come on.' Hanna beckoned Alice. 'I've just got time.'

5

Hanna turned the key in the lock and pushed the swollen and warped door past the point where it was jammed in the frame. She moved through into the dimly lit room at the front of the house and Alice followed, stepping into a room with a bowed linoleum floor, wood-panelled, and painted in what was now a dirty-blue. Immediately in front of the door, bisecting the room, was the dark wooden counter. Alice walked through, as if into the past. Across the back wall, behind where she had entered, she found the old cabinets and drawer units and the 1950s Coca-Cola sign.

Hanna wandered through the room, stroking the tops of cabinets, lifting up objects, some layered thickly with dust. The floor creaked beneath her feet. She explained to Alice the history of the shop. The cupboards revealed a few last remaining items of stock together with other, bizarre oddities.

'No, the shop that granddad ran sold everything – and I mean everything,' she said, 'Food, cleaning materials, charcoal, car parts, oil – you saw what remains of a petrol pump out the front...?'

Between two windows at the front there was an old bureau, Alice picked out objects. She found an old cash tin. Opening it revealed pockets of coins, which she sifted through to pick out the tarnished gold and silver coins.

Hanna followed Alice to the money. She picked out some coins herself. 'Some of these are probably fifty years old.'

'Just think of the history they could tell.' Alice smiled and flicked a coin into the air before catching it in her hand. She grinned. 'Virtually everything in this room could tell a story. Look–' She pointed across the room to a shelf.

Alice crossed the room to it, closing in on an old book and swiped it off the shelf. She opened it and laid it flat on the counter to leaf through.

'See – an order book. I can't read it because it's in Icelandic but look, who were these people. What were their lives like?'

'Farmers, fishermen...' Hanna shrugged. 'Don't forget the mad eccentrics.'

A little later and Hanna sat in her jeep watching in the mirror as Alice stepped away. She slipped the clutch into gear, and accelerated away, the tyres scrunching on the gravel. Glancing back she saw Alice turn and head back towards the house.

Alice stopped at the gate – a simple wrought iron affair with flaking paint and stained with rust. It loosely bordered the wild, unkempt garden. She looked along the front of the house to the windows which she supposed must open into the old shop. She returned inside, pausing in the kitchen to make a fresh mug of coffee which she clasped firmly in her hands.

She made her way back to the shop, setting her mug down on the counter and returning quickly to the shelf where she found the old order book. Smudging away the years of dust from the spines she thumbed through the collection, until her eye caught on one volume in particular; cracked, dry leather with gilded decoration, the book sat at odds with the row of order books to each side. She pulled it from the shelf and opened it. On thick, yellowed paper, the text was inked by a meticulous hand and - in English. Alice grinned and carried it to an old rocking chair in the corner to delve into the words, and quickly discovered it to be a journal. Within seconds she was lost in the stories it contained.

'Who was Solveig?' Alice asked later.

The family were gathered around the breakfast table. Baldur looked up at her; suddenly obstinately quiet in reaction to the question.

'Solveig.' Baldur corrected Alice's pronunciation.

Alice sat, expectant of more explanation whilst Baldur averted his gaze from her and returned to a conversation with his wife. Alice glanced around the room. She caught Eleanor's attention, and mouthed the question again.

'Uncle?' Eleanor asked, 'Who was Solveig, please?'

Guðni looked up towards his brother-in-law. He frowned. 'She – she was—'

Baldur snapped angrily in Icelandic and Guðni countered him, berating his brother. They got up from the table and passed through to the next room, arguing vociferously, gesticulating with their hands. Alice and Kirsten watched with bemusement and turned to Eleanor for translation. Eleanor shrugged and shook her head.

'Languages never really were my thing.'

'I'm sorry,' said Alice, 'I didn't know. Solveig; there's clearly some history.'

'Don't worry about it,' Eleanor reassured, 'Baldur, my uncle, he's not good at conversation at the best of times.' She put out a hand towards her own brother, casually flicking the back of his neck. 'Just like you, isn't that right, Ben?'

Ben glanced round and glowered at his sister but found it within himself to laugh.

'Anyway, Alice, are you going to show us this shop?' Kirsten broke the silence, as she got up to clear away the crockery.

Eleanor stood on a stool and reached up to one of the top shelves in the old shop. She was nine, or ten years old and teetering on the edge of the step for ... for what?

Eleanor looked at the stool now; a bit more battered and definitely dustier than in her memories. She glanced at the high shelf; not that high now that she was grown up. She crossed the room and reached up above her head to run her fingers through the dust until they found the cold metal. The memories came flooding back to her and she pulled the object down. A buckle – an old belt buckle. She didn't know why, but she slipped it into her fleece pocket.

On the deck at the back of the house, feet dangling into the long, lush grass of the garden, Alice sat between Ben, Kirsten and Eleanor with Solveig's book on her lap. She ran her fingers along the lines of text.

'I'm so glad she wrote this in English,' said Alice and glanced up briefly from the page.

'I guessed she used it as a kind of code,' said Eleanor, 'She was the only member of the family who could read anything other than Icelandic.'

As Alice returned to her reading, Eleanor leaned across her shoulder to scan the text and read odd snippets. She interspersed this with gazing over the meadow towards the shore and the sea. In the clouds she saw formations of patterns that worked themselves into pictures in her mind. On the other side of Alice, her brother fell into conversation with Kirsten. And then the book in front of Alice attracted her attention again.

Alice turned over more pages, and then flipped back a few to find her place. 'It mentions here—' She pointed to a section in the book. 'An old farm. They party at night it seems.'

'Like last night?' Eleanor pointed. 'This is the old farm.'

'No. I don't think so.' Alice shook her head. 'The one in here is definitely one of those timbered turf-roofed places – like you see on the postcards.'

'I don't know about that.' Eleanor shrugged. 'What about you, Ben? Have you ever heard of there being another farm?'

Ben glanced up from his conversation with Kirsten. 'Don't think so, no.'

Alice shook her head. 'It's definitely not here. She grabbed a map from down beside her and unfolded it. She began to re-read passages from the book and compared it to the map. 'Yes. Look here. It's on the other side of the bay but you said that was all your family's land.'

Eleanor peered at the map. She nodded.

'You think we could go and take a look now?' asked Alice.

They walked in a group, sometimes splitting off into pairs, down the track between two meadows, and across the salt-marshes, until the house was a single speck of light beneath the horizon from where the outdoor light was still on. At the far headland they turned inland up an overgrown track with bushes that clawed out at their arms and legs with the aim of tripping them. Climbing over the ridge, they saw it; the three-gabled turf roofs of the old farm.

'Looks like the place,' said Ben.

'It's funny though, how Dad never mentioned it?' Eleanor mused.

Beside her, Alice leaned across the turf-topped dry-stone wall.

'I guess we give it a look,' Alice said as she climbed over the wall. She was followed by Eleanor, and then Ben with Kirsten; jumping down into the overgrown garden. The four of them pushed forward through the long grass, towards the three-gabled timber front of the turf-roofed farm set back into the hill behind. Alice bounded forward to the door and traced her finger across the words carved into the frame.

Ben stepped up to her, 'That's our name.' He looked across at Alice. 'You were right. This *is* the old farm.'

Eleanor's fingers closed around the latch on the front door. She tried it. It opened. She pushed the door inward and it moved diffidently, graunching on its hinges and caught on the step.

Inside the old farm, Eleanor stepped through the dimly lit, timber-panelled rooms. The air was musty and she saw dust rising against the pale light that crept in through the door. The floorboards creaked beneath her feet, as she stepped on through, past rooms that were once kept for best but that had since been used to store hay and farm tools. Leaving the others behind, she ducked to the left, under a low doorway and carried on down a narrow corridor. Feeling her way along the side wall she discovered old wooden posts keeping the roof in place and walls made of turf bricks, which over the years had taken on the texture of old, brittle leather.

She ducked under another doorway, and the passage opened out into what was obviously a storeroom. Eleanor felt her way through a room that was almost completely dark save for faint light emanating from a single window, matted with cobwebs and set back some two feet though a turf dormer. She fumbled in her pocket for her torch.

'Stay.' A voice in the dark instructed her.

She swung round and her torch swept past crates and stacks of agricultural stores. In the darkest corner of the room, a man, tall and cloaked, stood with his hands aloft, flat-palmed, shielding his face from the torchlight.

'Please, enough.' The man's voice told her.

Eleanor recognised the voice to be that of the man from the mountains – the man who had sent her to that other world. She twisted the head of the torch and extinguished the light.

'What do you want now?'

With a wave of his hand he silenced her and summoned her closer.

'You can't feel it?'

Eleanor narrowed her gaze and shook her head. 'No.'

'The Old Peoples of the world are moving.' His tone was hushed. 'I have seen them. At night. In the day too, when folk are not looking; which mostly they are not. And you have seen them too.'

'I – I don't think so,' Eleanor answered.

The man said nothing but fixed Eleanor with a steely gaze. Subconciously, Eleanor reached into her fleece pocket and her fingers touched on something cold and metal. Stroking the smooth surface, she turned it over in her hand and clasped it; the buckle that she picked up earlier in the old shop.

Lights flickered. She swung round. Oil lamps flickered on the walls, casting pools of orangey light across the room. Her head turned again, back to the corner, but the man was gone. Her heartbeat quickened and she moved quickly into a run, back down the corridor. Ducking nimbly under the doorway she called for her brother and skidded to a halt in the parlour. No longer a storeroom and a pale imitation after years of neglect, but a functioning room lined with baskets and barrels of food and drink.

A young woman, a little older than Eleanor, with long blonde hair tied back tightly was at a table washing dishes in a large pewter bowl. She frowned at Eleanor, as if distracted by her sudden appearance at the door and yet she didn't appear to be able to see her. Eleanor gazed back, still silent; footsteps behind her; coming closer; and stopping. She froze.

'Eleanor?' Ben emerged out of the shadows and she breathed with relief.

'What happened?' he asked her.

Instinctively, Eleanor found her hand back in the pocket of her fleece, her fingers clutching the buckle. She turned to her brother. 'I don't know.'

They moved through to the next room where they found Alice and Kirsten, wandering amongst the beds and the loom, admiring the draperies and hand-stitched cloth. Both pairs of friends were about to speak, when from behind them came the clattering of a door and a gust of cold air blew through the house. They made their way down the hall. Outside, they found the sky black with storm clouds and cold winds blowing in from the sea with rain driving in across the front of the farm. Backing away inside again, they closed the door and returned to the bedroom at the back.

6

Charles Ancell drove the mountain pass, leaving a wake of dust behind him. As he approached the main gates of the factory he flicked at the remote and the large, steel gates swung back before him. He drove in past contractors at work, amongst the heavier machinery of the construction site, landscaping the car park. Charles grabbed his briefcase and laptop from the passenger seat next to him and headed across the car park to the offices. On the steps leading up to the doors, he paused to gaze out across the valley; three rigs are erected on large platforms, dominating the mountains behind. He smiled. Dust, kicked up from the worksite, blew in ballooning clouds across the site and left the taste of grit dirtying the air. He turned, and swiped his pass through the card reader.

Sweeping down the corridor, Charles arrived at his office overlooking the alpha platform. Kári, the leaden-faced and stocky Head of Construction was already at his desk. He looked up as Charles entered.

'Morning Chief.'

Charles nodded. 'What's the reach of the alpha drill shaft? Have we reached critical depth?' He began to set up his laptop and quickly accessed files on the Alcon network.

'We are just realigning the drill-heads now,' explained Kári, 'We had to withdraw the bore procedure during last night's storm – some of our temperature readings were off the scale.'

Charles shook his head. *Damn storms. Every time we have to reset the drill-heads it puts back the activation schedule.* He brought up system monitoring and stared at the diagrammatic representations of seismic activity plotted against thermo-geological readings.

'This is excellent. The temperature range is just as predicted.' Charles glanced up at his colleague. 'How close are we to the magmatic core?'

'Within tolerance levels,' answered Kári, 'We've lost three drilling heads, but we are on course to begin processing bauxite.'

Again, Charles nodded. He lifted his hand and pulled back the blinds to look out at the site, where heavy machinery was set against the backdrop of mountain ranges.

Hanna Katla glanced back over her shoulder; her boss was busy with clients behind a glass-panelled door. She focused again on her computer and Alt-Tabbed away from the booking screen into her web browser, and tapped in some words to Google. Seconds later her eyes were looking at the scrolling list of results. She clicked on promising looking links, searching out information on Alcon and their new plant. There were pages and pages of rumour and questions posted on various message boards and only a couple of relevant links. Everywhere, the Alcon company appeared synonymous with Charles Ancell, an American and Head of New Technology.

In the attic bedroom of the old farmhouse the four friends sat around the room amongst furnishings from a hundred or more years ago. Wind buffeted the front of the house and shook the window in its frame where the rain drummed against the glass. Long shadows, from an obscured sun, danced on the roughly hewn floorboards. Eleanor sat on the floor, knees hunched up in front of her, leaning on the bed.

'How did we get here?' Alice's voice was tempered with anguish, as she lay on the bed behind Eleanor staring up at the ceiling.

Alice's words merely echoed everyone else's thoughts and Eleanor felt the weight of responsibility.

'We could just be dreaming...' Ben said hopelessly. Eleanor could tell that he didn't really mean it.

Kirsten shook her head. She glanced towards where Ben was seated. 'No.' she grinned. 'I pinched myself earlier. We're not dreaming.'

'Which leads me back to my first question...' continued Alice, 'How did we get here? And how do we get back?'

Eleanor heard suggestions and droll comments bandied about by her brother and her friends as a white noise in the background of her thoughts. Sitting on the floorboards she felt so alone in the room. With her brain filtering out the external cacophony she found an unearthly quiet that weighed her down. Her hand slipped into her fleece pocket and fingered the cold metal of the buckle.

The buckle. It had belonged to Solveig – *was it possible?* And Solveig had disappeared, so what if she had disappeared into time. Could the buckle be a link through the years to her own ancestor? In which case the buckle brought them here. Eleanor looked up at the attic room, frozen in some distant time. But how? And why? If Solveig had been using the buckle herself to transport through time – she could have become separated from it and from there, lost.

In which case... her hands pressed deeply into the buckle till it hurt. She focused her entire mind and strength onto her buckle, onto her thoughts. She imagined the scene; and the time.

A cold draught rushed over her, and she blinked open her eyes. She was still sat on the rough floorboards of the attic, and around her were her brother and her friends. She looked again. Gone were the fabrics and the furniture. Eleanor jumped to her feet and crossed the room. She pulled back the trapdoor and all but slid down the stairs beneath. She moved down the corridor to the front door, not caring if anyone heard her footsteps. At the door she grasped the latch. The door stuck on the sill like before. Her hand felt for the buckle in her pocket. Her mind tumbled over her thoughts and her reasonings.

Though the storm had passed, dark clouds lingered over the mountains and a deep contrast remained between the sky and the almost golden light across the meadows. Occasional gusts of wind flushed birds into the air. Alice, Kirsten and Ben followed Eleanor outside. She glanced down at her hand, scarred red where the metal has been pressed into her skin. She turned it over and thrust it back into her pocket.

'You.' Ben stared at his sister. 'How did you do that?'

Eleanor drew back. She turned to face her brother now as she zipped shut her fleece.

'Where are we?' Eleanor said, '*When* are we?'

Ben shrugged as he looked about him, at the old farmhouse, with the grass reaching high and tangled with weeds. He muttered something about being home, but he didn't know, he had no proof. Eleanor trailed her fingers through the grass.

Alice pulled out her mobile: *registering*. She could only dare to hope. *Network found*. She smiled. 'We're back.'

'I thought,' said Eleanor quietly, 'I hoped. But I didn't know...'

'That was incredible.' Alice continued, 'What you did – *whatever* you did – what *did* you do?'

'I–' She couldn't say it. 'I don't know. Not exactly.'

Eleanor hid her face from Alice's probing gaze. A few moments later and Alice accepted the answer as unforthcoming. She turned on her heels and ambled the other way. Kirsten too, strolled in the grassland at the front of the farm. She cocked her head to one side and saw Ben seated, squat on a rock by the gate, sucking at a stem of grass and lost in thought.

'Ben?' Kirsten approached him. 'Ben, what's up?'

Ben nodded towards the mountains. 'Something's not right, Kirsten.'

Kirsten followed his gaze. Over the next ridge and beyond, the clouds were building, filling and darkening, second by second. 'It's like time-lapse photography?'

'I don't like it. It's not right,' argued Ben, 'Weather patterns can change fast – and in Iceland – the country's famous for it – but this? You're right Kirsten; it's like someone has filmed this scene in stop motion and is now playing it back at twice the speed.'

Bjäkk took the reading, measuring off the values and recording them in his logbook. Something was not right. He moved to another instrument and took that reading. No. He looked up. The clouds were moving fast. Too fast maybe? He moved quickly across the rooftop and let himself down the side wall by way of iron rungs. He jumped the last few feet and ran to – and slung himself into – his jeep. He grabbed up his phone and thumbed the number fast and erratically for. He dialled, and waited. The phone flicked to voicemail and he thumbed to cancel the call. He tossed the phone back onto the passenger seat, twisted the key in the ignition, and accelerated the jeep away from the side of the road in a scourge of gravel.

Back in his office, Bjäkk sat hunched over his desk inputting the afternoon's readings into the computer. Around him the encroaching dark accentuated the pool of electric light that illuminated his desk that was overrun with books, files, and piles of precariously balanced papers. He completed the data entry, snapped shut the logbook and leaned back in his chair. Out the corner of his eye, through the view striped by Venetian blinds layered with dust and grease, the scene was dark and foreboding. He crossed the room to the window. The mountains were shrouded in the blackest of black cloud; he could hear the wind rising in speed. Out to the north, the last of the setting sun reflected in an eerily silver band across the sea.

The four friends were striking out across the valley on the path home. Already they had put distance between them and the old farm. Ben glanced back, nervously over his shoulder. Then, forward again to the path ahead; then back again. Alice questioned his behaviour.

'It's nothing, I'm sure.' His tone was less than convincing and he knew it. 'How long did it take us to walk to this path when we came?'

'We didn't come on this exact path, but,' answered Eleanor, 'An hour? An hour and a half tops.' She looked along the line at her brother. 'Why?'

Ben pointed, over at the mountains beyond. 'That.'

The rest turned to look. Kirsten vocalised all their thoughts. 'What is it with these storms?!' Stopping for a moment they just stared at the looming clouds, building and blackening as they spoke. A cold wind swept across the valley, the wind picked up, and birds rose up from the marshes and meadow grass squawking.

Ben faced his sister. 'What is it with *you* and these storms?'

Upon pulling the door closed to her office, Hanna Katla broke into a run, crossing the street in the driving rain and ferocious wind. At her jeep she fumbled with her keys; and pulled open the door to find it wrenched from her grip in a strong gust. She regained her footing and dove into her seat and shut out the storm.

She sat for a moment, at the side of a Reykjavik street, as the windscreen was hammered with rain. Billowing sheets of water were driven down the street. A pulse of light illuminated the sky. She looked up and a few seconds later, the crashing sound of thunder followed it. *Not again. Dear God, not again.* She twisted the ignition key and flicked on the lights.

Eleanor and Alice ran, heads down into the driving rain, followed by Kirsten and Ben, along the threaded track that was pitted by jeep wheels and quickly filling with water.

Diana slammed shut the door to the house and slipped across the bolts. The wind crashed against the door and thumped it repeatedly. Cold draughts whistled in through the gaps around the windows. She stepped through to the back room where Guðni was peering intently round the back of a black and white television, fiddling with the aerial, and cursing and swearing variously in English and Icelandic as he berated it. He slapped the side and shook the casing with fading determination. Standing back he pushed the on switch one last time and a grainy, flickering picture appeared. A news bulletin on the sjónvarpið channel could be seen through the dancing lines of interference.

Guðni stepped further back, alongside Diana and slipped his arm around his wife's waist. 'If it holds out, we should get a weather report.' He glanced over his shoulder at the blackening view, '—see what we're in for.'

On the television they saw the shaky, hand-held footage of the storm battering Reykjavik. Diana gasped. 'My poor children.' She turned to the window as a fork of lightning bisected the view. The house shook with the crash of thunder that followed.

'Where are they?' She looked to her husband.

Bjäkk stood in the window with a can of beer in his hand watching the storm. Light from the lamps outside cast odd, streaking shadows across his face, as the wind blew against the trees and threw the rain at the windows. The clouds were heavy and black. The storm weighed in heavily. He checked his watch - not even three o'clock and yet it was as dark as a midwinter midnight.

The cloud had sunk low into the valley and the rain was whipped horizontal and stinging in its force. Eleanor struggled on. Hand raised to shield her face, she was bent almost double in her slow, struggling journey along the path. With her was Alice, fighting to push her wet hair out of her eyes. She heard her voice on the wind. And again; she stopped and turned. Ben, struggled in the wind with Kirsten, who was reaching out and calling for her. Eleanor called to Alice and they made their way back.

A fork of lightning fragmented the thick fog, reflected by the rain into a million shards. The thunder rumbled on round them; and then another fork of lightning; nearer this time. The path at their feet, became more of a muddy lake.

Ben was anxious. 'This is silly. We can't go on in this.'

'Ben, we can't stop here!' countered Eleanor, 'Can you see anything to shelter under?'

'We should have stayed at the farm.'

Eleanor stared at her brother. Her face soured to that of utter incredulity. She shook her head. 'But we didn't.'

'How far – how long would it take – if we go back?' asked Kirsten tentatively.

'Half an hour maybe?' said Eleanor, 'Double that in this weather.'

'We must be more than halfway,' said Ben. He glanced over at Kirsten apologetically. 'We'd best go on.'

Eleanor fixed a stare onto her brother. *What*, she questioned, *had we stopped for then?* Her face stung with the cold and wet. She felt the drips run off her fringe and down her face. She felt the rain penetrate the layers of waterproofs and fleece.

For a moment Eleanor found herself back on the mountain. Alone, cold and wet she wondered much longer she had to live. Beneath her layers of clothing her skin itched with the wet that had soaked through. She stared out into the fog trying to make out the shapes of anything – anyone who can be of help.

'Come on,' Alice encouraged.

Eleanor felt a short, sharp tug on her arm. She laughed.

'What?' questioned Alice.

'It's amazing,' said Eleanor, 'How do you always manage to have that grin on your face? Your unswerving optimism and determination is admirable.'

They battled on, along the track, but slower this time, and steadier. They were as wet and as cold as it was possible to be. Eleanor knew that they must not become tired, not at least, until they reached some form of shelter.

Guðni ran, head down across the yard and into the rain. He threw himself into the passenger seat of the jeep. Shaking off the rain, he lowered his hood, as Baldur climbed into the driver's seat alongside. Through a view broken by the distorting circles of raindrops on the wind-shield Guðni saw the figures of Diana and Lara silhouetted against the rectangle of the front door.

'You ready?' asked Baldur. Guðni turned his head and nodded. Agreed.

The wind howled mournfully as sheet after sheet of rain swept across the fields. The sky, black behind the fog, was lit in staccato flashes of lightning. Eleanor huddled with her friends behind a slab of rock that provided little more shelter than the open moorland.

'How much further?' Alice's voice was tired and stretched from the effort to keep going. She looked from face to face of her compatriots, seeking an answer. In each of their faces there was the same uncertainty.

'Is this what it was like for you?' Alice directed another question at Eleanor, 'When you were lost? Is it happening again...?'

Eleanor flinched, unable to face Alice's question. What happened could not be allowed to happen again. She turned her mind decisively and picked herself up quickly.

'We rested?' Eleanor recognised the tiredness and hopelessness on the faces of her friends. She tried to sound optimistic, 'See – look – there's more of these rocks, there – and there.'

Her meaning was unclear and she received blank faces from her friends.

'Don't you remember? Where we left the road, for a while it followed these rocks.' Eleanor tried to engage and encourage the others. 'Don't you see? We *are* almost home.'

Tyres screeched to a halt on the gravel road, kicking up stones and muddy puddles under them. Baldur left the diesel engine to purr in the rain. The headlights flooded the landscape, silhouetting the lines of rain in their beam.

'What is it?' Guðni asked.

Baldur raised his finger to silence him. He watched and listened and waited.

'You don't remember?' Baldur's voice was low and a little judgemental.

Guðni, turned his gaze from the road ahead to that of the profile of his brother. He questioned the accusation. Above him, the rhythmic drumming of the rain pounded on the roof of the car.

Baldur pointed. 'The Old Way.' He directed his brother to look across the road a gap in a fence. 'They said they were going to go down to the old farm.'

'If you've got torches with you.' Ben barked the command decisively. 'Put them on, now!'

Eleanor obeyed, knowing instinctively his plan. Kirsten and Alice paused in the gathering mud and delved into their rucksacks for torches. Quickly, they shouldered their packs again and moved to catch up the brother and sister, switching their torches on as they went.

Eleanor and Ben now led the way, quickening pace, but looking round often to ensure that Kirsten and Alice were still following. The four swept their flashlights from side to side and forwards across the road; hoping that someone may see the lights and come for them.

Eleanor stopped.

'What?' Ben asked in a hushed tone.

'Headlights,' said Kirsten.

Eleanor said nothing. Suddenly she broke forward into a run and pelted through the mud. She had lost all care for the weather. She had seen her chance and she was going for it.

The glow of lights, now visible as car headlights, began to move off. Eleanor screamed out into the night, flashing her torch wildly, she scrambled at the bank.

Baldur moved the car forward slowly. Both he and Guðni scanned the road and the landscape – as far as the thick fog would allow – for anything, any sign. Guðni slapped the dashboard firmly and barked his brother's name.

'There.' He pointed. 'A light – no two – maybe more...'

'Torches.'

Ben turned the head of his flashlight, flicking the beam on and off in a crude imitation of Morse code. Along the lane, Kirsten and Alice were copying the message. The headlights on the road above had now stopped again and now they could hear voices in the wind. Recognisable voices. Their own names being called.

PART FOUR

Midnight Research

1

William Tyndale surveyed the new day. From his vantage point just above the grey-brown snout of Skaftafellsjökul his eyes picked out the changing light across the horizon and the intricacies of cloud formations. There was a stillness and a quietness to the day, that was in sharp contrast to last night's storms. He watched Kathryn clamber up and over the moraine towards him. She arrived at his side, clutching a couple of printouts and a small logbook.

'I've got the results of the metrological analysis,' she said.

William nodded. 'I always knew that Iceland would be a key research area for my climate modelling.' He glanced at the papers. 'Is that it?'

Kathryn passed the documents to the professor. Her dark eyes looked up at him. 'That storm last night. It was quite incredible.'

'A late developing front I assume. What's so special?' William cast his eyes down at the printouts and readings seeing immediately something strange and of interest. He tugged the papers out of Kathryn's hand and took a closer look.

William barely heard his assistant, as he read through the document, flicking on and back through the charts, and beginning to do calculations in his head. Out of the corner of his eyes he saw Kathryn shuffle from foot to foot as she waited. He glanced around and saw Níls getting the equipment ready for the climb further up onto the glacier. He returned to his calculations, reading them through to the end, before sighing. He looked up, and out over the wide, flat beach of tundra that stretched for miles down to the sea. The great river cascaded out of Vatnajokull – far off past the headland to the right – roaring like a motorway and could be heard even here.

'You were saying?' He turned again to Kathryn.

'It's weird isn't it?' said Kathryn. She moved closer to him and pointed to the series of isobars and wind variants. 'Don't fronts normally track in across here, from the Gulf Stream and either go here, or here?' Her finger stroked the map to illustrate. 'But see here. Last night's depression came from nowhere. It didn't come from the sea, but from here, overland.'

'Impossible.'

Kathryn hooked back her fair hair out of the wind and nodded at what William said. 'Uh-huh. I double- and triple-checked the charts. It just spiralled out and deepened from this one area of the mainland—'

'The highlands? Like last time?'

Kathryn shook her head. 'Nearer the coast. I've left the computer back at base plotting the exact location. We won't know for several hours.'

*

William nodded, for a moment maintaining eye contact with his assistant. His gaze dropped back down to the notes and charts; the diagrammatic representation of pressure readings he found particularly curious. Drawing on years of research and study his mind computed the possibilities.

In the dim light of the 1950s wood-panelled interior Ben sat in front of the glow emanating from his laptop, entranced by the animated pressure charts showing the formation and progression of last night's storm. He leaned closer to the screen to concentrate on every isobar; his fingers moved over the touch-pad and mouse keys, deftly pausing the animation to step through the chart hour by hour.

Around him was a general hum of conversation. Occasional words of English and Icelandic from his father and uncle intruded into his thinking but it did not register with him. Above, floorboards creaked under the weight of footsteps and small wafts of dust and grit dislodged from between the floorboards fell from the ceiling onto Ben. He rewound the animation again and stepped through it, zoning in on a particular time stamp, repeating it over and over in ever decreasing graduations of detail.

In a little back room under the eaves with a ceiling that bulged alarmingly, Eleanor slipped her arms through the straps of her bikini top and fastened it. She stooped to gather up her thick, woollen, Icelandic jumper and towel and began to leave the room. She stopped, and returned to her rucksack. Lowering herself onto the bed she pulled a T-shirt from the bottom of the bag, unfolded it and took the buckle in her hand. She considered the buckle again. There was an all-consuming power within the cold metal and a sense of danger and foreboding to it. What she had found possible to do had proved alluring, even seductive, and she wanted to call on its power again.

And then she remembered the previous night with Kirsten and Alice, and Ben, caught in the most ferocious of storms...

Eleanor stood on the path, drenched, with rain seeping in through the layers of clothing to her skin. Nearby, Kirsten and Alice were with Ben, and each one was relying on her to bring them home safely. In her pocket, her hand fumbled with the twisted metal frame of the buckle. Did she bring on this storm? She felt the metal warming under her touch. Dare she prey on the power again?

Goosebumps rose on her arms. Eleanor felt the tingle of fear and uncertainty run through her. No, she realised she couldn't ever put anyone through that again. She sat, staring at the buckle in her hand, relieved with her decision, and yet also regretting the loss of an intangible, unfulfilled power.

No. She had made her decision. And before she could change her mind, she thrust the buckle deep into the bottom of her bag. *It was simply too dangerous.*

Eleanor pulled on her jumper and left the room, lingering for a moment by the light switch, before swiftly crossing the next room to the landing and descending the steep stairs.

Letting herself in through the back door, the swollen, twisted wood stuck on the warped frame. Kirsten padded through the small lobby in her bikini, a towel draped loosely over her shoulders. She pulled open the fridge and reached for a can of beer. Turning to go back outside she saw Ben across the far side of the back room, still working at his computer in a pool of light set against the encroaching dusk.

As Kirsten approached Ben, she saw more clearly the work that he was doing. His fingers moved fast over the keyboard, tabbing between different windows, he worked with system commands and code, writing the new computer model. She stepped up behind him and, setting her can of beer down for a moment, she fiddled with and tidied his hair.

'You not coming to join us?' she asked, 'The water's lovely. And you missed a good sunset...'

'Uh-huh?' Ben glanced up, but, preoccupied with his work he quickly returned to the coding.

Kirsten smiled. She leaned closer, laying her palms across his shoulders and gently began to massage them. Instinctively his head tilted back and round as he felt the ecstasy of her touch.

'A new idea, huh?' said Kirsten, still massaging.

'Yeah, the storm last night - it gave me some ideas - questions.' Ben turned and looked at her. His face was lit with the thrill of discovery. 'The pressure sequence I showed you. I'd never seen anything like it. Such a big depression starting and filling over land?'

'Do you know what could cause that?'

Ben shrugged. 'I don't know. I have some ideas. That's what my model is for - if I can just get it working.' He turned again to his computer to configure some options and parse the results. Moments later he cursed coarsely at the computer and bashed the keyboard with more commands.

Kirsten shook her head and slid round to the side of Ben. She lowered her face to the level of his. 'Come on,' she cajoled, 'leave this. Come to the hot tub.'

'Okay, yeah,' Ben agreed, 'You go on. I'll catch you up.'

Kirsten countered his agreement with suspicion. 'Yeah, really?'

'Honestly.' Ben told her, 'Go.'

Bjäkk returned the receiver to its cradle. He looked down at the core readings and shook his head. He grabbed up the receiver again, dialling the number with the same hand.

Hanna was applying her lipstick. With her hair pulled back into two pony tails, she fixed gold hoop earrings. Her phone rang and she grabbed her leather jacket, slipped her arms through the sleeves as she swung out of her bedroom and into the hall. She grabbed the phone from the side table and barked her greeting.

'Bjäkk?' she said.

What did he want at this time – doesn't he know she's late...? The doorbell rang. As Hanna spoke Icelandic to Bjäkk she threw back her head to let out a little silent scream of anguish and crossed the hall and pulled open the door.

On the doorstep was her boss and one of her colleagues. She ushered them in and through to the lounge whilst attempting to extricate herself from the conversation.

Ducking back into the hallway, her voice switched to English and she spoke with a hushed tone. 'I can't talk now, Bjäkk. Drive down tomorrow. We'll talk then.'

Bjäkk stood over his desk holding the receiver to his ear. He shuffled paperwork into his rucksack, as he spoke fast and enthusiastically down the phone to Hanna. He settled for a moment in his desk chair, and watched the computer finish burning a CD. 'When are you back tonight? If I leave now—'

'Stupid,' Hanna said with some affection, '—you'll be driving through the night. And you've caught me when I'm halfway out the door – and with my boss in the next room to collect some stuff.'

She stopped in front of her mirror. For a moment she stood still; staring at the painted face that looked back at her from the other side of the glass. She smiled weakly, 'I've got a gig to get to.'

*

Bjäkk held the phone in one hand by its cradle with the coil of flex pulled tight across to him. He continued to argue his plan down the phone. Eventually he hung up and sat and stared at the computer. He Alt-tabbed between the windows to the model running in the background and stared at it. Fiddling with the CD draw of his computer, he retrieved the disc.

Later, in the half-light of evening, Bjäkk ran from his small cottage to the jeep where its engine purred throatily. He threw his scruffy, mud-splattered, wind-worn rucksack onto the passenger seat next to him and slipped his foot on the clutch, pushed the car into gear and accelerated, steering with one hand as he fumbled with his seat belt. Beneath the jeep the wheels spun in a splatter of mud and gravel.

Alice hoisted herself out of the hot tub and followed Eleanor indoors. Ben's gaze closed in on the detail of every little droplet of water which fell to the cold decking and exploded in a waft of steam. His mind picked out the mathematical details of the chemical reaction. He blinked away the inconsequential thoughts as he focused again on Kirsten, now alone with him in the hot tub. Their knees met in the centre of the tub. Beneath the water, they tickled each other's feet with their toes.

Laughter subsided into quiet contemplation, and eventually Kirsten broke the silence. 'So what's your take on yesterday's events? Really, I mean...'

'The storm?' asked Ben. His answer was deliberately obtuse. 'The farm you mean? I would have said I was dreaming if it weren't for—' He quickly corrected himself.

'All of us?' Kirsten shook her head.

'Exactly,' said Ben, 'I don't know. I've read stuff, about shared dreaming, but it's all pretty inconclusive. Then again, so is time travel.'

He swirled his finger and made careful patterns in the water. Concentric circles and geometric shapes. He was lost again in thought and for a minute he was stepping again down the wood panelled hallway, past the half open parlour room door and those people... *Were they really his ancestors?*

'Has it occurred to you that there have been as many storms now, in as many weeks, that my sister has been lost in.'

Kirsten nodded. 'It does seem somewhat coincidental.'

'And this man that she said she met in the mountains. She said he taught her magic and that that somehow explained everything.' Ben threw his hand around in broad gestures and splashed water across the deck. 'It would explain *all* of today. If it were possible?'

Ben agonised over the impossibility of what he was talking about, forcing out the alien thoughts and reconciled his mind. 'I don't know how my sister did it, but that was some illusion that she put us all through.'

Kirsten smiled, torn between a desire for Eleanor's truth to be true and to hold on to reality with Ben's honesty. She beckoned him, comfortingly and edged round the seat of the hot tub to take him in her arms. Slowly, cautiously she snuggled up to Ben and allowed him the reassurance of laying his head in the hollow beneath her neck. She stroked his head.

Bold, punctuating beats were drummed out by Bryn in time with the lights, flares of colour into an otherwise darkened room. A sustained crash onto the cymbal that whispered into the darkness and the spotlights swept across the alcohol-fuelled audience before settling on the band. On opposite sides of the stage Jon opened the introduction on keyboards with Halldór on guitar. Hanna bounded energetically forwards from the shadows at the back of the stage, past Bryn and raised her mic to her mouth.

Hurting in my heart
Restless in my soul.
Your voice in my ears
Your face in my vision—
I am hurting;
Hurting for you.

Sticks of yellow flashed past on either side, the reflective markers to the side of the road that Bjäkk drove. Following the main road, he turned away from the coast to cut across inland. He felt the accelerator beneath his foot and pressed it further to the floor, stick-shifting down a gear to take the incline up the valley floor.

Standing at the foot of the stage, Hanna lowered herself closer towards the crowd, singing the more soulful balladry part of the song.

Last night
when you said goodnight to me
Last night
when you danced with me
You stole through my senses
You broke the lock off my heart and
Now I'm hurting;
Hurting for you.

2

An empty coffee mug. A can of beer. A notepad of squared paper ciphered over with mathematical formulae. Kirsten was reclined on the sofa and snuggled in Ben's arms, her head on his lap. Ben sat and stroked his fingers through Kirsten's hair as he reasoned with his climatic theorising and stretched to see where his notebook was. It was lying on the floor at his feet and he realised that he could not reach it without disturbing Kirsten. Part of him resented this inability to continue to explore his latest idea.

Resigning himself to not reaching his notepad, Ben relaxed again into his seat and tried to work through the calculations in his head. He used his right forefinger to write down calculations in the air. Then, keeping the figures in his mind, he saw them written against the backdrop of the room. He drew a graph and labelled the axis and shaded in the segments. Soon the room faded from view and the scene was merely a colourful backdrop to the page in his head.

A moth danced and flapped at the light in the room upstairs. Its shadows were thrown large onto the far wall. Eleanor and Alice sat with their legs beneath them on the mattress. Spread out between them were books pulled from the shelves of the old house with the family journal open next to them and the buckle lying on top.

Alice turned the buckle round in her hands and inspected its design of twists and flourishes. She matched it up with an illustration in one of the books – an encyclopaedia of Icelandic folklore. She pointed out the similarities.

Eleanor pulled the book closer and examined the words carefully.

Alice watched as she fingered the buckle. 'Can you read Icelandic?' she asked.

Eleanor looked up and shrugged. She admitted a passing familiarity with the language and joked that she was the envy of her history class because of it.

'It's—' Eleanor shrugged again. 'An old Norse design. Family unity. See...' She pointed out the one design around the edge enclosing a second in the centre. 'I think it's like two family emblems that form a new one.'

Alice stared more closely at the Icelandic text. 'Anything about magic properties?'

'There might be something here.' She pointed to the footnotes. 'It looks like it should be.' She moved the buckle closer to the illustration and then stared intently at and then to the other. She defocused her eyes and allowed the images to cross and converge. Overlaid one on top of each other, the image was cleaner and burned brightly in her mind. A face appeared in the design – abstract and indistinct – yet recognisably a troll of the old people.

And he was gone. Eleanor sat staring at the corner of the tent where the steam from a large aluminium kettle rose and clung to the inside of the tent as damp droplets. A face writhed and formed itself in the haze. Another one – a þursar companion. They were small; about three foot in height, one looked as if it wore wearing a crown of blue flame positioned as it was in front of the camping stove.

Eleanor turned to Alice, huddled at her side. She could tell in Alice's expression that she had seen them too. In the strange light of an Icelandic night that filtered in through the weathered and stained mess tent, the figures were formed solid; round of face and broad of smile. Their hair was thick and dark, and their skin was like tanned leather. Their eyes were wide and childlike. They were children who giggled and whispered in play.

One pointed with his fat stubby finger; directly at Eleanor and Alice.

A draught brushed through the tent and the candlelight flickered, dancing light and shadows up onto the girls' faces. The trolls were gone. Alice giggled and pulled a notebook out from under Eleanor's hands to write down a description of the strange creatures. Ideas were tossed between them, served up from the inner workings of creative minds and volleyed into play.

Alfar children played outside the tent, working with stories of their own, using slender limbs and pointed fingers to cast silhouette puppets into life on the canvas walls of the tent. Eleanor and Alice sat within, enraptured by the story played out before them and wrote it all down, embellishing it with ideas of their own.

And now the alfar scampered lightly across the bare floorboards and thread-worn rugs of the upstairs room. They hugged themselves close to the door-frame and peered round at the bedroom beyond where Eleanor and Alice sat with their books and the buckle. Through big, wide eyes, the alfar stared at the humans.

Downstairs, Ben's mind was in active contrast to the sedentary position that he found himself in. His fingers continued to stroke their way through Kirsten's soft fair hair, where she slept, head on his lap. His right hand delved deep into the pocket of his jeans and he pulled out a pencil. He reached again for the notebook on the floor beside him.

Guðni passed through the lounge to gather up his book and his glasses from the coffee table. He yawned. Pausing for a moment in the middle of the room he saw his son straining for the notebook and passed it to him. Ben received it gladly and watched as his father took the stairs on his way to bed.

Folding the cover back on itself, Ben found an empty page and scribbled down some sums with his right hand, whilst his left stroked and felt Kirsten's hair; the softness of her cheek through his fingertips.

Ben filled another page with graphs and equations. He tapped the point of his pencil on the page and considered his last supposition, before dismissing it and striking through it with a bold diagonal line. Folding back another page, he moved fast to redraw it.

With the harbour spread out at the lower end of Snorrabraut, the jeep approached the junction, headlights beaming and indicator lights flashing as it turned left into Laugevegur.

Bjäkk drove slowly, thumbs tapping the steering wheel and turned off the main street to park up at the kerb in a narrow side street. As he sat at the side of the road, a group of girls in short skirts and long black boots turned the corner and passed by, stopping a few doors further along outside the unprepossessing frontage of the nightclub.

Inside the club, Bjäkk pushed his way through the audience. He craned his neck forward as a couple of kids pushed past him to get to the bar. He moved forward, listening, remembering for a moment that year when he shared the stage with Hanna.

Hanna knelt, feet tucked behind her, at the front of the stage, microphone drawn to her face, her voice commanding the sea of people across the auditorium. Her words were softly sung and alluring with Halldór's gentle guitar strumming behind with Jon's keyboard ballad.

Alice lay on her bed, a sheet pulled loosely over her. Across the room, Eleanor lay on her front, propped up on her elbows writing in her notebook. She sketched out characters and settings, and allowed her imagination to run wild.

William rubbed his chin slowly and thoughtfully. He felt the stubble beneath his fingers, as he stared at the computer model and reached for his beer. Silhouetted in the shadows, staff moved in the bar, stacking chairs and mopping the floor as they closed up for the night. Somewhere beyond in the shop, fluorescent lights in the chiller cabinets cast oasis-like pools that were accompanied by a gentle hum. William continued to work at his computer, plotting data and watching the repercussions in his models.

The door crashed open and Kathryn and Níls burst through. Kathryn pushed past tables and slammed down her papers onto the desk in front of William.

'This, you have got to see,' she said. 'You see? These thermal readouts for Vatnajokul. It's getting hot down there.'

William cast a cursory look over the papers and looked up.

'We are overdue for another eruption. We know that. Everyone knows that. Yet this wouldn't cause the climatic variations that we've been witnessing.'

'What if it's another '96?' suggested Kathryn.

'I still don't see how it would cause these freak storms. See how they are centred so precisely.' He gestured at his own models. 'There's nothing to signify that this is going to result in any jökulslaup to rival the flood that tore through here a decade ago.'

Hanna pushed past the racks of electrics and speaker cables, and stepped out of the bright lights of the stage into the wings. She reached for a bottle of water and snatched it to her mouth. She blinked to adjust to the dim light off stage and stopped as she saw Bjäkk standing opposite her.

'How long have you been here?'

Bjäkk shrugged. 'An hour or so after your first set.' He watched her closely. 'You're good. The band's good.'

'Takk.'

He said something more but the next band had started playing and she could not hear. Hanna slipped her arm round his and led him further off stage, into a corridor at the back of the club. She turned to face him, staring up into his dark eyes.

'So what's so important? It's got to be big, for you to drive all this way.'

'It's something that Ben said,' Bjäkk was hesitant. 'It's best I wait till we are with him. It's a long explanation.'

Eleanor shifted in her sleep; her head moving across the pillow; her body curled in her sleeping bag, on the mattress on the bare floorboards. Ben crept across the room in his boxer shorts and t-shirt and, crouched low by his mattress, he slipped his feet and body down into the mummy bag. As he laid his head onto the pillow, he watched Kirsten through the open doorway, as she made her way to bed.

Monks, hooded and cloaked against the cold, walked through the field of lava. Hot pools pushed steam into the air. The monks processed with their cross before them, edging around a lake of flat water in which the mountains beyond were reflected in every detail. A music was cast out over the land that was accompanied by chants and the utterance of prayer.

Hanna's fingers clawed at the grainy black sand. Getting to her feet, she watched as the sand slipped through her fingers and drifted into the wind. She was flanked by Eleanor and Ben. The wind caught in her hair of obsidian black, and blew it into her face. She threw back her head and called out the song.

Within their church, the monks gathered in a circle before their altar. The priest with a face etched with age, stepped up to their altar as an incense lamp swung. The priest placed a shard of glacial ice into a groove in the centre of the altar and uttered words of an ancient tongue, before separating his hands over the ice as it burned blue.

Dark clouds rolled across the sky. On the opposite shore from the monastery, Hanna's voice rallied against ancient prayer. Shadowy figures walked the shore. Behind her, Eleanor and Ben echoed her words; voices of truth in the dark light of night.

Ben woke. Pulling his head from the pillow he sat up. Looking across the room he saw his sister waking and sitting up in her bed. She turned towards him. Without speaking they both knew what the other was thinking; the song held powerfully still in their minds.

A hundred miles away, in her house in the Reykjavik suburbs Hanna sat up in her bed. She swung her legs out of bed and set her bare feet onto under floor heated tiles. Her head stung with the power of song and the smell of incense. She looked down at her hands; a few grains of black sand were pressed into her skin. She reached for her phone and began to thumb out a text message.

'You felt it too?'

Later that morning Hanna stood in front of her cousins, as they all recounted as one, the strange tale from last night. As she spoke, Hanna ran her fingers through her fair hair now left with streaks of black. She reached out to Eleanor, and gently took hold of her hair to find the same black streaks. She glanced across at Ben; he too – even with his shorter cut.

'It really happened.' Hanna's words lingered between the three of them; their three minds coming to different explanations as to what happened.

Eleanor looked down at her feet. Standing on the gravel, her feet formed one point of a triangle with Ben and Hanna's. Beyond the triangle stood Bjäkk, where he remained by Hanna's jeep with the driver's door left standing open. Opposite, on the far side of the yard, was the corrugated iron facia of the family home.

'What are we part of?' Eleanor shook her head, 'Yesterday at the old farm we went back in time – last night – where were we?'

'It's like the old legends are coming true.' Hanna nodded.

'But why? And why us?' asked Eleanor.

The question hung in the air. A voice lingered in the wind; soft and mournfully it sung. It was left for Ben to break the silence. 'Ours was an old family. This land, the old farm, the diaries...' He nodded, 'We go back a long way.'

'Long enough to awaken things, things that are better left undisturbed?' asked Eleanor.

The three cousins stood facing each other in a triangle on the black beach. Across the water, behind outcrops lava and scrubby birchwood, incense burned, carried aloft in procession by a dozen monks, hooded behind dark tunics. Eleanor looked towards Hanna and nodded.

'Your hair...'

Hanna pulled a tuft of it in front of her eyes. It was as black as obsidian again. 'How?' Her face convulsed with confusion. She sought answers, and stared out at the day with her piercingly-blue, iridescent eyes. 'How are we supposed to know why it is that we are suddenly here, in lord knows what time, if we don't know how we got here?!'

3

Ben turned upon hearing his name. He stepped forward and crossed the yard as Bjäkk approached.

'Do you have your computer? I need to show you something that I've discovered,' Bjäkk said urgently.

'Sure. It's inside,' Ben replied, 'What have you found?'

He led Bjäkk into the house and through to the lounge. He lowered himself into the sofa and fiddled briefly with his laptop before sliding it round on the coffee table to face Bjäkk. 'Okay. Show me.'

Bjäkk leant forward – taking a few moments to take in the layout of a UK keyboard – before diving in with explanation and scientific reasoning. He slipped his memory stick into the USB port and called up a DOS prompt. Ben listened intently, following every word of climate dynamics and their effects on freshwater and ocean fish stock modelling.

Hanna's and Eleanor's interest wavered and they drifted away from the conversation. Kirsten lingered for a few moments longer but eventually wandered away to join the girls.

Stepping through the house, leaving the boys talking science in the lounge, Kirsten made her way to the back lobby, negotiating the chicane that was several doors. Finally she pushed open the swollen door and emerged out into the cool breeze onto the concrete around the hot tub.

The instantly striking smell of hot, sulphurous water hit her and stung the back of her throat. It transported her back through memories to a time a few weeks ago.

Some of her friends had already taken to the waters of the main pool, others including Andy and Eleanor were in the hot tub – an old bath sat next to the pool – in the corner.

Rounding the edge of the water that steamed in the cold air Kirsten passed a tall, elegantly slender lady. As they passed each other, Kirsten turned her head. The lady turned too and for a moment their eyes met. The lady held Kirsten in her mesmerising gaze and Kirsten felt a sense of some magic or power emanate from the lady.

'Finnbjörn?' The alfar lady called to her companion. Finnbjörn, a tall, dark haired, lean man of unquestionable beauty, stepped up out of the hot tub and followed the lady.

Kirsten's gaze lingered for a moment or two longer, before she herself made her way over to the hot tub.

In her attic bedroom, Eleanor sat cross-legged on the mattress. She turned the buckle over in her hands; examining it; wondering about it. She pressed it to her palm and emptied her mind to focus solely on the buckle. Around her, the room twisted and stretched, morphing into an earlier room - a room where the floorboards were newly laid, where the furniture was dusted and well kept. Instead of electric light, an oil lamp flickered from the corner of the room.

Eleanor relaxed her thoughts and the room returned to its present setting. A moth danced around the bare electric light.

Eleanor sat on the worn mattress in the old family home. She lay the buckle down carefully between her legs and removed her hands from its twisted metalwork. She allowed her thoughts to move once more. Closing her eyes briefly, she opened them again to find herself kneeling on a volcanic beach, her hands dug into the black sand.

Looking up across the lake, she watched light ripple over the surface like lines of silver. Hanna's voice hung in the air with the slow, remorseless chanting from monks on the further shore. She pulled her hands out of the sand and cupped them together.

The scene was gone. Again she found herself in the attic room, with the moan of the wind outside. Eleanor leant forward and stared at the buckle on the mattress in front of her. *What does it mean? How does it work?* She stared again, searching for understanding.

'It's nothing!' Eleanor declared. 'It's nothing but a red herring – a talisman. Worthless!' She skimmed the buckle through the air and watched as it clattered onto the floorboards and slid off into the corner. Almost immediately, her mind filled again. She was still in the same house, but once again in an earlier time. She heard footsteps on the stairs and voices on the landing. Icelandic voices. Her family – her ancestors.

Ben laughed. With the computer running a new model in the lounge, Ben pulled open the refrigerator for a couple of cans and tossed one to Bjäkk. They cracked open the beer and moved outside to settle themselves in the hot tub. Briefly disturbed by a call from an upstairs window, they returned to a conversation of beer-fuelled scientific insight.

Laughter filtered in from outside. Ben's was nervously self-conscious, and Bjäkk's; thick and gravely, and deep and resonating. Kirsten pushed open the door and stepped back out onto the decking at the back of the house. She smiled at the somewhat ludicrous sight of two hulking men sharing a hot tub and swigging back beer.

'You solved it then?' asked Kirsten as she stepped into the tub and eased herself down into the deliciously warm water. 'The mysteries of the world – have you got yourselves an answer?'

Ben turned his head towards Bjäkk, who nodded. 'I don't know if we've got anything so much as an answer, but we do have a theory,' says Ben.

Kirsten nodded and listened intently as Ben went on to explain how, in the course of Bjäkk's fish stock measurement he had discovered some odd correlations between freshwater and ocean temperatures. Whilst continuing to show interest, Kirsten couldn't pretend to understand the complexities of the links that they were suggesting with recent geothermal activity in the Highlands.

'It's the net growth of these three glaciers that confuses me though.' Ben was unstoppable once started on his subject of choice. 'The trend recently – going back for years – decades even – is for an annual glacial retreat of a couple of centimetres.'

'And all this is related?'

'It has to be.' There was hesitancy in Ben's voice. 'Definitely.'

Kirsten leant against the passenger side window of the jeep, watching the scenery pass by her on the journey north. Squeezed in next to her was Ben, chatting away to Bjäkk. She lost track of their conversation, caught up in the almost hypnotic way that Bjäkk illustrated his point by drawing graphs in the air with taps and sweeps of his thumbs and fingers on the steering wheel.

The jeep rattled across a long, low bridge and Kirsten looked again to the road. The next time she glanced round, she was, for a moment, sat at the front of the minibus next to her holiday leader. She turned her head and strained to look into the back of the vehicle, expecting to see all her new friends. In front of her eyes was the grit stained window overlooking the open back of the jeep.

Eleanor fastened the tarpaulin across the back of the jeep. She looked up into Hanna's gaze and smiled. Beyond, Alice was crossing the yard.

'You ready?' called Eleanor.

Alice nodded her head eagerly before turning her head and looking at the house and returning an expression that turned to slight dolefulness. 'I will be sorry to leave here.'

Eleanor agreed. Looking up at the window, for a moment she thought she saw the tall, slender figure of a woman looking down, across the yard at her. Briefly, their eyes were locked in the exchange, broken by the return of Alice's ardent enthusiasm.

'But we have work to do. Ancient scrolls to research...' Alice's face beamed with delight.

Hanna ushered them both into the cab, and soon they were off, turning right onto the road, south to Reykjavik. Eleanor opened Solveig's journal and spread it out across Alice's and her laps. Together they lost themselves in the words and the stories. Looking up occasionally, Eleanor found herself seeing alfar working in the meadows and playing in the yards of the small hamlets that they passed.

Within a few hours the single lane carriageway and fields on either side gave way to apartment blocks and the road was now multi-lane and well lit. The outskirts of Reykjavik were interspersed with outcrops of lava and grassy slopes carpeted with purple lupines; the houses were patchwork blocks of colour.

To the rhythmic blink of the indicator light, Bjäkk pulled on the steering wheel and took a left turn onto the smaller road to Hólar. He felt across the dashboard for a cassette and pushed it firmly into the tape player. After a discordant slur of an abused tape the heavy drum and guitar beats of American rock blasted from the speakers. Soon he was nodding his head to the beat and singing along.

Shafts of light broke through fractures in a sky of otherwise leaden cloud. The cathedral clock face was illuminated in the golden glow of evening and Kirsten watched the tower tilt and turn as she looked up at it from the moving vehicle. The jeep's roof obscured her view – but then there it was again, sliding out of frame as Bjäkk drove up to the car park at the front of Hólar Agricultural School.

Kirsten lifted her head from where she had rested it on Ben's shoulder and jumped down from the cab. She stood under the trees that were set amongst the green lawn and masked the entrance to the main building with its simple white painted façade and red roof.

For a moment, Alice was standing again under the exact same tree and pulling her rucksack from the trailer behind. It was twenty-two days earlier and the sights and smells and sounds of Iceland were still new to Kirsten. She walked across the car park towards the glass plated entrance hall. Following Eleanor and Andy, she heard him ask her if she had been here before.

'It only seems like yesterday,' said Ben.

Kirsten was jolted back to the present at the sound of Ben's voice.

'Are we sleeping in those classrooms again with the scary

portraits?' Kirsten asked Bjäkk as they crossed the grounds to the school building.

'Já, I think so.'

'Scary portraits?' asked Ben.

Kirsten laughed. 'Don't ask. The former headmasters - Alice was sure they were looking at her all night. All a bit Hogwarts I'm afraid.'

Ben grinned. Shortly they found their way to the classroom and dumped their bags down on the floor. Bjäkk left them to fetch out a couple of mattresses from the store cupboard and rearrange the desks to make room for them. Bjäkk soon returned with a selection of sheets.

Kirsten watched Ben, eyeing him carefully. She took in his every look and attempted to remember every beautiful feature about him. She loosened the straps of her rucksack and unpacked her sleeping bag.

He turned to face her and saw her gaze. She looked away, embarrassed at having been caught staring. Kirsten sensed Ben's desire to engage her in conversation. He looked at her diffidently as he fidgeted with his fingers. She could see that he found conversation awkward - or at least conversation without the structure of a time-specific, subject orientated focus.

Kirsten reached out and took his hand. His palm was cold and clammy. She looked up at him and wanted to hold him in a warm embrace but she knew that he was not ready for that.

'A week ago,' said Ben, 'if you'd asked me how my research project was going I would have said that I had reached an impossible conundrum.'

Kirsten could not hide her disappointment. Interesting as his scientific discovery was to her this was not the conversation that she had been hoping for. She found herself pleased though, with Ben's obliviousness and smiled and listened as he continued to outline Bjäkk's and his latest thinking. He outlined the agenda ahead of them tonight as he pushed the mattresses, into position on the floor. The focus of his conversation seeped away from Kirsten and back into the science-talk-mode that he shared with Bjäkk.

Kirsten stood at the window of the classroom looking down across the lawn and the car park to the collection of corrugated iron huts with old arched roofs. She could see Bjäkk and Ben crossing the grounds and followed them with her gaze until they disappeared inside one of the long, low concrete huts. She stepped back into the classroom, alone, with the portraits of the former Hólar schoolmasters watching over her.

From the front seat Eleanor watched her cousin in the wing mirror as she disappeared into her father's house. As evening faded fast into night she could also see Alice ambling along the driveway.

In the house, Hanna moved fast, passing the sideboard in the hall with the phone that blinked with new messages, down the stairs to the basement and to her father's book-lined study. She made straight to the desk and for the satchel propped up alongside it. Delving her hand into it, she rummaged for a set of keys. Holding them cupped in her hand, she looked at them, wavering for a moment over her decision, before clasping her hands shut on them and springing back out of the room.

Kirsten walked along the dimly lit school corridor, turned a corner and descended the stairs to the ground floor. The deserted halls echoed with her footsteps and silence weighed heavily on her. Brief bursts of laughter intruded from some distant room.

She arrived at the main entrance where an attendant sat at the front desk idly clicking away at the computer.

Kirsten stood by a carousel of postcards, giving them cursory interest before moving to the vending machine and the rows of candy and soft drinks. Her glance passed over them to a table to the left and to a crate of beer. She cast 250 Krona into the tray and took a bottle.

Outside, under the night sky, Kirsten forced the cap of the bottle across the edge of a wall. As the beer foamed up she snatched it to her mouth and drank.

Outside the large, floodlit museum just off the main Reykjavik High Street, Hanna pulled the car up to the kerb and the three girls piled out of the jeep.

'Are you sure about this?' Alice glanced at her watch.

They reached the top of the steps and crossed the open space at the front of the museum. Hanna looked reassuringly at Alice. 'Relax. My father works here. We're always coming to visit him after hours.'

'Yeah, *visit* him,' said Alice, 'He's currently a hundred miles away up some fjord.'

4

Kirsten walked the corridors of the agricultural school, sipping occasionally from her beer. Her footsteps echoed on the tiles. With no particular direction in mind she found herself at the door to the swimming pool. Through the wired-glass she saw the water dappled with moonlight and recalled a night, almost like this one, a month ago now—

Kirsten was in the pool, floating back in the water and there in front of her eyes, the hard-edged black silhouette of the mountain against a fractured sky. Alice was there, splashing in front of her. And there too were Eleanor and Andy; Claude with Emma and Michelle...

That night – their first in Iceland together – still only hours since their first meeting at Heathrow – she watched it from the other side of the door, drinking her beer and reflecting on all that's changed.

Kirsten wandered back along the corridor, drawn by the sounds of laughter that increased in volume with every step. Her mind continued to wind back over the past month. Ascending first up a half flight of stairs she then stepped down into the long, narrow canteen at the front of the main building. A group of Icelanders down the far end – postgrad students she guessed – were playing guitar and singing interspersed with jokes and laughter. She turned and looked the other way.

Her friends were sat at the tables with the hesitant and general conversation of a group of people she had only just met.

She recalled the singing of cartoon theme tunes from a shared past and smiled fondly at the thought.

Crossing the dimly-lit entrance hall, Hanna waved briefly to the security guard, exchanging a few brief words in Icelandic before she led Eleanor and Alice down some steps and into a small lobby. Their way was blocked by sealed, double doors, rigged up to electronic locks with blinking lights. Hanna swiped the access card through the machine and keyed in the pin.

'Magnus, the security guard,' explained Hanna, 'He's so cool. I've forgotten how long my pabbi and him have been friends.'

The door lights flashed from red to green and Hanna reached forward and pulled open the door. Another few steps down and they were crossing the floor of the exhibition hall under pale security lighting. They made their way past information boards, interactive learning zones and the large glass cabinets containing scrolls and books printed on vellum.

Eleanor held back slightly, as Alice moved forward quickly; drawn to the ancient texts.

'Look at this,' said Alice excitedly, 'Tell me I've not died and gone to heaven...'

Alice was drawn closer to the old books. She stared at the words, picking out the letters amongst the words in the paragraphs of text written by hand on stiff, firm parchment.

'Can anyone still read these?' Alice's voice was hushed.

'Any Icelander can,' answered Eleanor, 'It's a young language – compared to most that is.' She moved to another case, pointing out to her friends one of the earliest known transcriptions of Egils saga. As she told her friend about them, she kept watch on her cousin, as she worked through the security code at the small, partially-concealed door at the far end of the exhibition space.

A shaft of muted light broke across the room, as the door was swung inward. Eleanor left the display cabinets and followed Hanna into a back room. After a few moments Alice followed her friends. The walls were lined with papers and cabinets of document drawers. Hanna was already tapping through the catalogue on one of the computer terminals...

Kirsten crouched down next to her bed in the high-ceilinged classroom and pulled a notebook from her rucksack. She ferreted further for a pen and a few minutes later she was heading back downstairs; the sounds of laughter from the bar increasing as she approached.

Opening another can of Egils beer, Kirsten flicked through her journal and flipped the lid from her pen. Gazing briefly out of the window into the night she looked through her mirrored reflection in the glass and drew upon her inspiration. Her eyes flicked down to the blank sheet of paper in front of her.

Kirsten walked down the tiled corridor with Alice. It was now six hours since they landed in Iceland and already Kirsten could feel herself in love with the country. The drive north had been inspiring; the contrast of colours that they had seen even this afternoon had been dramatic; the harsh, dark grey, craggy peaks, the brown and grey ochre scree slopes that merged seamlessly with the lush meadow grass at the valley bottoms.

Alice was nudging her. Alice; she was such an incorrigible gossip, but you have to love her for it.

'What do you make of that Claude then?' She hissed in her Mancunian accent. 'In love with himself or what?'

'He creeps me out,' admitted Kirsten.

They walked on with the sound of the slap-slapping of flip-flops on the tiled floor. Around a corner they arrived in a lobby area flanked by lockers and a glass-panelled door to the outside. Approaching the door, they could see the steam rising from the outdoor pool.

Kirsten turned to her friend. 'You ready for this?'

Alice nodded and pushed open the door. As she did, it bashed into Andy – tall, dark and unashamedly aware of his attractiveness.

'Alice?' he said. Clothed only in sandals, swimming shorts and a towel draped across his shoulders, he offered Alice his hand. She looked him up and down, shaking her head at the confidence that he displayed.

'Get away with you.' Alice dismissed Andy's bravado and continued towards the pool.

Kirsten followed. Lingering for a moment she looked back. Out of the corner of her eye, she had seen something; shadows moving. She looked closer, two figures, shadows stretched tall against the walls. Shadows? No. They were looking at her. A man; and with him a lady. Tall and immaculately dressed, they were looking right at her with sharp blue eyes, searching her mind, Kirsten felt it burn and she blinked; flinching.

'You okay?' Eleanor approached Kirsten, rounding the corner of the corridor and approaching. The door to the pool swung slowly shut. Catching on its hinges the clicking sounds echoed along the corridor and through Kirsten's head.

'Fine.' Kirsten replied. 'Just tired. You know, the journey...'

Eleanor nodded.

'Your friend Andy,' said Kirsten, 'He's a bit full of himself isn't he?'

They emerged into the cold air outside; in the pool some of their friends were already enjoying the geothermal waters. Alice called out and Kirsten waved back. Eleanor watched as Andy dove into the water and surfaced at the far side of a girl.

'He's certainly not shy to impress,' agreed Eleanor. 'You ready?' She pushed down her drawstring trousers and unzipped her fleece.

Kirsten dipped her toes into the water. It's warm. Oh, so warm. She let herself down to the edge and sat for a while, legs immersed in water that seeped warmth into her skin and flooded up her body as the chill air bit at exposed skin.

'You gonna sit there all day?' Alice's gently mocking tone crossed the pool.

Kirsten laughed. She shook her head and was about let herself slide into the water when suddenly; out of the corner of her eye, there they were again. Her hands slid out from under her and she crashed down into the water. Her head disappeared underwater, eyes still open. Her vision swam in a blue blur of bubbles and the concrete sides – and the legs, arms, and shadows through the water of those two figures. Arms flailed, and her head bobbed back to the surface. Her friends were laughing. Kirsten laughed. The man and lady were gone. She pushed her arms back and floated and stared up at the moon; high in the pale, night sky.

Kirsten sat. She placed her journal and pen down on the classroom floor. No. Her memory was playing tricks. Her heart argued with her mind. It really happened. She looked down, at the can of beer on the parquetry floor. She smiled and lifted it again to her mouth.

Ben sipped his beer, lifting his eyes momentarily from data modelling. He glanced across at Bjäkk, 'What were those coordinates again?

Bjäkk raised an eyebrow to the question and pulled down a clipboard stashed with graph paper and computer printouts from a shelf above his head.

Eleanor stood over old parchment, studying the words. Alongside her were Hanna and Alice, bathed in a pool of light from the manuscript cabinet. Slipping her hand into a white linen glove she traced her words with her fingers.

'You have that map of the highlands, Hanna?'

Kirsten scribbled through a page of writing, before tearing it from her book, screwing the paper into a ball. She cast it aside and wrote again.

The cold fog pressed in on them. Grey and mercilessly, the fine rain stung their faces and penetrated their Goretex jackets. Slowly, steadily, they made their descent off the mountain. Conversation was muted, as they walked in single file, heads down, watching the footwork of the pair of boots in front of them. Kirsten turned her head, said something to Eleanor, behind her in the line. A response came. The subject; it didn't matter. Somewhere ahead a song was attempted, followed lacklustre by a chorus and it failed to hold the tune.

Kirsten looked up; across the room and out of the window. Clouds pulled across the sky, shutting out the moon. She got up and moved to the window, settling again on the sill and tucked her legs against the warmth of the radiator. She set her beer down on the ledge and focused again on her words.

The wind was stronger now, gusting over the ridge and funnelling down the valley. She couldn't help but think of her friends that didn't come on this expedition, sitting now in a warm bar with big mugs of hot chocolate served with a ball of ice cream floating on the surface and sprinkled with flakes of chocolate.

Cold shards of rain spiked her face and the warm, cosy images were gone. So too was the trail of boots that she followed. Her heart skipped a beat and raced. She moved forward at a quick pace and almost crashed into the back of Alice. She stopped for a second or two and composed herself, before setting off again.

Eleanor grabbed the map from Hanna's hand and straight away zoned in on the northern highlands. She fingered the contours of the mountain; she shook her head at the impossibility of what she realised.

'It's not possible.' Eleanor shook her head.

Kirsten looked up. Her eyes were wide and burning blue. Her mind was active in its realisation. She remembered with sudden vividness what she had thought she had forgotten and chased that memory.

'Eleanor!' Kirsten called her friend's name. She turned and ran back, calling out in desperation. The wind howled across the ridge and the rain drove at her face. Finnur's hands gripped her shoulders; holding her back, his voice was in her ear, instructing her to stay. She fought against her desire to run and returned to where the group were gathered.

'See. Look here.' Ben pushed the map in front of Bjäkk. 'See the coordinates for that first storm and the second? And the one two nights ago. That's just not possible.'

Bjäkk looked suspiciously at Ben. 'You are suggesting, that your sister—' He raised his eyebrows with wonder. 'That she is some kind of conductor for the weather.'

A tri-corder stood alone in the middle of the glacier. Lights on its headpiece blinked red and green in the lowering night. Its numerous arms of aluminium rods with the spherical sensors on each end stood silently recording. Eirný crept closer, joined after only moments by Greipur. Dark and slender silhouettes against the ice, they bantered in the old tongue. Cautiously they approached the machine, inspecting every appendage with keen eyes. They reached out to it with their long fingers but resisted the urge to touch it.

Away to the south, William sat in the mess tent in front of his computer watching the computations and examining the readings as they came in. The trestle table at which William, Kathryn and Nils were working was pooled in light from the gas lantern hanging from the ridge pole. Kathryn drew lines in pencil across a map with a ruler, whilst Nils analysed page after page of numerical data.

'I guess this is our next location?' Kathryn said, marking a point in the map firmly with the tip of her finger.

William glanced at the map, and then looked closer. He shook his head. 'I think not. Two nights ago we saw this storm come out of nowhere in a very specific spot. That's interesting, but it's not unique. In Reykjavik we had the same thing. The most violent storm we've ever seen came from nowhere and centred on one specific area.'

'You think there's going to be more of these?' Kathryn's question was rhetorical. 'Another storm in another place, equally inexplicable. How can we predict where that is going to be?'

William considered the question carefully. He shook his head, 'If we had some kind of common occurrence,' he said, and prodded at his temples as if willing his mind to cooperate. 'Think William. Think laterally.'

'It's ludicrous.'

'It's the only answer.' Eleanor rebutted.

Hanna reached out to her cousin, forcing her round to look at her. 'Eleanor, people have died in these storms. You can't possibly think that you are to blame.'

Eleanor remained silent. The words were in her mouth and ready to explode, but they lacked a voice.

'Hanna's right.' Alice echoed. 'It's stupid to think that just because you were there you caused it.'

'But I wasn't just *there* was I?' snapped Eleanor, 'I was at the centre of every storm. I got lost once – almost lost twice – and–'

Eleanor looked down. 'And Andy's dead because of me.'

5

'Of course she isn't.' Ben was contemptuous in his dismissal.

'Really? So what are you saying?' asked Bjäkk.

'You expect me to be able to answer that?' countered Ben. He looked again at the maps and the charts and mentally clutched at data matrixes and figures, searching for the pattern within. The numbers impregnated his eyes, morphing into abstract shapes and dancing shades of colour. 'She was there. At every storm – in the centre of it. When you look for answers you look for common threads.'

Bjäkk referred to his notes. Forty-eight hours ago he thought he was at the break through of discovery. Now there were just more questions. Ben threw his papers down and kicked himself off from the desk with his foot and wheeled back across the room in his chair.

'There's something she hasn't told me. I have to know what happened that night?'

Bjäkk remained silent. He lifted his head briefly. Nodding slightly, he looked idly down.

Kirsten lay on top of her sleeping bag, her legs curled on the mattress, with her notebook beside her on the pillow and the pen lying loosely between her fingers. A shaft of light triangled out across the room from the doorway. Ben stepped in and pushed the door closed behind him before tiptoeing across the floor. Kneeling at Kirsten's side, he remained for several long moments, just watching her breathing softly in her sleep. He reached out to stroke her hair. His hand lingered and then pulled back, afraid.

'You got your phone?' Eleanor held out her hand.

Alice shrugged and pulled her mobile from her jeans pocket; slapping it into Eleanor's hand. 'Who are you calling?'

'No one. Recording the evidence.' Eleanor grinned and quickly began to record the findings from the documents on the phone's camera.

A few minutes later, and they were crossing the foyer once more. Hanna waved to the security guard, and swiped their way out of the museum.

On the steps to the Culture House, Alice suddenly held back.

'What's the time?' Alice asked rhetorically, as she flipped up the lid to her mobile.

Hanna looked from the sky to Alice's phone. 'It's got to be one, two maybe at most...'

Alice grinned. 'Anyone for a drink before we get off home?'

*

Ben pulled his sweater off and eased his feet from his boots. Taking off his trousers, he slung them across the school table and moved to get into his sleeping bag. He paused and looked down at his bed for a moment and slowly pushed the mattress next to Kirsten's.

Relaxing into his sleeping bag he lay on his back staring up into the ceiling, his mind still chasing ideas and turning over theories. He glanced across at Kirsten and her peaceful sleep and was envious of her.

The sun, low on the eastern horizon, lit Hallgrimskirkja cathedral in an orange glow. The concrete columns that flanked the tower rose like beacons of colour into the sky. Lying on the floor at the foot of the tower were Eleanor, Hanna and Alice. Heads together, they formed a three-pointed star with their bottles of beer stood empty near to each of them. Against the clear sky of morning, Alice stared up at the white-faced clock at the top of the tower. The minute hand ticked onto the hour and announced the arrival of the new day.

The early morning sun crept down the western side of the valley, as it rose over the ridge opposite. Sheets of golden light were reflected back off the windows of the school and within one of the first floor windows onto the floor of the classroom. Kirsten woke, turned inward, and found herself face to face with Ben. She could feel his soft breath on her cheeks. His hand lay across her shoulders. She smiled.

Somewhere far off downstairs Kirsten could hear voices, and plates clattered. More prominent in her mind though was the silence of the morning in the high ceilinged classroom, with the clear northern light flooding through the windows. She reached for her notebook and held it aloft to read last night's words.

Turning back a page, she read her story in reverse. Another page after another and re-reading the story produced a whimsical smile as it brought the events back into her mind.

Kirsten bounded quickly, if carefully, across the small bridge and up the slope to the main path. Falling into line with Eleanor she followed Alice, who was some way ahead. They each carried their tall, plastic IKEA beakers filled with hot chocolate. Following the path, as it twisted and turned up the broken canyon wall with birch scrub and grass interspersed. As they reached the top at last they cut back on themselves to a rocky outcrop from which they could see the view. They gazed out right across the valley and the lush canyon floor at Vesturdalur one way, and to the other, a barren floor of rock and scree with the warden's hut behind its dry stone wall and its oasis of lawn and its two flag poles. It was like some frontier outpost – the last defence in a siege.

Yesterday morning they were standing in the middle of Heathrow; yesterday evening they were staying in a remote school in the north of the country; and now their tents were down in the canyon – their home for two weeks was in the middle of a canyon, forty minutes away down a track that was bad even for four wheel drive vehicles – forty minutes from the nearest hot showers and shop.

'This is great, isn't it,' Kirsten said enthusiastically. She stood on the outcrop of rock, drinking hot chocolate from the plastic beaker with a view to die for spread out beneath.

Kirsten smiled, finding pleasure in the re-reading. Carefully, so as not to wake Ben, she rolled onto her side, propped her head up on her arm and let the book rest on the mattress. She turned over the pages, dipping into the story and reading chunks of her memories.

'Here.' Sara led the group of British volunteers up a path, across a plateau to the cliff edge. The roar of the river churned, thick and grey at the bottom of the canyon, roaring like a motorway beneath. Grinning broadly, Sara beamed as the group gathered around her. She pointed

behind her, across the canyon to a huge cave opposite and an outcrop of
rock just beyond it. The river swirled around it, funneled through, back
and out in a frothing, confused mass of currents.

'Do you like stories?' Sara asked.

Kirsten remembered the words precisely; the way that their
Icelandic guide coiled them into the story. Even now she could
visualise the scene; and the story of how the cave and outcrop
came into being. She heard Sara's voice, as she read her own
version of words.

'Many years ago, on the shores of this river, at this place they call
Hljóðaklettar – you saw back there how the cliffs are castle like – there
lived two trolls called Karl and Kerling and they were very much in love.
Karl wanted a child, a son, an heir to bring up as his own. Kerling,
though she loved her husband, did not feel the same way.'

'Kerling agreed to have a child with Karl, but only if he fulfilled
every task she set him for one month and a day. Karl loved Kerling so
much he would have agreed to anything, and he did. Within a day,
Kerling had made her first demand. She wanted the cave where there
they lived to be bigger. For seven days Karl worked tirelessly in the gloom
at the back of the cave, pulling the rocks apart with his old, trusted
pickaxe. For seven nights, he carried the spoil out by hand, crossing
the great river to be rid of the rocks. At the end of the seventh night, he
pronounced it finished and asked Kerling again for the child. Kerling
thanked Karl for the task now done. When morning came and they
retired to bed, she refused him access to her chamber. Karl sat up in
the entrance cave, as close to the sun as he dared and cried. He cried
so many tears for Kerling that the river swelled and flooded the valley.'

'You've seen already how the river has carved this new path to the
sea and created the forest at Ásbyrgi? This then is how this place became
known as Cruel Kerling.'

'The next night she demanded fish. Fifty cod, this night and next,
for she wanted to make a pie. Karl agreed, such was his devotion to

Kerling and his desire for an heir. Wading down the river, he fished in the bay all night, only getting back to his cave just as the sun was rising. The next night, the same thing; Karl went out to catch enough fish for Kerling to make her pie. And what a pie; it is reputed to have been one of the best ever made. But still, Kerling forbade Karl access to her bed chamber before the month and a day was up.'

'The next night, just as the sun set, Kerling told Karl of her third task. This time her beloved husband must build her a bridge, for she wanted to visit her clan on the west bank...'

Kirsten looked up from her book. Was that the last of Karl's tasks? She thought so; and cursed herself again for not writing down the whole story at the time. Whilst not exactly how it came about, she remembered the ending vividly. She could see Sara's face still, possibly embellishing the story.

'On the last day before the month was up, Karl was desperate in his task – the hardest so far – working till sunrise he almost made it back to his cave. It was not to be; for Kerling realised her mistake and ran to help and she too was caught in the sun's rays. And there, remaining for all time, are Karl and Kerling, petrified trolls standing on the gravel bank by the river.'

Kirsten moved forward, taking a step past Sara to the edge of the cliff and looked down at the churning water that separated them from the two trolls. As she looked, she saw their features; Karl's big forehead and Kerling's ample bosom. Now birds roosted on their heads and the water had cut gouges out of their feet. She felt sad for them.

'We really ought to get off home.' Hanna said suddenly.

Eleanor and Alice turned to look at Hanna.

Alice glanced back up at the sky and shrugged. 'When does that coffee shop open, you know, the one down on the main street in the basement?'

'You mean Kofi Tómasar Frænda?' answered Hanna, 'Soon I think. People go there before work. It's just at the other end of this street.'

Walking back down Skólavoórðustigur in the early light of morning, the streets were quiet and the day seemed at peace. Passing the distinctive blue and yellow frontage of 12 Tónar, Hanna lingered at the window displays of the music store. Eleanor and Alice, soon returned and joined her. As they stood browsing the selection of CDs, Eleanor suddenly became aware of a face reflected next to her in the window. She found her eyes refocusing on it; on the fringe of untidy blond hair, the blue eyes and – and that smile.

'Finnur!' She said his name with joyful exclamation and turned instinctively, uninvited, to hug him. 'How long have you been standing there?'

'Eleanor,' he said, 'It's good to see you.' He took her in his arms, taking time to look at her. 'So well.'

'I've been stood there about as long as you. I was coming up the street, thought we would pass. Then I saw you go back to the shop.' Finnur said as he glanced past Eleanor. 'And Alice. It's good to see you.' They hugged. 'It's been too long.'

'But what are you guys doing here?' He laughed. 'This shop doesn't open for another two or three hours.'

Eleanor looked at him, studying his face, remembering those nights in the ranger's hut; sitting up with the guys all night playing cards; laughing and telling stories. 'It's a long story.'

Finnur nodded. 'I know. Eleanor, *where* were you?'

Eleanor cowered slightly at Finnur's words. 'We were just going for a coffee. Do you want to come?'

At one end of a leather sofa, a young woman in her early twenties hugged a big mug of coffee close to her, reading her book before work. On another sofa, a young male student read from his book, lifting his eyes frequently to check out the girl on the other sofa. Occasionally she looked up at the same time and their eyes met. They smiled. In the far corner of the room, a businessman, sharp-suited and with thin, receding hair, checked his email.

At the bar, Finnur ordered the round of drinks, returning to the table in the middle of the room to pull up a chair alongside Eleanor, Hanna and Alice.

'You're looking well, Eleanor.'

'Thanks,' she replied politely, if uncomfortably. She began to speak, and stopped. Again she could't. Her mouth was suddenly too dry to speak. The silence lingered uncomfortably as they waited for their drinks.

'So Finnur, what brings you back to Reykjavik?' Alice knew how, given the choice, he preferred canvas for a roof and the nearest neighbour being in the next valley.'

'Yeah. I'm missing some good treks, but you know – meetings with my bosses. You should have seen me yesterday – suit and everything. It seemed that the National Parks are reviewing the access to the Highlands. My bosses are cutting back on the routes on which I can operate.'

'Is this because of…?' Alice stared incredulously at Finnur. 'Not because – surely?' Glancing briefly towards Eleanor she looked again to the mountain guide.

'Ah,' Finnur ignored the question. He glanced up, 'see the coffees have arrived.'

Mugs were passed to Hanna and Eleanor, while Alice and Finnur received their hot chocolates; Alice revelled in the wide brimmed bowl of a mug, with the ball of ice cream floating on the top and the chocolate flake stuck into the top.

'I'm sorry.' Eleanor said eventually. She looked directly at Finnur. 'I'm really sorry. If I'd stayed with the group, got down off that mountain—'

Finnur cut across Eleanor's apologies. 'It's really not your fault. It was a bad storm. We were so lucky it wasn't any worse. You didn't choose to get lost. You didn't bring the storm.' He laughed. His laughter was met by empty silence, save for the sound of three cups, being placed back down on their saucers. Finnur looked from one girl to the next girl and to the next.

'Okay. What have I just said?' Finnur was suddenly hesitant and unsure of himself.

Alice and Hanna looked to each other and then at Eleanor.

'I'm definitely missing something here. Eleanor. You didn't cause the storm.' His eyes flashed back across the table to Alice. 'She doesn't really think that – does she?'

Eleanor looked up. Her words were plainly put and matter of fact. 'The storm three nights ago; I caused that. Why not the others?'

6

Kathryn pulled back the zip and poked her head out of the tent. She rolled back the door and pushed her feet out, before slipping on her boots. As she tied her laces she looked out at the day and at William where he was striking his tent, his rucksack packed and fastened nearby.

'Are we going?' she asked.

'Yes. I had a call. A colleague in Reykjavik,' replied William, 'We'll finish up our current set of tests and leave.'

'Where're you going? Back to Reykjavik?'

'By way of the Highlands, yes. Something you said to me yesterday, it's got me thinking.'

Kathryn looked inquisitively at William.

'No.' He stuffed the last of his tent into the bag. 'I'm not going to elaborate.'

Nils returned to camp clutching his toothbrush and paste with his towel slung over his shoulder. 'Wouldn't tell you either?' said Nils. 'He is – what would you say – an enigma.'

Kathryn smiled. Yes, that summed William up perfectly.

Kirsten carefully moved Ben's hand. Careful not to wake him, she eased herself off the mattress. Scooping up her journal from the floor, she laid it down again on of the school desks next to her bag and changed quickly into her swimming costume, artfully slipping on her bikini top beneath her T-shirt. She grabbed her towel and made to leave. In mid-step, her mind changed and she returned for her journal.

'So that's it, I guess.' Eleanor glanced down at her empty coffee cup and at the swills of coffee grains left clinging to the inside. Her hands subconsciously traced the rim of the cup. She shrugged. 'That's my story.'

Finnur nodded. He placed his hands together at their fingertips in consideration of everything that Eleanor had said. 'It's some story.'

'You don't believe me?' queried Eleanor.

'I didn't say that.'

Finnur's words were greeted with surprise by Eleanor. Hanna and Alice leaned closer across the table.

'This man. This Gunnlaugr,' said Finnur. 'Describe him some more?'

'I think I said everything.' Eleanor tried to recall again the exact circumstances of their first meeting. 'He was old, dark hair, very tanned skin. *Very* weather-beaten – like he'd been hung up at the end of some fjord on one of the racks they use for the fish. Long legs – and he walked with a staff, carved maybe; but not I think because he needed it. Just because he did lots of walking.'

All the time Finnur nodded.

'You know him?' asked Hanna.

Again Finnur nodded. 'Yes, I've seen him around.' He paused for a moment over his thoughts. 'Not that I've heard of him go by the name Gunnlaugr before. Gyrdir is his name,' said Finnur, 'If it's the same man and it sounds like it is. I've seen him on occasion in the mountains. Never normally that far north though.'

'Is he – dangerous?' Hanna glances at her cousin.

'Personally?' Finnur reflected, 'I wouldn't trust him. But dangerous? I don't think so.'

Silence surrounded their table, as Finnur left them with that revelation. At least, Eleanor thought, she didn't dream it all. Gunnlaugr did exist; he did meet with her. She looked up, and narrowed her gaze on Alice. She was preoccupied by something in the room.

'Alice?' asked Eleanor.

Alice started, woken from her day-dreaming.

'What've you seen?' Eleanor glanced round in the direction of Alice's gaze, before turning back to her friend.

Alice shook her head. 'I don't know. That girl over there – the one reading her book and the guy on the next sofa. I don't know why but–' She stopped with a sudden intake of breath. 'She's coming over.'

The girl had closed her book and placed it down firmly on the table. She unfolded her long slender legs, rose , and brushed down her dress before approaching. Instinctively Alice raised her hand and waved.

'Excuse me. You don't mind if I join you?'

And without invitation she pulled up a chair to Eleanor's table even before they had agreed.

'I'm sorry. I couldn't help but hear your conversation.' The girl continued. 'I know Gyrdir. And he is very dangerous to my people.'

Her statement was met by blank looks.

'I'm Jóhanna,' she said.

'Hi. That's nice.' Eleanor shrugged. 'But who *are* you?'

'I'm Jóhanna.' She repeated her words, this time directing it towards Hanna, 'You at least should know who I am Hanna Katla Baldursdottir.'

Hanna's eyes widened. She shook her head, 'I'd like to say you'd made some mistake, but that is my name. How...?'

'My family and your family have lived entwined in each other's lives for centuries.'

Jóhanna's proclamation came with a precise lilting tone that seemed to accentuate her sharply defined physical features; her long fingers; her iridescently blue eyes; and her fine cheek bones.

Hanna laughed. 'I've never met you, or your family!'

'No,' says Jóhanna, 'But we have met *you*. Have you never sat in your room, with your guitar in your hands and played your latest song and felt you were with somebody?'

Eleanor watched her cousin, and the strange woman who seemed to be able to see inside their minds.

'It's not just music!' Jóhanna argued defiantly. 'You always think that. You've never wanted to accept us, not really. You make up stories about us – some of you even say you believe. But no, you are all the same. None of you really believe in us; and we live with you – protect you...'

Hanna stayed silent. Eleanor remembered her first meeting with the þurs, and suddenly she knew before she was told.

'We are huldufolk,' said Jóhanna, 'We are your brothers; we are your sisters.'

*

Kirsten slipped down into the water as steam rose from the pool and into the air in the early morning. She pushed back her head and stretched out her arms. The water lapped gently around her face. *It was always bliss to have the pool to herself*, she considered.

'Kirsten!'

Kirsten blinked her eyes open and floundered. She choked on some water. She steadied herself on the pool bottom. *How?* Facing her across the pool was a tall, young woman with the blondest of blond hair and piercingly blue eyes. With her was a man of similar age and similarly fair features; his eyes were blue and alluring.

'Kirsten Elisabeth Ball?' The woman's question was pronounced rhetorically.

Kirsten stammered and stuttered, 'How do you...?'

'You don't remember us?'

The man was surprised when Kirsten shook her head. 'We met you and your group when you were here before. You must remember, you beat us at cards.'

Kirsten racked her brain. She remembered that day and night a month back when she journeyed north with her new friends. She remembered the game of cards and Alice winning every one – hustler. She grinned.

'No, sorry,' answered Kirsten.

They both looked upon Kirsten with curiosity and faint surprise. The man stepped forward towards her. 'I am Finnbjörn and this is my beautiful Eirný.'

Kirsten looked from man to woman; from Finnbjörn to Eirný.

'We have been travelling with you and your friends for some time now.' Eirný's voice was as crisp and clear as mountain water.

Kirsten laughed; a laugh that subsided into uncertainty. 'You're kidding me?'

'It's true.' Eirný continued, 'We have become part of your lives. You could say that we have been watching out for you when you've found yourself in danger.'

'What?' asked Eleanor, 'When have you saved us?'

Jóhanna reached across the table and took Eleanor's hand.

'You of all people should know the answer to that question.' She held Eleanor in her gaze. 'Think what has happened to you. Can you really explain how you have survived?'

'You?' Eleanor found her emotions torn; unsure of just what to believe.

'There is so much you have to learn, Eleanor Ármannsson.'

'You're being serious?' said Kirsten, 'Aren't you?'

Finnbjörn smiled coyly and reached out to stroke Kirsten's arm with his long, fingers.

'You guys, you really are elves.'

'Alfar,' Finnbjörn answered, 'The huldufolk.'

'I didn't realise. I thought that – I knew the Icelanders – that the humans believed in you. But I still thought you were myths.' Kirsten had difficulty finding her words. 'Is it all true? That you live under rocks, that you stop roads being built in the centre of Reykjavik?'

Finnbjörn looked to Eirný. They laughed at Kirsten's tales.

'We let them think these things,' said Eirný, 'It pleases us.'

'You say that you know Gunnlaugr – Gyrdir. How?' Eleanor leant across the table towards the alfar lady. 'Finnur says he's not to be trusted. You say he's dangerous. He saved my life...?'

'He had you running errands for him?'

'Yeah, but...' Eleanor stopped herself. 'How do you know that?'

'There are many things that we know. Remember, we live behind the rocks, in the fabric of this land. We see most things.' Jóhanna's words hung in the air. Her revelations were not easy to answer. Eleanor, Hanna, Alice and Finnur all felt uncomfortable in Jóhanna's presence.

'So what do you know of Gyrdir?' Eleanor asked finally.

'He killed my father. And his father too.' Jóhanna spoke the truth plainly. 'For many years now he has been attempting to infiltrate our world. So far he has only scratched our doors, but he is determined and I fear he will succeed.'

Eleanor's jaw dropped as she remembered. 'The rune stones I gave him?' She found it hard to admit what she had done. 'I've helped him haven't I?'

'Perhaps,' said Jóhanna, 'But you kept the cup from him.'

Eleanor started suddenly upon realising how much she already knew.

'Yes. Yes I know about the cup. You did not deliver it to him. Remember, my people have eyes everywhere.' Jóhanna paused for a moment before continuing, 'We are lucky. Without the cup, Gyrdir does not have the key of how to use the rune stones.'

William Tyndale watched the valley unfold in front of him as the gravel road dipped down a slope and forded the fast flowing river to reach the compound of huts at the foot of the lava field. As the bus pulled into the car park William glanced quickly at his watch and got up to retrieve his coat and bag from the overhead locker. He made his way, stop-start behind other passengers, down the length of the bus and finally stepped down to look out at the valley he found himself in. The mountains sloped down towards him as blends of iridescent, ever changing coloured scree. Nowhere else on Earth was quite like this place, he decided. He turned his attention to scour the crowd. Having only spoken to the man on the telephone he had no idea who he was looking for until he saw him; and William knew straight away. Waiting for him was the tall, gaunt man with a sharp, angular face and piercingly bright eyes. William weaved through the throng until he reached him.

'Gunnlaugr?' said William.

'And you, Professor Tyndale.' Gunnlaugr smiled. 'I've heard so much about your work; it's good to meet you at last.'

'Your correspondence intrigued me.' Professor Tyndale remained formal, suspicious of this stranger and his wild ideas. 'Shall we go?' He gestured towards the accommodation hut.

'Jóhanna, why did Gunnlaugr kill your people?' asked Eleanor.

'Revenge,' said Jóhanna, 'When he was cast out, those that had assisted in the endeavour became his enemies. My cousin Solveig was the only one to escape.'

'Solveig? We've heard that name before,' exclaimed Alice, 'The journal. She wrote the journal!'

'Not necessarily, it's not an uncommon name,' said Hanna.

'Uncommon enough though.' Jóhanna turned to look at Hanna. 'Do your family talk about her?' Jóhanna asked.

'You saying that one of my ancestors is an elf?!' Hanna shook her head. 'I believe in the old legends, but...'

'Solveig was as human as you and your cousins. Pétur, her beloved, he was as alfar as I am; and she loved him, but your family wouldn't understand.'

'You're lying,' Hanna said firmly.

'Do I have a reason to tell you anything but the truth?'

'You've been spying on us. Creeping into our lives and changing how we see the world?!!' Hanna countered. 'And you talk to us about truth? How long have you been watching us, biding your time before you make this approach? You could be working with Gunnlaugr for all we know!'

'Elves?' Ben folded his arms. 'Yeah, right!'

'It's true.' Kirsten couldn't think of anything more to reason with him. She stood on cold tiles in her bare feet, her towel pulled around her and her hair and skin dripping water onto the classroom floor. 'They want to meet you. Eirný and Finnbjörn, they are amazing and they have such wonderful stories. Do come...'

Ben looked at her. He saw her smile and was caught in her seductive gaze.

'This is insane.'

Ben grabbed his swimming shorts and followed Kirsten down to the pool. He faced her in the water. She was beautiful and he reached out towards her. She pulled away and led him over to Eirný and Finnbjörn where they were whispering to one and another and introduced Ben to them. Eirný greeted the newcomer with fondness.

'You are just as beautiful awake as you are asleep, Benjamin Ármannsson.'

Ben narrowed his gaze at the stunning blonde with sharp, precise features.

'Don't be surprised. We have visited you and Eleanor – yes we know about your sister – often as you sleep. We have taken care to watch over your family for longer than we can remember.'

Ben winced. 'Nice act.' He pulled Kirsten away. 'You're huldufolk yeah? Spiritual beings from another dimension. Well spirit this – prove to me who you are.'

'Ben!' Kirsten rounded on him, shocked by his tone and his manner. She felt his arms protectively around her waist.

Eirný closed the distance again between herself and Ben and Kirsten; Finnbjörn with her. She stroked patterns into the air with her long fingers. 'Our world is your world Benjamin. But you want to see magic?' She flicked her hand across the pool, casting ripples in the surface and droplets of water to scatter. Light refracted in the water and danced around them and—

'What have you—? Where are we?' asked Ben. They were all still in a pool, but one far away, high in the mountains, with a glacier looming over them; a pool warmed by the natural geothermal springs.

'Could anyone who is not of the huldufolk do this?'

'Or this?' Finnbjörn clicked his fingers and day was plunged into night. Above, the aurora borealis rose and fell in the sky above. Kirsten looked up and pointed, entranced by the ever-changing colours.

'Do you still disbelieve our heritage?' asked Finnbjörn.

Ben and Kirsten glanced from the sky to each other; and from each other to Finnbjörn.

'You don't like it?' Finnbjörn snapped his fingers again. Daylight returned. 'Do you see? Benjamin Ármannsson, how can you doubt us now?'

Ben felt uncomfortable. He knew what he had just seen but he could not reconcile it with his logical mind. He turned to Kirsten. 'You trust these people?'

Kirsten nodded.

'Kirsten, if they can pull stunts like this—' He shook his head. 'And I don't know how – they can trick us into believing anything.'

Eleanor hugged Finnur on the street corner outside the coffee shop. She held him in her arms before they parted and he stepped away and began the walk down the street into town. Eleanor returned to her friends. Glancing round she offered him a wave goodbye as he disappeared into the early morning pedestrian traffic. She turned again to Hanna and Alice and shrugged. Hanna reached out and took her cousin's hand; fingers between fingers. She looked over, offering her every support that she could. 'It's your decision.'

Eleanor nodded. She turned, and looked beyond Alice, through the window of the coffee shop. Through obscuring reflections and lettering painted onto the glass, Jóhanna was there, seated at the table. She looked up and her gaze met with Eleanor's. She stood.

'Right,' decided Eleanor. She returned to the coffee shop and as she reached the step, putting out her hand to the door, it was suddenly open and there facing her was Jóhanna; her blue eyes piercing in their intensity.

'I don't know if I trust you,' said Eleanor, 'But you know stuff. Stuff that I – I don't know how you know.'

Jóhanna began to answer but Eleanor silenced her with a determined look and a wave of her hand. 'There's something happening this summer; something that I'm involved in. I don't understand exactly what – and whoever you are – I think you do.'

There, it was said. She watched as Jóhanna nodded, slowly and deliberately and Eleanor stepped back to allow the alfar lady to step out onto the street.

Jóhanna's hair caught in the breeze. She stopped and turned. 'Come.' Her voice is lilting, 'I'll show you.'

PART FIVE

Huldufolk

1

The children of the alfar laughed and played in the garden. Wisps of smoke released from the chimney drifted up into the sky above the small turf-roofed farm perched out at the end of the peninsula. Across the bay fishing boats worked the waters. A young Jóhanna with fair hair and blue eyes stumbled in play, and picked herself. She crouched down again and remained still for a moment, low to the ground, watching her face reflected in a pool of water. Her face was reproduced in perfect clarity before her; mesmerised by it she reached out and tentatively prodded the mirror.

Her face became distorted as the water rippled outward. She cocked her head to one side and watched as the water cleared and the image settled again. This time it was of a different scene. On the far side of the water, three children played; a boy and two girls. They played in the yard outside of the house with the painted roof surrounded by the white picket fence.

The girl through the water crouched down beside the pool, face close to the water, hair shifting in the breeze. She chewed on her lip and watched as a boy ran through the grass, stopping to stoop low and hide as his sister chased another girl. They whooped and screamed in the garden beneath the water—

Eleanor chased her cousin across the grassland at the back of the family's old farm. Her feet stepped awkwardly over the hummocks of grass and she tripped and fell. Her hands crashed down into a puddle and shattered the stillness of the water. She withdrew her arms and lingered for a moment by the pool. The water settled and a face stared back; a girl's face.

Jóhanna stared back at the other side of the pool. On the far side of the shimmering water, Eleanor matched every quizzical expression with her own.

'Góðan daginn,' said Jóhanna.

The nine-year-old Eleanor jumped with surprise.

'Gódan daginn,' Eleanor replied without a moment's thought that she was addressing a reflection in a puddle.

Jóhanna, now tall and fifteen years older, lowered herself to scoop water from the pool. At first she let it trickle between her fingers and watched as the drops hit and danced across the surface of the water. She scooped another handful and splashed it across her face. The cold water tingled on her skin. Eleanor stood alongside the alfar lady.

'That was you?' Eleanor didn't really need to ask.

Jóhanna nodded. 'I didn't know who you were, at that time, of course. I didn't know we were related.'

The child Eleanor blinked and peered to look at the alfar face. 'Solveig?'

The wind blew ripples across the surface of the puddle. Eleanor's face was gone and Jóhanna launched herself to her feet. She turned and scampered across the field, climbing back over the dry stone wall into the garden.

An old woman with white-blond hair was sitting in a wicker chair outside the house with a book laid open on her lap. She gazed out across the garden.

'Jóhanna!' The old woman called.

The girl quickened her pace and ran towards the old woman. She slid to the ground at the old woman's feet and thrust her face up onto her lap. The old woman smiled and stroked the girl's face.

'Do you know how very old I am, Jóhanna?'

'Solveig is many, many years old.' Jóhanna trilled quickly.

Solveig smiled. 'It is true.'

'Solveig,' Jóhanna began. She looked up with wide, questioning eyes, at the lines of the old lady's face, drawn long over the years. 'What do you write in that book?' She reached out to touch the dry parchment, feeling the inked words beneath her fingers.

'This?' Solveig glanced down at her own old hands that held the book. 'This is my life. Have I told you of my life Jóhanna?'

Jóhanna tucked her legs under herself and settled in for the comfort of the story. 'Tell me again, Solveig.'

Solveig lay a comforting hand on the child's hair. She looked down at the child as Jóhanna looked up. Solveig nodded.

'How old am I Jóhanna?'

'Very old.' Jóhanna replied with a child's honesty and Solveig smiled, amused by this.

'You are the mother of my father's father's father,' Jóhanna continued.

'That's right Jóhanna. And I am mortal born. And you know what it means to be mortal born?'

'You were born in the other world, amongst men. You are not true alfar,' said Jóhanna.

Solveig heard the words and allowed them to linger in the air. 'No. I am not truly alfar. I do not have the abilities that you and your kin have. Stretched as my life is, I grow old. You see that now and one day I will fade from this world. But in joining with Þórarinn I have lived for centuries longer than ever I would have in the other world,' she laughed, 'I live to speak to you now.'

'Of course, I can never leave this world. When my family still lived I could never visit them. At most I could watch them through windows, like you were just now, in that pool.'

'That was the other world?' Jóhanna gasped; this part of the story at least was new to her. 'Was that girl of your family? I thought I could see a resemblance...'

Solveig smiled, her lips stretched thin across her dry face.

'Yes and no.' Soleveig recalled the family history and the heritage. 'She is of my mortal family yes, but just as I am also of your family, so is she part of yours.'

Eleanor stood in the garden of the old farm. With her was Jóhanna, in her fine satin robes with her long hair tied back in plaited bands. She looked at her alfar cousin and wondered.

'So Solveig married into the huldufolk,' Eleanor said. 'Is she still alive? Can I see her?'

'No.' Jóhanna shook her head sorrowfully. 'A year after, she faded; became a ghost to both worlds. She lives still, but only in legend.'

'But—' Eleanor protested. 'You've seen her – and – all those times when I've travelled in time? I've seen things that by the laws of science that my brother believes in, I really shouldn't have! Surely it is possible for me to meet with Solveig?'

Jóhanna silenced Eleanor with one look and a raised hand.

'Then why? You bring me out here, but for what?' Eleanor argued with this strange and new-found relative; this creature of the alfar – a huldufolk – who lived in the shadows of her own world.

Wind gusted sheets of rain across the deserted forecourt under a leaden-grey sky. A van with blacked-out windows stood alone by the petrol pumps with its tarpaulin-covered trailer buffeted by the weather. Inside the service station Eleanor sat opposite Andy next to the steamed window. Around them were their other friends from the holiday. Eleanor cupped her hands around her bowl of hot chocolate.

At the table next to them a man and a woman sat staring into each other's eyes and whispering. Across the room two young men in football shirts played pool and spoke only to congratulate or commiserate over the game.

Eleanor smiled and remembered the holiday so far. Her attention drifted into the conversation alongside her. The ranger was telling another one of her stories, leading those around her into believing as truth the tales of huldufolk.

Eleanor looked up to see Jóhanna was now across the garden with Greipur, her dark and brooding lover. The sharp features and black hair of the man flashed through her mind. She turned as Alice and Hanna approached.

'How can the old stories be both so right and wrong about the alfar?' Eleanor kicked the gravel under foot.

'She believed in our stories—' Hanna suggested.

Alice grinned. 'Like all good Icelanders you mean?'

'Já.' Hanna nodded. 'There's a lot of truth in them. Are you ready?'

'You heard from Ben?' asked Eleanor.

Ben stashed his bag into the back of Bjäkk's jeep and reached to pick up Kirsten's from the floor. As he turned he spied her approach, carrying a small box of food and drink.

'Provisions for the road,' she said.

Ben smiled and peered into the box. He delved his hand down, and brought out some sweets. 'Yum. Chocolate raisins...'

He was about to scoff a handful into his mouth when the ground beneath them pulsed and the mountains growled. The chocolate raisins flew from his hand. Kirsten stumbled forward and caught hold of Ben's fleece to steady herself.

'What the...?' Kirsten looked across the valley where a flock of birds took to the sky in one black, twisting cloud; squawking.

'That's not good,' said Ben.

'Earthquake?' Kirsten looked closely at Ben's troubled face.

He shrugged. 'I don't think so.'

A glass danced across the table and plunged off the edge to explode across the floor. Eleanor looked up. Around the room, pictures clattered against the wood panelling. Rising cautiously from the arm chair she crossed the floor of the house, quickened her pace and burst out into the garden beyond.

'Did you feel it?' asked Eleanor.

Hanna and Alice turned to her face her. *Yes, yes they have.*

'It's started.' Eleanor nodded; looking from her friends to the wider hills beyond.

'That was a volcano?' Alice's question was mostly rhetorical.

'I think so,' said Hanna. 'We get these, from time to time. It's not unusual.'

The jeep lurched to a halt, spinning gravel out from beneath the tyres. Inside the cab, Kathryn and Nils fell back into their seats. They turned to face each other. Glancing into the rear view mirror Nils saw the reflection of the land behind tremble. A noise like thunder rumbled out of the mountains.

'Shit!' Níls jumped down from the jeep.

Kathryn joined him. Beyond the next ridge, far up over the vast Vatnajókull glacier, ash billowed into the sky.

William kicked back his chair and crossed the room to the window. He stepped out onto the decking that surrounded the mountain hut. The thunderous rumble had faded and the tremors had eased. In the valley, between slopes of iridescent colours and the breaking cliff face of lava, people had stopped to stare up at the mountains.

'What the hell?'

William returned to the hut, pausing with his hand on the cold aluminium of the door handle before going straight to his laptop. Tapping into his university pages he brought up the seismic chart, and the distinct and sudden readings. He grabbed his pen and began to make notes and work through equations.

A thunderous roar echoed around the council chamber. Round faces argued every position into the rocks they sat on. Clothed in garments of seal skin, their fingers adorned with silver work, the þurs elders were days - weeks or months maybe - from any decision being reached.

'Four point five.' Bjäkk called out as he pulled shut the door to his office. He crossed the roadway and grassy bank to where Ben and Kirsten were waiting.

'Definitely a volcano. Up on Vatnajókull. You should hear the radio traffic - it's a buzz,' Bjäkk continued.

'Don't tempt him,' joked Kirsten. She nudged Ben in the ribs.

Eleanor broke away from her friends and tore across the yard to a stile into the field at the back of the old farm. Slipping over the uneven ground and grassy hummocks she arrived at the side of the pond with a surface of mirrored water. She stopped and lingered for a moment on the bank. She heard the call of her name carried on the wind and glanced back towards the house. Hanna and Alice could only just be seen, flashes of colour that worked their way through the garden.

Eleanor turned back to the pool and looked down into the clear water. She saw Jóhanna and a little drummer boy. Jóhanna was beckoning. Eleanor jumped; and as she leapt through the air, time slowed. Legs bent, her feet splashed down through the water and her body followed.

Instead of sinking deep into a murky pool, Eleanor found herself pass through the water and out the other side where the world seemed to swirl about her until she landed, with a jolt and bended knees amongst the long, lush grass. Glancing up she watched the dissipating ripples of water across the surface of the pool in which she now saw Hanna and Alice looking down at her.

'It worked.'

Looking about, Eleanor found herself in a world that echoed her own in so many ways yet was subtly different in so many others. Gazing out over the fields and flat pastures all the way down to the sea, men and women worked the land and tended to their cattle. In the yard children were playing, and there, standing beside her, was Jóhanna. Without a word Jóhanna disappeared around the corner of a house. Eleanor followed.

Driving defensively down out of the mountain roads, Bjäkk steered for the centre of the road and breached the single-track bridge that spanned the wide chasm with the small but gurgling stream. The jeep lurched almost to a stop as he leaned on the brakes and swerved around recent rock fall in the middle of the road.

River water surged and spun around the monster wheels of Níls' jeep as he forded the crossing and drove himself and Kathryn along a road that was little more than a beach to the fast flowing mountain river before it tacked back up the dark, gravelly, volcanic slope. Braking suddenly, Níls brought the vehicle to a halt.

'Why have we stopped?' asked Kathryn.

Níls silenced her with a wave of his hand. 'Listen,' he said.

Thunder rumbled across a sky flaked with cloud.

'Another eruption?' asked Kathryn rhetorically.

'I think not. Still part of the same one.' Níls was guarded. 'Come. We must get to Professor Tyndale.'

Kicking out stones from the loose road surface, the wheels spun as the engine growled under acceleration. The jeep lurched forward and climbed to the top of the moraine.

Eleanor was taken through the house to a vestibule beyond the parlour and to a staircase which was revealed behind a large wooden trapdoor. The young alfar who accompanied Eleanor gestured for her to descend. Eleanor's curiosity outweighed any hesitance and fears as to where she may be heading and with the dry, flaked wood beneath her fingers, Eleanor descended the ladder-like stairs into a dimly lit cellar beneath the house. Stooping slightly to avoid banging her head on the low ceiling, she crossed the uneven stone-flagged and partially-boarded floor.

As Eleanor followed her instincts down the dark, occasionally candlelit corridor, footsteps resounded across the floorboards above her head. Occasionally small pockets of sand and dust caught in the crevices exploded and cascaded down. Finally, at the end of the corridor, she reached a door, fastened with a wooden latch. She knocked lightly and pulled back the bar. The door creaked on stiff wooden hinges and Eleanor stepped forward.

The room opened out into a larger space, lit by candles and the light from a blazing fire in a stone opening. Immediately, Eleanor recognised the tall, slender figure of Jóhanna, silhouetted against the fire, in conversation with another fair-haired lady. Eleanor knew instinctively who this lady was, even before she was introduced. The lady turned and beckoned Eleanor closer, her face half in shadow and half lit by the fire light.

'Solveig?' asked Eleanor.

2

Light from the single window at the end of the dormitory attic room cast sharp shadows deep into the corners. Most of the space on the two enormous bunks – one down each side of the room – was taken up with Professor Tyndale's scientific equipment. Both William and Nils were busy connecting the computers and climatic processors together.

Kathryn surveyed the room. She remembered the drab lectures back in Southampton; this, now, was a proper research lab on the frontier of new discoveries; taking over the upper floor of a hostel in the process. Her gaze settled on a box of antennae dishes and cables. She grabbed them and squeezed past the professor. Throwing open the window, Kathryn climbed out gazelle-like, onto the roof with aerials slung over her shoulder and wires between her teeth.

Exposed on the roof, her legs straddling the ridge, Kathryn felt the full biting cold of the wind as it blew in across the dark, shadowy, pitted lava-field. She strapped the radio receiver to the chimney and twisted at the screws with numb fingers.

She stopped. Out of the corner of her eye she had seen something. She looked again, across the lava field at the twisting turning pathways along which dark shapes moved. At first she took them for hikers heading back home after a day's walking; but no, she could see them now. They were not like any human hiker she had ever seen. Some were half naked and clothed only in roughly-fashioned leather jerkins and tunics of heavy cotton. She pulled her binoculars from the pouch on her belt and narrowed her gaze on them. They worked amongst the rocks; barefoot and nimble.

'William!' Kathryn called out and immediately wished she hadn't.

William's head poked out from the attic window. The strange creatures amongst the lava field vanished, shyly retreating into the dark corners and caves.

'Nothing,' Kathryn answered.

Professor Tyndale smiled and ducked back inside the room. Kathryn turned back to the mountains to scour the pathways and outcrops for any sign of movement.

'Let me look at you.' Solveig reached out to Eleanor. 'I see it in you my child. The power burns strongly within you.'

Eleanor winced. 'You mean – elven power – the alfar?'

Solveig nodded solemnly and drew Eleanor in to sit with her by the fire. 'Do you understand, Eleanor?'

Eleanor shrugged. She cast her gaze about her. The subterranean room was in a time and a world that was distinctly separate and yet linked in some way to her own. She returned a questioning gaze.

'You are my ancestor. You married into the alfar people and – and—' Eleanor stumbled over the words. 'Somehow I can do things that my brother would say with his scientific reasoning were impossible.'

Solveig nodded slowly and reached for an iron poker with which to stoke the fire. She dislodged the logs and prodded at the embers. The burning wood spat and the sap crackled and hissed.

'Your family dismissed my existence and forgot all but my name.'

Eleanor recognised the truth in Solveig's words.

'That, Eleanor, is not the whole story.'

Solveig allowed her words to linger in the dimly-lit cellar room. She controlled the pace of the exchange between herself and Eleanor. Her piercing blue eyes burned as brightly as the fire she stoked.

'See how the embers burn, my child.'

Eleanor looked to the grate. She saw in the fire, the flames that burned and the orange glow of the embers with the dark black shapes of the remaining wood. In them she saw a land of dark hills and burning fire. She saw the land burn and people living in the land.

'Your family?' Eleanor asked.

'Our family,' answered Solveig.

Kathryn left the technical conversation between William and Níls behind her as she crept downstairs into the spacious hall that smelt of wet walking boots and dripping jackets. Retrieving her boots from the shelf by the door, she slipped them on and pulled on her coat. Minutes later she was leaving heading out towards the lava field and feeling for her torch in her pocket in the lowering light.

Uncertain of exactly what she sought, Kathryn was certain that stealth was of the utmost importance. She placed her feet carefully, as she ascended the steep wall of twisted lava into the maze of paths and channels of the field proper.

Eleanor was transfixed by Solveig's words as she conjured scenes from history in the grate of the fire. Silhouettes of men moved quickly, working the land, whilst children played and danced by a house.

Eleanor turned to her storyteller. 'How did you meet?'

They sat in the cellar room of the old farm by the flickering light of the fire. Occasionally footsteps clunked about overhead, and small releases of dust wafted down from the ceiling onto the boarded floor.

'Like you, I believed in the old stories. I wanted to meet with the huldufolk. Our worlds are as joined as they are separate. I met my love and that was it.'

'And the þurs people?'

'They live in our world too, but they cannot cross over into yours as we can.'

'But,' began Eleanor, 'I think I've seem them. I'm sure—'

'Shadows,' explained Solveig, 'Echoes from this world into yours.'

Silence lingered heavily in the air. Solveig held Eleanor's attention with a single look. 'People in your world do not see the shadows from other worlds because they do not have the time to look for them. But they are there. As are we.'

'Before though—' Eleanor remembered a detail. 'When I was in the mountains and Gunnlaugr sent me to fetch those rune stones from the trolls. The þurs – they had a way to cross over. A bridge. I used it to get back...'

'The Bifrost,' said Solveig, 'Yes, it is an ancient path.'

'They – the þurs had a silver cup and some rune stones. I stole them.' Eleanor felt the need to make her confession, 'I'm sorry. Gunnlagur asked me and I didn't know any different.'

Eleanor was held in Solveig's steely gaze. She shivered as a cold draught brushed past her.

'I'm sorry,' said Eleanor, 'Did I do wrong?'

'You gave the rune stones to Gyrdir, yes?'

Eleanor nodded. 'I really am sorry. If I'd known...'

'And the cup?'

'No.' Eleanor shook her head. Looking at Solveig, she did not see surprise in the old woman's face. 'I don't know why, but I kept that. It didn't seem necessary – he only wanted the rune stones – I've got it back–' Her voice stopped as she remembered. 'I mean, upstairs in this house in my own time – my own world...'

Solveig said nothing. Eventually she stood, slowly, and unsteadily crossed the room. Her still slender figure was bent with age. She moved to a table upon which stood a copper pan with a wooden lid. She beckoned to Eleanor.

As Eleanor stepped up next to her, Solveig removed the wooden lid to reveal a shallow pan of water that was still and mirror like.

'See.' Solveig directed Eleanor to watch closely. With her long fingers she flicked the surface of the water and watched the surface ripple outwards and reflect back inwards.

Tiny waves crossed the small pool in the copper pan; and pictures swirled in the water. Images – fragments of the past – formed themselves into visions of reality. Eleanor found herself looking down into a room, lit by an oil lamp. A man; a father is sat on a bench hunched over a piece of bone, carving it with a steel blade. At his feet, children played. They arranged small tablets of stone – or bone – on the earth floor and pushed them around in some variation of a game of dominos. Certain moves brought rewards and the winning child snatched his counters. Eleanor looked deeper into the vision and at the runes carved into the tablets. She gasped.

The vision was gone but Eleanor continued to stare into the pool of water, and wait for more. Solveig replaced the lid.

'You saw, yes?' asked Solveig.

Eleanor looked up into the old lady's eyes. 'The rune stones?'

'A child's game.' Solveig smiled thinly. 'We still play it. A variation of it.'

'Gunnlaugr – Gyrdir – wanted a child's toy?'

Solveig shook her head.

'I don't think he knew what form the key to the Bifrost took. He knew it was crafted by the alfar and was now in the þursar world. It's the cup, Eleanor. Do you understand now, how you use it?'

Even before Eleanor could answer, Solveig reached out her hand and lay it on Eleanor's cheek. 'Understand Eleanor.' She spoke the words softly and locked Eleanor's sight in her own.

'And go now. You know what is needed.'

Hanna strummed her fingers across the strings; fingering chords. She tried words, allowing her mood, her instincts and the tune to carry her. She sat forward, stopping occasionally to put down lyrics into her notebook. Across the room, Alice sat in an armchair poring over the old family journal, tracing words and ideas into her Moleskine.

Last night;
you took me in your arms.
You said my name;
you told me the word
I told you.

Hanna winced and struck the strings again, teasing the rhythm out of the guitar. She looked up and stared across the room at nothing and allowed her fingers to move as they pleased. She found a phrase. She repeated it. And again. She smiled and noted it down.

Down the hallway there was a fumbling at the latch and the old, weather-warped front door was pushed and cajoled open with an accompanying creaking and groaning. Voices echoed across the threshold; footsteps down the hall...

'Eleanor?' Alice cast her book aside and made for the door. She was followed by Hanna, clutching her guitar at the neck.

Ben and Kirsten entered the lounge followed by Bjäkk.

'Oh. You're back already.' Alice winced.

'So where's Eleanor?' asked Ben. His voice is tinged with suspicion and annoyance. 'My sister hasn't gone missing again has she?'

His words hung in the room, with the stale odour that wafted throughout the old house. Alice looked to Hanna.

'Not exactly, no,' said Hanna.

'We met with Finnur again, in Reykjavik,' began Alice, 'and then with this woman – she ended up being one of the elves. That's when we came back here. Jóhanna – the alfar – she had something to show Ellie ?'

'Show her? Show her what? Where's my sister?'

'Umm, with Jóhanna,' said Alice, 'But it's fine.'

Hanna stepped up to her cousin. 'It is. It seems that Jóhanna is our family too.'

Bjäkk stepped across the decking and looked out across the meadows to the hills beyond at the far end of the bay. He pulled a crumpled cigarette packet from his back pocket and cupped his hands to light a cigarette. He drew on the smoke.

Behind him wisps of smoke drifted upwards from the chimney. He looked out. Birds swooped low over the meadow.

How will they react to this changing land? Do they feel it when the earth growls beneath the ground and vents its energy? But wait? There in the grass? What's that?

Bjäkk called out Hanna's name and threw his cigarette to the ground as he jumped down the steps and sprinted across the garden and the wall at the end of it. Behind him, Hanna and Ben and the others were on the deck and following him, as he landed in the meadow, on his knees, at Eleanor's side.

She lay peacefully, sleeping. Gently, Bjäkk leant over her and touched her cheek. He checked her pulse. The others arrived alongside him and Ben fell to the ground at his sister's side and took her in his arms. She blinked her eyes awake. Before Ben could speak, Eleanor silenced him.

'We have to go back into the mountains.' Eleanor said with the determination. 'This time I need your help.' Eleanor looked beyond her brother and cousin to her friends, and to Bjäkk. 'All of your help.'

Upstairs in the bedroom, Eleanor stood over her bag. She pulled open her rucksack and threw her clothes onto the bed and delved into the rucksack for the carved silver cup. In doing so, her hand touched something else. She returned to her bag and brought out the buckle. She shrugged and gathered both items up before heading downstairs and going to join her friends outside on the deck.

Eleanor sat with the cup before her. Alice looked on as Hanna examined its carvings and its construction; in wonderment of it and confused by her own legends.

'I've never heard of this...?' admitted Hanna.

Eleanor stared at the cup. 'I thought it was the runes that were important. But the cup?' She shrugged. 'I guess I just thought it'd make a good souvenir.'

Eleanor took the buckle up in her hands and flipped it into the air, catching it in her palm. 'And to think I thought this was what held the magic!'

Hanna looked up from the box towards her cousin.

'So how does it work?' asked Alice.

Alice thrust a big glass jug under the tap and twisted the tap. The pipes gurgled and spluttered around the house; the tap physically jolted forward as it coughed out first dregs, then running water, stained with an orangey-brown mist. She carried the jug carefully outside for all to see and couldn't help but smirk as she spoke.

'Pure, clear, Icelandic water, yeah?' Alice shook her head.

'Anyone got bottled water left?' asked Eleanor.

'Not pure enough,' said Ben, 'The additives that they put in. Sure it's clear, but it's not so much pure.'

Bjäkk lifted his gaze from the jug of discoloured water. 'Wait. I have an idea.' He clambered to his feet and stomped into the house, returning after a few minutes with a bottle still frosty with condensation.

'Pure Icelandic water yeah? That should do you.'

Alice took the bottle and looked to the label. Characteristically black, with the bold sans-serif lettering on it. Brennivin. She looked up at Bjäkk and shook her head.

'Black Death?' exclaimed Alice, 'Are you serious?'

'So it's 40% proof, but it's still water,' Bjäkk said, 'It's still the clearest you'll get.'

'I guess it's worth a try.' Eleanor took the bottle from Bjäkk. She smirked as she unscrewed the cap and began to pour.

'I can't believe that you are actually pouring a bottle of schnapps into a silver cup!' Kirsten said.

Eleanor placed the cup down in front of her and waited for the surface to stop shimmering. As a perfect mirror presented itself she leant over it to look directly into the vessel and waited.

'What are you...?' Alice began to ask, but Eleanor shushed her, concentrating all the time on the cup of still water.

3

As a large, orange sun sank low over the horizon it cast ripples of colour across the bay. The sunset was broken only by thin streaks of clouds. On the decking Eleanor sat with the cup in front of her. She stared into the water, seeing herself reflected back in the perfectly still surface. Around her, her friends were silent, watching her, waiting for it to happen. Eleanor continued to sit and watch and wait. Still nothing.

'At least it's a nice evening for it,' mused Ben.

Eleanor glanced up and shot her brother a glowering stare.

The sun sank lower, and below the cloud; rays of rich orange light filled the sky, and reflected on the windows of the old house; and round the rim of the cup.

Looking down, Eleanor saw an orange disc in the cup that shimmered a little, and the delicate, razor-thin lines sparkled in the sunlight. Around the outside of the cup the etched design, a pattern of swirls and knots was illuminated, and reflections of the design bounced back onto Eleanor's hands and the ground around it.

Across the valley shadows lengthened, slowly and patiently as the sun sunk lower in the sky so the light in the cup burned brighter. Eleanor was caught in awe, unable to comment, as the light radiated out and refracted through the purity of the water within, like a multitude of rainbows. Shining out, first across hands and faces, the rays of light and beams of miniature rainbows converged on the wall of an outhouse. Eleanor snatched glances at the wall, hardly daring to take her eyes off the cup. The others stepped a little closer to look.

Where the light had radiated now there showed an outline of lines on the wall. Within the outline, more lines, words even; and symbols.

'It's Iceland.' Alice leapt up excitedly, looking at the dancing, glistening shapes on the walls.

'It's true,' agreed Bjäkk.

'You can see every fjord – see.' Hanna gazed upon the map.

Eleanor glanced away from the wall to look again at the cup. She inspected the design etched to its outside and saw that where she had seen before a random collection of patterns, now she could see how from their reflections to create the map.

Ben lurched suddenly from his place and delved his hand into the cold remains of the barbecue for a stub of charcoal and dived towards the wall. Keeping low, spread out on the deck so as to minimise any blocking of the light he began to trace the design onto the wall. Kirsten backed slowly towards the barbecue and chose her stick of charcoal. She approached Ben and joined him on the floor to trace the intricate western coastline. Close to the coast she drew a star onto the concrete to mark where a particular intensity of light had fallen.

'It's a proper treasure map,' said Eleanor. She scrambled to her feet and pointed, commenting to Alice who was now stood beside her.

'It's weird how this house has all the right angles to reveal it.' Alice tapped the decking with her foot.

'I guess it just happens that it fits to here.' Eleanor shrugged. 'Ben would know better.'

Ben glanced up. 'The relative angles from the sun. Yeah, it wouldn't be unique but it is damn lucky.'

'Or coincidence.' Alice mused.

As they sketched the dark stains of charcoal to the map the sun sank lower and the light faded. The last of the strokes were added to the wall as the light finally left them.

Eleanor sat amongst her friends and family on the decking in the half light of a sunken sun. The colours of day were bleached. They sat and stared at the map sketched on the wall. Footsteps echoed across the deck. Bjäkk returned from the house; a collection of shot glasses in hand. Eleanor looked curiously at him.

'What?' Bjäkk shrugged. 'It's a shame to see a good drink go to waste.' He began to scoop out shots of the alcohol from the silver cup.

'We have done good work here, I think.' Bjäkk raised his glass; nodded. 'Skull.'

Around the group, the others raised their glasses, each with varying amounts of enthusiasm and trepidation.

'Skull.'

They downed their shots. The cold liquor burned at the back of their throats, but its effect was not entirely unpleasant.

'We can't leave it like this.'

Ben looked towards to his sister.

'If it rains.' Eleanor nodded towards the wall. 'It's only charcoal. Even if it doesn't go completely then we still won't be able to read it.'

Silence. One by one they turned to look again at the wall and the map.

'Not just that either,' said Alice.

Heads turned and eyes stared at her.

'What's up there, yeah,' continued Alice, 'It's some great secret – it's been hidden all this time and we've exposed it. We can't leave it like that, that's for sure.'

'Alice is right,' says Hanna, 'The alfar directed us to this, but there are others out there who shouldn't have this information. And if there's one thing I've never been more certain of, it's that we've awoken something – stirred the interest. We will be watched and people will come here and look for us and see what we've done.'

Ben shook his head dismissively. 'You can't know all of that cous—'

Hanna Katla glared at her over-analytically minded cousin. 'Maybe not, Ben. But can we really take that risk?'

'Gyrdir,' said Bjäkk, 'He will come.'

Eleanor turned towards Bjäkk, as did the others.

'How do you know of Gyrdir?' asked Hanna.

'I work in the north, Hanna. I hear the stories of the mountains and of the people who roam the wilderness at night. Gyrdir will come.' Without waiting for any reply, Bjäkk, turned and crossed the deck to enter the house.

A few moments later he returned, passed Eleanor her digital camera and directed her towards the wall. As she began taking pictures Bjäkk circled the group, handing them each paintbrushes and rollers that he had found in the house. Lastly he turned to the collection of dented, stained tins of paint. Crouching by them, he attacked the lids with screwdrivers and prised them open. Ben soon joined him, with sticks he had found, jabbing them down into the skin that had formed on the surface and stirring up the semi-liquid paint.

'Dad's going to so love us...' Hanna shook her head, looking at the shades of colour, and beginning to imagine the mess that they were going to make.

'But Bjäkk's right,' voiced Eleanor as she spread out her pitiful amount of paint across the wall. 'They will come. If not Gunnlaugr, then something.'

Ben looked to his sister. 'We'll leave first thing in the morning.'

Eleanor shook her head, but it was Bjäkk who spoke. 'We should leave now.'

Silence. There was no answer to the grim mood that had overtaken them. Quietly painting away at the bottom of the wall, Alice pushed paint into the crevices with a stiff and ruined brush. She slapped watery paint across the surface.

'Where will we go?' asked Alice.

Eleanor began to wonder herself. She turned and looked with wide, searching eyes at her cousin, and to Bjäkk

The wind picked up, gusting across the valley. Darkness spread out across the landscape, enveloping corners in darker shadow. Within the house, Eleanor and her friends moved urgently, packing their belongings any which way they could and running from the porch door to the two jeeps to stow their gear.

'Alice, what are you doing?!' Kirsten demanded as she paused by the door to the old shop. Alice was packing books into old apple crates.

Alice turned; smiling innocently.

'We don't know what's important. We have to take everything remotely useful with us.'

'We haven't got time,' Kirsten pleaded.

Bjäkk lingered for a moment as he rushed past the door. 'We can't afford not to.' He switched his gaze from Kirsten to Alice. 'Good work.'

Rain swept across the front yard, in gusts of vigorous wind. The front gate swung on its hinges, clattering constantly on the latch. Ben ran, head down into the driving wet and flung bags into the back of the jeep under the tarpaulin. He slammed the tail-gate back up and ran again for the house, passing Hanna on her way out.

The sky split open with light before being plunged into darkness again. The valley resounded in thunder. Hanna ran back to the house. Slamming the door shut behind her, she pulled back the hood of her coat and wiped away the rain from her face.

'We can't go driving in this,' said Hanna, 'It's madness.'

Bjäkk answered with cold honesty. 'We don't have a choice.'

Hanna shrugged. She had voiced her opinion; now she looked to the others.

'I think Bjäkk's right.' Eleanor spoke cautiously, 'But I'm not the right person to judge danger am I?'

'We should ride out the storm here,' said Ben, 'We don't know what the road's like—'

'A week ago I would have agreed with you.' Alice cut across Ben's words. 'But we've seen things. We've all seen things that we can't explain. If Eleanor and Bjäkk sense there's a danger coming then I say we go.'

'When we were driving down – wasn't there a service station – guesthouse place?' asked Kirsten, 'If we got as far as there – it's still not late – we could stay the night. Then go on in the morning.'

Hanna looked towards her cousin. Ben remained silent, and whilst still seemingly troubled by the suggestion, looked to be relenting. He looked up and caught her gaze, and she felt the weight of responsibility.

Eventually, relenting, she allowed herself to answer. 'It's an option.'

The engine growled beneath the bonnet and the windscreen wipers pushed channels of water across the glass. The headlights cast beams of light onto the half-timbered, half-concrete front of the service station. A neon light swayed erratically in the wind. Hanna pulled out her phone and flipped up the lid. Glancing across briefly at Eleanor and round at Alice in the back seat, she thumbed through the numbers and hit dial.

Diana paced the kitchen of her brother-in-law's Reykjavik home, listening in to her husband's half of the phone call. Guðni lapsed between English and Icelandic, asking questions, gathering information and pursuing answers. Diana prompted questions continually; almost snatching the phone away for a moment, were it not for Guðni's measured actions and calming tone. After a while he switched completely into Icelandic, an often practised skill for maintaining secrecy and playing back a composed series of events.

Hanging up the phone, he barely had time to step back across the hall before he was pounced upon by his wife, insistent to know every last detail as to what was happening.

'What's our daughter up to now?' snapped Diana.

'It was Hanna I spoke to,' Guðni attempted to calm his wife, leading her to the kitchen table where he poured another mug of coffee. 'They've left the old house. Driving north apparently – some mission...' He explained how they'd joined up with an old friend of Hanna's; that they would keep in contact; but that Ben was after some scientific discovery.

Diana stared into her husband's eyes. 'Ben?' She shook her head.

Guðni remained silent. He knew exactly what Diana was inferring and he agreed. A smile drew over his face. Kids; he mused.

'It could be something to with Ben's project. The weather conditions that we've been having – it could be true–'

'You don't believe that.'

Guðni frowned and shook his head slowly. 'No.'

Hanna sat in front of her jeep, holding her phone in her hand, staring at the display: call ended. She sighed, tears forming in her eyes. She clutched at her face and tried to compose herself.

'I can't lie at the best of times.' She looked across at her cousin. 'And your Dad. He's the worst. There's no way he believed me.'

The guesthouse sign swung in the wind, beaten this way and that by the rain. Lightning flashed and thunder rolled down the valley. In the sky above, clouds moved, dark greys and shadowy blues, pitted against cavernous wells of black swirls. Faces formed and figures wrestled and fought in the dark shadows of a fractured sky.

Finally, Hanna cut the engine and clicked off the lights. For a moment or two longer she remained seated in the jeep with Eleanor and Alice. Again, she sighed.

'Let's get out of this cursed weather.'

The old farm sat on the edge of the wide, flat valley. Along the shore, waves crashed, churning up sand and shingle. Along the road, a single car made its way. Across the fields at the back of the farm, dark figures stalked. Eyes burned brightly and the slender figures climbed the walls to encircle the house. Untroubled by the wind and the rain, they appeared at windows, crawling out from the darkest of shadows; more and more they came.

Glass broke and shattered inwards onto the floor. Wind gusted through and blew the curtains into the room. Svart-alfar, clad in black, climbed in and stole further into the house, sniffing all the time as they searched every corner.

Outside, Gyrdir stood tall against the wind and stared at the freshly painted, erratically coloured wall of the outhouse. A svart-alpha leader approached Gyrdir.

Hanna and Ben returned to the dimly lit breakfast room of the guesthouse with mugs of steaming, potent smelling hot chocolate. They set them down at the table in the corner lit by a single table lamp, around which were seated Eleanor, Kirsten, Alice and Bjäkk. Behind them windows rattled in the wind; and a chill draught crept in through the walls of the old building.

Hanna Katla moved her chair slightly to reposition herself alongside Eleanor and saw on Ben's laptop the photographs of the map painted on the house wall.

'So what have we decided?' asked Hanna, 'Where does the map lead us?'

Eleanor laughed. 'You're not going to believe this!' She pulled out a map of Iceland and lay it across the keyboard and began to trace her finger over the northern Highlands and then pointed out parts of the map in the photograph.

'You see these symbols? They correspond to the area where I was lost – and here – if I'm not mistaken this is where they are building that new aluminium plant.'

Hanna glanced over at Ben, who reacted with an expression of incredulousness equal to her own.

'The proposals for that development that I found – it did look odd,' said Hanna.

'And Gunnlaugr.' Eleanor stared. 'Gyrdir – whatever his name is – I know we can't trust him but he did say that these people were damaging the Bifrost.'

'And the huldufolk.' Hanna added.

Silence. They sat around the table considering the maps in front of them. Alice eventually reached out and turned the laptop to face her; staring into the map.

'So we know where we have to go. And I guess we have to stop this factory being built.' Alice bit on her lip. 'But what can we do?'

Gunnlaugr stood on the road above Hanna Katla Baldursdóttir's family home. Below him, he watched the house and the flames that burnt within. As he watched the roof collapsed inwards on itself and the house exploded. Sparks flew and metalwork twisted, warped and melted. The svart-alfar retreated, away from the carnage that was left at the head of the valley. Gunnlaugr smiled, thinly.

Kirsten turned over in her bed, back to the room and pulled the covers up round her chin; snuggling. 'Good night Alice.' Her tone was firm and signalled the end of the conversation.

Alice giggled from across the room and shot a conspiratorial look of amusement at Eleanor.

'Goodnight sister-in-law...' Eleanor added gleefully; and laughed.

Behind the cover of bedding, Kirsten smiled wistfully.

The sky flared with light; and a noise like thunder rolled round the mountains and continued to roll across ridges and down valleys.

The window banged; the glass trembled in the frame. A glass of water fell from the bedside cabinet. It smashed on the floor; a pool of water that exploded outwards.

Laughter ceased. Kirsten sat up again. Alice stared at the broken glass on the floor. Both turned and looked up at the dormer window, and Eleanor and Hanna did the same. Climbing from their beds they padded barefoot to the window, they pulled back the curtain to stare up at the mountain behind. Nothing but the night and dark clouds thrown across the sky by the wind could be seen.

'Did you hear it?' Ben was at the open doorway, looking in on the girls in the room. His question was rhetorical. Kirsten pulled down her T-shirt, preserving some modesty. She stepped back across her room and ushered Ben out, reassuring him that they were okay; and that they could talk in the morning.

'We are safe here – where we are going?' Alice's voice was tinged with concern.

'Here, yes.' Hanna responded reassuringly, 'And we won't go anywhere where there's any risk.' She shot a confirming glance across at Eleanor.

Kirsten crouched beside her bed, carefully picking up the pieces of glass. 'It is scary though. All of it.' She stood and looked back across the room at her friends. 'The volcanoes. Gunnlaugr. The world's falling apart – all of it. It's all scary.'

4

Dark swells of ash billowed upwards, choking out the half light of early morning. In the sky, a helicopter flew over, circling the black cloud as it filled and pushed on upwards, shrouding the top of the mountain from view.

Miles away, nearer a quieter western shore, a light wind blew in from sea across the valley. On the edge of the gravel forecourt with its weather-beaten, salt-aged carcasses of gas pumps was the smoking remains of the old farm. Fragile relics of a wooden frame stood open to the sky and blackened sheets of corrugated iron hung precarious and lonely. Within the footprint of the house, piles of ash were heaped with the stinking, charred remains of the house. Soot blew finely in the wind and drifting smoke stained the air.

*

Live pictures of the eruption were broadcast on a flickering television screen. Ben and Eleanor and the others sat around with their breakfast watching it in the dining hall of the guesthouse. Ben sat with his hands clasped around his coffee mug unable to take his eyes off the screen.

'I said to my mates that this was going to be a holiday of lifetime.' Alice laughed nervously. 'I couldn't have been more right!'

'Volcanoes doing this – it's not uncommon,' said Hanna. 'This one though, it does seem – well – we have been expecting something big.'

'You can't think that this is a natural thing though...?' said Eleanor.

Hanna gaped, and even Ben turned his head. 'How do you mean?' he said.

Eleanor pulled out the map of the highlands together with the illustrations in the morning's paper. Lastly she grabbed the photo of the map they painted on the wall of the old farm.

'Don't you see? It's the same place.'

Kirsten picked up the map. 'It is, you know. The same volcano...'

'Ben?' Eleanor glared at her brother. 'You've got to agree this time? The link, it proves something.'

'It proves the random shifts of probability, yes,' Ben analysed.

Eleanor sighed. She turned to Hanna and Alice. 'I sometimes wonder if my brother would accept that I existed if it wasn't for my birth certificate. Else I may be an example of random shared belief.' She shook her head. 'It is the same volcano. The aluminium plant, Gunnlaugr's hideout, the alfar map? It's clear.'

Eleanor crossed the floor of the guesthouse reception hall and stepped out into the fresh new day. Ben was already there, stowing bags into the two jeeps, and chatting with Alice and Kirsten.

'Today's the day then?' Alice asked rhetorically.

'You think?' laughed Ben.

Eleanor grabbed Ben by the arm and pulled him round to face her. 'The Þurs people started this for me. It's time I met with them again.'

'And you think that's safe?' asked Ben.

'The Bifrost hasn't broken yet.' Eleanor nodded. 'I have to try.'

'I wasn't talking about the Bifrost.' Ben gestured to the mountains. 'Out there, the mountains are tearing themselves apart. Toxic gasses are spewing into the atmosphere and you want us to go on a journey underground?!!'

Eleanor stood, silent, and simply looked at her brother. She found it hard to comprehend how, even now, he refused to see what she had for so long seen.

'He has a point you know,' said Kirsten.

Eleanor turned to face her.

'Your brother,' Kirsten continued, 'how many times have you almost died in the last month? How does he explain this to your parents?'

Eleanor stood still. She heard what Kirsten said and she did understand.

'It's difficult, Kirsten. What I know and what I feel – I do see how it can seem to be more of a story, but also I have seen these things. It is real. I can't not help.'

Charles Ancel sat behind the wheel and pressed the ball of his pen down onto the clipboard to sign off the paperwork. He passed it to Kári. 'Keep drilling. We can't allow anything to delay the opening of the Thermo-Tunnel.'

Kári nodded.

'What we are doing here is no longer a secret.' Charles' voice was filled with distaste. 'Questions are now being raised in government and across Europe. They want us to stop construction; to look at the plans *again*—'

Kári shook his head. 'Haven't they already been through all the necessary consultations? I thought they had held the public enquiries and heard representations from these spurious environmental groups already?'

'Quite so. We took the plans through every hoop they asked of us and they flagged it through. Well enough is enough,' Charles continued, 'the thermo tunnel must open on time. We simply cannot afford any more delays.'

'It won't be easy. After last night, we lost another twenty men,' said Kári, 'you can see why. They have families. We are working in the shadow of volcanic activity. It's a risk...'

'And the others?' Charles Ancell knew the numbers of staff on his payroll and he knew that twenty men were easily replaceable.

'Still with us, at the moment,' Kári confirmed. 'If we make an adjustment to overtime payments we can secure them for as long as needed.'

Charles nodded. He waved through the suggestion and looked up at the construction site through the windscreen. The gaunt steel rig was rapidly taking shape around the cavernous opening to the Thermo-Tunnel.

A helicopter pushed on upwards over a ridge and dipped again, ducking down over the valley beyond. William watched from the valley floor. He glanced round, at the live TV footage which Níls had hooked into on the laptop. Cameras trained on the ground beneath showed the thick smoke and steam venting from the mountain.

'Nils, you're too good. How do you get connected to these networks?'

'It's easy. Journalists – the TV companies are the worst – they never secure their networks.'

William glanced round the valley, as more vans and jeeps with their satellite dishes and cameras arrived. He laughed. 'Looks like we won't be short of choice, then!'

Eleanor stood with Ben, Kirsten and Alice in a car park by the quayside at the edge of Akureyri, as Bjäkk climbed up into Hann's jeep and they drove off together.

'Where are they off to, again?' asked Alice.

'Food,' Eleanor replied, 'for up in the mountains. So what shall we do in the meantime?'

'I guess,' said Alice, 'I wonder if that little hot dog stand is still there. They were delish—'

They began to wander back onto the road and into town. It didn't take long. Two blocks later they were standing at the top end of the high street. Eleanor stepped on ahead with Ben, and Kirsten dropped back with Alice. She watched Eleanor; the turn of her head; the way her arms gesticulated as she enthused over something with her brother. A memory stirred in her mind; the nod of Eleanor's head.

Kirsten nodded towards Eleanor, where she walked ahead, chatting away with Sara. The tall, long-shanked figure of Andy was next to Eleanor, his hand trailing across the small of her back.

'They are so much more than friends,' said Kirsten.

'You think,' Alice said with a grin. 'There's something sexual there?'

'Undoubtedly.'

They walked on into the centre of Akureyri.

Ahead of Kirsten, Eleanor walked on ahead with her brother.

'I owe her an apology.' Kirsten glanced at Alice, next to her.

'What, Ellie? Why?' asked Alice.

'There was nothing like that,' Kirsten said, 'not between her and Andy.'

'You think he's really dead?'

Kirsten nodded sadly. 'That's how I know that there was never anything between them.'

They crossed the street at the corner and passed a book store on their way down a pedestrianised street.

Alice laughed. She called out to Ben and Eleanor. 'I still can't get over this is a second city of a country. How long did it take us to walk here from the outskirts?'

Kirsten smiled at Alice's comment. At the end of the street was a kiosk, from which the air steamed with the smell of hot dogs, onions and mustard. Kirsten, Alice and Eleanor gathered as Ben juggled notes and coins with baps.

Andy stood amongst the groupon and took a large bite out of his hot dog. Grease and mustard smeared his lips. Kirsten saw him catch Eleanor's eye as she turned and glanced over her shoulder. She grinned and reached out to wipe away the food.

Eleanor shivered. She turned to face her friends. She looked down at her partially eaten hot dog.

'Eleanor?' asked Kirsten.

Eleanor started; awakening from a dream.

'You okay?' Kirsten repeated, stepping closer towards her friend.

Eleanor scanned the street quickly. 'Fine. I think so.' She took a small, tentative bite from her hot dog and swallowed.

'For a moment I thought Andy was here.'

Kirsten looked to her friend, with compassion. 'You too? It's weird. In this street, it's like he should be here.'

The same street. A simpler time. Half of the dozen friends and compatriots of the holiday are gathered eating hot dogs, under a blue sky and in crisply cold air.

'I hope I can do this,' said Alice.

Andy grabbed Alice at the waist and hugged her. 'You've seen the route. It's a good track, Finnur says.'

Alice laughed. 'It's a mountain, Andy! You and Eleanor are always fell running back home. Me? I walk to the pub in the centre of Oldham if I'm feeling energetic!'

'Well, if you want to think about it like that...' Andy grinned. 'There is a pub and a round of drinks at the end of the walk–'

'Or rather a gas station and round of hot dogs...' added Eleanor.

'It always comes down to hot dogs.' Eleanor smiled as she remembered.

'Well they are the best!' Alice said.

Hanna Katla frowned. 'They're hot dogs. Snack food. Good, but–' She chortled.

Gurgling, frothing, fresh mountain spring water tumbled down the mini waterfall, bouncing over rocks, sucking and surging round the shore of lush, thick grass and breaking around stepping stones before cascading down again into the canyon to join the surging, roaring power of the melt water that formed the arterial Jökulsá á Fjöllum.

Mattocks and rakes lay beside the path and Eleanor and Kirsten and their other friends sat and lay in the grass; or, like Alice, filled their water bottles from the clear spring water.

'He can't just sit,' said Eleanor.

Kirsten glanced from Eleanor to where Andy was crouched by the cooking stove and the big aluminium pot watching the pink sticks of hot dogs boil; poking them occasionally with a pair of tongs.

'He always has to be doing something. If he's not walking – climbing some mountain, then he's – you've seen him – shifting on boulders or working on footpaths, or now cooking. I'd just wish he'd just come and sit,' Eleanor continued.

'I guess I'm a fine one to talk,' laughed Eleanor.

Kirsten smiled, sharing in the enjoyment of just sitting. She slid her feet out of her work boots and pulled her socks off, allowing her toes to scrunch and curl and feel the grass.

'Even when I'm sitting here, seemingly doing nothing,' Eleanor plucked blades of grass with her fingers, 'my mind is working, playing through the words, the stories, working out how things go.' She reached for her notebook and biro, thrusting it into the air as evidence. 'See. I can't even go out for one day heaving boulders and de-braiding eroded footpaths without having this close at hand in case of ideas.'

The conversation faltered. The quiet tumbling and gurgling of the fresh waterfall jostled with the deafening and continuous drone of the great river beneath them in the canyon floor.

'Mustard? Onions?' Andy called across the stream. She nodded and reached for the hot dog he passed to her.

'We all have our weaknesses I guess.' Kirsten considered the recent past, stroking the lines of a piece of street sculpture in the centre of Akureyri.

'Huh?' Eleanor turned her head towards her friend.

'You stepped away from the path – possibly distracted by stories – we don't know. You got lost,' said Kirsten, 'And Andy. He couldn't stand around and do nothing. If he'd stayed with us, instead of going off after you, he wouldn't have been alone in Snorri's the night of the storm—'

Kirsten stopped. Even now she couldn't bring herself to admit what had happened.

'He wouldn't have,' Eleanor said flatly.

A fork of lighting cut through the sky. The Reykjavik skyline was lit for a fraction of a second before being plunged again into darkness. Andy woke and pulled himself from his bed and approached the window to watch the storm.

Another fork of lightning lit the sky, followed almost immediately by its thunder, and there, the face in the window; sharp and angular, thinly featured. She looked in on Andy through dark eyes shrouded in black hair.

For a moment, Andy was confused as to what to do. Another strike of lightning, out across the harbour and a flare of light in the sky that rolled with thunder; he twisted up the latch and pushed open the window. The girl, clinging to the first floor ledge, climbed in, drawing up her skirt over her pale leg as she slipped into the room. She straightened up, looking beguilingly into Andy's eyes. He watched her in return, wondering who she was.

'Who...?' he breathed.

Valdís silenced Andy with a single look and kissed him softly. Andy stared at his night time visitor, who stood before him, cloaked in black. Another fork of lightning echoed by thunder and in the double flash of light that illuminated the room, he saw the points to the girl's ears poking out from beneath the long black hair.

Andy glanced out of the window, at the clouds seemingly exploding and ever-changing in shape and position. Rain hit the glass in loud percussion-like rhythm. He looked again to this elf – this alfar lady – who was before him.

'It's quite some storm, isn't it?'

Valdís stepped closer towards Andy and reached out to take his hands in hers, entwining his fingers with her own. She held him, pressed herself closer, and kissed him. A fork of lightning and a crack of thunder shook the house from top to bottom. It exploded in light and flame. Andy and Valdís were gone.

Andy lay on a bed of straw and dirt at the base of the open sided cave. The dark, spindly shape of the svart-alfar woman moved away from the shadows and approached his cold body. Looking at him with dark eyes and from behind a curtain of black hair, she stood over him, feet either side of his body. She lowered herself down and took one of his hands in her own.

Seated astride Andy's still body, Valdís stroked the sides of his face. She lowered herself closer and breathed his name. A fine mist-like condensation drifted over him and enveloped his face. It glistened slightly in the light. She repeated his name, saying it in the old language. He blinked his eyes open, choked, and breathed again.

5

Water, churned and frothed, powering down through the canyon, carving out its path from the basalt columns on either side. Stained with the colour of the rock detritus and sediment, the glacial melt water was not pretty but unrelenting. The river plunged into the pool beneath and cascaded back up, showering spray far into the air, rising like steam out of the tundra of rock and grey sand. Half a mile across the bleak plateau, the minibus with trailer hitched up behind stood alone in the small car park.

Alice dived out of the toilet hut to join Kirsten and Andy unloading rucksacks.

'There it is,' said Eleanor, stepping up behind Alice, 'Not so far away – is it, Dettifoss. But you can always hear it.'

'I'll miss it.' Alice laughed. 'It's not a beautiful thing at all – in the usual sense – but in its awesomeness–'

Alice watched the spray from afar. She turned and moved to retrieve her rucksack. As she straightened herself back up, she saw Andy, standing ready, pack shouldered, booted and jacketed, standing on one of the rocks that marked out the perimeter of the car park, staring out across the landscape beyond to where it sloped up, gently at first, to the rising peak of Krafla.

'And so to our next adventure,' said Alice. She looked round; she saw Kirsten and Eleanor; they grinned with enthusiasm for what was to come.

The end of the bridge
and you're on the way home
The end of the bridge
and you're half way there.

Hanna sat with her legs swinging from the open front door of her jeep, letting her fingers find their way across the strings. The words came to her and she sung, feeling the emotion; her fingers echoing the voice.

Beneath her feet, the ground throbbed. Above her head, a helicopter circled.

'There's that many people here now – scientists – press – we're in tents I'm afraid,' Eleanor said as she returned to the jeep, gesturing back over her shoulder, 'Ben's sorting out a pitch.'

Hanna nodded. She glanced down at her guitar and continued to try out chord combinations. She looked up again. Eleanor was back with her friends, talking.

Later that night, in the dim half-light of late-August Hanna stood by her tent gazing over towards the hut, listening to the laughter and conversation that spilt out from it on the decking. She saw Bjäkk, drinking and chatting with the guides on the decking. For a moment she remained still, watching him; before ducking down and into the mouth of the tent.

Inside, Eleanor, Alice and Kirsten were sprawled on their sleeping bags poring over the books, cross-referencing places and details again to the map.

Hanna sat down with her friends.

'How are you getting on?' asked Hanna.

Eleanor was about to answer when the ground convulsed beneath them, and the whole campsite echoed over and over to the rumbling; deep and throaty, round and back; slowly fading.

'You sure we're safe?' Alice asked nervously.

Eleanor looked to Hanna, who shrugged in response. Eleanor shrugged too. 'I think so.'

Kirsten slid her legs out from her sleeping bag and crawled from the tent, pausing to slip her feet into her boots before moving to the next tent. She slid up the zip. 'Ben, are you decent?'

The zip to the tent door was tugged upwards and Ben's head popped out. He grinned and ducked back in. Kirsten crawled inside the small two-man tent to find Ben sat, legs crossed in the centre with a flask of hot chocolate beside him, working on his laptop.

'What you working on?' Kirsten lay down next to him, glancing between the complex mathematical computer modelling and Ben's face.

'The guys out there, they've set up a wireless hub. It wasn't hard to get in.' Ben brought up his web browser. 'See, the amount of data on this eruption already on the net is amazing.'

'Anything on the last tremor yet?'

'There are message boards – yah.' Ben laughed, 'Ódinn's unhappy – *apparently*.'

Kirsten grinned. 'He might well be. If the þurs and alfar are really stirring, it wouldn't be if surprise the Gods were in on it too.'

Ben frowned. 'You've been spending too long in the company of my sister.'

Eleanor stood on the edge of the campsite staring out into the chill night and pulled her fleece round her. Behind her; the party was still going on in the hut and the car park of camper vans and 4x4s created an unearthly silhouette of shadows in the mountainscape. In front of her there was solitude; a plateau of rocks and a mere of standing water. Patches of birch scrub; it all lay before her as graduations of muted colour and shades of shadow. The rocks and the mountains beyond were darker layers still of shadow. As she gazed out, dark figures moved across the landscape, working their way round the water's edge, foraging for food. They waded out into the water, moving swiftly to pick out fish.

Eleanor stood, transfixed by people that few ever saw; too busy with their own lives, to look, to care.

'Greipur is dead.'

The voice came from her side. Eleanor jumped round to find Eirný standing next to her.

'Gyrdir killed him,' continued Eirný, 'He cares nothing for our kind.'

'How? When?' Eleanor remembered the soft lines of Greipur's face and his caring nature. 'Why?'

'Even for Gyrdir it was cruelly done,' Eirný said 'He had the svart-alfar kill him right after they burnt your uncle's farm.'

Eleanor gaped. 'The farm? Gone?'

'You left there just in time, it seems.'

Eleanor stuttered and started. 'I knew there was evil coming. I sensed it. But – but this – the farm? It's all gone?'

The ground shuddered beneath her feet and the mountain growled again.

'Gyrdir. Where is he?' Eleanor asked, urgently.

Eirný was gone. Eleanor pushed her hair back and looked this way and that. She called Eirný's name but no answer came. She shook her head, hardly believing her own eyes any more, doubting herself; had she imagined Eirný's presence? The farm? Was it really gone? Eleanor felt her toothbrush between her fingers and she remembered her purpose for crossing the campsite. She turned and made her way to the wash basins.

She stepped up onto the wooden platform and to one of the sinks next to where Kathryn stood, brushing her teeth whilst gazing up into the night. Eleanor put back her head and looked up at the sky, patched with clear sky and stars twinkling, and thick cloud; and there too, a dark stain of black smoke from the mountains.

She's suddenly aware of the girl next to her watching her. She spat toothpaste into the basin and looked back. Kathryn glanced away. Eleanor rinsed the brush through and continued. This time they both looked up. Eleanor found herself thinking that this girl was strangely familiar.

'You want something?' asked Eleanor.

Kathryn shook her head and moved away. She headed back along the decked walkway to the hut.

Radios blared and engines turned over. Hanna lay still, in the moments before sleep, and listened she picked out the individual voices from the clamour and her face twitched with curiosity.

'Hanna?' Eleanor asked from alongside her.

Hanna sat upright and pulled down the zip of her bag. She got up quickly and pushed her feet down into her boots as she stepped out of the tent in her long-johns. She passed an old, battered VW campervan and recognised it instantly.

'Jon!' The call was more of a question than anything. She broke into a run and threw herself up the steps onto the deck and round to the front door of the hut. Inside she kicked her boots off towards the racks inside the door and continued on into the kitchen. She stopped and stared. Staring back at her, in the middle of a game of cards, were her bandmates Halldór, Bryn and Jon—

The end of the bridge
and you're on the way home.
The end of the bridge
and you're half-way there.

Hanna leant into the song, her face taut with emotion; wind blowing through her hair. Alongside her Halldór fingered the chords on his electric guitar. They were flanked by Bryn, beating out the rhythm, his drum kit amongst the rocks on the ridge, and by Jon standing against the fractured sky, a silhouette with his keyboard. High up in the mountains, they were singing; words and nature bound in one.

'What are you doing here?' asked Hanna.

'We're here to take direct action,' said Bryn, as he left the table to greet Hanna, 'In the last few days it's been all over the press. What Alcon are doing up here.'

'You wouldn't believe,' said Halldór from over his coffee, 'Since the eruptions started Alcon have been in a media storm. They say there's no link and they've got scientists arguing for them – but then these others – it's one big argument.'

'Great TV.' Jon nodded.

Hanna looked up, glaring severely at Jon. 'This is a bit more serious than a TV show.'

Halldór laughed and draped his arm across Hanna's shoulders and squeezes her close. 'He knows that, don't you Jon?'

Jon nodded, mouthing a meek apology.

'It is good, very good, though,' said Halldór. 'With the succession of storms and now the eruption, people are finally taking notice.'

Eleanor crawled back into the tent, where Alice and Kirsten were already ready for bed. A burst of laughter from across the campsite echoed over to them.

'Rowdy aren't they, these scientists,' said Eleanor. 'It's some party they are having.'

'Seems somehow wrong to be partying, doesn't it?' mused Kirsten.

Alice lay in her sleeping bag, her head propped up on her arms. 'Do you remember our last-night party?'

'That was so cool. Talk about perfect endings—' remembered Kirsten.

The music blasted from a ghetto blaster echoing beyond the ranger's hut and out across the canyon floor. Chairs and tables have been pushed to the edges of the room, now lit by the flickering night-lights placed on every surface and up the stairs. The gang danced; Alice in that pink skirt moved freely, she cast her head back. Her gaze was thrown upwards to where, through the skylight she could see the clear sky.

She twisted and turned on the floor, pulling the boys into her moves. Above them, through the skylight, lights began to dance in the sky; shades of green and blue, clouds of colour in the night.

'Hey, look up there.' Alice stopped and pointed. Kirsten, and Eleanor and Andy all stopped and looked. Then they were tumbling outside with their other friends into the cold wilderness, and staring up into the sky, awed by what they saw.

'Days like this.' Kirsten breathed the words. *'It's these that I'll remember forever.'*

She gazed up, up into the never-ending sky. Flares of colour seemed to reach out from the canyon walls in the west; arching up into the night. Morphing; they grew and contracted, moving higher. Predominantly green, the lights were tinged with other colours. Shades of blue and purple strengthened and dimmed.

'It was amazing,' said Alice. She looked round, towards where Eleanor lay in her sleeping bag. 'Ellie?'

Eleanor looked up and saw Alice's slightly concerned expression. She nodded. 'It was good, yeah, but...' She blinked away. She couldn't look at her friends. A cold draught seeped through the tent, and tickled her skin. Suddenly she was back there.

In the cool of night, her sight fixed on the changing, bewitching sky above, as the lights began to sink into the eastern cliffs, Eleanor felt Andy's hands on her waist; fingers finding their way beneath her top and stroking her.

'You said you'd show me things I'd never seen before,' Andy *whispered to her and kissed her neck.*

Eleanor pulled back, easing herself from Andy's hold. 'Andy, don't.' She smiled, weakly.

Eleanor sat, hunched in the tent, and felt the pain of her dream. Vaguely she saw her friends gather closer to her, reaching out to her. She sobbed as she remembered her best friend. She saw him, on the first day of term in her first year at university. She looked to her side and saw him next to her in the lecture theatre. She turned and there he was, with her in the fells; a number pinned to his back and the finish line up ahead.

'I'm sorry—' She choked on the words.

With her vision blurred by tears she pulled herself from her sleeping bag, and rushed from the tent, pausing only to slip into her sandals, she ran through the campsite. She left her friends behind, where they called out after her.

Valdís sat by Andy, on the tomb-shaped stone. She reached out her slender fingers and took his hands.

'Forget her.' Valdís suggested to Andy. 'She left you. Remember that.'

Valdís turned Andy's head and held him in her sight. 'You owe her nothing.'

Silence. Andy found himself mesmerised by this woman's beauty. Words come to him diffidently, but once spoken they were bold and honest.

'I know.'

Against a scarlet sky stood two figures, high above on the ridge; cloaked and hooded, against the biting wind. In the valley floor, amongst the pitted rocks and scrubby birch, Eleanor hid herself from view. Next to her in the wilderness was Jóhanna. She turned her attention down river to where Finnbjörn was making his way along the valley floor towards an opening in the rock.

Eleanor turned to Jóhanna. 'It's time?'

Jóhanna nodded and Eleanor turned again; looking down the valley and to the cave. It was time.

PART SIX

Ragnarok

1

Ash and black smoke vented into the atmosphere from high up on the glacier. Miles away, on a campsite, the sun shone and a gentle breeze blew. A young boy stood motionless holding the Frisbee in both hands whilst his friends called at him to throw it. He was transfixed by the sight of the eruption. Around him was the distinctive winnowing of the snipes as they swooped down. Reluctantly, the boy turned and returned to the game. He threw the Frisbee and watched as the plastic disc arced high, turned and swooped downwards towards his sister's outstretched hands. The ground heaved beneath their feet, and both sister and brother were thrown to the floor. They tumbled to the grass awkwardly as birds scattered, and the mountain roared.

*

Charles Ancell clutched the cold steel rungs of the ladder, as around him the construction site and the mountains tremored. He looked up at the industrial rig with its central shaft and gritted his teeth. As the shaking subsided, he continued up to the viewing platform where he turned to Aðli.

'How long before we tap into the magma?' barked Charles, staring at his employee with wide, bright eyes.

'It's not that simple.' reasoned Aðli, 'Drilling this tunnel. That was easy. Now, with the pressures below, we have to work carefully. One mistake and it will take the whole mountain out.'

'How long?' Charles asked again.

Aðli shook his head solemnly. 'Next we have fit the Thermo-Valve and set up the remote drill. Then we begin drilling through.'

Looking down on the glacier, a tiny private plane flew over the black cloud of noxious vapours. A journalist sat next to the pilot and recorded the images.

Eleanor paced the ground in front of the huts, glancing often at her watch. She kicked at the dirt with the toe of her boot and checked her watch again. Nearby, Ben sat waiting with Kirsten.

'Look who I've found.'

Eleanor turned on hearing Alice's voice. Both Alice and Hanna were approaching from the direction of the main hut.

'Where have you been?' Eleanor asked Hanna accusingly.

'Ellie, relax...?' Hanna said calmly.

'Relax!' Eleanor reacted incredulously. 'The world is being torn apart and you want me to relax? The alfar have shown me where we must go. Now let's—' She turned on her heels. 'Ben? Kirsten? You ready?'

'Ellie, you're not understanding me—' said Hanna, 'The guys I met up with last night. They're from my band. They want to help.'

Hanna stepped closer to Eleanor and stayed her stride. 'Gyrdir is dangerous. You told us that he's killed already, and he's destroyed the old farm. We need safety in numbers.'

As Hanna spoke, Bjäkk crossed the open ground from the hut, and with him, Halldór, Bryn and Jon.

'It's cool, Ellie,' continued Hanna, 'They understand.'

Eleanor looked from her cousin to the advancing friends, all dressed for the outdoors with sturdy boots and packs on their backs. She even spied an ice axe hanging from the straps of Jon's rucksack.

'Fine.' Eleanor was resolute. 'Well, if we are all ready, let's get moving.'

The group shouldered their bags and set off, led by Eleanor away from the huts and the steaming hot pools and the trucks rigged together with cables and satellite dishes. Leaving the flat, grasslands and pools behind they followed the river down a narrower rift valley. The sides came down sometimes as scree, and sometimes as jagged, rocky outcrops, twisted and overhanging into caves.

'Why do I get the horrible feeling, that we are being watched?'

Eleanor glanced over at Alice. 'I think that we are. No. I'm sure of it,' she said.

'This valley,' said Hanna from other side of Alice. 'It's perfect for an ambush. It's good that we have the guys for safety.'

All three girls looked back, over their shoulders at where Ben and Kirsten were lagging a bit behind, and a little further back still were Bjäkk and Hanna's bandmates.

Further on, and the path took them over a craggy rise in the valley floor, where the sides were pinched in closer before sinking lower into boggy ground. Eleanor stopped, halting the party whilst she pulled out the map again.

'You think we are there?' asked Hanna.

347

'Almost,' Eleanor answered and pointed, 'You see that overhanging rock?'

Hanna followed Eleanor's directions and looked too.

'I just have this feeling, but I think it's there,' said Eleanor, 'See how the rocks above make a bit of a face.'

'With a hooked nose, yes.' Alice grinned.

Eleanor marched onward, now at a brisk pace. She slipped and slid down the path, and splashed through the bog to the river. She forded it via stepping stones and scrambled up the cliff on the other side. Arriving at the cave entrance she glanced back. The others were following her, and she entered the dim interior of the cave. She stopped after a few paces and blinked. Slowly her eyes adjusted to the light and she stepped on into the cave.

Facing the back wall, Eleanor was flanked on either side by her friends. She lifted her hand up to the cold, damp surface and traced the natural patterning and the etched lines of the rock.

'You sure this is the right place?' asked Ben. He glanced from the cave wall to the photographs and maps.

Eleanor swung round and snapped at her brother. 'Yes, we're in the right place.' Her eyes burned as bright as fire. 'Finnbjörn led me here last night. The alfar. They know the secret entrances. Can't you sense it? Can't you sense where we are?'

Ben stood his ground, feet firm, eyes fixed. He stared his sister out. 'Maybe?' He continued to hold her with his gaze. 'Maybe not? Wherever we are don't you think you had better get on with it?'

'I'm working as fast as I can,' snapped Eleanor, 'but if we hadn't had to have waited for *some* people—' As Eleanor swung round she cast a mean stare towards Hanna.

Eleanor walked away and explored deeper into the cave, inspecting the rocks and tracing her fingers over fractured walls, as she sought out something. She stopped at a section of cave wall.

'I think, it's here.' Eleanor placed her hand to the wall. She sensed an opening. In the fractures between the rocks a doorway began to show itself. Behind her, Ben stepped back and ambled to the cave entrance.

He emerged out into the open, his hand trailing through the ferns that grew by the entrance. Jon stood nearly talking with Bryn, and a little further off were Hálldor and Bjäkk.

'For the life of me I don't know why we are here.' Jon shook his head. 'For every minute we stand around here we could be taking direct action up there.'

He pointed at the mountain. Ben followed his gaze.

'You're right of course,' said Ben. He peered into the dim mouth of the cave, picking out only Alice - maybe Kirsten - from the darkness. 'Of course I've seen some things over the last few days that if I didn't know better–' He stopped himself.

'Hey Eleanor!' Ben called out and his voice echoed across the valley, 'You done in there?'

'She's away with the fairies.' Ben shrugged. 'Or the elves.'

'The huldufolk,' said Jon. He kicked the ground; playing with the gravel with his boot. 'That said, I still don't see how the storms that we've been having are related to them, or to dormant volcanos.' Jon swung his foot and kicked the stone into the cave. He looked up at Ben blankly.

A svart-alfar foot soldier, dark and slender in his features, moved forward, always spying around rocks. He signaled to accomplices across the valley. They moved on, finding new vantage points, each a little nearer to where they could see and not be seen by the humans down by the cave entrance. Sindri hissed contempt. Looking over his shoulder, he saw his master, standing proud, back down the valley. He turned again and moved closer, listening with acute hearing to the conversation by the cave.

'Can we help you?' Jon took a step towards the new arrival.

The stranger stayed Jon with his hand. 'Please. Gunnlaugr Olafsson,' he said.

'Gyrdir.' Ben hissed the man's true name under his breath.

Gunnlaugr laughed. 'Where have you heard that?' His smile was deceptive, friendly and unthreatening. 'I told you my name. You do not tell me yours?'

'Me? I'm Ben,' answered Ben, 'I'm the brother of the girl you abducted a week ago.'

'Abducted?' Gyrdir appeared surprised. 'Oh. You mean the girl I found wandering alone in the snowstorm and whose life I saved? I am pleased that you have both been reunited.'

'You lie,' said Ben flatly, 'What do you really want?'

'The same as you. To understand—' Gyrdir reached out and gripped Ben's arm. Images flashed through Ben's mind; boiling clouds and mountain ranges that spat fire. Winds and rain ravaged the land, and equations and graphs seemed to leap from the back of his eyes and flick before his field of vision.

'So, you're a scientist.' Gyrdir spat out the words and released Ben from his clutches.

'Eleanor!' Ben called out, diving out of Gyrdir's reach, 'If you are going to do it, now would be a good time!'

Inside the cave Kirsten turned on her heels and stepped across the uneven floor. 'Eleanor! Listen to Ben. Gunnlaugr, Gyrdir – whatever his name – is out there.'

Eleanor didn't answer. She turned her head and looked at the rock at a different angle. She brought in her left hand; piecing together the riddle in her mind. And suddenly the rock flared with colour. Eleanor was breathless; the rock, in a haze of light seemed to morph beneath her touch and the cave appeared to go on further.

'Ben!' Alice called sharply. Through the cave entrance, Alice could see Gyrdir advance towards Ben and Jon. She tried to reach out and stop them, but Bryn and Hálldor were already leaving. Alice turned on her feet and saw Eleanor and Hanna by the opening in the cave wall. She turned again. 'Ben!!'

'Don't go, Ben.' Gunnlaugr reached out, fingers outstretched, tugging at invisible strings.

Ben shook his head. 'Who are you?'

'A friend.'

As Gunnlaugr stepped up towards the cave he was joined by Sindri and other svart-alfar foot-soldiers. Ben heard Alice's call to him from behind.

'And they are?' Ben was dismissive. 'Friends as well?'

'I can help you understand everything Benjamin Ármannsson.' Gunnlaugr's tone was persuasive. 'Isn't that what you want, above everything?'

Hálldor descended out of the cave watching the stranger carefully; observing the cloaked figure, fixed by the darkly etched lines in his face, the silver eyes, and the thin, ambiguous smile. Sketched lines and picture books flashed through his mind.

A young boy with ragged fair hair sat by his father's side. In his tiny right hand he clutched tight a small piece of soft cloth. He looked up engagingly into his father's eyes as he pointed with his left hand, his forefinger long and straight, at the picture book from which his father read.

Hálldor's father nodded and said the man's name, 'Óðinn.'

The child looked again at the picture, a sketch of chalk and charcoal, with accented pen work, scratched and rough in its design. The man, the monster, the creature on the page, with that weather-etched face, the cloak;

the dark hair and silver eyes – the frightening expression... The picture both frightened and delighted the imagination of the young Hálldor. He stared transfixed. And as he stared, the face seemed to stare back.

Gunnlaugr stepped closer, a gnarled and weathered hand on his staff. Hálldor stepped forward suddenly and pushed Ben back towards the cave.

Hálldor reached up and took down the book from the shelf. He sat on his bed and looked at the cover; an illustration of the man that had haunted him all his childhood. He smiled, as the memories came back. He turned the pages, reading the text and bathing in the images, he devoured the story. It was as haunting and as beautiful as he remembered, with the same, shocking and terrifying ending. He snapped the book shut.

'You're not what you say you are,' spat Hálldor, 'You're nothing. You're a myth. You're a legend. A character from a storybook.'

Gunnlaugr said nothing. Looking from side to side, he signaled with his hands and summoned his army of svart-alfar. Wraiths of men appeared from behind rocks and out of shadows.

'Really?' Gunnlaugr's tone was mocking, 'I'm nothing more than a storybook?'

'Go.' Hálldor looked to Ben. 'Your sister needs you.'

Ben began to protest but Hálldor was firm and Jon and Bryn were in agreement. He turned and launched himself towards the cave entrance.

Gunnlaugr brought down his staff onto the rock. The sky darkened almost instantly. A fork of lightning cut through the sky and thunder cracked open the heavens; Ben stopped in his stride and he turned to look back. In those few moments, Gunnlaugr pushed aside Hálldor and his two friends, the svart-alfar close in and Gunnlaugr reached out with a shadowy claw-like hand. Ben turned and lunged into the cave.

'In!' shouted Eleanor

Alice turned one last time; at Ben, behind in the cave. She looked up briefly into Eleanor's eyes and saw the nod of the head; and stepped through.

'Ben!' Eleanor snapped sharply. As he neared her, she reached out and grabbed him by the sleeve and pushed him through. Nearer the mouth of the cave, Hanna's band mates were struggling with Gyrdir and his followers; holding them back. For a moment Eleanor met Bjäkk in her gaze. She silently pleaded for him to hurry. Glancing round she saw the doorway begin to fade. She pleaded to them.

'Eleanor Ármannsson – the task I set you is not finished.' Gunnlaugr pulled free of Bryn's grasp and was halfway across the cave before Jon intercepted him.

'Go, Eleanor!' Bjäkk shouted, 'We'll sort this!'

Eleanor turned, the gateway softened and shuddered. She turned one last time; saw the struggle; saw Gyrdir break free once more and Bjäkk lunging towards the lean man with all his thick-set weight. Eleanor turned again at the last minute and dived through the gateway.

Gyrdir hit the cold stone wall of the cave. He spat anger and contempt and laid his fingers on the rock, feeling out the patterns; sensing for energy.

'You're too late.' Jon stood tall, arms crossed.

Gyrdir turned, slowly. Any trace of cordiality was gone from his voice. 'You made a bad choice. A very ill-thought out choice.'

Eleanor collapsed onto the floor, exhausted. She glanced up, across the stony floor, where her friends and brother were fallen. She looked further down the passageway to where Hanna was already exploring.

'We should get moving,' said Eleanor as she picked herself up from the floor and moved to retrieve her rucksack.

2

Eleanor lead the way through narrow passageways and down stairs carved from the stone. They moved from chamber to chamber, working their way between caverns filled with stalagmites and stalactites. At the top of one, they stopped and looked over the edge and shone their torches over the edge. They could just make out the surface of a pool water that was who knows how deep.

'This place is amazing,' remarked Alice, 'Can you imagine if the tour companies knew that all of this existed...?' She reached out her hand to touch the walls.

'Alice, don't!' Kirsten called, just as Alice pulled back her hand. 'You mustn't touch. Down here, the acid on our fingers can destroy the microorganisms that grow on the rocks.'

Kirsten glanced towards Ben for confirmation and he nodded.

They moved onwards, taking new passages, and ascending stairs to other chambers under Eleanor's instinctive, unquestioned lead. They walked on in silence, breaking it only to warn about uneven or loose steps. The darkness oppressed all other conversation.

Eventually, whilst stopped for a breather, Alice broke the silence and asked, 'What happened back there?'

Eleanor turned round and looked at her brother. 'Ben?'

Ben looked back at his sister. *Why me?* He returned her gaze.

'Thought you might have a scientific, rational, explanation,' Eleanor said.

Ben remained silent. He couldn't explain what happened. He knew what he had seen but it also didn't make sense. Where they were now didn't make sense either. He reached out towards Kirsten and stroked her hand lightly. She turned and waited for him. Their fingers entwined and their hands closed around each other. Down here in the dark of this cave, Ben clung to the only thing that his brain could make sense of.

'What's happened to the others?' Alice quickened her pace towards Hanna.

Hanna felt the chill of the question. What had happened out there – her friends – she couldn't think of anything *but* that they were alive. In her mind she saw Bjäkk through the opening in the rock, forced back by Gyrdir, crashing into the cave wall, winded. Again, her mind replayed the scene, but each time it ended with Eleanor lunging through the entrance as the door sealed itself again.

'I'm sure they'll be fine.' Alice lay a hand on Hanna's arm reassuringly.

At the bottom of the natural, dripstone, cavern, just before it plunged into a deep underground lake, a shaft, hewn from the rock broke off and curved round further into the mountain. Presently the tunnel ended in a spiral staircase that lead further down, lit at intervals by flaming torches. The stair seemed to go on for ever and Alice and Hanna, on more than one occasion, lost count of their number.

At the foot of the stairs they emerged into a side passage and from there, into a street, deep underground; half-carved out the ground, half fashioned by nature. Þurs moved in the street, lumbering slowly about their daily tasks.

'There are shops...?' Alice was wide-eyed and awestruck.

'You didn't mention this before?' Hanna prompted Eleanor.

'It's just like in the sagas. Karl and Kerling, Alice, you remember?' Kirsten nudged her friend.

Eleanor turned to her brother. 'Now do you believe me?'

Again Ben didn't answer. He held Kirsten's hand tightly and stepped forward towards the street. His attention latched onto a single þurs worker that lumbered past, his short stubby legs and big, bare feet treading the dirt. In each stubby-fingered hand, he held a roughly hewn wheelbarrow that he pulled behind him.

'Ben?' Eleanor was behind him.

Ben turned to face his sister. He tried to answer, but his words stumbled over his thoughts. He laughed and shrugged.

'Where now?' Ben tightened his grip on Kirsten's hand.

'We have to find the council chamber,' said Eleanor.

Hanna tugged at her cousin's sleeve. 'Is it safe? The þurs – won't they see us – object...?'

'No.' Eleanor shook her head confidently. 'I don't think so. I haven't been here before. Gunnlaugr – Gyrdir – sent me much closer to where the council chamber is, but the þurs, when I met them, they just seemed to accept me.'

'You'll forgive me if I tell you how incredible that sounds,' Ben quipped dryly.

Kirsten scowled at Ben and he looked down, sideways towards Kirsten, his mouth twisting with meek apology.

Eleanor led her friends down the crowded, bustling street, sometimes weaving in single file, and sometimes in pairings between the friends that changed from time to time. At times separated from Kirsten, Ben felt adrift and he felt the need to catch up or slow down, anything to regroup and have their hands link again.

Lining the sides of the street, sat on roughly made wooden stools, þurs women gutted fish for the night's meal and worked swiftly with fat fingers to mend fishing nets and make rope. From time to time they looked up at the strangers who walked through their community, watching the humans closely if silently.

As he walked, Ben studied the faces, picking out characteristics of this alien race. He observed the fat faces and the big, thickset and wide eyes and the enlarged foreheads. The females had their long dark, and straight hair pulled tight back across their heads and platted into long ponytails. The men – the boys even – had thin, wiry and wild hair which showed off the size of their round heads.

Ben called out to his sister. 'How did you do it?'

Eleanor glanced back at her brother blankly.

'The way in? Through the cave...?' Ben clarified. 'Was there some kind of door?'

Eleanor nodded. 'Exactly. A door. I guess I just found the key.' She grinned and turned to continue to lead her friends through the streets.

The darkness seemed to spiral up forever, fractal-like into the rock that was dripping with stalactites; cones of calcium that hung down from the ceiling in frescoes of colour. Pétur stood in the centre of the hall staring up into the roof and watched the colours of the rocks seemingly dance before his thickset, bulbous eyes, in the unearthly light beneath the mountain.

In his mind, Pétur heard his master's voice and lowered his head as he remembered his task. He scampered away as fast as his squat little legs could carry him. He ran up the grand staircase flanked on either side by statues of þursish dignitaries, trailing his stubby fingers on the stone balustrade, to the street above. He stopped, and waited; eyes scanning the street ahead.

Eleanor stepped onwards. With each step, Pétur matched her movements and blocked her.

'Excuse me.' Eleanor laughed to herself at her use of the peculiarly English expression.

'Pétur,' said Pétur, and nodded his head to the human girl, 'You?'

Eleanor stuttered and stammered in front of the þurs – a child – she supposed. She moved to sidestep the þurs boy and he moved to block her. Again, they dodged and blocked, dodged and block...

'My father is expecting you,' said Pétur, 'Follow me.' Spoken without thought to any possible disobedience Pétur turned quickly and moved down the street, descending the stairs again into the hall. Eleanor found herself stood amongst her friends, each waiting upon the other. For some reason, either Eleanor found herself unwilling or unable to make a decision.

Eleanor stood amongst her friends upon the outcrop of rock overlooking the plunging depths of the canyon. Her fingers closed around the wooden handle of the mattock. She looked towards other watchful people. Kirsten returned her gaze.

'I guess,' Kirsten suggested, 'We better do it.'

Eleanor nodded in agreement. They moved off again, following the þurs boy through the subterranean street and down the widening steps into the open cavern. They found themselves looking this way and that, awestruck by the size and splendour of the cavern. In the centre, beside the gnarled and twisted dead tree, Pétur waited for them.

'What is this place?' asked Hanna. She pushed to the front of the group to address Pétur directly. Gesturing towards the natural domed roof her fingers reached out to touch the dead tree.

Pétur slapped Hanna's hand down. 'No. Do not touch the Ash of Yggdrasil! Come, we will be late.' He began to lead them away again.

Hanna pulled back obediently.

'The tree of life?' Hanna looked again at the dry stalks and twisted branches of a long since dead tree.

'Pétur...?' She hurried ahead of the þurs child, cutting him off and pointed him back to the tree.

Pétur ignored any attempts at distraction and pushed past, beckoning as he went for the group to follow. Eleanor squeezed her cousin's hand comfortingly as she passed. 'Come on. We'll get you an answer – I promise.'

On the downward side of the slowly sloping great hall, Pétur led them on a path down the side of a chasm. The still silence within the great hall that they had left was replaced by the churning froth of a subterranean river plunging out of a cleft in the rock and falling into a deep gorge below. The path they took, hardly wide enough in parts for a procession of mules in single file, clung to the edge of the gorge, overhung, sometimes very low, by more rock.

Pétur took the path quickly, and barefoot paused only occasionally when he realised the others had been left behind;

their progress slowed by the need to stoop – bend almost double at times – beneath an overhang.

Reaching up, Alice clutched at the smooth-faced shafts of basalt that twisted and curved into the path they walk. She delayed for a moment, leaning out as far as she dared to gaze down into the gorge below. She watched the main stream of the river funnel through and tumble out of pinch points in the rock, eddying back into pools of translucent stillness. Ben lowered himself to his knees and crawled forward to the edge. He shone his torch down; the beam of light reflected brightly on a pair of shining eyes. A þurs male, waist deep in water, turned and looked up. Ben was joined on the floor by Alice and Kirsten. They all watched as, out of the shadows, more rocks seemed to move and reveal themselves as more members of the þurs fishing party.

Ben lifted his head and looked up into the roof of the canyon. Twisting around above him were columns of basalt, overhanging the underground river and somewhere, high above, a narrow slit of sunlight.

'Come.' Pétur returned to them. 'We must be going now.'

Ben glanced back over his shoulder, at Pétur far off down the path and at Eleanor and Hanna, waiting closer by. Slowly and carefully he pulled himself back from the edge and stood.

Alice moved to catch up with Hanna and then Eleanor, whilst Kirsten waited with Ben. They moved off, following the others down the path that descended the side of the canyon. He felt reassuringly into the air beside him and his fingers found Kirsten's hand. He slipped his hand into hers.

'You okay?'

Ben looked towards Kirsten. *Of course he was – a silly question.* But not silly – he knew exactly to what Kirsten was referring. He thought of the trolls down in the bottom of the canyon, fishing.

He thought of the boy Pétur leading them – *leading them to where?* And they followed this guide, trusting him completely...? His mind buzzed with the irreconcilable conflict of mythical creatures and science.

'You think they're still a trick of the mind?' asked Kirsten

'Like I can answer that!' Ben shook his head.

They continued on in silence, minding their step, occasionally catching sight of the torrent of water flowing beneath.

Eleanor called out. She was standing at a section of path which widened out under a section of overhang that came down to meet the floor.

'What's up?' asked Ben, 'Where's our trollish friend?'

'This is the way to the council chamber.' Hanna took the lead, gesturing towards a dark hollow in the rock that seemed to seep into nothingness. Ben stepped into the hollow, feeling at the solid rock before him. He turned, directing his gaze quizzically towards his cousin and his sister.

'There's nothing here,' he said simply, trying to convince himself that the appearance of the þurs – these people of the rock – were nothing more than some shared vision and a trick of their minds.

'What?' Ben recognised the expression of disbelief – the infuriation towards his obstinacy – on Eleanor's face. 'This isn't another door?'

Flames burnt brightly from the walls around the chamber. Eleanor and her friends were ushered onto wooden stools that were hastily fetched for them. Room was made for them around the large stone table, uneven, yet polished on its surface and filled with beautiful, swirling colours. Ben reached out and stroked the surface; in awe of the geology. Eleanor shrank back, suddenly feeling small, surrounded by the large, rounded forms of the þurs elders.

3

Bjäkk stared at his blood-stained hands; at the thick lines from where more blood seeped. He lifted himself up and propped himself against the cliff. His eyes throbbed and he squinted for a while before slowly his sight focused again. Hálldor was further down the slope, picking himself up and stumbling towards him. He moved to help Jon. Slowly Bjäkk's breathing returned to normal. His tongue felt the inside of his mouth and tasted blood.

'Bryn?' Bjäkk's voice was husky as he called out his friend's name.

Hálldor and Jon leant on each other for support as they made their slow, stumbling way across the slope in front of the cave to join Bjäkk.

'Can you see him?' Bjäkk scanned the valley.

'There!' Hálldor pointed and called out.

Bjäkk followed Hálldor's gaze. For a moment he couldn't see anything. Then, amongst the scrub and meadow grass down by the river, they saw the leather coat and jeans that were unmistakably Bryn's.

'I'll go,' said Bryn

Ash billowed out into the cloud, and stained the sky with sulphur and pumice. At the top of the mountain; the crown of the glacier was cloaked from view, disguising the destructive power that was welling up underneath. A clear sunlight glistened across the ice. In the campsite, William stood staring at the mountain. Glancing over his shoulder, he watched his two assistants plot today's geophysical measurements.

Out of the corner of his eye, he was momentarily distracted by a group of four young men, limping back into camp using each other as props. Rock climbers having attempted the impossible he supposed. Shaking his head, he returned his maps and charts.

Bjäkk and Hálldor helped Bryn to the hut. Inside Bjäkk began to sponge Bryn's face and clean the worst of the blood from the scar that ran down his cheek. He rinsed the cloth through and flushed a red stain through the bowl of water.

'Is it bad?' Bryn's voice croaked dryly, 'What am I going to look like at the gig next week?'

'Just surface wounds I think.' Bjäkk washed dried blood out of matted hair. 'Who were they?'

Silence. Bjäkk looked from the bucket of cold, blood-stained water to Bryn, and to Bryn's two band mates. No one wanted to answer. Bjäkk doubted that there was any answer to give.

'Ódinn.' Hálldor said the name reluctantly, 'It was Ódinn.

'Of course.' Bjäkk pulled back, 'The chief god. The wanderer. God of fury and destruction.'

'No shame then.' Bryn managed to laugh. 'To be injured by him, I mean.'

Bjäkk looked up at Hálldor. 'Do you think the others know? How did you?'

Hálldor shook his head. He lifted his hand to his head and pressed his palm into his forehead, and winced. 'It sounds silly.' Slowly he looked up and glanced around at his friends. 'I had a storybook – as a kid – of our oldest legends retold. That man. He was on the cover – on every page – I just know. He was Óðinn.'

Kathryn stood on the other side of the door, standing in shadow. She listened to the Icelanders' talk of gods and of myths and legends. A draught hit her, swirling around her feet and clinging to her bare arms. She turned. Nothing. She turned back to the door and listened for more.

Finnbjörn stepped out of the shadows again, moving silently, carefully in just behind where Kathryn was standing; listening too.

'Does Hanna know?' asked Jon, 'Did any of them know what they were fighting?'

The question hung between the friends. Slowly Bryn shook his head. Bjäkk picked up the words for him. 'I think, not.' He shook his head. 'They knew that Gunnlaugr – Gyrdir – was pursuing them. I don't think they knew who he really was.'

'Gunnlaugr?' repeated Hálldor, 'I've not heard that name before. But Gyrdir, it's an old alfar word for Gangleri. Gangleri the walk-weary.'

Jon nodded. 'And another name for Ódinn. Cast out by his own people in the world of men, unable to return.'

'It all makes sense,' Bjäkk agreed.

The door slammed shut. William looked through the dimly lit hall, seeing his young assistant standing prying beneath the stairs and behind an open door.

'Kathryn.' His voice sounded more abrupt than he meant.

Kathryn jumped back, startled. She relaxed on seeing William and pulled away from the door to go to him.

'What were you doing?'

'Nothing.' Kathryn bit her lip, 'Just–'

She saw Professor Tyndale watch her quizzically; expecting more by way of an explanation. He reached out a fatherly hand towards her and took hold of her arm.

'Are you sure?' he asked, 'You know that you can tell me anything, don't you?'

For a moment Kathryn considered telling him her thoughts and what she heard. She looked up and into his eyes. She blinked her gaze away.

'How's Nils getting on with those calculations?' Kathryn asked.

William looked more closely at his assistant. Kathryn caught his gaze and knew that he suspected that there was something more.

'Interesting.' William nodded. 'Actually there's something that I wanted you to have a look at.' With a subtle positioning of his hand into the curve of her back William directed Kathryn through the front door and back out into the open.

Charles Ancell climbed the ladder onto the open platform, gloved hand over gloved hand on the cold steel rungs. He swiped his security card through the lock and pulled open the hatch before stepping into the warm interior of the control room.

Aðli was bent over the control desk checking settings with another of the operatives. He looked up and nodded towards his boss, finished checking the settings with the junior and then went to Charles.

'Are we ready?' Charles asked.

Aðli nodded. 'The tunnel is complete. We still have building works to undergo but we can send the first shipment down.'

Charles nodded. He had waited long for this day. He considered the billions of dollars that his company had outlaid on this project. Crossing the room now to gaze through the window he was able to enjoy seeing the expanse of the aluminium processing plant spread out before him and the first of the five rigs poised above the landscape.

'Begin final preparations,' instructed Charles, 'We start at noon tomorrow.'

Kathryn sat in front of the laptop in the dimly lit attic room of the hut. He   r concentration waned as her attention drifted out through the window and across the mountain. She saw figures move through the darkness, seemingly living amongst the lava fields and remembered the talk she had overheard downstairs. She remembered the earnestness with which they had spoken of gods and mythical creatures.

Footsteps on the landing and the door opened and shut and she looked up briefly to see that Níls had stepped into the room. She looked back at the laptop; at the facts and figures of this latest volcanic eruption. She lifted some paperwork and looked through the data they had culled from the recent storms. She glanced up again at Níls, holding back her questions and wondered whether she should give voice to them.

Nils looked back at her, expectantly.

Kathryn bit her lip as she deliberated her uncertainty. 'Nils?'

Nils nodded.

'You know how Icelanders – how they really do believe in elves and trolls and all those Norse gods and...' She felt the weight of Nils' gaze upon her. 'Is that true?' She shrugged. 'Do *you*?'

Nils recoiled slightly, shaking his head involuntarily. 'I don't know. I guess.' He moved to take a seat at the other laptop opposite Kathryn. 'Yeah, we all do, at some level. It's like your country and King Arthur. We like to believe they existed, but we know they don't really.'

'What do you know of Ódinn?'

'One of the gods. *The* god, if you like. Good, yet fearsome – wise but reckless.' Nils gazed across at Kathryn, unable to hide his confusion at the direction in which Kathryn was taking their conversation.

'Reckless?' Kathryn asked, 'How do you mean? What happened?'

Nils shook his head. 'How is this relevant Kathryn?' He returned to his papers and sifted through the data, referring often to the computer for models.

'I don't know.' Kathryn sighed, 'It's probably not. No–' She turned her head back to the computer and refocused her eyes to the screen. Using her thumb as guide, she read that day's calculations and tapped them into the field. Sliding her middle finger gently across the scratchpad, she clicked to run. The usual status bars built and disappeared, replaced by another, the programmes and function keys flashing through too fast to read, as the system processed the latest results.

The god of all gods. Good yet fearsome. Wise but reckless. Kathryn heard Nils's scant explanation over and over in her mind. She ducked her head to one side. Níls was hard at work. She sighed and moved to the window to look out onto the area of decking, the grassy meadowland and the swarm of television crews, and journalists doing their pieces to camera. She looked up, at the mountain beyond, smoking in its toxic fumes.

'I guess I'm just interested,' she said.

Níls looked up; then back at his work.

Kathryn turned to face him. 'Just tell me – if you know. I've been in your country for going on six months now and I know precious little about your culture.'

Níls looked up momentarily. 'It's not important.'

Kathryn approached her colleague by a few more steps.

'No.' Her tone was firm. 'It's probably not. But all this science, this theorising – these last couple of weeks have been intense. I need some release from it. I don't think I realised, not really properly, but science isn't everything. It doesn't have all the answers.'

Bryn slammed the beer can down onto the table, reached for another slice of smoked trout and draped it over a piece of flatbrauð. Taking his beer again he washed down the food.

'So Óðinn is here, right?' began Bryn, 'I'm guessing he wants to return to his world. And we stopped him? That's got to make us unpopular.'

'It's Eleanor that can open the door. He knows that,' said Bjäkk, 'I don't think he will be attacking us again.'

'Until Eleanor returns with Hanna – and the others–' Bryn shook his head. 'He was watching us before. Him or his spies. They're out there.'

'Why now though?' Hálldor leant back in his chair. 'What's special about now?'

Bjäkk stared across the table at his friend, not completely understanding what Hálldor was getting at.

Hálldor slowly nodded. 'Well it's like storybooks, já? He's been cast out of his world, yes. And he's been walking through ours for what, centuries and he wants to get back. So what makes the now special?'

'Eleanor said that when she met him first in the mountains, he mentioned Alcon's new factory,' said Bjäkk, 'That they're digging deep beneath the mountain—'

Beyond the table where the four friends sat, William Tyndale was preparing food and washing up, increasingly slowly, stopping frequently to listen to the conversation across the room.

'The burning mountains.' Hálldor remembered stories told during his childhood and legends of his people. 'The bridges between the worlds. He wanted to use Alcon's drilling as a way to break through back into his world.'

Bryn nodded. 'Cunning...'

'And dangerous,' said Bjäkk, 'Consider the temperatures and the pressures involved.'

The conversation fell to a silence that weighed heavy over them. Voices and laughter from other rooms seeped through the woodwork; and footsteps echoed across the floor above. Wind picked up and pressed in noisily onto the windows of the hut and a draught blew in under the door.

William turned away from the counter, drying his hands on a cloth. He approached the table around which Bjäkk and his friends sat. Hálldor looked up with questioning eyes.

'I'm sorry.' William's voice was polite and well-spoken. 'I didn't mean to listen, but I heard you talking. The eruption – the storms we've been having – you know something about it?'

Hálldor laughed. 'Everyone knows it's happening. It's no secret.'

'But you implied – I'm sorry – that someone,' William said hesitantly, 'someone was affecting it in some way?'

Hálldor continued to stare quizzically at William. He shook his head.

'I am William Tyndale,' said William, 'Professor William Tyndale. Myself and my colleagues have been studying the recent climate anomalies. I'm interested if you have any theories.'

Hálldor laughed. 'I'm a rock star – not a scientist–' He shook his head with incredulousness, 'Bjäkk, what do you think? What theories do we have for the nice scientist?'

Bjäkk turned his head, smiling at Hálldor's sardonic tone. He looked up at William and nodded.

'Take a seat.' Bjäkk gestured to the chair at the end of the table from which he removed his feet. 'A lot has happened in the last few weeks, William. Science isn't the only system at work here.'

William watched Bjäkk closely, listening and taking passing glances at Hálldor and on occasion to Jon and Bryn.

'Are you ready to open your mind, Professor…?' said Bjäkk.

4

Ben eased himself into his seat at the vast stone table, feeling inexorably small amongst the moot of a dozen þurs. He reached out for Kirsten's hand and she let his fingers slip between each of hers and close into a clasp of security. They exchanged a reassuring glance before Ben looked back the other way. Alice, Hanna and Eleanor were seated around the table too.

Wood echoed on stone, resounding powerfully around the vast chamber. Ben looked to the front – along with his friends – across the swirling, polished colours of the stone table at Bergur, the large and rotund þurs leader. Like all of his kind he had round eyes close-set into a podgy face, with wrinkles that were deeply etched behind wild and hair that was so thin he was almost bald. Around his body he wore more fur and animal hide than his comrades and a broad leather sash across his chest that was decorated with bronze and bone detailing.

Bergur rapped the thickly hewn wooden hammer down three further times. He rose from his seat and leant on the table in front of him, with his knuckles pressed down into the basalt. For a moment he held each of the humans in turn in his gaze.

'Eleanor.' He directed the full force of his gaze across the table. 'First born of Guðni Ármannson, you return to us. What news of the man we seek?'

Eleanor felt the weight of responsibility and shrunk back into the hardness of the wooden chair, as two dozen þursar eyes all turned and fixed their gaze on her. What did *she* know? Her discoveries, her eagerness, seemed so unsure and inconsequential now. Held in the gaze of the þurs elder, Eleanor listened to the silence that awaited her to break. It was painful in its emptiness.

Slap-slap. Slap-slap. Eleanor's head turned towards the source of the noise, tiny and unimportant as it was, it deafened her mind. Drip-drop, slap-slap. Droplets of water fell and hit the stone table, breaking and cascading outwards. She glanced upwards into the cavernous roof and the stalactites that dropped downwards into the space. Her eyes picked out the water that seeped from the columns, swelled and filled at the tips until they dropped free, thrown downwards. Drip-drop, slap-slap, onto the stone table.

Eleanor looked up at the Þurs elder.

'I don't know. Not really,' Eleanor stumbled over the words. She reached down and loosened the cords of her rucksack. Delving her hand deep, she fingered and pulled from the bag, the carved silver cup. She stood it on the table and rose from her seat long enough to slide it forward towards the centre. 'I'm sorry. I took this, last time I was here.'

A stir of disquiet rumbled round the council table.

'Óðinn's cup.'

Bergur rose and slammed the wooden hammer down onto the table. He roared out Eleanor's name and she fell back into her seat and pressed her bones into the thickly carved wood, unable to stop herself tremble.

'You took this from us. And you gave it to him?!'

Eleanor shook her head, defiant. 'No.'

'Why did you take this?' Bergur stepped away from his simple throne and followed the circumference of the table, his close-set, bulbous eyes fixed all the time on Eleanor. He neared her.

'You took, our property, too *him*.' The Þurs leader spat out the words. 'Why?'

Eleanor clambered out of her seat, and edged backwards along the row. Her friends moved to join her, but were pushed back into their seats as the Þurs passed.

'I told you we shouldn't have come,' Ben told his sister.

'Shut it Ben.' Eleanor silenced him with a sharp tongue and a withering stare.

'You should listen to your – brother.' Bergur advanced still further. 'Why did you come?'

'To warn you.' Eleanor saw her opportunity and stepped forward determinedly. The þurs leader stopped momentarily, caught off-guard by Eleanor's advance. 'Gunnlaugr – Gyrdir – he tricked me. You know him, I know you do. You know what he's like.'

'You betrayed us.'

'No!' Eleanor shook her head. Glancing round she saw a face at the table; a Þurs elder whom she recognised. 'There! There he is, the þurs who showed me the bridge.' Around the table, the þurs elders followed the direction Eleanor pointed, to the youngest elder; the þurs whom Eleanor had met weeks ago on her first visit.

'Erik,' the þurs leader stopped and turned, 'What is the meaning of this?'

Nervously, Erik rose to his feet. 'It's true. I showed this girl to the Bifrost to her way home. I did not give her Ódinn's cup.'

With her long, pale and slender fingers, Valdís positioned the small tablets of bone. She sat on the ground, reached out, and took Andy's hands. She gazed upon him, giving him gentle instruction as to what to do with the counters in her soft, beguiling voice.

The wooden door to the shelter slammed open and shut. Both Valdís and Andy looked up as Gyrdir, tall and cloaked stomped into the room. He marched straight up to them and kicked at the floor before them, sending the tablets of bone scattering.

'She has learnt well, that girl.' Gyrdir's voice was deep and growling.

Valdís pulled back from Andy, stepping low over his body, the folds of her clothes brushing over his head, she ducked forward and went to Gyrdir. 'What is it? You were unsuccessful, lord?' She reached out and stroked the angular, weather-worn face of her master, drawing her long finger nails seductively and affectionately down his face.

She rose herself up on her toes, bringing her face level with his and spoke in a soft whisper to him. 'The boy is developing well. He is almost ready.'

Gyrdir looked into the eyes of his svart-alfar mistress. He nodded and pressed his lips to hers.

'You left me with it. You told me things. You wanted me to take something – to do something.' Eleanor took a step closer again to the table, staring across the stone, circled with þurs, at Erik.

'She speaks the truth?' Bergur asked Erik, who became visibility weakened by the force of the confrontation.

'The legends are vague. She was asking questions – I may have hinted–' Erik stopped. The argument was meaningless. He reached across the table and took the cup in his hands and inspected the runes etched into its surface. Silence befell the council chamber, disturbed only by the slow, noisy breathing from the þurs and the continued drips from the roof.

'This is ridiculous.' Ben got up suddenly. He kicked back his seat. 'Eleanor where are the maps? Show them.'

Eleanor turned, shocked by her brother's response and his sudden belief in her ideas.

'Hanna,' Ben continued, 'Pass it to me.' He gestured to Eleanor's day sack.

Hanna leant forward and scrabbled for the bag. She pulled it up and onto the table. Pulling back the cords, she eased out a microfleece out, a water bottle and notebook; then the envelope of papers. She slid the other things away and pulled out the maps and photographs from the envelope and arranged them in front of her.

Ben looked round the room at each of the þurs, at Erik and at Bergur. 'You call it Ódinn's cup yeah?' He intensified his stare on Erik. 'Yes?'

Erik nodded.

'Right?' Ben pulled the sketch of the map on the farm wall and the photograph away from Hanna. 'So you know what happens right, when you fill it with the purest water and hold it to the setting sun?'

The þurs muttered and conferred with one another in an ancient tongue.

'No?' Ben held up the photo. 'Those runes – they let the light through. Held up against the sun, the light refracts through the cup of water to show this – a map of your land. And here – this is where it is being destroyed from.' He pointed to the picture of the map and the sketch.

The þurs elders remained silent. As the slow drip-drip of water from the colonnaded ceiling reverberated around the chamber, they sat and stared.

Ben shook his head in disbelief. 'You have no idea what this is about?'

Eleanor stepped towards her brother. 'Do you?' she asked him. 'You accept it now?'

Ben heard his sister's comment and tried to ignore it, but couldn't avoid a fleeting exchange of gaze. He returned his attention to the þurs elders.

'You see this map, which your special cup drew for us. You see what's marked here? Vaðalda. Not far is it? From where an aluminium smelting company are building a big new factory – boring right into the volcano – and you're worried about what some pathetic wandering man is going to do with some of your artefacts?' Ben shook his head. 'Your world is going to be ripped apart by forces you don't even understand.'

Eleanor reached out towards her brother. She begged softly. ' Ben, are you sure you understand it?'

Bergur strode towards Ben and snatched the map out of his hands. His whole face twisted with a threatening snarl as he tossed the map away. He looked down on Ben contemptuously.

'And you think you understand my world more?' Bergur spat gobby phlegm in Ben's face and turned away.

He barked his orders and a dozen guards stepped forward out of the shadows and seized Eleanor and Ben, and then their friends and dragged them, protesting, from the chamber.

Bundled at a fast pace, they were taken down dark side passages into a colder, darker, and damper part of the mountains where the roar of water intensified before they were thrust forward and down into a cell. The entrance was sealed behind them; a solid wall of rock faced them.

Water dripped down the algae covered rocks; the rhythmic, regular sound of every drop resonating round the cell as each hit the rock beneath. Two flaming torches were wedged into the rock halfway up opposite walls and the flickering light cast long and wavering shadows across the room.

Ben swung round to face his sister. Before he could speak, his cousin was on her feet and interceding.

'Eleanor's got a point, you know,' Hanna reasoned. 'The cup. What did they call it Ben?'

Ben shrugged. 'I don't know. Ódinn's cup or something—' He stopped, and then repeated himself.

'Yeah...' Hanna nodded. 'And that man. If he's Ódinn?'

Ben was dubious, 'Ódinn's a god. Why does he need to resort to trickery - and *us* - why Eleanor? Can't he just use his godlike powers?'

'Ben, you remember the old stories...?' Hanna said wearily. 'He was cast out centuries ago for one misdemeanour or another - thrown out of his kingdom. The þurs and the alfar have been keeping him from it ever since.'

'And he taught me how to get in, so that I would take to him something that would open a door for him.' Slowly the truth dawned on Eleanor. 'I've betrayed the huldufolk,' she added quickly.

Hanna shook her head. 'Gunnlaugr betrayed us all.'

Eleanor shook her head again, slowly and sadly; she looked up into her brother's eyes, narrowing her gaze upon him. 'And now, thanks to you - we are stuck down here in some troll prison. Thanks for everything Ben.' She turned and walked away from her brother, pulling back the fur hanging at the end of the cell and stepping past into the dark.

'My fault is it?' Ben called after his sister. 'When you are looking at where to place blame, just who was it who got us into this?' He turned and stepped away into the opposite corner.

Hanna Katla Baldursdóttir, was left standing in the middle of the room hearing the determination of the scientist from one side and the passion of the mythologist from the other. She kicked her heels into the dirt and tried to make first for one cousin and then the other. Her head turned again, this way and that. She wanted to go to Eleanor. She wanted go to Ben. Sighing heavily she sunk to the floor, tucking her feet under her, cross-legged in the middle of the cave. A stillness descended around her and she lowered her head into her hands and pressed the tips of her fingers into her face.

Behind Hanna, in the shadows of the cave, Alice and Kirsten watched their friends, listened to the arguments and felt their concern.

Ben put his hand out to guide himself down into the lower section of the cave, stooping as he stepped through a low archway. His eyes slowly adjust to the dim light whilst inside his head his mind tumbled with facts and figures and the reality of this fantasy world he found himself in. The þurs are creatures from a storybook – mythical creatures – creatures that he had just argued physics with.

Kirsten stepped down through the cave behind Ben, slipping her hands gently round his waist. She tucked her chin onto his shoulder.

'You okay?' she asked.

Ben sighed softly. He shook his head. 'I don't know. What happened back there? How did I end up doing that?'

'You care,' Kirsten suggested, 'Maybe?'

Ben turned to face Kirsten, his arms slipping around her waist. 'I'm finding it hard to know what I believe anymore.'

Ben felt comfort in the warmth of Kirsten's breath and the softness of her touch. 'I argued with things - with creatures - that in my head shouldn't exist.'

Kirsten didn't answer. She just held him longer and pulled him closer into their embrace.

Hanna squatted low to the floor of the cave, putting out her hands to the rock as she had seen Eleanor do. She blocked out all thoughts and turmoil from her mind, cleared her head of clutter and attempted to tune herself into this new environment.

Hanna stood before the wall in the setting sun, outside the old farm, staring at the map painted on the wall. Her eyes were fixed to one small area, daubed roughly in paint and accentuated with charcoal she saw in the marks, a face. Her face.

Below her hands, Hanna began to sense it. Beneath her finger tips, Hanna began to sense the stirring of power. It felt electric; sharp bolts of feeling through her nerves and a rippling, tingling sensation that stung her from within.

'Hanna?' Alice's voice came from out of nowhere.

Hanna turned and saw her friend stepping out of the darkness. She returned her gaze to her own hands; staring at them as if imagining the sight of the power stirring within them and rippling up and down her arms.

'What's up?' asked Alice.

Hanna laughed. 'I think I'm understanding - look—' With confidence, Hanna reached up and pulled back the air in front of her. Like a curtain it was pulled back to reveal another world beyond. Alice gasped at both the sight and at the power that Hanna had demonstrated.

'How did you do that?'

'I'm not sure.' The curtain of air, time and space that Hanna had pulled apart rippled backwards like folds of soft cloth. She and Alice stopped, captivated by the scene that was scarcely more than a few feet from them. Huddled around a trestle table in a mess tent, around which hung a stale odour of damp condensation, were Eleanor and Alice in the midst of a conversation, and Kirsten turning over the cards of clock patience. Alice remembered the night clearly; the story that she had been creating with Eleanor; a tale of saga-length proportions breathed with the life of Icelandic legend.

As Alice and Hanna watched the scene, so the other Alice and Eleanor from a far off time looked up. Alice realised immediately what it was as the scene twisted back round on herself and she remembered. She remembered clearly sitting in that mess tent, the air thick with damp condensation from the gas stove in the corner, seeing the outlines of figures moving in the tent entrance and shadows thrown up onto the canvas.

'It was us all the time,' said Alice.

Hanna looked between the Alice standing next to her and the Alice from another time. 'They saw us.' Hanna winced as her brain struggled with the concept. 'You saw us then...?'

Alice nodded, differently and uncertain, 'Couldn't tell. We thought we were—' her voice trailed off as she realised how silly her words were sounding, 'I guess alfar or þurs? Now I think about it though, yes, if it hadn't seemed so unbelievable then yes. Yes we could.'

Hanna Katla nodded. Without uttering another word she turned aside and lifted up her hand to draw the window closed. Beyond where the mess tent once stood, the dark corners of the cave now remained.

'How did you know...? Did you learn this from Eleanor?'

'Something I saw.' Hanna shrugged. 'A combination of things I guess. Things I've learnt over the last few days – weeks. I just had a feeling. I can't explain it.'

'Can you open the window anywhere else?' Alice asked.

Hanna smiled wistfully in return and set her mind to empty itself and drew again on the power.

Valdís lay her pale, slender fingers across Andy's face; flicking undone the buttons of his shirt with her long nails and a wave of her fingers. She sat astride him on his stone bed and stroked his torso and leaned close to breathe his name softly.

She stopped. Her arms were clasped firm, relenting into a gentle embrace. Andy looked up from his bed.

'I'm yours Valdís,' he said.

Valdís smiled and pressed her lips to his mouth.

'Andy?!' Alice clutched her hand over her mouth to stifle her shout. She stood transfixed at the window that Hanna had opened; the window from one dark cave to another.

'That's Andy...?' Hanna's question was rhetorical.

'He's alive!' exclaimed Alice.

'I don't know.' Hanna shook her head, 'It could be real or a dream, I just can't tell—'

'No, he's alive.' Alice was adamant. 'The alfar have rescued him. I knew he wasn't dead.'

'Alice, no.' Hanna was cautious against her friend's optimism.

Across the gravel floor of the cave, in that other cave, Valdís, sat astride the half-naked lean body of Andy, turned; her eyes piercing and bright.

'You!'

Hanna or Alice thought for only the briefest of moments that the accusation was aimed at an unseen comrade in the other cave, as they quickly realised that Valdís' attention was on them.

From out of the shadows around her emerged other svart-alfar and amongst them the tall, striding figure, of Gyrdir.

'Baldursdóttir,' he addresed Hanna, 'I knew you would realise your place in things. You shall take your place in the world, I will see to it.'

Hanna stood frozen by the confrontation as she attempted to understand what she had done. Her thoughts trailed away into an emptying mind in front of Gyrdir.

'Andy! Get away from them!' Alice stood at the edge of the window pleading with her friend.

Sitting now on his bed, finding it hard to recognise the figures across the void he reached out for Valdís' comforting hand. Then he rose up and stood behind her, embracing the svart-alfar lady.

'Andy!' Alice called. Her head turned, in time to see Gyrdir's approach flanked by his svart-alfar followers, swelling in number. She turned again. 'Hanna, close the window. You have to, now!'

Gyrdir stepped forward, slowly advancing towards the window.

Alice turned away from the scene in front of her and reached out to grab Hanna by the hands. She shook her awake and pleaded again to her to close the window. Hanna nodded and drew her hands through the air. As the window closed, Alice screamed again for Andy, but it was too late. The window closed with a last lingering view of Gyrdir's twisted and stretched face and his controlling hand reaching out.

Alice sunk to her knees and mourned the loss for a second time of her friend. Hanna moved to comfort her, as first Eleanor, then Ben and Kirsten returned to the cave, drawn back by the shouts and the commotion.

Alice looked up as Eleanor approached. She shook her head. 'Andy. He's not dead.'

Kathryn pulled herself from her sleeping bag and from the dark corner under the eaves of the attic room. She pulled her combat trousers on and took her coat down from the peg, stopping and wincing as it rustled, the noise seemed to echo around the room dreadfully. She retrieved her torch and grabbed her small day sack before stepping slowly and quietly from the room, pulling the door to behind her until the latch was just resting on the frame.

On the landing she paused for a moment longer and considered her actions. She frowned and quickly descended the stairs. At the bottom of the stairs her hand trailed behind her on the rail as she pushed onwards to the kitchen, dimly lit from one of the security lights. Pulling a glass from a shelf she twisted the tap on, gushed water into it and drank. She turned and leant back against the counter, gasped and blinked.

William stood framed by the dark oblong of the doorway. Kathryn gulped down more water and slid the glass back onto the drainer then slipped her arms into her jacket.

'I thought you were asleep,' she said.

'As I did you,' William returned the observation. 'Where are you going?'

'Out.' Kathryn didn't feel like talking. 'Couldn't sleep. Needed a walk.'

'At this time of night?' William asked, 'What's the matter Kathryn?'

Kathryn looked up at her boss. She couldn't answer. *How could she answer what she herself didn't understand?* She shouldered her rucksack.

'I'm sorry. I can't.' As she pushed her way through the door she heard William's last words drift after her. 'Can't? Or won't?'

William remained a few moments longer, standing in one doorway looking at another. He turned to go back upstairs when he saw movement. He looked closer. The door was still closed – but there – figures were looking at him.

'He's seen us.' Hanna panicked and pulled shut the curtain. She turned her head and looked towards her cousins.

William stepped forward quickly and inspected the corner. He threw open the door and looked out into the night. He called a greeting and returned indoors and looked at the room; empty as before. He scratched his head, puzzling over what he had seen. What he had thought he'd seen.

'That was a way out,' Ben reproached.

'And there was someone in the room.' Hanna reminded Ben, 'We can't go walking through from one world to another in front of complete strangers. You of all people should know that.'

'Why do we want to leave anyway?' asked Eleanor, 'Gyrdir wants to destroy or damage this world. We can't let him do that to the þurs.'

'The þurs don't want our help.' Ben forced the words. 'Look at us. Look at what they've done.'

'But I started this,' said Eleanor, 'I took the cup. I gave the runes to that man, that thing...'

Ben shook his head and looked to the others for support. He saw Alice mouth Andy's name. His cousin kept silent. He looked to Kirsten and she shrugged.

'Eleanor, I'm certain that you didn't start this,' Hanna Kanna said boldly. She waited patiently until she had everyone's attention. 'Think about it. Gunnlaugr - Gyrdir - Ódinn - whatever his name? He found you. And Solveig? She was of our family. The old farm and my dad's maps - his books - I don't think any of this is chance. It's not your fault.'

Eleanor shrugged. 'It doesn't change anything.'

Hanna shook her head. 'You're right. But it does show us that this is not because of you—' She remained silent for a few moments before adding, 'Alone.'

Kathryn took a path into the heart of the lava field, in the dusky-blue light of night, slipping from one dark shadow to another. She avoided using her torch and instead forced her eyes to adjust. She looked keenly for the huldufolk, still unsure of exactly why she sought them but sure that she must.

The earth shook violently and the rock walls convulsed. Hanna was thrown from her feet, crashing backwards into her friends and fell to the floor.

'The mountain.' Ben tried to pick himself up from where he found himself trapped by his sister's legs. 'It's tearing itself apart.'

The sky flared orange before descending again into night. Kathryn scrambled to her feet and found herself face to face with a pair of large, round eyes and a face with marshmallow lips. She gasped and recoiled. The face was joined by another; þursar scouts who jumped down from their ledge and approached Kathryn cautiously. The first of them drew a knife in front of him. Kathryn backed away.

'I'm not going to hurt you,' she said and showed the two þurs the palms of her hands.

The second þurs put his lips together and whistled a signal into the night. Almost immediately two more þurs joined them and began to circle Kathryn. She pressed herself back so far and so hard into the sharp, irregular shape of the lava that it hurt. The first and she thought senior scout stepped right up to her and reached out a thick, podgy hand and swiftly touched Kathryn's arm, withdrawing it immediately. He rolled his eyes and stared closer.

'I'm Kathryn.' She trembled as she spoke. 'I want to help.' She shook her head as she realised how silly her words sounded. She didn't know that they needed help. And even if they did what arrogance it was of her to think that she could help. What did she know? She cursed herself under her own breath.

Again the þurs scout stepped forward, this time with his friend alongside. They rose up on tip toe and sniffed at Kathryn and she could smell their oily, fishy pungency. It turned her nose. Again, he reached out, this time towards her face.

And suddenly, as quickly as they came, the þurs left her. As swiftly as they could on their little legs they ducked back into the shadows, scattering out amongst the lava field. Just as Kathryn was beginning to wonder what was going on, the ground began to throb beneath her feet. Dust and gravel was dislodged and flung up into the air or fell in showers from the cliff above.

Once more the ground shook, this time stronger. The tremors built and Kathryn ran from the wall of lava. Above the mountain seemed to roar with anguish and even in the night sky she could see the ash cloud billow from its summit. Far above her, the mountain seemed to explode, rupturing with a deafening noise that echoed back and forth across the valley. The ground shifted violently and threw Kathryn to the floor sending her hands scraping through the gravel and her face into the dirt.

In the mountain hut, William picked himself up from the floorboards. Bags lay upturned on the floor where they had been thrown. A glass lay smashed and water seeped down into the cracks between the floorboards. Out, across the hillside, in a sky stained with smoke and ash, dawn began to break.

Dust fell like a thin curtain glistening in the light from the torches. Hanna, Eleanor and Ben picked themselves up along with their friends.

'It's ripping itself apart,' said Alice with fear in her voice.

'Hanna, a door,' Ben pleaded with his cousin, 'Get us out of here.'

Hanna Katla nodded. Attempting to blank her mind from fear she focused on the world outside and felt her power flow through her arms. As she reached up and closed her hand around a pocket of air, Eleanor rushed back through the cave and stayed her cousin's hands. She shook her head.

'No need. The tremor – it's broken through the rocks. We can get back out to the passage!' Eleanor looked intently from cousin to brother and from brother to friends.

Hanna relaxed out of her state of trance and nodded in agreement. 'Let's do it,' she said.

Torches; ripped from the walls by the violence of the mountain burnt the cloth and animal hide drapes. Bergur attempted to restore order to his council chamber, as his fellow elders panicked and fled. Sunlight refracted across the stone table and a shaft of light sliced through the cave from a vast and distant crack that had been opened through the roof. A þurs elder screamed and Bergur called out the name of Lárus. Caught in the sun's rays, the life drained from Lárus as his skin returned to the rock from which he was made.

'The sun is in our own chamber!' Bergur spat the words contemptuously. 'We are lost!'

5

Dawn. The tyres of Charles Ancell's jeep skidded on the gravel as he accelerated away from the hut. Eighties rock music warbled and crackled from the stereo. He leant on the accelerator and steered hard into the curves of the track up onto the ridge, from where he could see the mountain shrouded in a thick, dense ash cloud that stained the sunrise.

Driving up to the main gates, Charles pulled the handbrake and flicked the car out of gear as security let him into the compound. He drove forward into the car park already half-coated in a first layer of asphalt and pulled up alongside half a dozen other jeeps and vans. Killing the ignition, the music drained away and he pushed back the door and stepped down. He took in the view of his factory. Around the compound, many of the buildings were still of gaunt steelwork shells but in the midst, the first rig was finished; standing with clean lines against the mountainous horizon and the glacier beyond.

Charles couldn't hide his gleeful expression. Today was the day; the day that he would make history. He strode off quickly to climb the steps of the control tower.

Inside, Charles stopped, immediately.

Gunnlaugr turned and faced Charles. 'I thought I was going to have to start without you.'

Dials danced on scales, oscillating violently over the red; digital displays flashed up numbers and electronic recorders sounded tones and signals. Nils glanced from machine to machine and from reading to reading. Lost amongst the activity he cursed and questioned Kathryn's absence.

'She'll be back soon,' William said calmly.

Kathryn sat, hunched against the wall holding a svart-alfar blade. The edge was notched with the victims of previous battles but it was still dangerously sharp. The flat surface was dulled and fogged with tarnish and the handle was of grubby bone. She stared in fearful confrontation at the slight, tiny, wraith-like figure opposite.

Kathryn saw in the wide, staring eyes, a haunted, scared child that was stripped of its weapon, trapped with its human adversary. Kathryn had the idea to take the creature back to the hut, although she was not entirely sure why she thought this was necessary. Slowly, keeping her eyes fixed on the creature, she raised the knife in readiness. With her other hand she slipped her rucksack from her shoulders and stripped away one of the straps. Cautiously she approached the child. With one hand outstretched she reached out with the other and lunged. At the last minute she grabbed the child's thin wrist.

'Heimili!' The child screamed.

Even under the screeching, anguished tone of the child, Kathryn recognised the Icelandic word for 'home' from conversations with Níls over the last few months.

'It's okay,' Kathryn said firmly and clearly, praying that the child would understand. 'I'll take you home.'

She bound the child's wrists together with the nylon strapping from her rucksack and pulled them tight, before dragging the child to its feet.

'Come,' Kathryn said and led the child down through the pitted paths of ancient lava. Crossing the field of gnarled and pointed black rocks they eventually descended down the short but steep path onto the marshy plain in front of the mountain hut.

Kathryn pushed the child ahead of her, up the stairs and into the dormitory. She pushed the child back onto the bed, where it cowered in the corner. Kathryn stared across the room at Níls.

'What are these creatures that attacked me?'

Níls turned from his computer and looked first to Kathryn and then to the child that was even now crawling itself into a whining and sobbing ball. He looked back at Kathryn, as did William, both bewildered by the change in behaviour of their colleague.

'They attacked me. This thing, attacked me,' explained Kathryn.

William approached Kathryn and the girl. He looked carefully and curiously at the svart-alfar girl with her pale, thin face, her slender body and her long, dark hair.

'What is she?' He took the girl's knife from Kathryn's hand. 'An elf?'

'Svart-alfar, I think,' said Níls, 'a dark elf. You shouldn't have brought her here, Kathryn.'

Kathryn stared back at Níls. In her gaze she questioned his cryptic, half-said answers.

An explosion ripped through the room, thundering around the walls and physically convulsing the floor. It threw the scientists to the floor and the svart-alfar girl across the bunk and into the pit of darkness where the roof converged with the top of the bunk. Vibrations continued to oscillate through the timber room as the thunder-like noise rolled across the valley. William crawled to the window first, followed by Kathryn and Níls, and peered up at the mountain and at where the ash cloud stained the sky black with flashes of red across the horizon.

'It's begun.'

The voice was small and highly pitched. Kathryn turned, closely followed by her colleagues. The svart-alfar child looked back at them with piercing, silver eyes.

'Ragnarok.' The child stood, now more confident. 'The end of things has come.'

Charles picked himself up from the floor of the control room. He eyed Gunnlaugr where he stood unmoved as if the volcanic eruption had passed him by. Computer screens and temperature control scales were oscillating in the red. Around the plant sirens blasted and wailed their synthetic song.

'The smelter?' Charles scrambled to his feet.

'It's working,' Gunnlaugr replied. 'Just as I told you.'

'The temperature's too high.' Charles began frantically to alter variables, one eye on the various lights and dials and one on the darkening, threatening sky.

'The temperature range is within normal tolerance.' Gunnlaugr offered his calm reassurance.

'Maybe for the centre of the Earth!' Charles shook his head. 'If I don't lower the temperatures here the whole factory is going to blow.' Charles glanced round at Gunnlaugr. The man stood tall and vitriolic. He gazed out at the mountain that continued to spew out ash and smoke and smiled.

The boy froze, as the Frisbee flew past his head. His brothers and sisters were staring too. Across the campsite – out over the ridge – high across the glacier, the sky was black and choked in ash. The noise was an endless roar; a perpetual drone and it intensified still further.

A young girl, kneeling on the ground, felt the pulsating of the soil beneath her, cried. The thundering roar intensified; a growling, angry noise that penetrated the ear drums and pierced the heart; a noise with no cause; a hidden threat.

Across the campsite a siren wailed. Suddenly the parents were running to grab their children as rangers circled the site in their jeeps calling out the emergency.

Alice and Hanna ran ahead, storming up the stone stairs. Charging forward, they emerged out of the entrance and skidded to a halt as spray hit them full on. Eleanor, Ben and Kirsten piled in behind them. The cavern had split into two and water was surging out into the narrow gorge and the spray filled the space like fine mist. Hanna, with water dripping off her face, turned to her friends and after checking first that they were okay, led them back up the narrow cliff-side path. Around them the hard rock walls creaked and groaned under the pressure of escaping water.

Reaching the top of the gorge, they paused momentarily to look back down at the churning froth of foam and water and mountain debris. The vibrations within the stone walls intensified. The whole cavern visibly shook and the walls reverberated with the roar. Noise built and built until an explosion brought down the roof. The gorge broke further down the river and sucked water through. Hanna and her friends were thrown to the floor as dirt and grit was flung upwards. Hanna spat and coughed out ash. Her friends too, spluttered sand and clambered to their feet.

Across the gorge, a shaft of sunlight descended through the dark from a new hole in the roof. The mountain continued to growl around them; Hanna beckoned them onwards and led them through an arch of rock back towards the grand hall.

'Wait!' Eleanor called out. Her face was dripping with water and smudged with dark, volcanic sand.

'Look.' Eleanor took hold of Hanna's arm and brought her back over to the edge. She pointed up towards the fracture in the cavern ceiling from where the sunlight now broke.

As they watched, blinking away the fine spray and squinting against the light, the spectrum of light arced down towards them.

'The Bifrost.' Hanna whispered.

'It's beautiful,' said Alice.

'And dangerous,' warned Eleanor.

Ben found his gaze drawn to it but scoffed, 'It's a rainbow. The sunlight, the water droplets in the air – it was going to happen.' He felt Kirsten squeeze him tightly by the hand and urged him to be quiet.

6

Bjäkk stood at the back of his jeep loading bags. He fastened down the cover with bungees stretched across the side as raindrops, large and loud, smacked the nylon. At first slow and deliberate, the rain increased. Bjäkk looked up at the sky and grimaced. *Hanna, where are you?* His heart pined for his friend. Around him, cars and jeeps were leaving the site leaving a scarce few trucks belonging to scientists and media crews.

'Bjäkk! Hurry!' Hálldor leant out the driver's window of his campervan. 'We've got to go!'

Bjäkk turned to his friend. He shook his head. 'I can't. My friends...'

'The mountain's going to explode, Bjäkk. Today's not the day for heroism. Hell, even the capitalists behind the Alcon plant think it's finished.' Hálldor reasoned. 'The only people staying 'round here are scientists and the press.'

Bjäkk stood in the car park holding his keys and looking from Halldór to his jeep. He glanced up at the mountain and the mushrooming ash cloud. The side door of the van slid back and Bryn, still clutching at his injured ribs looked out at Bjäkk. His face was stretched, tired and exhausted.

'Come on mate,' said Bryn, 'There's nothing we can do now. We've seen the enemy.' He choked. 'We've fought it. If Hanna and that lot are still alive, they can survive this. If they can't, then they are lost already.'

The rain started in earnest; heavy and humid. Bjäkk considered Bryn's words. He pulled up the collar of his jacket.

'I hear what you're saying, I do.' He shook his head. 'Like you say the only people staying are the media and scientists. And I'm a scientist now.' Bjäkk smiled wryly and slid back the door, slamming it shut.

Hálldor accelerated, and drove away leaving Bjäkk standing watching, wondering if he'd done the right thing. He turned, pushed back the tail gate of his jeep, and slammed the bolts back into place. He walked away and returned to the hut.

The temperature gauge oscillated high into the red. Charles stared at the needle until his eyes were sore. Slowly, he turned his head towards Gunnlaugr and scowled.

'What have you done?' Charles spat the words. 'You promised me the world's riches?'

'I promised myself the world – my world. And look, it comes to me after so many years.'

Charles' lip quivered. He stared at the man that he now found impossible to understand. A gust of wind forced open the door to the control tower. Sand and gravel blew in. Rain hammered thickly on the observation windows as darkness swept in; a darkness that was punctured by a shaft of sunlight that broke through a crack in the stormy clouds. Charles turned in time to see a spectrum of light arcing towards the factory.

'My world,' said Gunnlaugr, relishing the moment.

'Is now really the time to be chasing rainbows?' Charles choked on a laugh. 'Next you will be singing Julie Andrews.'

Charles looked round for his mobile and found it on the floor under his chair. He thumbed through the phone book for Kári's name.

'The bridge between the worlds,' Hanna said simply. She stood, oblivious now to the continual spray and stared at the rainbow of light as it formed itself into the Bifrost.

'It's amazing,' said Alice.

'It's a way home?' asked Kirsten.

Ben squeezed Kirsten's hand and looked narrowly into her eyes. He shook his head.

'It's *a* way home,' Hanna answered.

'But—' Alice said tentatively.

'It's not safe,' Eleanor interrupted. 'Ragnarok remember. If the worlds are being torn apart do you really think a bridge is the safest place to be?'

Ben had stepped up to the foot of the rainbow and was exploring the strange light that surrounded him, commenting over and over on the impossibility of the situation and reminding himself about the science of rainbows. He tapped one of a pair of statues that now flanked the end of the bridge; a tunnel of spectrum light, yet with a substance, a solidity, that he could step onto.

'It looks safe enough,' Ben commented. 'I say we try it.'

*

Andy felt the fine workmanship of the bone handle and the silver detailing at the hilt of the sword which Valdís had slipped into the leather sheaf now fastened to his belt. In the dark cave he stood tall. Barefoot and bare-chested he wore trousers of coarse linen and a leather jerkin and his eyes shone like silver.

'Come.' Valdís beckoned. 'It is time for us to join our master.'

Andy reached out for Valdís and caught hold of her wrist. 'Wait!' He pulled her closer. She looked up at him, curious of his intentions.

'Before we go—' Andy pulled her closer, stroked his hand through her long, black hair and pressed a kiss to her lips.

Smoke poured out in plumes from the factory as flames leapt higher out of the murk and explosion followed explosion. Gunnlaugr stood on the jagged ridge above the site as rain and wind flooded the hillside. Each drop of water stung his skin with ash. Out of the gloom, a refraction of light and water brought with it a spectrum of light that formed in front of him.

Across the slope, Valdís and Andy made their approach to join Gunnlaugr at the foot of the Bifrost.

'You join us?' Gunnlaugr looked upon Andy, his newest recruit. 'You choose wisely.'

Andy nodded. This man and – he glanced at Valdís – this woman; they had given him a second life. He breathed in sharply and turned to face the Bifrost with his companions. Within the radiance of light before them, an entrance to a stair crafted from stone appeared. Partially translucent with the mountains visible beyond, Andy had no fear as the three of them took their first steps into the entrance and began their ascent.

*

Ben tried his footing on the first step. Even though the stones were partially translucent, they were still firm and secure. He tried another and turned to face the others. He nodded.

'Of course it's safe.' Eleanor countered, bounding forward and taking the stairs two at a time past Ben. 'I told you didn't I? This is how I got out before.' She stood on the stairs several metres above her brother.

Hanna was next to take to the bridge. Kirsten and Alice followed last, with Kirsten falling in alongside Ben as Alice joined the others ahead. Together, the five of them climbed up the ancient staircase, deep into the bridge and the space between the worlds.

'At least we know when we're halfway!' Alice tried a joke.

The growling, tearing sound beneath the ground reached deafening proportions. At the snout of the glacier, ice fractured, seared off and fell into the moraine. Crevasses widened and new ones split as rivers of water spilled out, first as a trickle, then as a gush until suddenly and explosively the snout of Skeiðarárjökull was ripped apart. Six thousand cubic metres per second of glacial water mixed with dirt and rock were pouring out into the river and ripping rocks and soil out of the ground as it went. Crashing past power cables and telegraph poles, they flipped them out of the ground like straws and snapped them like twigs.

Miles away across the plain, a driver slammed on the brakes and skidded his bus to a halt. The driver assessed the encroaching wall of water with the upcoming bridge. He flung the bus into gear and accelerated, pumping the pedals for power and steering for the middle of the long, low, single-track bridge across the river. A third of the way across and the wall of churning water was looming nearer. The driver floored the accelerator as he realised too late his mistake.

Two thirds of the way across the bridge and the violent, malevolent river hit the bridge, twisting the girders on impact. The driver steered the bus through a skid, saw the end of the bridge and cursed out loud as he watched the road buckle and split. The iron supports of the bridge twisted and stretched like sinews until finally they snapped, thrusting the bridge along with the path of the river and the bus tumbled and spun off into the river, smashed and broken and cast out towards the sea.

Bjäkk stopped outside the ranger's office, watching the scenes of devastation on a live 24 hour news channel. Impassively, he realised he had just watched the deaths of maybe forty innocent people. He couldn't take his eyes off the screen as the helicopter born camera zoomed in on the bus as it was swept down river. For a moment, he thought he glimpsed a child's face pressed to the window. He turned away.

Kathryn turned to see the svart-alfar girl, tucked in the shadows of the corner, beginning to work magic with her hands.

'Stop her!' She screamed and launched herself towards the girl at the same time as William. Together they both grabbed for the girl's wrists. The girl lunged forward and bit Kathryn's hand. She looked up, and through the slits of silver eyes, showed her feral and dangerousness. Kathryn withdrew and looked down at the blood seeping from the puncture wound.

On the stair, Hanna stopped.

'What is it?' asked Ben.

Hanna nodded her head forward and pointed. Ahead of them, in the dark of the shadows three figures were advancing towards them. 'We are not alone.'

'Gunnlaugr?' Eleanor choked on his name.

Hanna nodded to Eleanor, 'It would make sense.'

As the others fell in alongside them, they looked ahead again. Now more figures came into view, smaller, and further off behind the advancing three. Along the bridge, the air and the rocks all shimmered with the spectral light of the Bifrost. Obsidian glimmered and reflected through the walls. Hanna felt the danger and cast out her hands. She felt a power flow through her arms and put up some kind of invisible shield. The three figures advanced closer and they watched them carefully.

A storm raged, somewhere out over the mountains. Flashes of lightning seeped through the translucent walls of the bridge. Another fork and for a moment Eleanor could make out the features in the faces of the advancing people. Another flash as the thunder continued to roll and she could see him again.

'It can't be?'

'What is it Eleanor?' Hanna quickly asked.

Eleanor didn't answer straight away. She reached behind her and pushed Alice and Kirsten to the front. She nodded to the second tallest of the figures. 'Tell me that's not Andy?'

A triple flash of lightning and the face was unmistakable. The short cropped hair; the dark, unshaven beginnings of a beard on his chin; it was the face of Andy. Eleanor shook her head. He was walking shoulder to shoulder with Gunnlaugr – with Gyrdir.

'No!' Eleanor ran forward, discounting any fear, she scrambled up the steps, slipping a couple of times before stumbling past Andy. She turned and reached out to him. 'I thought you were dead?'

'Eleanor, don't!' Hanna screamed.

Eleanor ignored her cousin. She had to get through to Andy. She sidestepped Andy and positioned herself in front of him, putting out her hands to grab his shoulders. She looked up into his eyes imploringly and saw the silver shining through.

'Andy?' asked Eleanor. 'What's wrong? Why don't you answer me? Your eyes...'

Andy stepped on, in step with his companions and pushed past Eleanor as he went. Eleanor was left, fallen on the stair as Gunnlaugr advanced on the others.

'No.' Hanna Katla confronted Gunnlaugr. He stopped, two steps up from her, and smiled; a thin, sly smile. At Gunnlaugr's side Andy closed his fingers around the hilt of his sword.

'It's too late.' Gunnlaugr laughed. 'I've been let in.'

Hanna shook her head, dismissing his assumption. Glancing back she saw the old world, the world of the huldufolk. Turning again, she saw her own world, with the mountains venting fire and ash and the glaciers ripping themselves apart. Looking up, the sky was a ferocious storm of churning clouds splintered at times with lightning. Out in the east, the sun still found a way to break through the darkness.

'Not too late, no,' Hanna stood firm. 'You are taking the old sagas far too seriously. We know what you are planning.'

'Would you be this brave if you knew who you were defying?'

'I know that you say you are Gunnlaugr.' Hanna was equally determined in her response. 'And I know that Gunnlaugr is simply a corruption of Gangleri. Gangleri the walk-weary?'

Gunnlaugr laughed off Hanna's words. He gathered his companions together and took a step forward. Hanna held him back with the power that she drew through herself and out through the palms of her hands.

'Do you prefer Gyrdir? That's what's the alfar call you. Svipal maybe? Vak or Ygg? Bolverk maybe suits you better?' Hanna took a slow, deliberate step closer. She gritted her teeth in anger. 'The þurs don't call you anything other than what you are. How many names do you have, Ódinn?'

For the moments following Hanna's utterance of his real name, the worlds went quiet and the storm subsided. Gunnlaugr's face was twisted and he recoiled at Hanna's words.

'We kill them now master.' Valdís drew her sword, a svartalfar blade forged from silver and glinting with the light of the Bifrost. Andy too, began to pull his blade from the sheath. Gunnlaugr stayed both their hands.

'They are nothing. They are human children. They cannot stop us.' Gunnlaugr lifted his hand and plucked at the threads of Hanna's magic. He laughed. 'Come. My world awaits.' He snatched up the invisible threads and cast them aside and Hanna fell to the ground with them. She looked up from the floor as Gunnlaugr pushed past her friends. As Andy passed Kirsten and Alice they tried to attract his attention but he stared through them, blanking their existence and their friendship.

Hanna began to pull herself to her feet as Eleanor chased down the steps after Gunnlaugr. 'Wait!'

'By the descendancy of Solveig!' She screamed. 'I command you to stop.'

She stood still, looking down on the man – the thing – the stranger from the mountains. She watched him stop and linger in his stride. She waited and–

'Solveig.' Gunnlaugr nodded. He turned slowly; his mouth all but snarling. 'Of course, Solveig. What of her?'

'The blood of Solveig. It runs through me – through us.' She reached out and pulled her brother and cousin close, clasping their hands with hers. 'We have power. Go now and leave this place while you still have a chance.'

Gunnlaugr laughed. 'The blood of Solveig. That witch!' You're right of course, the blood of Solveig runs deep and runs far.' He turned his head slowly and bowed his head to Andy. 'Doesn't it my friend.'

'Andy?' questioned Eleanor. Her face winced with uncertainty.

'It's true.' Andy stepped forward. 'Thank you Eleanor. It is a great gift you've given me. I have my friends here to thank for recognising it.' Slowly he drew his sword, and raised the blade lie on Eleanor's face. He stared down the line of glistening sharp edge.

'Now you leave whilst you still can. You might yet escape the mountains before the close of Ragnarok.' Andy nodded.

Eleanor flinched.

'What just happened there?' Ben pushed his hand through his untidy mop of wet hair. Silence dwelled around him on the ancient stair – the Bifrost – the bridge between the worlds.

'What did he mean, *thank you Eleanor?*' Hanna looked to her cousin.

Eleanor sat on a step, her face buried in her hands.

'It's obvious isn't it?' said Kirsten, 'He doesn't fear you as descendants of Solveig, because he has his own descendent.'

Hanna shook her head. 'The blood of Solveig runs far?'

'Along those lines,' reasoned Kirsten. 'You three are not the only descendants.'

Ben and Hanna turned to look at Eleanor.

'No Eleanor. Tell me you haven't?' Ben looked away.

'Eleanor?' Hanna asked. 'You said that you and Andy – that there was nothing–'

Eleanor forced her head further into her hands. Thoughts entered her mind and she pushed them away. Tears began to well up and soak through her fingers as she tried to comprehend what she had done. Slowly, she lifted her head. In her mind she could see the scene so clearly.

Andy stood, framed by the doorway to her college room. Tall, toned and beautiful in his favourite checked shirt tucked neatly into his Levis. Eleanor's expression recoiled with her body in anguish over her feelings. She shook her head.

'Oh, thank god—'

Eleanor watched the relief flow across Andy's face. In an instant, she knew that she had made the right decision. She stirred from her daze, with Andy perched on the bed in front of her and reaching out his hands to hold her; to comfort her. She looked away.

'It's okay.' Andy held her close. 'It's what we wanted.'

'Shit.' Alice bit her lip and slid it out between her teeth.

'Your first year at uni...?' Ben struggled to understand his sister. 'Is that why you didn't come home that Easter?'

Eleanor looked up. She nodded hopelessly.

'We were going to go fell running. Regional finals if I remember. And you were what, having an abortion?'

'I'm really sorry Ben.' Eleanor felt small, looking up at her brother, 'We wouldn't have won anyway. I hadn't exactly been keeping up the training.'

Hanna reached out to support her cousin. 'It's okay Eleanor, Ben didn't mean to be so insensitive.' She glanced over her shoulder and glared at Ben.

'And Andy never knew?' Hanna knelt down in front of her friend.

Eleanor shook her head. 'Neither of us were ready for that. It didn't seem worth destroying both our lives,' she said. 'Better that I just did what needed to be done. Keep it simple.'

Hanna pulled her cousin into an embrace. Kirsten reached out for her friend's hand.

'I didn't know Andy was going to die.' Eleanor looked up. 'That was never in my plan.'

'You didn't kill him. What you did – or didn't do – it was the storm, it...' Ben told her with hard accuracy.

'If I told him – how do you know we'd still have been friends. He still had feelings and I never...' Eleanor sighed, too tired to think straight. 'He would have met someone else. He wouldn't have come to Iceland.'

'You don't know that. You don't know how he would have reacted because you didn't tell him.' Ben crouched down. He reached out and took his sister's head in his hands, and stared directly into her eyes. 'You never gave him the choice. That's what I don't understand.'

Kirsten grabbed at Ben's sleeve. She whispered, 'Ben? This isn't about you...'

Eleanor gazed down the length of the Bifrost, at the ever-darkening, gathering storm clouds. In the distance lightning flashed. 'You heard Gunnlaugr. I gave him what he needed. If it wasn't for me he may not have found a way.'

Silence. Suddenly the danger they faced gripped them all. Alice watched her friends, each in turn, from her space on the step next to Eleanor hugging her knees close to her breast. She glanced from Eleanor and Hanna Katla, to Ben and to Kirsten. She watched how Ben and Kirsten's gaze always came back to each other.

'Sadly I think you are right, Eleanor,' Alice said flatly. One by one her four friends turned and looked to her, each with variations of the same questioning expression. Alice nodded towards Kirsten and Ben.

'The way I see it, Gunnlaugr doesn't care. He needed Eleanor, but he wouldn't. So when Andy fell victim to him, and let's face it, with what happened to him he wasn't going to object...' Alice put her reasoning honestly and simply. 'There's three of you with the blood of Solveig running through you. Are you telling us there's no one he could have used? And Ben, I'm not saying that you and—' She nodded to Kirsten. 'But you have to agree there's a possibility...'

'Alice!' Kirsten rebuffed sharply. She began to continue but her words stumbled and failed her and she fell back on Ben's support only to pull away when Ben offered her a kiss. She shivered.

'Still,' continued Alice, 'at least we know where Gunnlaugr gets his power from. So presumably we know how to take it away.'

'Já. Of course,' Hanna agreed. 'He's drawing on the oldest power he knows. Solveig is the link to the alfar - to the huldufolk.'

'And Andy is the link.' Eleanor uttered the words simply and quietly.

'We have to break the link,' Hanna nodded.

'It's down to me then.' Eleanor looked up, her eyes bright and blue. 'I have to finish what I started.'

7

Looking down the length of the Bifrost, the mountain hut could be seen across the plain. Eleanor stood with Alice and Kirsten. Her breath was fast – she took Alice's hands and placed them palm against palm and looked directly into her friend's eyes.

'You do understand don't you? You have to go. We three have to do it alone.' Eleanor glanced round at Hanna and Ben.

'But thank you.' Eleanor found it hard not to cry. 'You've been great. More than great – we couldn't have got this far without you.'

Ben stepped forward and embraced Kirsten. On the steps they kissed and embraced tighter. They whispered words to one another and again kissed.

'Come on bro,' Eleanor called him, sympathetically.

Eventually Ben released Kirsten. His hands, entwined with hers, slowly let them slip away. He looked at her and carefully memorised her every hair and every freckle.

'Ben?'

Kirsten nodded to him. 'Go. Go on. Laters—'

Ben turned and joined Eleanor and his cousin. They began to ascend the Bifrost once more. Stopping after a few metres, they turned. Alice and Kirsten were where they had left them. All three of them ushered their friends to go; to be gone.

Once more Hanna and her two cousins turned and they made their ascent, pausing only twice more to look over their shoulders. The first time they saw Alice and Kirsten making their final, fast descent towards. The second time they saw the stair empty and suddenly so quiet, and so still. They were alone. The three descendants of Solveig once more crossed the bridge into the world of the huldufolk and the world of gods; the world of old magic.

Across the horizon, a long dormant mountain, ruptured across its peak and exploded with a force that sent fractures through the ground. From the hot pools around the mountain hut, a sleeping geyser woke.

In the upstairs dorm, a computer screen blinked with new geothermal activity. William moved round and leaned over the screen.

'A second volcano,' said William. He navigated around the computer, flicking between screens and typing in codes. In the background the geothermal readings blinked out a third volcano. William flicked back in time to see a fourth volcano scored on the screen. 'The world's tearing itself apart. This isn't right.'

Behind William, the door squeaked open and Bjäkk pushed in. He stopped upon seeing the odd collection of a greying man bent over a computer and a young man pinning a girl with strange pointed ears to the bed whilst another young woman tied up the girl's wrists.

'What is this?' asked Bjäkk with sarcasm. 'A laboratory? Or an orgy?'

'It's private that's what it is.' William replied without even looking at the newcomer.

'Bjäkk?!' Kathryn exclaimed, almost simultaneously. 'What are you doing here?' She pulled the knot tight around the girl's wrists and got down from the bed to greet Bjäkk.

'You know this man?' William asked, still without turning around to see Bjäkk.

'Yeah.' Kathryn walked up to Bjäkk and looked into his face. 'He oversaw my project – when I was at Hólar.' She laughed. 'Bjäkk. The fish man of Hólar. Long way from the sea?'

'Geothermal activity affects land and sea Kathryn,' Bjäkk answered, 'and this–' He looked around the room at the stacks of data and instruments. 'There's going to be some serious after effects. Quite some setup you've got here Professor Tyndall.'

William lifted his head from his computer and turned. He saw a stockily-built man in jeans and leather jacket with dark-hair and a recently scarred face. He saw Bjäkk turning his attention now to the feral girl on the bed.

'I'm intrigued as to what you actually intend to find. And the svart-alfar girl – that's just added confusion.' Bjäkk's tone was mocking towards the scientist.

William looked again to Bjäkk. 'You know who the girl is?'

'She's svart-alfar. She's a dark elf – a creature of evil.' Bjäkk crossed the room and took the girl's sword in his hands. He inspected the blade and the hilt for its fine workmanship. 'Why do you have her?'

'She attacked me!' Kathryn rushed to say. 'I don't know why I brought her here - maybe - recently I've begun realising that what we've been chasing—' She nodded towards the computers and all the sensing equipment. 'That it's not the whole story. There's more that we can't track and that we can't model. It's crazy I know...'

'It's not crazy.' Bjäkk shook his head. 'Our job is to record what has happened, track what is happening and attempt to predict what will happen. The worlds' work according to the laws nature gives them but we effect change. So do other worlds and other peoples.' Bjäkk turned the sword over in his hands as he spoke, feeling its weight and taking a measure of its handling. He tried a lunge. And again. He nodded. 'Impressive.'

'Bjäkk?' Kathryn looked concerned for the fish man.

Bjäkk stepped a little closer to the svart-alfar girl to examine her fine, pale cheek bones, her long black hair and the silver in her eyes. 'Will you take your leader a message for me?'

The girl looked up from where she lay on her side, small yet still ferociously independent. She muttered something in her own tongue and spat her response. He nodded and lowered himself to the level of her eyes and spoke his words sincerely. 'Tell Ódinn that he'll never succeed.'

Bjäkk stood and turned. Without further warning he swung round once more pulling out the sword and lunged forward. He pierced the girl's heart—

Valdís threw back her head, screaming in anguish. She fell to her knees clutching at her heart. Slowly she pulled her fingers away and saw blood. She muttered words in the svart-alfar tongue as Andy fell to her side to tend her and inspect her wound. He watched as Valdís lay her fingers to the wound and stemmed the bleeding with a lightness of touch.

Gunnlaugr turned towards Valdís. 'How? How have they done this?'

'They are attacking our brethren.' Valdís looked up at her master and spoke. Her voice was etched with the pain of silver ripped through her heart. 'They've killed my sister.'

'Then they have signed for their own death.' Gunnlaugr turned angrily and reached out to the gnarled and twisted ash tree in the centre of the cavern. As his fingers closed round the slender stemmed branch, it flaked to dust in his hand. He smiled and laughed.

The ground quaked and fire breathed again out of desolate mountain. Hot lava boiled over and scorched the earth beneath the summit. The air thickened with a toxic mix of smoke, ash and sulphur.

Water burst out of a second hole in the glacier and surged forward to join the flood as it spilled out across the plain towards the sea. On the main road, a van was parked up, as a film crew captured pictures of the jökulhlaup that pulled apart the tarmac and uprooted power cables.

Gunnlaugr stood in the Great Hall beneath the mountain, vaulted with hexagonal basalt columns that stretched out over him and black obsidian that shimmered with an ethereal light. Gunnlaugr looked back at Andy. He gestured for the boy to get up and Andy obeyed him. Gunnlaugr snatched Andy's arm and pulled him closer.

'Take it!' He nodded towards the dying tree. 'Take Yggdrasil in your hands.'

Andy returned Gunnlaugr's gaze. He nodded and freed himself from the man's grip.

'The tree of life.' Andy grinned broadly. He reached out and seized the trunk; the dying trunk of a twisted tree. His fingers relaxed and he almost let go of Yggdrasil. He sneered at it and looked away, catching the gaze of Gunnlaugr.

'Take it. Give it time. You have the blood of Solveig in you.'

Andy looked again at his right hand and watched as his fingers closed tight again.

'I feel nothing.'

'Give it time,' repeated Gunnlaugr.

Valdís picked herself up from the floor and slowly approached Gunnlaugr and Andy, but her gaze was on the tree; the dead tree that slowly, almost imperceptibly, began to bud. The buds began to swell and unfurl. Lush new growth with a dusty white residue opened and grew before their eyes. Andy smiled and reached out with his free hand and touched the new growth, soft and velvety beneath his fingers.

Sunlight broke through the clouds and the storm clouds began to dissipate. High in the mountains it even seemed as though the volcano may have been easing its attack on the land. A few birds circled the sky and the rainbow began to fade.

Ben's jaw dropped. Pausing in his descent, he looked back at the darkness at the top of the bridge as it gave way to daylight and the stonework began to crumble. He cried out but his voice was lost and his feet rooted to the step. Eleanor called out to him, begging him to run. Just behind her, Hanna turned and grabbed her cousin, pulling him on and the spell was broken. All three of them ran headlong down the stair, falling out at the bottom as the Bifrost faded from view.

'It's gone.' Ben glanced back at the open cavern, still flooding through with torrential water. 'If ever we had to go on.' He laughed nervously before turning and finding himself staring at two pairs of huge, leathery-skinned hairy feet. He looked up from where he was crouched on the floor. Erik and Pétur are stood in front of him. Ben glanced to either side at his sister and cousin where even now they were picking themselves up off the ground. Erik and Pétur, were stationed with fellow þurs foot-soldiers around the cavern armed with bows and daggers.

'Hey!' Eleanor greeted them like old friends. 'Where's Bergur – your leader?'

'Bergur is of stone now,' replied Erik, 'I have been appointed our chief.'

'So, Chieftain Erik of þurs, congratulations.' Eleanor stood before the immense figure of the þurs adult. 'Are you not going to ask why we've returned?'

Erik rolled his thickly set eyes and was about to speak. Eleanor silenced him. 'Because you know it's a funny thing. We met someone – three people – crossing the Bifrost and I think I understand. You want to know how to defeat Gyrdir. No wait, your people choose only to call him by his real name.' Eleanor nodded, impressing herself with her own surety. 'You want me destroy Óðinn.'

'You do not understand of what you speak.' Erik interrupted sharply. 'I trusted you with our runes—'

'No, maybe not,' Eleanor nodded, 'But do I have huldufolk ancestry.' She saw Erik look again towards her. She directed her gaze into his eyes. 'I've even spoken with Solveig.'

'You lie. Solveig is dead.' Pétur was adamant.

Eleanor shook her head. 'Give me your sword.' She said the words simply enough, but found not just Erik looking at her with curiosity and confusion. Catching her cousin's eyes she saw concern in Hanna's face and heard too the sharp intake of breath from Ben behind.

She returned her gaze on Erik and nodded to the dagger that he wore at his side. Slowly Erik drew his weapon and passed it to Eleanor. She took it and pulled the blade back across her palm and watched as blood ebbed out.

'Eleanor no!' Ben leapt forward and pulled the dagger from his sister's hands, casting it aside at Erik's feet. He pulled a handkerchief from his pocket attempted to wrestle it into Eleanor's palms.

'Ben, no!' Eleanor flicked her wrist and scattered droplets of blood onto the ground.

'What are you doing?' Ben rounded on his sister. He grabbed her by the shoulders and stared into her eyes.

'Proving my heritage.' She offered the explanation simply and pulled free. 'See.'

Ben turned, as did Hanna, as they followed Eleanor's gaze. Where blood had fallen on stony ground, ash saplings were growing; pushing their way through the soil and unfurling leaves.

'You see?' Eleanor looked around in desperation at the other þurs.

Erik stared at Eleanor for what seemed like an age. He flicked his gaze between each of the three mannfólkið. They were so small and fragile and yet, he looked down at the lush new growth – yet so powerful.

Andy laughed. The tree was blossoming now and thick with fresh new growth. He threw back his head and stared up into the dome of rock where shafts of basalt and obsidian reflected the lights. They twinkled like stars against a sky and water lapped at the shore.

Andy pulled back. He released the tree from his grasp and looked about himself. With him were Gunnlaugr and Valdís, but the three of them were no longer in an underground cavern, but on a beach of black sand from which Yggdrasil grew. Surrounded by water they were on a lake bordered by mountains. The sky was overcast with clouds and a mist descended over the far off hills, shrouding the water and closing in on the water.

'Seize the tree.' With firm words Gunnlaugr directed Andy.

Andy grinned as strength surged through his blood once more and he turned and grabbed again at the twisted trunk. Beneath his feet, the ground broke apart as the roots grew.

Rock fell and cascaded into the cavern and into the surging waters beneath. Hanna looked up and saw the tree roots, writhing like snakes in the roof.

'Mimir's well,' said Hanna.

'Mimir's what?' Ben asked over the roar of the water.

'Keep up with your Norse mythology, Ben,' Hanna quipped, 'Mimir's Well is one of the three wells that lie beneath Yggdrasil.'

Ben shrugged a response, and shuffled on his feet for a bit. Next to him, Eleanor's hand was already heeled behind the thin line of a scar.

'Eleanor Ármannsson!'

Ben looked round upon hearing his sister's name. Next he heard his name too, and that of Hanna's in a strong, male voice. The three of them cautiously approached the end of the canyon and looked down. Beneath them, on the river were long boats, and in one, Finnbjörn stood, calling up to them.

'You are known to the alfar leaders.' Erik nodded slowly to Eleanor. 'You are indeed of some heritage.'

Finnbjörn called again. His crew were now tying up their boats to a now rocky ledge at the foot of the cliffs.

'Will you let us go?' Eleanor asked the þurs man.

Erik remained silent for a few moments. He took the sword from Eleanor's hand and inspected the craftsmanship. He passed it back to Eleanor.

'And you shall keep this sword,' Erik told her, 'Petur, see to it that the others are given swords of equal quality.'

As Petur scampered away, Erik turned again to the three cousins.

'I fear that you will need them where the alfar will take you, but they should protect you well.'

Three boats broke through the mist, guided by alfar oarsman in the stern. Hanna, Eleanor and Ben sat tucked into the bows, one in each boat. A mournful, piercing song ebbed and flowed on the wind and permeated the mist.

Valdís saw the boats and drew her sword. She threw back her head and called out to her people as lightning forked through the clouds. From out of the mist black figures waded through the water. At the shore, the boats grounded on the beach, scrunching through the black sand. Eleanor leapt out over the bow and splashed through the shadows. Across the beach, she saw her brother and cousin and in the centre, a twisted, blossoming tree and Andy in the thick of it. Behind her, Finnbjörn stepped through the water, oar in hand, using it as a walking stick. He stepped up to her, laying his other hand on her shoulder.

'Eirný and Jóhanna,' Eleanor nodded towards the alfar figures standing alongside Ben and Hanna.

'You must do what you must do.' Speaking in a hushed voice, Finnbjörn nudged Eleanor's gaze back to the tree – to Andy.

Andy, who, feeling centuries of magic coursing through his veins held his left hand outstretched towards Gunnlaugr. Slowly Gunnlaugr stepped towards his boy; the human child and reached out towards Andy's outstretched hand. A bolt of lightning broke the sky and a gust of wind threw dust into the air.

Eleanor ran forward across the beach and drew her sword. Valdís stepped in front of her master and blocked Eleanor's approach. Sword met sword, metal clashed with metal and

Gunnlaugr grasped Andy's hand. Light flared from the joined hands. Gunnlaugr threw his head back and screamed, calling out his victory. Black mist swirled and lightning cracked across the sky. His eyes burned like fire as he called out to his followers; he laughed at his enemies as he sucked the old magic out from the old world.

Blade on blade, Eleanor fought Valdís. Every attacking strike was met with another that blocked it. Out of the black mist, more svart-alfar came, drawing their swords and meeting Ben and Hanna separately in conflict as they tried at points around Yggdrasil to fight their way through to Andy.

Eleanor glanced towards Andy, caught between Gunnlaugr and the source of his power, Andy looked tired and stretched. Eleanor choked for her friend and distracted, glanced up just as Valdís' sword came down towards her. Eleanor deflected the blow, but felt herself falling backwards onto the ground. Her sword, wrenched from her fingers, slid out of reach. She lay in the sand and looked up as Valdís neared.

'My master gave you a chance,' Valdís laughed, 'I couldn't take that risk.'

Eleanor watched as Valdís lifted her sword above her and took aim. Her fingers grappled at the sand as she felt for her sword. Valdís' sword came down towards Eleanor and she saw it near her. Her fingers felt the smooth touch of the sword and closed around the hilt and thrust it out above her head. Eyes squeezed shut she felt a moment of resistance before she let go and flung herself sideways. For minutes after she lay face down on the ground, face in the sand.

She lifted herself up, spitting the dirt from her mouth and looked sideways, at the body of Valdís and the red stain of blood on the sand under her. With her own sword still rammed through the svart-alfar body, Eleanor stooped and picked up

Valdís', peeling the girl's fingers from the hilt. Eleanor stood and turned towards Andy and then to Gunnlaugr.

'Let him go.'

Gunnlaugr stared with faint irritation at Eleanor. Slowly a smile drew across his face. Eleanor ignored the response. She stared firmly at him and rose up as tall she could. 'Let him go,' she repeated.

'Of course,' answered Gunnlaugr. 'I never wanted to hurt you or your friends.' He looked across, down the length of his arm at Andy's hand, held in his. He released his grip and let Andy go.

Within seconds Andy let go of the tree and fell to his knees, exhausted and spent.

'Andy!' Eleanor rushed to her friend, throwing her sword to the ground and taking Andy in her hands instead. She lifted his head and looked into his eyes; blank and empty.

Eleanor swung round and stared up at Gunnlaugr. 'What have you done to him?'

'Nothing.' Gunnlaugr shook his head. 'Nothing that fate has not already dealt him.'

Eleanor's face twitched with confusion. She felt for Andy's pulse. It was there, if weak – he was definitely alive. Her face stung with emerging tears and she reached out and kissed her friend. 'I'm sorry Andy. What have I done to you?' She held him close as the storm above intensified. Out of the corner of her eye, she spied the black steed, galloping through the water, kicking its hooves through the sandy shore and rising up in front of Gunnlaugr.

'Eleanor!'

She looked up at Ben's calling. And Hanna too, she was screaming at her cousin not to forget. *Forget what?* In Eleanor's hands she felt her friend's head. She heard his breathing. She took his hand in hers, closing her fingers within his. Across the beach, Gunnlaugr mounted his steed, once again wearing the clothes of Ódinn. The horse reared up again at Gunnlaugr's bequest, as he called out victory. Eleanor lifted up Andy's hand in her own, looking at the fingers. It's the hand that had held the tree. The link. She dropped Andy and got up, taking up her sword again and stepping back to look at her friend.

'I'm sorry Andy, really.'

Eleanor gritted her teeth and stepped up to her friend again and slowly, deliberately pushed the sword through Andy's chest. Blood oozed out and he screamed.

Gunnlaugr screamed and with a deafening crack of thunder, the lightning struck.

8

Ben sat in front of his computer watching the computer model draw itself. He sighed and picked up the printouts of the past week's eruptions. The figures blurred into one as he stared at them; a haze of calculations at odds with one another. He picked up a newspaper and leafed through the pages looking at story after story of devastation. Full colour pictures leapt out at him from every page. Volcanic eruptions, roads ripped to pieces by floods and a school crushed under the weight of a mountain.

He turned back to the computer and slid his cursor along the task bar brought the web browser back up. He stared at the news site, clicking through the galleries of photos; the tearful relatives and the stunned and shaken tourists. His head slid back down into his hand. As his fingers clawed around his glasses he pulled them from his face. His hand closed tight around them and he thumped his forehead with his fist.

Eleanor stood on a sandy beach holding a bloodied sword. Andy lay at her feet, on blood-stained black sand. Ben and Hanna closed in on Eleanor, standing alongside her, opposite where Gunnlaugr stood on the beach by his fallen steed. He turned and laughed mockingly.

'Don't think you've defeated me.'

'It's over,' answered Eleanor, 'the link is broken.'

Gunnlaugr took steps towards the family. 'But at what cost?' He shrugged towards Andy. 'Your friend dead and you trapped. There's no Bifrost here. It's a cold dark place which even the alfar have left.'

He closed the gap between them, snarling out his words, 'I am stranded here once more. My horse is dead and I am once more cast out from my own world, but so are you.'

'All I wanted was my freedom.' He walked the shore, kicking at the sand as the wind blew.

'You tried to destroy the world,' countered Eleanor.

Gunnlaugr swung round and towards the others. 'I wanted to go home!'

Ben's glasses lay on his laptop. Ben sat in front of the screen, head in hands, attempting to press the tears from his eyes. He felt warm hands on his shoulders, around his neck and a sweet perfume.

'It's okay,' Kirsten told him softly.

Ben lifted his face and turned to face Kirsten. He pleaded to her with wide eyes and a twisted smile. She read his trouble and hugged him. Again, she reassured him.

'It all makes perfect sense? I should like that—' Ben pulled back. 'I run through the figures Kirsten and it's all there. Climatic shifts, temperature variances, thermo-dynamic waves. Put it all together and you've got one hell of a catastrophe.'

'It's good isn't it?' Kirsten held Ben's head and looked into his eyes, 'It's not like the people out there – politicians, scientists – the public – that they are going to believe what really happened.'

Silence. Ben just stared at Kirsten, still in doubt at what she said.

'But the Alcon plant – they are never going to build another. Not now—' Kirsten told him. 'We kind of won...'

Slowly Ben nodded. Kirsten helped him up and together they walked across the room, the sitting room of the family home in the tree-lined Reykjavik street. They stood at the window and looked out into the garden. Alice sat on a swing, laughing and chatting to Eleanor, who lay in the long grass under the Birch tree.

Smoke filled the control room and sparks flew from partially functioning computer terminals. Charles Ancell picked himself up from the floor, red in the face and choking. Through the windows, smoke-stained and broken, he could see flames reaching fifty feet or more out of the factory. He pulled his handkerchief from his pocket and clasped it to his face, as one-handed he began searching through a cupboard. He pulled out an old leather-bound book and stuffed it into the top of his trousers before grabbing a necklace of precious stones and bottle of incense and stuffing them all into his pockets.

Another explosion in the factory and Charles was thrown against the wall. He turned and looked around at the factory he had built and the riches that it had promised, now up in smoke. He dived to the door, thrust it open and began to descend the ladder. Another explosion, this time blasting flames through the control room and Charles felt the iron rungs of the ladder seem to fly from his fingers as he was thrown free and fell.

Another explosion ripped from the factory, and beyond the mountains spat fire from its summit. Charles Ancell lay on the ground at the foot of the ladder. He picked himself up and, bruised and blackened by smoke, he limped across the car park to his jeep. He pulled open the back door and dragged a plastic crate onto the gravel. He grabbed a bowl from the crate and emptied the contents of his pockets into it. He then took the book and flipped through the pages, studying the text carefully. Kneeling on the ground, he began to pull other objects out of the crate. He arranged a series of cans in a circle around himself, which were revealed to be candles once opened and lit. He lifted up the necklace of stones and slipped it over his neck. Then, after sprinkling incense into the candles, they flamed higher and brighter. He stood and began chanting.

Ben stood at the window, looking out at his sister and her friend.

'He saved us in a way.' He turned to look at Kirsten. 'I don't know where we would be without him – in the end.'

Kirsten squeezed his hand and hugged his waist. She smiled.

Hanna knelt on the black beach, focusing her mind and willing her power to open a window. Nothing. She tried again, mouthing ancient words, but found herself unable to cut through the worlds. She hit the sand and cursed loudly. Turning swiftly she threw a handful of sand at Gunnlaugr and cursed his name.

'Your cousin made her choice,' said Gunnlaugr from where he quietly sat on the sand. He looked up, offering only resignation. 'Blame her not me.'

'What?!' Eleanor turned on the man. 'You were going to destroy our world. For what? So you could go home!' Eleanor marched over towards Gunnlaugr and stood above him, pushing him to the floor, no longer fearful of the once-god.

'Why didn't you just leave me alone? Why did you have to single me out?' Eleanor attacked the man fearlessly. 'Me getting lost in the mountains. That was no accident, was it?'

'Do I need to answer that?'

Eleanor stared at Gunnlaugr scarcely able to comprehend his indifference. Ben approached his sister and tugged at her arm. He beckoned her away.

'There's no use talking to him,' Ben told her.

'But we can't just give up!' Eleanor shook her head, 'We have to get home.'

Hanna picked herself up, sand trailing through her fingers and blowing in the wind as dark smudges in the air. 'Andy was the link. To defeat Gunnlaugr you had to break that link.' She looked at Andy's body. 'But breaking the link in Gunnlaugr's also broke our own power. Look how the alfar have gone. They can't reach this place either.'

'But the tree – Yggdrasil – it lives,' insisted Eleanor. She turned towards the tree and stared at the green lush growth – the only colour in this grey world. Ben and Hanna looked too, staring at the fragile, intertwining branches of the world's oldest tree. As they stared at it, a leaf curled and died and snapped free, floating on the wind until it lay in the sand. Another and another followed.

Eleanor stared at the tree with disbelief. 'No–'

'I'm sorry.' The tone of the man's voice was not apologetic. Eleanor swung round with Ben and Hanna to face the newcomer. Charles Ancell stood on the beach, his face scarred by fire; his clothes, ripped and dirty.

Charles looked down at Gunnlaugr, almost mockingly. 'I'm sorry.' He repeated his words and reached out and grabbed Gunnlaugr and pulled him to his feet. Gunnlaugr allowed himself to be manhandled despite his taller, broader, more dominant appearance opposite the slight, thin and wiry form of Charles.

The sea lapped at the shore, closer at each wave to Charles and Gunnlaugr's feet. Charles yanked up his opposition by the neck and stared into his eyes. 'You lied to me,' he snapped, 'you promised me riches.'

Gunnlaugr laughed. 'Would you have built a factory for me if I hadn't?' He knocked Charles' arm away and pulled away from his grasp. 'You're a fool, Ancell.'

'I'm a fool am I?' Charles grinned. 'Who is it who can come and go through the worlds, whilst you are trapped here–' He glanced around at the three young cousins. 'With kids?! You trusted to old magic and you lost.'

The two adversaries held back and stared at each other. Charles snarled at Gunnlaugr, baring his teeth wolfishly.

'You don't recognise me?' barked Charles. 'Call yourself a god, Ódinn? I work in the metal industry – you bound me in the human world, but you still relied on me to break through the worlds.'

'Fenrir.' Hanna stooped over Andy's body and took the sword from the beach next to him. She stepped towards Charles. 'You look like man, but you are a hunter. You are Fenrir.'

Charles swung round. A brightness in his eyes, he snarled, breathing slowly and deeply. Gunnlaugr's confidence was suddenly weakened.

'Fenrir?'

'Master.' Charles bore his teeth once more, saliva drooling over sharp incisors. He leapt at Gunnlaugr and closed his jaws around Gunnlaugr's neck. Gunnlaugr screamed and fell to the ground as Charles took on his wolf-shape once more. Hanna stepped closer to both of them, holding the alfar sword in both hands. She must kill one of them and be free, but which one? She breathed fast looking from wolf to god; from god to wolf; she lifted her sword.

Ben watched from afar. No, he thought. He watched as Hanna took aim at Gunnlaugr's heart. He shook his head, not knowing exactly why, but sure that she mustn't. Waves lapped more frequently now on the shore. The sand under his feet was wet. He screamed towards his cousin and lunged towards her. Pushing her off her balance he grabbed the sword from her hands as she fell and swung round bringing the sword with it. He lunged it into Fenrir's throat.

The wolf howled and fell. Gunnlaugr and Fenrir lay as man and dog, bloodied and dead.

Hanna Katla Baldursdóttir sat at the base of Yggdrasil with her two cousins, Eleanor and Ben Ármansson, at either side. Night fell and a cold wind drifted over the water. Looking up through the silhouetted branches of the ash tree, the northern lights ebbed and flowed across the sky.

'It's over.' Eleanor looked up at her family, 'We can't go back.'

Silence. Ben, his head on his cousin's shoulder, gazed up at the lights as they danced across the sky. He smiled. 'We might be at the end of the world, but it's not ended. It still lives. They do have another chance.'

A cool breeze washed over them. Hanna hugged her cousins closer and slowly the music found her. She settled the rhythm and softly sang—

Into the north we went

Into the north we came;

Wonderful things we saw

Amazing things we felt.

Both Eleanor and Ben smiled at the sound of their cousin's soothing voice. It was almost as if they could hear the music of the ballad on the wind, drifting over them.

Ours is a family of the north

Ours is the family of amazingness.

Take my hand,

and lead me through.

Walking on the river—

of the rainbow bridge.

Trust me; take me;

Hold me hear.

Listen to the sounds of the north;

See the sounds of the north;

Find our way back from the north.

Across the water Finnbjörn steered the narrow alfar boat. With him were Eirný and Jóhanna. Under the sky of dancing lights they journeyed across the water to a tiny beach entirely surrounded by water with a solitary ash tree growing from its centre. Eirný leapt from the boat into the shallows and pulled the boat up the beach. Jóhanna and Finnbjörn went with her across the beach to where Hanna and her two cousins lay sleeping. One by one, they carried each one of the family back to the boat, all the time intoning spells of long sleeping.

Laying them down, still sleeping, still peaceful in the flat bottom boat, they set off back across the water under sky still singing in light.

Ben woke. Blinking his eyes open he felt disorientated as daylight flooded into the room. Under him was the cosiness of a soft pillow and quilt. He picked himself up and looked around the room again; his room in Reykjavik. And on the bed opposite was his sister. They were both in hiking gear and their boots were over by the window? He put his hand up to his chin and felt the thick layer of stubble.

'What on earth?' He got up and crossed the room to the window, looking out over the Reykjavik skyline and the church of Hallgrimskirkja above it all. He turned towards his sister, 'Eleanor. We're home – how...?'

Eleanor opened her eyes and, with the same confusion, sat up.

'Ben?'

'I know.'

They looked at each other and then, simultaneously called their cousin's name. Throwing themselves out of the room, they charged up the stairs, around the landing and skidded to a halt at Hanna's door. Ben knocked, tentatively. Eleanor passed her brother a despairing look, tried the handle, and pushed their way through.

Sitting on the edge of her bed, Hanna Katla looked up. She smiled.

'The alfar,' Hanna said with a shrug. 'I'm guessing.'

Eleanor nodded. 'But how?

'Does it matter?' answered Ben. 'Magic?'

Eleanor turned and looked at her brother, hardly believing her ears. She smiled. Ben grinned and moved forward drawing Eleanor and Hanna together into a hug.

Hanna stood by the polished lines of the Viking ship, gazing out across Reykjavik harbour and chatting on her mobile. At the blast of a car horn she turned to see Hálldor leaning from the window of his van. Hanna grinned and waved, lingering by the sculpture to finish her conversation.

Bjäkk snapped shut his mobile phone. He looked out at the mountain, smoke still drifting in the air and steam rising from the fresh lava field. He kicked a lump of pumice across the deck outside the mountain hut and returned indoors and crossed the hall to the kitchen. Kathryn looked up as he entered.

'Everything okay?' William asked.

Bjäkk nodded. 'The alfar took them home – they think that's what happened.'

'Do you think we'll see the huldufolk again?' Kathryn paused as she chopped vegetables.

'Can't say,' said Bjäkk. 'If their world is in danger again – maybe?'

Silence. The four scientists considered the prognosis and it weighed heavy.

'Well then,' decided William, 'in that case, much as I would love to meet these huldufolk, once we have this meal – we have work to do.'

Lights swirled, picking out people in the darkened room, filled with a throng of people all watching one thing. Lights on, lights off. Face there, face not. Eleanor and Alice – and Kirsten and Ben. Happy, excited, and expectant. Drum beats, a guitar that kicked into the song with keyboards. The lights swooped around the club and picked out the band on the stage and Hanna Katla in the centre, opening the night in song.

AUTHOR'S NOTE

Thanks for reading. I would like to thank Anna Shannon, Caroline Simms, Cat Dix, Catherine Cragg, Catherine Hodgkinson, Deborah Shepherd, Elizabeth Ewing, Emma Shepherd, Gregor Hutton, Helen Dann, Jane Edwards, Jane Rawson, Janet Ingolfsson, Jenny Owen, Kelly Atkinson, Kirsten Summers, Kirstie O'Connell, Kirsty Harris, Laura Fishenden, Louise Robb, Lucinda Frew, Lucy Howard, Lucy Wainwright, Rachel Baguley, Rachel Turner, and Ros Letellier for spotting spelling mistakes, typos, and all those niggling grammatical errors. If you've spotted something that you think should be corrected, let me know and I will add you to this roll call.

If you enjoyed this story, please do return to its page on Amazon and leave a review, or talk about the book on Facebook www.facebook.com/TheEndOfAllWorlds

You can find out more about my writing on Facebook at www.facebook.com/teshepherd or follow me on Twitter at www.twitter.com/shepline

Talk about the book: #TheEndOfAllWorlds

www.words.shepline.com/books/end-of-all-worlds/

19463579R00231

Made in the USA
Charleston, SC
24 May 2013